Centrifugal Force

A Novel of a Possible Future

Vaughn L. Treude

Nakota Publishing © 2012

Centrifugal Force

Copyright 2012 by Vaughn Treude

http://vaughntreude.com

Cover Art by Kyle Dunbar

ISBN: 978-0-9882442-0-7

Published by Nakota Publishing

http://nakotapublishing.com

In memory of my father, Lowell Otto Treude. He never fought in any wars, but he was a hero in his own right.

Acknowledgements

I would like to thank the following people:

My mother, for giving me her work ethic and love of learning

My friend Joel (no relation to any fictional character,) for being my first collaborator back in grade school

Harry Browne, whose book gave me the belief that freedom was possible in an unfree world

My friends and fellow writers of Nexus and the Grendelmen, for their critiques, feedback and motivation

Sandra Bowen, for her meticulous editing (see her books on Amazon)

Arlys, for being a test subject for the first readable version of this book

And her daughter Arlys-Allegra, for her unwavering support and encouragement.

Chapter 1 – They Used to Call It a Free Country

Joel Walter stood on the side of the highway, hands cuffed behind his back. He gritted his teeth as he watched the highway patrolman approach his daughter.

"Step out of the car, Miss."

Esther opened the passenger door and got out, glancing nervously at her father. The stocky patrolman, whose name badge described him as Officer Labarre, directed her to stand next to a nearby truck scale. Though the weigh station was closed, it provided a convenient spot for a law enforcement checkpoint. *What's that little storm trooper up to?* Joel wondered. The dash cam on the patrol car wouldn't record him over there.

Meanwhile, Labarre's colleagues, who wore the uniforms of Immigrations and Customs Enforcement, proceeded to search Esther's Honda Accord. The first agent, a petite blond woman, checked the passenger compartment. The other Federal agent, a tall black man, opened the trunk and began rifling through their luggage.

Joel had been driving when Labarre waved him to the side of the road, then asked for 'permission' to perform a search. When Joel politely refused, they pulled him bodily from the car, then cuffed and frisked him. Labarre even confiscated the cigars he found in Joel's shirt pocket, no doubt for his personal use.

Why, Joel wondered, had they been selected for this search? Surely they didn't fit the profile of terrorists, gang members, or drug dealers. They were simply driving home to Arizona after a family gathering in Chicago.

Labarre was speaking to Esther, possibly some kind of interrogation, but they were too far away for Joel to hear. Joel was sick was apprehension, but at least there was plenty of traffic on the highway. Hopefully that would prevent these cops from trying anything too egregious.

The patrolman took a step closer to Joel's daughter. In a loud voice, he said, "Stand with your feet apart. Raise your arms."

Her mouth fell open. "Sir, I request a female officer. Especially since you do have a woman present." The blonde, who was checking under the Accord's floor mats, stood up and glanced at the other Federal agent. He shook his head. She shrugged and began perusing the contents of the young woman's purse.

"Raise your arms!" Labarre repeated. Wincing, Esther complied. As he'd done with her father, the cop started at the underarms and moved down, but in this case he paused at her ample bosoms. He squeezed and prodded as if he expected some sort of contraband to be hidden in her brassiere. Under her long dark hair, Esther's face flushed red; she clenched her teeth in indignation. She'd been practicing *krav maga* since second grade; had Labarre been a civilian, he'd have been lying cold-cocked on the pavement.

Joel turned to the ICE agents. "You see that? He's molesting my daughter, stop him!"

The black officer looked up from Joel's suitcase, the contents of which were spilled all over the road. "Sir, I'd advise you to remain calm. The pat-down search is within Federal guidelines."

"Guidelines my ass!" Despite his arms being bound, Joel charged at Labarre like an enraged bull. "Get your filthy paws off my daughter!"

In one quick movement, Labarre stepped away from Esther, drew an Air-Taser from his belt and fired at Joel.

"Aagh!" Joel's cry was involuntary. He fell to the ground, twitching.

"Stop it!" Esther shrieked. "My dad was only trying to protect me!"

After reeling in the electric projectiles, Labarre stepped closer and kicked Joel twice in the ribs. Joel tried to roll away, but he was unable to move his legs. He was relieved to hear the crunch of gravel under booted feet; surely the black ICE agent was stepping in to prevent any further abuse. To Joel's surprise, the second man delivered a kick of his own, even harder, to his other side. As the kicking continued, Joel drew up his legs and curled into a fetal position.

"This is totally illegal!" Joel's voice was slurred. "You're going to hear from my attorney about this!" The black man paused for a moment, then resumed kicking. Labarre pulled out his baton and began hitting Joel on his shoulders and the side of the head.

"Stop them!" Esther shouted at the female officer. "They're injuring him!"

"He assaulted a law enforcement officer." The female agent's voice sounded strained and tired. "The camera will confirm that he made a threat."

"In my purse," Esther hissed. "The card in my wallet, behind my driver's license. My mother works for the Arizona Attorney General. Tell your men to back off or face charges."

The woman found the card and read it. "Guys, that's enough! You've made your point!"

A short time later, Joel was in the Accord's passenger seat, his face scratched and bleeding from the gravel and bruised from Labarre's club. Esther got behind the wheel and started the car.

Labarre, standing well away from the car, bent down and peered through the window. "I'm letting you folks by with a warning. Don't let me catch you in Missouri again, you hear?"

Without a word, Esther rolled up the power window and drove off, then stared at her father. "What on earth are you smiling about?"

"Stupid yokel. You hear the way he said 'Missourah' instead of 'Missouri'?"

"Don't be a bigot, Dad. Though he certainly was a thug and a pervert."

"Just like I was saying earlier." Joel's voice was thick from the clotted blood in his nose. "Every day it's more like Stalinist Russia. And what's the reasoning behind this outrage? The shooting in Nashville? Or is it some other bit of police state *dreck*?"

"I'm sorry, Dad. I can't handle your drama on top of everything else." Despite Esther's stony expression, her eyes glinted with barely suppressed tears. "Bad enough we just buried Grandpop." She sniffled loudly. "I'm furious, too, but you've got to keep a low profile until things calm down a bit."

"So I should just stand there and watch that *goyische* pig rape you?"

"With a thousand people driving by? Don't you get it, Dad? He was groping me to get back at you, because you mouthed off to him when he stopped us."

Joel laughed out loud, then stopped immediately. "Ouch, I think the black one broke my rib." His face looked puffy and monstrous in the rear view mirror. "What bugs me the most," he continued, "besides the beating, of course, was the fact that they wouldn't tell us why they were stopping us, or what they were looking for."

"It had to be the Nashville thing," Esther said.

Earlier that same day there'd been a mass shooting in the Music City, which one radio commentator described as "the worst terrorist incident since 9/11."

Joel nodded. "I can see that being the rationale, but what's the point? The shooter is already dead. The news didn't say anything about any co-conspirators." According to the media, the man was Israeli, a former West Bank settler evicted from his home by the recent peace accord. "Hey, do you think it was racial profiling? Maybe they saw your 'Jewish World Service' bumper sticker."

"Very funny, Dad. Personally, I think they saw you coming. Anybody else would just let them do the search, but you had to make a fuss. Which gave them the excuse to paw my boobs and then kick the crap out of you."

"Esther, my daughter, I love you, and I'm sorry for what happened, but I can't accept what's happening to my country."

She gave her father a weak smile. "You used to be so cheerful, always laughing and joking. Now you just obsess about politics. Are you channeling Grandpop? "

"And what's wrong with that? He was a war hero. He lied about his age to get in the Service. On D-Day he stormed the beach at Normandy. The fighting spirit is in the blood."

"I know, Dad." With her right hand she dug in her purse, produced a Kleenex, and dabbed at a drop of red trickling down her father's face. "Next time, try not to lose so much of it."

Joel shrugged. "I'll do my best."

One year later

Joel rolled down the window of his truck and felt the Phoenix summer heat wash over him. For once, the hundred-ten degree air made him happy. He'd spent the last couple days stuck in an air-conditioned courtroom, testifying in a Federal case involving a former client of his accounting practice. It aggravated him, being forced to waste his time there, to be questioned and grilled about financial transactions about which he had no knowledge.

The defendant's attitude really bothered him. Maybe because the guy was Albanian, he'd expected to get off easy by bribing the authorities, like he could have done in the Old Country. In any case, he sat there giving Joel the evil eye the entire time he was on the stand. Did the guy think he had a choice whether or not to testify? *Definitely not the sharpest tack in the box.*

It had been over a year since Joel had last been to Phoenix. He was happy to keep it that way, until that ridiculous subpoena. He'd gone to court for clients before, but the others were all tax cases. This was the first one involving terrorism. *Oy, Mom and Pop thought accounting would be a safe profession!*

For Joel at least, the ordeal was over. He handed the parking voucher to the attendant, a young Hispanic man with a shaved head and a tattooed neck, who inserted it in an electronic reader. The screen flashed '0.00.' "Have a good day, Sir," the attendant said without a trace of enthusiasm.

Joel nodded. "You, too." *I'd be unenthusiastic, too, if I had to work in this heat.* It would be almost as hot back home, but at least he was on his way. *Thank God.*

As Joel stepped on the clutch to put the old Ford F-150 in gear, there was a deafening boom, followed by a shock wave that rocked the truck where it sat.

13

"What the hell was that?" He twisted around in his seat, unable to see anything but smoke issuing from the parking structure behind him.

"Shit! Manuel, you there?" The attendant shouted into a walkie-talkie. "Manuel, answer me!" He left his post and ran off into the dark cloud.

Should I stay? What if somebody needs CPR?

Then Joel remembered something they'd said in Israel, where he'd spent a semester of college. *One attack is often followed by another.* The terrorists would plant a bomb in a crowded marketplace, and when the good Samaritans came to help the injured, a second explosion would finish them off. Joel decided to leave this one to the professionals. *Best get the hell out of here!*

He hadn't driven more than a couple blocks when he heard the sirens. As he pulled over to the right, three fire trucks came screaming past. For a few moments he sat there, heart hammering, until some guy in a sports car behind him began leaning on his horn.

"OK, OK, keep your shirt on." He put the truck in gear and started off again, but the impatient driver had already zipped around and cut in front of him. Usually he'd have a few choice words for that kind of behavior, but today it just didn't seem important. He'd lost his appetite as well, after feeling ravenous just a few minutes before. *Might as well go straight home.*

The drive gave Joel a chance for reflection. It was two years now since his father's passing. As much as he missed his Pop, he was glad the old man never saw what had happened to this land he loved. All the violence and chaos, even as the government got more repressive.

Like what the Feds were doing to Enver Ahmedaj, Joel's former client. Poor guy was collecting money to help out his cousins in Kosovo, and they hit him with a charge of 'material support for terrorism.' Even if the Albanian Relief Fund *was* a terrorist front, was that any business of the US government? The Albanians in Kosovo had no beef with Americans, just the Serbs. Maybe they had a legitimate need to defend themselves.

Still, it really pissed Joel off that Ahmedaj seemed to think he was a squealer. It wasn't him, it was the people at the bank who'd noticed all the cash transfers to the Balkans and alerted the authorities. And what about Enver's brothers? He should have been angry at *them,* not being there to testify on his behalf, despite a court order.

By the time Joel reached Sun City, KTAR radio had a special bulletin on the incident. A bomb had detonated in the trunk of a car, injuring six people and killing a Federal judge. That judge was James Roller, who'd been presiding over the trial where Joel had testified. It may have been a bizarre coincidence, but Joel had a bad feeling about it.

Joel reached in his pocket for a badly-needed smoke. *Damn, out of cigars!* Luckily he was only a few miles from Wickenburg. He stopped at a drugstore there to buy some Garcia y Vegas. After a quick smoke, he went to the deli next door for a bite.

Back on the road, Joel's stomach was doing flips. The corned beef on rye was good but he'd been so anxious to get back home, he ate it much too quickly.

A couple hours and several stogies later, Joel pulled into the driveway in front of his house. He glanced at the truck's dashboard clock, and remembered he was supposed to meet his friend Nephi at the Java Jolt this evening. Though Joel was in no mood to see anyone, he wasn't sure he wanted to sit at home alone, either.

He sat there for a moment, trying to decide whether to put the truck in the garage and call it a day. Finally he decided against it. He was far too keyed up to rest, and after a day like this, it wouldn't hurt to have the sympathetic ear of a friend.

Joel got out of the truck, and headed over to check his mail. The mailbox was located in front of his neighbor's house, the left-most of a cluster of four. For a moment he hesitated, worrying about what he might find inside of it. Lately he'd been receiving death threats from persons unknown. Probably it was just somebody's idea of a sick joke, or perhaps it was some Neanderthal who found

Joel's on-line political postings offensive. Still, a person had to be careful these days.

Get it over with, he told himself. *Like jumping into a cold pool. Why prolong the agony?* He popped open the door and stuck his hand in. A stabbing pain caused him to yank it out immediately.

"Aagh! *Scheissen!* Motherfucker!" Joel was too shocked to go on cursing like he might have done in less painful situations. Out of the mailbox fell an angry diamondback, which immediately coiled up on the ground and rattled, threatening to strike again.

Through the haze of pain, Joel remembered something he'd heard on a TV documentary on reptiles. Chilling the wound would slow the effects of the venom. He ran to his front door, but in his panic he couldn't get the lock open, especially not with his left hand.

At that moment Mrs. O'Reilly emerged from her house. "Is everything all right? I heard shouting. What happened to your hand?"

"Got bit by a rattlesnake. Damn it hurts! I need to get to the hospital! I was just gonna get an icepack."

"Goodness gracious!" the white-haired lady exclaimed. "A rattler, here in your yard? Just a sec." She returned with a towel and a baggie of ice, which she handed to Joel, now at her doorstep clutching his injured hand. "Should I call the ambulance?"

"No, it'll be quicker if I drive. Damn, we can't just leave the snake. I don't want anyone else to get bit!"

"Don't worry, I'll call Animal Control. You get going. Good luck!"

"Thanks, Sal, you're a lifesaver." Joel hopped in his truck and peeled out, steering awkwardly with his left hand.

Lord, what *meshuggah* times these were! A man couldn't even get his mail without risking his life. At least now he had proof the threats were no joke. When he'd first started getting them, he brought the letters to the local police. "We need more evidence," the detective said. The cheap Chinese printer the bad guys had used was totally untraceable.

When he reached the hospital, Joel barreled in through the automatic doors, ice dripping all the way. Thankfully the emergency room was empty, but then, Kingman, Arizona, was a fairly small city. At the front desk, a plump nurse infuriated him by insisting on photocopying his insurance card. "Hey, I could be dying here!"

"It'll only take a minute. I've sent one of the aides to get you a fresh ice pack." She ushered him into a tiny examination room. As the pain ebbed to a dull throb, Joel noticed how dark things looked. Was the poison attacking his nervous system? *No, you schmuck, you're still wearing your sunglasses.*

Once again he reminded himself not to *kvetch*, because a lot of people had it much worse. Like Enver Ahmedaj, who might be facing decades in prison for his so-called 'crime.' Or the rest of the guy's family, who'd be in big trouble with the court for declining to appear. Most likely they'd lose their trucking business as well, since Enver had used company computers to transfer the money overseas.

Plus I have my health– assuming I survive this snakebite. The throbbing in his hand was getting worse. What was taking them so long? Joel popped his head out the door, about to yell for help, when the doctor arrived. He was a dark-skinned baby-faced fellow with a badge reading 'V. Gupta.' Joel glanced at his watch and realized it had been only a couple of minutes.

"Let's take a look, shall we?" The doctor took Joel's hand. "Nasty bite. You're quite sure it was a rattler?"

"If it was a cobra in disguise he did a pretty decent impersonation."

The doctor smiled wanly. "It's lucky you got here so quickly. Just one moment." He disappeared. A minute or two later, a nurse appeared with a syringe. It hurt like hell; Joel bit his lip and concentrated his attention on the woman's ample bosom.

"That'll fix you right up," she said with a smile. "Now just relax and wait here, we need to make sure you don't have an adverse reaction to the anti-venom."

After the nurse left, Joel tried unsuccessfully to call Animal Control. He needed to tell them to keep the snake, rather than releasing it in the desert somewhere. It might provide the evidence the cops could use to catch the perpetrator.

Then he called his daughter and got her voice mail. "Hello, Esther, I'm at the hospital. Had a little mishap. Don't worry, nothing serious. Call me when you get a chance." Esther worried about him far too much. When she heard what happened, she'd probably flip out. Her mother, on the other hand, might decide to root for the snake.

Once again, the wait seemed to take forever. Joel was getting irritated. He really needed a smoke, and wished he had a book or something to distract him.

He pulled a news magazine out of the rack. With all the cell phone browsers and e-Readers these days, he wasn't used to seeing dead-tree periodicals. The cover story was "The Rebirth of Organized Crime." Inside was a discussion of the major immigrant groups that were horning in on the Mafia's business. To his great amusement, there was a big section on the Albanians. *Why am I not surprised?*

Finally young doctor Gupta returned, examined Joel's hand once more, and did a brief check of his vital signs. "It's going to be pretty tender, so I'll have the nurse wrap that up for you, then you're good to go. Just try to take it easy on the hand for a while."

No kidding. "Thanks, Doc." Luckily the nurse didn't keep him waiting. The second she was done, Joel rushed past, eager for a cigar and some well-deserved rest in front of the TV. As he reached the hospital doors, he remembered– damn! He'd left his sunglasses in the exam room.

As Joel passed the admissions desk once more, something unusual caught his eye: two young men, wearing long sleeve shirts and ties despite the sweltering Arizona heat. He distinctly heard one of them say 'Walter'. Quickly Joel went back down the hallway, out of sight of the desk, and pretended to read a sign promoting flu shots. He held his breath and strained to hear what they were saying. The next bit made him shudder involuntarily.

His initial suspicion was correct; the men were FBI agents. Could this be about the Albanians? Or maybe they wanted to question him about the bombing, since the garage recorded the license plates of all visitors, and he'd left at a very suspicious time. It was not a situation to take lightly. These days, the old rules no longer applied. Joel needed to talk to his attorney, just in case the Feds decided to hold him incommunicado for 'national security' reasons.

No, Joel decided, he didn't want to face the Feds unprepared. Instead of exiting through the emergency room door, he headed the other direction down the hall. He could get out the main entrance and circle around to his truck before the agents came looking for him.

Minutes later he was driving away, puffing furiously on a cigar and glancing nervously in the mirror. Eventually he'd have to face those agents. The sooner he contacted his attorney, the better. He pulled into a grocery store parking lot and got out his cell phone. It rang repeatedly, then went to voice mail. "Sarah, it's Joel. Please call me ASAP." Now what?

Oh damn. In all the excitement he'd forgotten to call Nephi and cancel. At this point, he might as well go. He could use the distraction, and a good strong cup of coffee so he'd be alert when Sarah called back. Besides, the kid said he had something interesting to show him.

He needed to call Esther again, though he was dreading it. She'd give him the third degree, followed by a good scolding. Definitely got that from her mother.

It was a warm, humid day in Chicago, ripe with the smells of blooming flowers and fresh grass. The locals had been complaining about the weather, unusually hot and muggy for this time of year, but Siri loved it. Maybe that was because it reminded her of growing up in Sri Lanka, where heat and humidity were the norm.

Today she took a direct route across the quadrangle so she could tread on the sweet green lawn. The shortcut helped her avoid the stares of the male students. Siri was tall and slender, with glossy black hair falling halfway down her back. She was frequently mistaken for a student– which she had been, not too long ago.

Being on the faculty was more stressful than Siri had expected, even though she was teaching some of the same classes she'd taken here as an undergrad. It was too bad she couldn't have stayed at Stanford, where she'd gotten her doctorate. The lifestyle there was more laid-back. Still, it was nice to be back at her alma mater; and considering the University of Chicago's world class reputation, the perfect place to use her math / economics PhD. Plus she could stay close to her parents, especially since her father was not doing so well these days.

Siri walked up the steps of the familiar Eckhardt hall, and had to force herself to turn left to go to her new office. She said a little prayer to the Buddha– *please, no students waiting at my door today.* All she wanted to do was go home, get something to eat, stretch out on the couch with her cat and watch some sci-fi on the satellite.

Her prayer was answered, but not in the way she'd hoped. The two men waiting by her office door were definitely not students. They were clean-shaven, grim-faced, and wearing conservative suits. One was short, black-skinned, and muscular, the other tall, thin, and pale.

"Doctor Sirimavo?" the black man asked.

"It's Doctor Jayasuriya, actually. Sirimavo is my first name."

The black man smiled. "I'm sorry. I thought the surname came first in Sri Lanka."

"It does," she explained as she swooshed the fob on her key chain to unlock the door. "But my family's been in America awhile, so we use the western name order. And you are?" She eyed them expectantly.

"I'm Agent Ron White of the Department of Homeland Security, and this is Agent George Kudrmas." He produced a cell-phone-sized device from which erupted an official DHS hologram logo, plus his name, 3D photo and badge number. Siri's eyes widened involuntarily.

Kudrmas, smiled. "Don't worry. You're not in any trouble."

White put away his badge. "As a matter of fact, we're here because we've taken an interest in your work. May we come inside and talk?"

"Sure." She was still nervous as she pushed open the door. "Come on in. Please excuse the mess, but I didn't know I was having visitors."

"No problem, Doctor." White and his partner followed her in. "I must inform you, the content of this conversation is confidential, by the Terrorist Surveillance Act, section 32 dash 5."

"I understand."

While White made small talk, the other man waved a device around the room. It looked like a tri-corder from the original *Star Trek*, only smaller. It emitted short chirping noises. He scanned Siri's pictures of Gandhi and Ludwig von Mises and stopped at a vintage *Firefly* poster, framed and autographed by Nathan Fillion. "Loved that show," he said.

"Me, too." The casual chatter made Siri nervous. Couldn't they get to the point?

Kurdmas smiled and returned the gizmo to his jacket pocket. "We're with the DHS Electronic Intelligence Division, or EID, formerly known as the National Security Agency. You're probably familiar with our work. We're always looking for new talent in communications theory and analysis. We reviewed your doctoral dissertation and were quite impressed."

"You mean, 'Trust-Based Schemes in Anonymous Economic Transaction Markets?' I didn't know the EID was interested in economic theory."

"It's not so much the theory as its potential applications," said White. "I have a math background myself. I've read your paper; it's brilliant. But we need to consider the effects on society. We at the EID believe that there's a serious potential for abuse. Consider how much funding the Federal government currently loses through tax evasion, and multiply by ten. An idea like yours, implemented in software, could have a disastrous effect."

Siri could guess where this was going. Were they threatening her with some kind of restraining order? Her stomach knotted in fear, which slowly morphed into anger. She forced herself to smile and remain calm. "I believe your superiors may be giving me too much credit. Black markets have always existed. I'm describing how they work, not causing them. I mean, did Newton invent gravity?" She followed with a nervous little laugh.

"You're right," Kudrmas nodded. "Which is why the EID has no intention of preventing you from pursuing your research. We just want to make sure it proceeds in the right direction. This is why we're offering you a position with our agency."

"I'm flattered, but I've just started this job, and I don't want to leave the University in a lurch. Besides, I like it here, and I like being in Chicago, near my parents."

White's face grew somber; the tone of his voice subtly changed. "Maybe we haven't impressed on you how important this is. How seriously it could affect other people. You grew up in Jaffna, right? A Sinhalese in an area controlled by the Tamil Tigers. Which, frankly, we didn't expect to come back after their so-called 'defeat' in '09, but you can never underestimate the tenacity of terrorists. Surely you'll do anything you can to oppose that kind of evil."

For a few seconds she was speechless. Of course they'd checked her background. They knew about the bombing, her long stay in the hospital, and her sister Daksha's death. She wanted to scream: *You have no right to snoop in my private life!* Or to imply that her work could cause the deaths of more innocent people.

"Ms. Jayasuriya," said Kudrmas, "I'd like to apologize for my colleague. He's passionate about his beliefs, and he sincerely wants you to work for the EID. It was insensitive of him to mention your family's loss." He shot White a reproachful glance. "The job we're offering you would have a much higher salary than your current position at the University. You could afford to fly back to Madison anytime you wanted to see your parents."

White started to speak, but Siri cut him off. "What happens if I don't accept your offer?"

White folded his fingers into a tent and exhaled. "Of course you have the right to decline; it's a free country, after all. But we'd have to consider carefully whether you'd be allowed to pursue this line of research. In any case, the University has close ties to the government, and would frown on any project that didn't have DHS approval."

"I understand." She took a drink from her water bottle, now warm. "How soon do you need my decision?"

Kudrmas smiled. His fatherly image was enhanced by the crinkles around his eyes. "We know it's a major decision. Take your time, talk it over with your parents. Not the specifics of our conversation of course, but the move to Virginia, and what it would mean for your career."

White was more brusque. "But definitely don't take too long. No more than a few days. Otherwise we can't guarantee that this opportunity will still be available."

Siri had an impulse to shout, "Never!" and order them out of her office. But it wasn't wise to arouse the ire of the DHS. She had to calm down before making any major decisions, or doing something she might regret.

Maintaining her composure, despite the knot in her stomach, she said, "Thank you gentlemen. I'll think it over carefully and get back to you within the week."

The men left. She put her face in her hands and sighed. Then she took out the tiny 'forbidden due to fire code' coffee pot from the bottom drawer from her filing cabinet, and filled it with water from her unfinished bottle. Soon she had a hot cup of Sri Lankan tea, though this time it didn't make her feel better.

Unlike a lot of her people, Siri had never hated the Tamils, even though the Tamil Tigers had practically invented suicide bombing. Every group had its bad apples. Ironically, the man who'd turned Siri's life upside down was a fellow Sinhalese, infuriated by the partition of his country. Like any terrorist, he must have believed his goals justified hurting innocent people.

The memory was vivid, as much as she wanted to forget it. Siri and Daksha had ridden to the market, to buy pineapple and honey to make their father's favorite cake for his birthday. She could still feel the hot sun on her neck, smell fruit and spices, and hear the clucking of chickens.

The girls walked their bikes between the crowded stalls. While Siri stopped to examine some sweet, juicy dates, her sister kept going, and was soon four or five stalls away. Suddenly there was a sound of gunfire, and screaming. The crowd pressed forward like a single organism, sweeping Siri along and forcing her to drop her bike. Her mind raced in panic, first with the terror of being crushed, then with worry for her sister.

Siri's thoughts were interrupted by a deafening noise. She flew through the air, directly into the big stomach of a man by the onion seller's stall. That was all she remembered when she awoke to the white walls of a hospital room, her head bandaged and her left leg in a cast.

She looked around, her head foggy from pain killers. "Where's Daksha?" Her mother started to weep.

Siri finished her tea, a tear rolling down her own cheek. Homeland Security had no doubt investigated more than her childhood. They'd know about her father's radical views, how she'd followed in his footsteps. Plus all the anti-war organizations she'd joined. Maybe that was what had attracted the Feds' attention.

"Well," as her father would say, "I warned you it wouldn't be easy." An independent-minded economist, her father had raised her on the great free market thinkers from Smith and Locke to Hayek, von Mises, and Rothbard. Not to mention Ayn Rand– a bit didactic at times but still one of the greatest exponents of liberty.

Most people would have jumped at the chance to be on the Federal payroll, with the job security, health benefits, and proximity to the halls of power. Not Siri, who considered government to be, at best, a necessary evil. If the EID wrote her paychecks, it wouldn't be just to keep her work on barter under wraps. No doubt they'd want her to develop algorithms for spying on people through their economic transactions; an activity she couldn't condone.

What would be the safest way to turn them down?

★  ★

This was really awkward. Joel was carrying a king-sized latte in his left hand, plus a heavy laptop bag on the same shoulder. Despite the thick wrapping of bandages, his right hand was too painful to use. He could have left the computer in the truck, but since the break-in last month, he didn't feel safe doing that. Besides, he'd been hoping Nephi could help him with a spy-ware problem that had slowed his system to a crawl.

Halfway to his destination, the strap started slipping off Joel's shoulder. He tilted his body to the right and quickened his pace, hoping to reach the table without dropping the bag.

"Hey Joel, you need help with..."

Joel looked up and ran headlong into his friend. Startled, he dropped his drink to the floor of the coffee shop, causing a brown flood at his feet. Only the quickness of Nephi's reflexes kept Joel's notebook computer from suffering a similar fate.

Joel forced a smile. "Nephi, when I said let's get together, I didn't mean it literally!"

"Sorry, I thought you saw me. Holy crud, what a mess!" Nephi set the computer down gently on the table next to his own. "It's my fault, I'll get it." The young man went to the counter. "I need a bunch of napkins, please."

"Oh, don't worry about it." Jasmine, the pretty young barista Joel was always flirting with, emerged from behind the counter with a mop.

"Uh, thanks, Jaz." Joel ordered a new latte and threw a couple bucks in the tip jar. Returning to the table, he sat down across from his friend and sighed.

Nephi looked at him and grinned. "Having a rough day?"

"You might say that."

Nephi took a sip of his fruit flavored herbal tea. "You have to admit it was an impressive entrance. Excuse me a sec, I need to finish this before I forget what I was doing." He looked back at his own notebook, a black Dell three times the size of the trendy silver portables most of the shop's patrons were using. Its appearance was deceiving. Within the archaic case were the internals of a high speed micro-

notebook, which made room for an extra battery and enough drive space to house the Library of Congress.

Joel had been friends with Nephi Snow since their chance meeting in Phoenix's infamous Tent City Jail. They seemed like an unlikely pair. Joel was a bit stocky, with an olive complexion and wavy salt-and-pepper hair, and looked every day of his fifty-plus years. He liked to joke that at six feet, he was 'a Jewish giant.' Nephi was only a few years out of college. He was tall, slim, and fair, with muscular arms from helping out on his uncle's ranch. At six-four, the young man made Joel feel like a runt.

As always, Nephi typed with Uzi-like rapidity. "There!" Hit the 'Enter' key with a flourish, then snapped the notebook shut. "Sorry 'bout that. I hate to lose my train of thought."

"Not a problem." Joel took a sip of coffee, savoring its robust flavor. Even in the worst times, life had its simple pleasures. "I'm just glad to be back in town."

"Oh yeah, you were in Phoenix, weren't you? What were you doing there, anyway?"

"Testifying in Federal Court about some former clients. What a pain in the ass! Though I shouldn't be kvetching, I could be one of the guys being investigated."

"I hear you. Did you get caught up in those road blocks after the bombing and stuff? You were right downtown, weren't you?"

"I sure was. Thank God I got out before the incident. I hear traffic was a nightmare."

Nephi nodded. "So what the flip happened to your hand?"

"Now there's a story. Would you believe I got bit by a rattlesnake?"

"Yeah, right!" Nephi laughed. "That's a good one, Joel. What really happened?"

"I'm serious, it really happened." Joel related the day's events: his brush with death in Phoenix, the surprise in his mailbox, his visit to the hospital, and his near-encounter with the FBI agents.

"They came looking for you at the hospital? They sure must've been anxious to see you. I wonder how they knew you were there."

"Probably talked to my neighbor; Mrs. O'Reilly is the biggest busybody on the block. But also a real sweetheart; she got me a bag of ice so my hand wouldn't fall off."

Nephi shook his head. "Something doesn't add up. You were in Phoenix this morning, where they easily could have found you, and they had to come all the way to Kingman?"

"I'm the last person to make excuses for the government. But assuming this is related to the bombing, I was leaving the parking garage the moment it happened. No doubt they photographed my license plate on the way out. Makes me look kind of suspicious, actually."

"That's why they need cameras everywhere," Nephi said, "so they can always have someone to blame. Which reminds me, there's something I need to show you. You remember that whistle blower website from a few years back, the one that moved to Switzerland, then Iceland, before Uncle Sam finally got it shut down?"

Joel sighed; he was at this very moment being pursued by the FBI, and this guy was off on politics again. "Of course. They got a lot of flack for exposing government secrets, even more than Wikileaks. You yourself said they went over the line sometimes."

"True, but I'm not so sure about that anymore. Your case is exactly what we're worried about," *we* obviously referred to Nephi's mysterious contacts in the hacker movement, "the misuse of surveillance, to harass people, and scare them out of exercising their God-given rights. Or to manufacture evidence against law-abiding people. Which is why we've started our own underground police leaks website. This is a perfect opportunity to..."

"Hold it right there, Neeph. In principle, I agree with you totally. But those radical friends of yours will get you in big trouble. There's this thing called 'obstruction of justice'..."

"I'm aware of the law, Joel. And I didn't say I was actually working on that site, though I may have done a little consulting about Internet security. Nothing illegal about that. Hold on a sec." He opened his laptop again and resumed his furious typing.

"What are you searching for? Details on the bombing? I've been listening to that crap on the radio all day."

"This is stuff you won't hear on the radio." Nephi sat silently for a few seconds, then his eyes widened. "Good gracious. We need to get out of this place." He pushed the 'moon' button and the computer screen went dark. Snapping the notebook shut, he stuffed it in its bag.

"What? What did it say?"

"Not so loud." Nephi glance left and right nervously, and continued in a whisper. "I'll meet you at the south side of Andy Devine Park in ten minutes or so and we'll talk about it."

"You have my cell number, just..."

"No!" Nephi grimaced, then lowered his voice. "Turn it off, now, and take the battery out. It's like carrying a homing beacon in your pocket." When Joel opened his mouth to protest, Nephi shushed him. "I'll explain everything there. Go now, I'll leave in a couple minutes."

Kingman, Arizona, was not a large town. It only took a few minutes for Joel to drive to the park. It was busy, with lots of moms, a few dads, and dozens of noisy little kids. That was not surprising, because with the brutal desert summer just around the corner, now was the time to enjoy the outdoors. Personally, Joel found it a bit warm for his taste already.

He looked around nervously as he pulled up to the curb on the park's north side. What the hell was up with Nephi? The kid wasn't one to fly off the handle over nothing. Joel took one more drag on his cigar, stubbed it out in the ashtray, and opened the truck door. At that moment, a familiar white and blue van pulled up. The passenger side window came down.

Nephi was visibly agitated. "Get in, quick! Grab anything you think you might need, we may not get to come back."

Joel trotted to the back of his truck and threw open the hatch on the topper. The urgency in his friend's voice had him spooked. He grabbed the suitcase he'd packed for the trip to Phoenix and hadn't put away. Luckily the snake had prevented him from unpacking.

He opened the van's sliding door, put the computer bag and suitcase in back, then hopped into the passenger's seat. Nephi immediately headed down the street, away from the park.

"OK, you want to tell me what the hell is going on? If this is some kinda joke, you got me. My blood pressure is going through the roof."

"It's no joke, Joel. I wish it were. I've saved the data on my phone, here, take a look."

"Hey, you said I shouldn't use *my* phone."

"They're not looking for me. Besides, mine's modified to be untraceable."

"All right, give me that thing already." Joel looked at the tiny screen and pulled his reading glasses out of his pocket. "How do they expect people to read this stuff?"

It appeared to be a scan of an official document. Joel read aloud: "Department of Public Safety– Internal Use Only– All Points Bulletin." He stared at the photograph for a second, unbelieving. "*Oy vey*, this is me!" He looked at Nephi, who was staring straight ahead as he drove, a grim expression on his face. "They think *I* planted the bomb in the courthouse parking garage? What the *hell* would make them think that?"

"This *was* the same judge you wrote all those critical articles about, wasn't it? And you *were* in the area."

"For the record he treated me quite fairly. I was just torqued about how he handled that lawsuit, where the ICE guys killed that illegal alien. Violating immigration law shouldn't carry the death penalty. Assuming we still have that barbaric form of punishment."

"They also said something about personal effects found at the scene." Nephi's brow furrowed in concentration. "Didn't you say your truck was burglarized a few weeks ago?"

"Yeah, but they only took some random crap, clothes, shoes... wait a minute, you think somebody's setting me up?"

Nephi shrugged. "It's a distinct possibility. Scary, 'cause if it's true, whoever's doing it is also crazy enough to try assassinating a judge. Assuming it's not some kind of Alex-Jones-type false flag operation."

"Oh my God, I'm a dead man!" Joel cradled his face in his hands. "Unless I can get into some kind of witness protection program."

"Problem is, you don't have any information you can trade with. I hope you have a really good attorney. Assuming they allow you to pick your own. If it's a terrorism tribunal, they assign you some junior level hack from the military."

Joel laughed mirthlessly. "You sure are optimistic," Though he was trying to keep a brave face, his heart was pounding and his stomach churning. The kid was right. Sarah was a great lawyer, but not a criminal defense specialist; he hoped she had a good referral for him. He looked back at Nephi. "Have you been replaced by a pod person? You're always the one telling me things are getting better."

"Gee, I'm sorry. I don't mean to be so negative! The way things have been going lately, even I'm having my doubts."

Joel sighed. "Yeah. You know, all these years I've been saying America's becoming a police state, but I never really believed it. Just didn't seem real. Now I'm thinking I need to go underground, or even flee the country. Too bad Mexico's such a mess right now." He glanced at the street signs; they were stopped at a light on the town's main street. "So where're we going?"

"Nowhere in particular. Maybe we should go to my house, give you some time to plan your next move." He put his blinker on and eased into the left turn lane. "On the plus side, the cops haven't gone public with the arrest warrant. If you left town, it wouldn't be unlawful flight."

"If I'm already a suspect, it would make me look totally guilty."

"True. Though if you were camping out in the desert somewhere, and it turned out they only wanted you for questioning, you could say, 'Gee, I didn't know you were looking for me.'"

Joel shrugged. "You think they haven't heard that one before? Though I probably ought to make myself scarce, just to be on the safe side. I don't want to end up like those Pakis who went to the FBI with a tip on a terrorist attack and ended up in prison themselves."

"Yeah, people are really skittish these days. They don't trust the government, but the terrorist thing's got everybody too freaked out to do anything about it."

"Well, first of all," Joel said, "I'd like to get a few things from my house."

Nephi was silent a moment before answering. "Not a good idea. They're probably staking out your house right now, if they came after you at the hospital. I don't think it's safe."

"Good point, but if they are staking the place out, hopefully they're out front. I have a secret back entrance. I could just get in, get my stuff, and get out." Joel looked at Nephi with his best impression of a wide-eyed little kid. "If I had somebody to drive me."

Nephi laughed. "I suppose. But I'm not eager to get in trouble with the law. That one time at the protest and half my family was ready to disown me. If the Feds take you in, you didn't tell me anything about this, right?"

"My lips are sealed." Joel made a zipping motion. Nephi's mention of 'the protest' brought back a rush of memories. Their chance meeting had been a pivotal point in the young man's life; now this random event would also have a serious impact on his own. It was almost enough to make a life-long skeptic believe in Fate.

"How do we get there again? I've only been to your house one time."

"North of the Interstate, remember? Head for Canyon Avenue and I'll tell ya when to turn." He patted the young man on the shoulder. "Don't worry, I've got this figured out. So... what was it we were talking about before we fled the Java?"

Nephi's mouth settled into a grim smile. "Weird coincidence, how relevant it is to your situation. I've told you before about the hacker network, but I held back a lot of the details. Not that I don't trust you, I just thought being a non-technical person, you'd find it pretty boring."

Joel nodded. "I understand. But I'm not sure you should be involved, either. Especially not that 'police leaks' web site. You're asking for big trouble."

"But it's totally in line with our mission, which is to support the right of the people to life, liberty and the pursuit of happiness. We're not encouraging law breaking, just self-defense. We support the police, but somebody has to keep an eye on them, hold them accountable."

Those words brought a smile to Joel's face. "I knew you were a bit of a rebel, but it surprises me to hear you talking like this. I thought Mormons were supposed to be for law and order, not making common cause with those pinko ACLU liberals."

"Hey, don't believe the stereotype of LDS folks. Remember Jack Anderson? One of America's greatest investigative journalists, thorn in Nixon's side? He was one of us. Not to mention Brigham Young, who had his share of troubles with the authorities. Anyway, the network has people of all creeds and color. The only requirement is to care about defending the Constitution, which is what the politicians and bureaucrats are *supposed* to be doing."

"Point well taken. If that hacker stuff can keep my *tuchus* out of the slammer, it's got my vote. But enough of the techno-geek details. I'm a little too stressed to concentrate right now."

Joel directed Nephi to his neighborhood, but when they reached the turnoff for his street, he told him to keep going. They drove a few blocks more, parking in front of a small evangelical church. As he got out, Joel said. "If I'm not back in 15 minutes, leave without me. If I think I'm going to be caught, I'll call you if I can."

Nephi gave Joel a withering look that brought an image of his dearly departed mother to mind. "No phones, remember? They'll check your records for sure. I don't need my number in there any more than it already is. Good thing I've been using encrypted email."

"And I used to think you were being paranoid! OK," He glanced at his watch. "It's 6:35 now, don't wait for me past 6:50, OK?"

Joel headed down the sidewalk, as fast as he could go and still look casual. He often took walks around the neighborhood, so a lot of people knew him. His next door neighbor– not Hannah, but the guy on the other side– even knew about his 'secret entrance.' That could be bad, if the Feds talked with too many people.

The 'secret entrance' came into being somewhat accidentally. Behind Joel's back fence was a strip of grass his home owners' association insisted be kept mowed, yet their rules forbade putting a gate there. Naturally, he'd been compelled to defy those arrogant pricks. It was a stealth gate, a half dozen wood slats fastened together on the back side. The lock was mounted behind a convenient knothole. Joel inserted the key, which he'd mounted on stubby screwdriver to make it reach. With a little jiggling, he got it unlocked, the boards swung back on a hidden hinge. He stepped in carefully through the fence frame.

Joel crept through the yard to the back door, then hunted nervously for the right key. As the door creaked open, he knew something was wrong– the security system was off. Somebody had been inside, maybe still was. His stomach lurched. *Of course, the kid was right!*

Luckily this door led directly to the master bedroom. There in the walk-in closet was the rifle-sized safe where he kept his most prized possessions. *After all these years, my paranoia has paid off.* Heart pounding, he dialed the combination. He quickly selected a few things: cash, gold coins, passport and a couple of special mementos. These he slipped into a blue nylon duffel bag. His handgun, unfortunately, was in the locked drawer of his nightstand. *Should I go for it?* Crouching like a guy in a bad action movie, Joel duck-walked across the room, only to step on a crumpled antacid wrapper that had somehow missed the garbage.

"Williams, did you hear something?" The voice came from the living room.

Damn! In an instant, Joel was out the door, without the gun. He detoured around the lawnmower shed, out through the make-shift gate. It was really hard to act casual, but his luck held out; he didn't encounter anyone on the walk back. Nephi was still sitting there waiting.

"You made it, just barely," Nephi said. "Though I decided to wait five more minutes before abandoning you." He grinned. "Actually, I was on the phone with one of my hacker associates, and I lost track of time."

Joel pulled a pack of cigars from his shirt pocket, then remembered where he was, and put them back. His hands were shaking; he really could have used the smoke. "The Feds are in my *house*, man!"

"Good gosh, I hate to say it, but I told you so! Wait, how can you be so sure? Could they be the guys who put the snake in your mailbox?"

"No, I imagine those guys would sound like a bunch of knuckle-dragging Neanderthals. This fellow sounded professional, and totally calm, like he wasn't worried about the cops showing up. No, they had to be some sort of cops themselves."

"You are so lucky they didn't catch you. I sure hope we're not being followed." Nephi glanced over his shoulder to the back seat. "That is one huge duffel bag. And that other one, is that a guitar?"

"Shh, it's actually my Tommy gun," Joel laughed. "Seriously, though, I got just about all the really important stuff. And you're right, I was extremely lucky not to get caught. Thanks for stopping, Nephi, you're a real *mensch*. Now let's get the hell out of here!"

Chapter 2 – On the Lam

Joel pushed himself back from the table and put a hand on his stomach. "Thanks, Bud. A good meal does wonders for my mental state. Even if my entire life's screwed up."

"Just try to keep a positive attitude. The Lord will provide a solution if you keep an open mind." Nephi stood up and started clearing the table.

"I sure hope so. Hey, don't do that, I'll clean up. You were brave enough to take in a fugitive as a house guest."

"OK, thanks. Just load it in the dishwasher. I need to go send a few emails."

"It's a deal." It only took Joel a couple minutes to throw away the steak bones, load the dishwasher, and wipe off the table. *Time to sneak out to the backyard for a smoke.*

Joel glanced around nervously as he slid open Nephi's patio door and slipped out. Good, the block walls were high enough, and the neighboring homes were single story. As far as he knew, the Feds hadn't yet put his name and face on the 'Most Wanted' website. But he still needed to keep a low profile.

He pulled a cigar out of the pack, bit off the end, and lit up. He puffed on the stogie and enjoyed the first sweet drag. Even when times were bad, life could be good.

Nephi's yard was as he'd expected it, immaculate, with lush grass and ornamental shrubbery. As the sun disappeared below the neighbor's house, the lights winked on. The sprinklers sputtered to life, adding moisture to the desert air. A humming sound alerted Joel to a security camera attached to the house, slowly panning the yard. *High tech, what a surprise.*

He'd only been out there a few minutes, puffing and pacing nervously, when the patio door slid open and Nephi appeared. "I was wondering where you went off to. Nothing about you on the news sites. How you holding up?"

"Good as can be considered." He noticed Nephi wrinkling his nose. "Oh sorry, smoke bothering you?"

Nephi rolled his eyes. "Besides the obnoxious smell, no. I'm not going to lecture you on the health hazards, I'm sure you know all about those. It's just that none of my neighbors smoke cigars, and nobody in my family smokes at all, so–"

"A security breach, eh? Oops." He stubbed it out on the bricks lining the flower bed. After cleaning off the ashy portion, he slipped the rest in his pocket. "On the good side, I think I killed a few mosquitoes. You can thank me when you don't get West Nile Fever this summer."

"And maybe I just added a few minutes to your lifespan. Thirsty?" He held up two bottles of water.

"Sure, thanks." Joel cracked open the bottle and sat down at the patio table next to his friend. He took a long drink, then sighed. "What am I gonna do, Nephi? First time in my life I'm completely at a loss."

"Just a sec." Nephi held up a finger to his lips. From his pocket he produced a small remote control. He pushed a button, and music started playing from well concealed speakers.

Security consciousness, that's good. Joel recognized a song that had been big on the alt-rock radio scene a few years back. Maybe Nephi was hipper than he'd thought. Then he recognized the band: the Seagulls, from Salt Lake City, not to be confused with the Flock.

Nephi took a long drink of water, set the bottle down on the patio table. "Seems to me you have three options: turn yourself in, wait for them to come get you, or flee."

"Hmm, I guess it comes down to which course of action is less risky—being taken into custody, or being out in the world, where somebody is obviously trying to kill me. Maybe they'll try something more effective next time, like a pipe bomb."

"Wow, in all the excitement with the FBI, I completely forgot about the snake incident. Who in the world would want to kill you? And why? I mean, you're nobody important."

Joel let out a guffaw. "Thanks for the vote of confidence! Well, for starters, I was in that debate on Colorado Valley Public TV, where I came out against the Nigerian war. Got a whole bunch of hate mail from that. Then there's that skinhead group White Cross. When I did the blog post against Arizona's immigration law, they threw a brick through my window."

Nephi shook his head. "I'm sorry I was skeptical when you told me about the threatening letters. I figured it was just some lunatic who'd singled you out randomly for harassment. Did the notes actually say they were from White Cross? Was it just anti-Semitic rambling, or was there anything more personal?"

"Not really. Hebrew treachery, betrayal, and the wrath of God. Typical nut ball stuff."

"Hmm, that sounds familiar. Do you think these people might be Muslims? The Koran has some verses about Jewish treachery."

"Huh? What's a good Mormon boy doing reading the Koran?"

"You forget, I did my mission in the Philippines. They have a large Muslim minority. If we're going to convert people, we have to understand the local culture, right?"

Joel thought for a moment. "Well, my former client, the guy who's on trial in Phoenix, is a Muslim from Albania. Not very devout, perhaps. Besides the terrorism thing, he was accused of drug smuggling, supposedly to raise funds for the cause. Does your leaks site have anything about criminal investigations? Guy's name is Enver Ahmedaj." He spelled it out.

"I recognize that name. The family owns a trucking company, don't they?" Nephi entered the name in his smart phone. They were quiet for a few moments as they awaited the response, which, as Nephi had told him before, was slow because of the proxy servers and security filters.

"Got it, finally." He let out a long whistle. "Now this is interesting. There's an APB out on your Albanian buddies. Except for Enver, the entire family vanished. As potential witnesses, their father and the two brothers, Emal and Egon, were under court orders not to leave the state. Nothing about the Phoenix bombing, though I'd think they'd be prime suspects." He looked at Joel. "Muslims have an exaggerated sense of honor. It wouldn't be surprising if they wanted revenge against you, too, for your testimony against their brother."

Joel held up his bandaged hand. "I'd call that a fail. Though the bombing, that might just get me. One of the things stolen from my truck was a silver butane lighter with my initials on it. Want to bet that was the 'personal effect' they found on the crime scene? Though it might not have been the Albanians. Wouldn't be the first time the Feds tried to frame an innocent man."

"Yeah, but assuming somebody in authority wants to frame you, why would they stoop to murdering one of their own people? While they were breaking into your truck, they could've just as easily planted drugs in there."

"Good point. Better yet, child pornography, make everybody hate me."

"Besides the Ahmedaj family, or maybe White Cross, who else could it be? Who else might have a beef with you?"

"My ex and her family?" Joel laughed. "I've been pretty naïve. Of course the Ahmedaj's weren't happy with me, but I had no choice but to testify, did I? Guess I shouldn't assume other people are rational. Now that they've disappeared, I'm pretty sure they were the snake handlers."

Joel finished his water and crushed the bottle in his uninjured hand. "Though I can understand why they went on the lam. The Feds will probably end up seizing their business. So why stick around and risk being arrested, too? I just wouldn't blame my accountant." He sighed. "Wish I'd kept up with my Spanish. You'd think with all the people I meet, I'd have kept in practice... but illegals don't have much use for tax accountants."

Nephi's eyes widened. "You thinking about skipping the country?"

"What's to think about? If they can pin the bombing on me, I could get the death penalty. At best, I'll be in prison the rest of my life. Even if I appeal, I'm not a young man anymore; I don't have that kind of time."

"Especially if you don't quit smoking." Nephi smiled.

Joel shrugged. At least the kid could nag in a good natured manner, which was more than he could say for his ex-wife. "George Burns smoked twice as many cigars as I do, and he lived to be a hundred. But that's not the point. Of course I'd try and fight this thing, but if it's a national security issue, I probably won't be allowed to pick my own lawyer, or even see the evidence against me. That's hardly a fair trial."

Nephi nodded. "Yeah, I've heard a lot of horror stories. At first it was just Muslims, but now they do it to anybody who's stepped out of the mainstream. He emptied the bottle with a long drink. "I'll check with my uncle in Nevada. He might be able to help you. He's a retired US Marshal, knows what he's talking about."

"Really? So he's one of the good guys now?" Joel instantly regretted the flippant remark.

Nephi laughed. "Let's just say his bosses pushed him too far, so he opted for early retirement. Only thing is, he's paranoid about the phone; prefers to use shortwave radio, and we have to speak in code. He totally refuses to use the Internet. So if we want his help, we have to go to where he lives, which is in the middle of the Nevada desert."

"But you've got a job. I can't ask you to use up your vacation for me."

"No, actually it works out. I was planning to take all next week off to go see friends in Salt Lake. Luckily tomorrow's Friday, Dad won't mind if I take an extra day 'cause things are slow right now. And it's been too long since I've seen Uncle John. So what do you say?"

Joel rubbed his forehead and considered for a moment. "What do I have to lose?"

Joel woke with a start. It sounded like someone was trying to break down the door. "Don't shoot, I'm unarmed!"

"Very funny!" Hearing Nephi's voice reminded him where he was. "Time to get up!"

"OK, keep your pants on!" He sat up, tried to clear his head. What a crazy dream he'd been having! The Albanians were chasing him with venomous snakes. He reached the top of a hill and found himself surrounded by dark-suited FBI agents, who raised their guns fired. *Bite me, Sigmund, no fancy symbolism there.*

He glanced out the window. It was still dark, and the sun came up early this time of year. His back hurt from the too-soft bed in Nephi's guest room. Joel got up and rummaged through his bag for a clean shirt. As he pulled on his clothes, he reflected on the strangeness of the last couple days. He also felt a stab of guilt. What was he thinking, letting Nephi get involved?

Nephi knocked again, driving those thoughts from his mind. They'd loaded the van the night before. All Joel had to do is stumble around, get dressed, brush his teeth, and dash outside for a quick smoke. On the way out of town, they stopped at a McDonald's drive-through for breakfast. Which was good, because Nephi didn't own a coffee pot.

They headed up Highway 93 to Las Vegas. The state had finally finished its never-ending construction, and there was freshly surfaced freeway all the way to Sin City. Nephi turned on the radio, and the two sat silently as he drove.

As he finished his coffee, made tolerable by one creamer and two packs of sugar, Joel began to feel human. "You think it's safe to..." he glanced around the van, then at his friend.

"If the van was bugged, they'd have us already. Besides, I sweep it for bugs every week." He grinned. "Uncle John's given me a healthy sense of paranoia. Not to mention being hauled off to jail for trying to take a picture."

"A conservative is a liberal who's been mugged. A libertarian is a conservative who's been arrested." Joel had to smile to himself, remembering their first encounter. "So tell me more about this uncle of yours."

"Like I told you, he spent thirty years as a US Marshal, but he got fed up. Bought a ranch and started raising sheep, like his daddy and my granddad used to."

"How'd he end up consorting with radical-type people?"

"His last few years in law enforcement he got real disillusioned. Lots of times he didn't like what he had to do, didn't feel like justice was being served. The last straw was when he had to apprehend a little old lady who'd been growing marijuana for her son who had AIDS. She was very polite and apologetic as he arrested her. She said she wasn't jumping bail, she just wanted to visit her sister in the nursing home in Arizona. He submitted his resignation the next day."

"Wow. That must've taken a lot of *chutzpah*, after all those years in the system, to say, 'I've had enough.'"

"He's a brave man and I admire him tremendously," Nephi said. "He's also the black sheep of the family for leaving the church. My folks hardly speak to him. My brother and I keep in touch, we go up to his place sometimes." He laughed "We just don't discuss religion."

The conversation died as they drove on. Joel gazed at the scenery, trying to get his mind off the guilt. As his father used to say, "Son, to get yourself in trouble is bad enough. But when you pull in those around you, shame on you!"

His pop's words had been prophetic. What Nephi was doing right now, aiding and abetting a fugitive, could easily land him in prison. True, his association with the so-called 'hacker network' might eventually get him into trouble on his own. Still, he doubted his young friend would have otherwise done something this serious.

Joel yawned and stretched in his seat. "You know what this reminds me of? The 1960's, when people used to run to Canada to dodge the draft."

"Why, were you one of those?"

"How old do you think I am? That ended years before my time. But if I'd been drafted, I'd have gone to Canada. The Viet Nam war was senseless. Had an older cousin who did go."

"Where? Viet Nam, or Canada?"

"Canada. Came back when Jimmy Carter signed the pardon."

"You were lucky. They drafted me a few days after I got back from my mission."

"*Oy!* That Nigerian war's just as stupid as Viet Nam was. Only instead of Communists, it's Muslims– and oil, of course. I'd have dodged that one, too, if I were your age."

Nephi laughed. "My family would have disowned me if I'd have done that. I was lucky to get Conscientious Objector status, though I'm not technically a pacifist."

"They were lenient at first; they didn't want people rioting in the streets."

"You're right. They've been getting gradually stricter with deferments, must figure most people won't care enough to make a fuss." They were now passing the last of the Vegas sprawl. "We're making good time! Only 200 miles to go."

★ ◎★ ★

"Hey barkeep! Another scotch and soda. With lots of love, if you know what I mean."

"That's what I like about you, JL, you don't beat around the bush." The bartender set the drink in front of the big man and looked at him with narrowed eyes. "So what's goin' on? Eleven-thirty in the morning is way early even for you."

"Mind your own goddamn business" Jon Larsen snarled, raised his glass and drained it in one prolonged swallow. He set the empty glass down and laughed. "I'll tell you the sad story some other time. Right now, I'm in a shitty enough mood as it is. Give me another, OK?"

Suddenly there was a hand on Larsen's shoulder. He spun around on the barstool, an arm half raised, ready to punch the would-be assailant. When he realized who it was, an embarrassed smile crossed his face.

"Christ, Jon, chill out!" The man behind him was like himself, quite stocky; not just heavy, but well-muscled from years of physical labor. By some quirk of nature he was also three inches taller. "I thought I'd find you here. Figured you could use a little cheering up from your favorite brother."

Larsen laughed. "Screw you. Unless you're here to drink with me."

"Sorry, it'll have to be a Coke. Got to get back to work in an hour. Lars, we'll have a large basket of fries." He turned back to his brother. "Tell you what, I'll smoke your ass in darts."

"Ha ha, that's a good one, 'little' brother. Everybody know who the dart-meister is around here." He got up, a bit unsteadily, and followed Dave to the other side of the bar. "You go first."

"No, you're the expert, show me how it's done." Dave handed him three red darts.

The elder Larsen turned to face the board. He sighted along the dart with one eye, then threw. "Twenty points." He threw again, this time hitting the outer bull's eye.

Dave threw his first dart, hitting the one-point section. The second time, he missed the target entirely, embedding the dart just below the outer ring. "Shit, should've warmed up a bit."

"Problem is you're not drinking, bro. I've got killer aim with a couple under my belt." Jon Larsen walked to the board to collect the darts. When he returned his smile was gone. "You know what pisses me off? What pisses me off is we didn't even have a chance. Our technology was cheaper and more efficient, so they banned it. Not those frickin' Aussies, though, their shit was barely functional. Bunch of corrupt weaselly cock sucking..."

"What's that, JL?" At the pool table next to them was Bill, one of Jon's high school classmates. The guy practically lived here. "You talking about the Winergy project? On the Web they said the EPA nixed it on account o' the migratory bird hazard."

Larsen snorted. "So what? We kill a hundred times more than that every hunting season. The Aussies' crappy windmill kills only like ten percent fewer. Guess they had the money to buy off a few Congressmen." He threw, hitting a five-pointer on the double ring. "See what you made me do?" He chuckled bitterly. "Did I say ours was way more efficient?"

Bill nodded. "Yeah, it sucks, we could've used those hundred jobs. But you've got all that land, so you don't have to worry about that, eh, JL?"

"You'd think so, wouldn't you?" Dave let loose another dart, hitting the fifteen this time. "He sank all his savings into the project. I told him he shouldn't put all his eggs in one basket, but he's the perfect example of a stubborn Swede."

"I'll say." The man circled to the other side of the pool table, searching for the best shot. "Remember in high school, that fight with Rasmussen, Jon kept swinging even after..."

"JL!" The bartender yelled. "Is this your phone on the bar? With the god awful ring tone?" The voice of David Lee Roth singing 'Jump' could barely be heard over the Garth Brooks on the jukebox. "Must be why nobody swipes your fancy phone." Larsen ambled over, took the phone from him, and flipped him off as he walked away.

"Jon Larsen?" said the voice. "This is Nephi Snow."

Feeling the effects of quicker-than-usual whiskey consumption, it took Larsen's brain a moment to make the connection. *Young fellow, tall, Mormon, smart as hell.* Where had he met the guy, anyway? Must've been DEFCON, where else would it have been?

"Hey Nee-phy, good to hear from ya. Just a sec, man, I gotta take this outside, kinda loud in here." He headed out the back door into the bright North Dakota sunshine. "What's up? Testing the voice encryption app? Signal's clear, though it still sounds a bit noisy on your end."

"I'm on the road. The noise must be on your end; I spent months on the decompression, to get the sound quality up to par. I had a question for you. You go to Canada pretty often, right?"

"Used to. Not so much anymore, too much hassle at the border. Why, planning on dodging the draft?"

Nephi laughed, a high pitched giggle that caused annoying distortions in the voice decoder. "No, I've done my time. I've got a friend who's in some serious trouble. I think he might need to relocate to a friendlier climate. You know anybody who might have connections in immigration up there?"

Larsen shook his head, then remembered it was an audio-only call. "Sorry, man. I only go up there to hunt and fish. I stay as far away as possible from anything governmental."

There was a pause on the other side. "Uh, you still got a lot of hacker contacts, right? You know somebody north of the border?"

"A couple," Larsen admitted. "I'll ask around, but no promises. In the meantime, if your friend needs a place to hide out... uh, he didn't rob any banks or anything, did he?"

Nephi's laugh brought back the distortion. "No, of course not. You know how things are these days, you don't have to do anything to get in trouble. But I appreciate your kind offer. Way things are going, we may need to take you up on it, Jon."

"JL, remember. All my friends call me that. And if there's anything you need, don't hesitate to call." He shut the phone and sighed. *Those goddamn Feds just can't leave anybody alone, can they? Oh well, maybe it's a chance to strike a blow for the good guys...*

★ ◎★ ★

Joel stared at the screen of his notebook computer. It was difficult to put what he was feeling into words. "My Dearest Esther, I am terribly sorry I had to leave so suddenly, without saying good-bye. You must be out of your mind with worry." Though who would blame her if she'd given up on him? He'd embarrassed his daughter many times in the past, but this would top them all. Was there even a point to this? He needed to ask Nephi, was there a safe way to send his daughter an encrypted message?

The stress and worry of the last few days had been exhausting for Joel. Nephi, bless his heart, had stowed the camping table so Joel could rest on the tiny bed. At first, it was a nice change from the passenger seat, which didn't have enough support for his back. But Joel couldn't sleep, too much on his mind. He tried reading one of the books he'd rescued from his house. Lord knew he needed to get his mind off his troubles for a while. But the bouncing of the van made it difficult to read. He realized he'd never called Esther back;

46

somehow he had to let her know he was alright, even if it was a risk. Surely the FBI was keeping close watch on her.

How could he explain how much it hurt to abandon the only family he had left? Joel was at a loss for words. He shut off his computer and put it back in its case. Fighting a bout of nausea he crawled to the front and squeezed into the seat next to Nephi. *Serves me right, should've stayed up front and kept the kid company; this is an enormous favor he's doing me.*

Joel looked out the window. The landscape was even more barren than northwestern Arizona. "I see we're off the highway."

"Good observation! We're almost to Uncle John's."

"He really lives out in the sticks!" Joel felt in his pocket for his cigars, remembered it wasn't his vehicle. "Not that I'm complaining! I feel at home in the desert. Maybe it's genetic."

"I have to warn you about Uncle John," Nephi said hesitantly. "He doesn't know you're Jewish, so he might say some really un-PC things. But the man doesn't have a bigoted bone in his body. Except about gays, and even then, it's not the people, it's the behavior he hates."

Joel rolled his eyes. "Don't worry! I'm not easily offended." *What the hell am I getting myself into? Nephi's going to give his uncle the benefit of the doubt. For all I know, the guy might have a closet full of brown shirts and jackboots.*

"And try not to mention the war or the draft. He's pretty open minded on a lot of issues, but being a war veteran, he's a bit touchy about the Service."

"You got it, Boss!"

They rounded a curve and saw a house up ahead, on the right side of the road. Low slung and tan, it blended in with the landscape. Somewhat incongruously, the dwelling incorporated an old fashioned porch made of well weathered cedar. Behind the house stood a long barn or shed, also desert tan;

beyond that, a flock of dusty sheep. The color was on the flag pole, the Stars and Stripes flapping in the breeze.

"The fifty star flag!" Joel exclaimed. "I'd forgotten how pretty it was. I remember when they changed to the one big star made of fifty-one little stars, how everybody hated it, especially when they made the blue part bigger so it'd fit. But people got used to it."

"Don't get Uncle John started on *that* topic. He *hates* the new flag, cause he doesn't think the District, I mean Free Columbia, should be a state. He says the founders had a good reason to make the capital city separate."

"But Nephi!" Joel feigned astonishment. "Free Columbia is mostly *African American*. Anyone who's against it must be *racist*."

Nephi smiled. "You're incorrigible."

Two big German shepherds ran up to greet Nephi's van as it rolled into the yard. One stationed itself on Joel's side of the vehicle and barked and snarled, showing yellowed teeth.

A tall thin man in blue jeans and a white cowboy hat emerged from the house. "Hans! Herbert!" he yelled. The dogs rushed to his side. Nephi got out of the van, and Joel followed.

A smile cracked the lines of the man's sun-weathered face. The hair showing from under his hat was white, and his nose had a bump, probably it had been broken long ago. "Nephi! It's been way too long since you've come to see us! Last time, you were barely old enough to drive."

The younger man grinned. "Come on, Uncle! It was just two years ago! Though, it *has* been too long. This is my friend Joel Walter. The guy I was telling you about."

"Glad to meet you, Joel!" he said. "Call me Jack, only my relatives call me John." He extended his hand to shake.

Joel hesitated, then offered his left. "Sorry, my right's out of commission for a while."

"I see," Jack said. "What happened, if you don't mind my asking?"

"Rattlesnake bite," Joel said. Seeing Jack's eyes widen in curiosity, he added. "It's a long story. Too long to explain standing here in the hot sun."

"Well, come in then! Walter, isn't that one of the more common Jewish surnames?"

"You're saying it's not also a common Gentile name?" The man's bluntness was amusing. Joel's ethnicity was an easy guess, with his prominent nose and wavy hair. Not to mention the habitual Yiddish-isms he'd learned as a child from his grandpop. Still, it never hurt to be cautious among the *goyim*.

"My uncle's incurably politically incorrect," Nephi said with a grimace. "Don't get the wrong impression. Growing up LDS, we take an interest in surnames and genealogy."

"*No problemo*. I'm Jewish as apple kugel, and proud of it." *Even if I haven't been to Temple in over a year.*

"Well, I hope you like Mexican food." Jack Snow motioned for them to follow him into the house. "Rosa's cooking some machaca enchiladas. That's beef, by the way."

"One of my favorites." Joel decided not to mention he wasn't observant of the dietary law, so pork was no big deal. It was best to appear devout among religious people, and despite Nephi's explanation, he wondered just how far Jack had fallen from the Mormon tree.

"Nephi! And you must be Joel!" Jack's wife Rosa was a short stout Hispanic woman, with the deep brown eyes and shiny black hair Joel had always fancied. She was pleasantly curvaceous, and appeared to be ten or fifteen years younger than Jack.

Jack surprised Joel again by getting himself a can of beer from the fridge, and offering him one, which he gratefully accepted. Despite being domestic, it tasted like ambrosia. The enchiladas smelled wonderful. He desperately wanted a cigar, but didn't want to push his luck.

They sat down and waited with heads bowed as Jack said a quick grace. Once finished, he looked at Joel. "Try Rosa's tortillas, they're homemade."

"Everything looks wonderful," Joel said. "Thanks so much for having me."

Conversation was put on hold as they all helped themselves to Rosa's simple but hearty cooking. When time came for second helpings, the pace slowed a bit.

"So Joel," Jack said, "I understand you're in need of special services. Nephi couldn't say anything about your situation over the radio, so you'll have to fill me in."

Joel looked up from his beans. With a totally straight face, he said. "You've heard about the bombing at the Federal Courthouse in Phoenix? Well, I didn't do it." Jack and Rosa responded with puzzled looks; Joel laughed. "Not that it makes much difference to the Feds. The FBI is looking for me as we speak."

Jack gave his nephew a stern expression. "I had no idea this was so serious." Nephi opened his mouth to say something, but Jack raised his hand. "No, it's not your fault, we need a better method of secure communications."

"I keep telling you, Uncle, we have one now! Our Griffin application allows secure untraceable anonymous..."

Jack's face reddened. "I've warned you before, you shouldn't be messing around with the Internet! You may think they're not tracking your every move, but they *are*."

Everyone sat in an uncomfortable silence. *Didn't expect him to be that adamant,* Joel thought.

Rosa looked at her husband. "Jack, why don't we save this until after dinner? Give everybody a chance to relax a bit before we get into the serious business, OK?"

"OK." He gave them an unexpected grin. "She's right as usual. So Nephi, how's that brother of mine? Is he still talking about retiring?"

"He keeps saying he's gonna, but I don't think he quite trusts us kids to run the company. Even if he does retire, he'll still have his fingers in it."

They talked amicably about Snow family business, with Rosa asking Joel the occasional question about his life and upbringing. He responded with lavish praise for her cooking. For a moment Joel almost forgot he was a fugitive.

When they finished eating. Rosa cleared the dishes; Nephi got up immediately to help. Jack looked at Joel. "Shall we retire to the porch?"

Joel looked at Rosa, who said, "Go on, this'll only take a few minutes."

The porch was charmingly old fashioned, with a wooden bench and two rocking chairs. Jack motioned to Joel to have a seat on one of the rockers, choosing the other for himself. Then Jack surprised Joel again. "Since Rosa gave up cigarettes, she won't let me smoke in the house anymore." He reached into a pocket and produced a briar pipe and a pouch of tobacco.

"I guess you won't mind if I light up one of these, then."

"What's that? A Mirabella? On one condition– if you have an extra one for me."

The two men sat in the evening quiet, smoking and sipping their beer. One of the dogs sidled up to Joel, soliciting a pat on the head. Nephi emerged from the house with a Pepsi in hand. Joel looked at him and grinned. "Ooh, get the man away from home and he goes wild."

"Very funny. A lot of us don't object to colas, for adults, in moderation."

"Definitely my favorite adult drink," Jack said with a laugh. To Joel, he continued, "Yes, I grew up LDS, but I'm not one of those angry fallen Mormons. It's just that after I met Rosa, I decided the Catholics are more fun."

They fell silent after that. The stars were thick in the sky. In the distance, a coyote howled and the rest of the pack joined in.

Finally, Jack spoke. "Back to the matter at hand. I'm not as involved in the Patriot and militia communities as I once was. Person has to be pretty careful these days; they'll haul you in with the slightest excuse. At the same time, I'm not ready to concede defeat. I'm not going to let a bunch of Marxist one-worlders take over my country."

Joel nodded. "I hear you." The guy's rhetoric was a bit right-wing, but they were on the same side. "I've been writing for years on my blo– um, column, about how we're losing our freedom. May be partly how I got myself in this mess."

Nephi laughed. "That, and having a Muslim immigrant family for clients, who happened to be mixed up in organized crime."

"Unbeknownst to me, of course. I should've suspected, since they were Albanians, but I don't like to judge people based on the nationality."

Jack blew smoke into the darkness and grinned. "I dealt with a few of those Albanian mafia types when I was a Marshal. Those people are into everything." He took a sip of beer, then another puff, and continued.

"Normally what we'd do is try to find a legal way to settle you out of the country. Legal according to the host country, I mean. My nephew mentioned Canada. Normally, I'd be for that; the Canucks are big on granting political asylum. Sometimes Australia or New Zealand, they haven't gotten too bad. Problem is, you're charged with a terrorist act, so they won't touch you."

Nephi interjected. "But that's not fair! All the Feds have to do is make an accusation, true or not, and the person has no place to go."

Joel shrugged. "Maybe the Iranians would take me."

Jack ignored Joel's joke. "Mexico is another good choice, if you speak the language. They'll take anybody with enough money to bribe the right officials. Unfortunately, with the drug war down there, I wouldn't recommend it unless you have a death wish."

"No thanks. I do speak a bit of Spanish, but I can't afford the bribes. Luckily, I had an emergency stash of cash in my safe, which I was able to grab before I went. By now, I'm sure they've frozen my bank account."

"For you, Israel might be an option. Unless they might tie you in with the Albanians."

"They probably wouldn't want me anyway, with those right wing Likudniks in charge. I've been publicly critical of the ethnic cleansing of Jerusalem. Assuming anybody noticed."

Nephi suddenly chimed in, "What about Costa Rica? Lots of Americans go there."

"For someone in Joel's situation, that's a possibility. He'd definitely have to adopt a new identity, in case the Feds tried to extradite him. Better yet, Belize or the Caymans; the more local corruption, the better. The problem is, you'd have to get there by sea. You don't want to cross Mexico by land. And the Coast Guard's in high alert because of the Port of Newark bombing. These days the Feds are after you coming or going."

Joel sighed, put a hand to his forehead. "Lord help me, what am I going to do?"

Jack put a hand on his shoulder. "Don't give up. The high alert can't last forever. Much as I hate to say it, going underground is your best option, for now. Until things calm down and we can find someone with a boat to get you to some friendly Caribbean country."

"Sounds like the Underground Railroad," Nephi observed.

"Exactly like that. Ironic, since my forebears in the Marshal Service had to go after runaway slaves. Not something we're proud of."

"So then," Joel said, "I assume there's somebody in your network who could help me with that sort of thing. Is there? I'll pay what I can for the service."

Jack finished his beer, set the can down with a clank. "I wish to God there was, Joel. I've never wanted to cross that line, not so much for my own sake as for the fugitives themselves. I know how easy it is to slip up, I've spent years on the other side. And it seems like the options are disappearing. Sometimes I think Rosa and I should get out before it's too late." He took a drag on his cigar, made a face. Joel produced his lighter and relit it.

"Thanks." He took a puff, then continued. "Still, I love America. It'd break my heart to leave her. It'd piss off Rosa, too, after all she went through to get citizenship." He chuckled. "I wish you luck. These days, it's easy to get burned by the government by no fault of your own."

"Don't I know it! Well, if you think of anybody..." Joel forced a smile, but he felt like he'd been punched in the gut. *What a totally wasted trip.*

Joel looked at Nephi. In the light from the window he could see the disappointment on his young friend's face. Joel felt a stab of anger at himself. *I never should have let him bring me here. Maybe if I turn myself in, he won't get in any trouble.*

Surprisingly, when he realized he still had that choice, it felt like a great load off his shoulders. He took a last drag from his Mirabella and stubbed it out in Jack's cowboy hat ashtray. He had to smile, despite himself. *I'm a fugitive. Wanted by the law. My Pop always warned me I'd end up this way. Once again, he was right.*

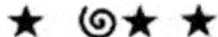

Emal Ahmedaj awoke from a wonderful dream, basking on a nude beach full of doe-eyed big-breasted playmates. For a moment, he was angry to be back in reality. Judging from the light, it was early, not yet time for work. He could wake up the wife for a quickie. She didn't complain as long as she could go back to sleep for a while.

He rolled over, expecting his wife's delightful body. Instead his face ran into musty couch cushions. He heard the snoring of his five-year-old son, his brother, two nephews. His father was loudest of all due to his emphysema. *Shit!* He remembered why he was here.

He was not in his two story house in Arizona. He was in a two room hovel in the Fort Worth barrio, sharing sleeping quarters with all the males in his family, while the women and girls slept in the other. He quickly hopped off the couch to claim the bathroom before it became occupied. A little voice inside scolded him for not being grateful. As bad as the situation was, it was far better than indefinite detention in Guantanamo.

When he got out of the bathroom he stared at his old man for a while, watching the bushy mustache moving in time to his labored breathing. As a child he had worshiped the man. God, how he hated him now. He fantasized about replacing the old man's oxygen bottle with nitrogen; put the old bastard out of his misery.

A horrible thought, but his bitterness was justified. If not for the old man, they'd be in their own homes, still driving their shiny Kenilworth trucks. It was bad enough they'd been transporting narcotics. In the Old Country, Emal Ahmedaj Senior had always stayed a step ahead of the law. You just had to bribe the right officials. Here in America they had the protection of the Albanian Mob. As long as the Corporation got a piece of their action, all was well.

But as the man got older, and his health started failing, he'd got religion. Emal Junior, who had been reading the Koran daily for three years, found it a little too convenient. As if going to the mosque on Friday would make up for all the years of smoking, drinking, and crime; the last two of which the old man still did. Still, it was a step in the right direction, until he'd started sending money to the Shqiperian Liberation Army. (*Shqiperia* was the official name of Albania in Albanian.) Emal Senior probably figured it would compensate for his sins, and put Allah on his side. Even worse, his father had let his youngest son take responsibility for his crimes.

Emal grabbed a pita and some hummus out of the fridge, and ate it cold. He imagined a breakfast of pancakes and eggs, and fumed at the unfairness of it all. Years ago, the USA had helped his brethren in Kosovo. Now if you supported Albanian causes, you were a "terrorist". You went to Gitmo if you were fortunate, or were sent to Syria to be tortured if you weren't.

The bedroom door opened and Esma emerged, yawning. "Good morning, Dear. How's your back?"

Emal kissed her on the forehead. "I'll live."

She gave him a groggy smile. "I almost miss our morning sex. Ylli snores like a buzz saw, and little Jeelah kicks like a mule. You men are lucky to have the living room and all the couches. *We* have to share beds with the children."

Emal shrugged. He loved his wife dearly, though he'd never admit it to his father and brothers. Emal Senior had often slugged their mother (in a tragic irony, now dead from cancer) when she got too mouthy. A terrible example for his sons. Maybe the Koran allowed it in special circumstances, Emal thought, but not such casual brutality. Not that the Book ever mattered to his Marxist farther, until he started worrying about the afterlife.

"I have to make some deliveries," he said, glad to be getting out before the others got up. "Kiss Ylli and Jeelah for me."

"Emal," she said as he was heading for the door. "Do you think we're safe here?"

"Probably, if Papa behaves himself. At least we don't have the Jew to worry about." He laughed quietly. "I wish I could have seen his face when he opened his mailbox. He must have survived, though, because I heard the police are looking for him."

"That was bad enough. Even if Walter informed on Enver, that doesn't justify revenge. But the bombing– Emal, please tell me again you and Egon were not involved."

"I swear I had nothing to do with that. You think me a total fool?" His rage was partly from fear. Though his brother had claimed to know nothing, Emal was far from certain. Egon had been associating with some ruthless characters. Although it was a necessary risk of their occupation, even more so now that legitimate enterprise was closed to them.

"No, but I do not trust your brother's influence."

"I don't think you trust me, either." Her worries echoed his own, but he was loath to show weakness. As the eldest brother, with their father ailing, he was supposed to be in charge.

"The behavior of the males in your family doesn't inspire a lot of confidence."

He nodded and grunted, imagining what his father would have done. Esma would have had a loose tooth at this point. As irritating he found his wife's westernized ways, the thought of physically hurting her made him sick to his stomach. He swallowed his anger, kissed her, and headed into the muggy Texas morning.

★ ✪★ ★

Joel strained his eyes to read the clock on the mantle. It was six AM. An ungodly hour, but with the sun shining through the gap in the curtains, he hadn't needed an alarm clock. He'd been awake for some time, worrying about his situation, and pondering the best course of action. No answer had been forthcoming.

Beside him, Nephi dozed on the recliner. Joel got up, his back aching from the too-soft furniture, and closed the blinds. *One more reason Jack and Rosa don't often have overnight guests*. Returning to the couch, he dug around in his bag and found the book he'd been reading the day before. Lately he would always start one but never have a chance to finish it.

Then Joel smelled coffee perking, and he realized there'd be plenty of time for reading on the road. The prospect of decent java made the day look brighter. First, he needed to change. Rather than dumping his hastily packed clothes on the couch, he grabbed his bag and headed for the hall bathroom. When Joel returned to the living room, Nephi had already gotten up and put the blankets away. That was lucky; otherwise he might not have noticed that his cell phone battery and fallen out of his pocket and was lying on the couch.

"Good morning, Joel!" Rosa smiled as he entered the kitchen. "Breakfast is ready."

"Buenos dias, gracias." Rosa's smirk told him his pronunciation was as bad as ever.

"Morning, Joel." Nephi was already at the breakfast table.

"Coffee? Hot chocolate?" Rosa offered.

Joel gratefully took a cup of coffee and sat down. "Where's Jack this morning?"

"He went to the north section to check on the flock," Nephi said. "He can't stick around to eat with us late-rising city folk. Poor Aunt Rosa, she had to make breakfast twice."

"De nada. We have toast, eggs, and..." Rosa let out a little gasp. "My goodness, I feel so foolish! I should have made something else besides bacon!"

Joel chuckled. "No worries, I'm not exactly Mr. Kosher." He speared several strips with his fork and took a bite. "Mmm, this stuff is to die for! Oh, Rosa, I've been wanting to ask this, but Nephi warned me it was a sore point with Jack. Can I use your phone line to get on the Internet? I don't need broadband, just need to check my email."

"That Nephi does like to exaggerate. It's not that Jack is *against* the Internet, he just doesn't trust it. Because he was law enforcement, he knows how the government spies on people and how easy they can break that encryption stuff."

"Besides Joel," Nephi said, "I wouldn't advise it, not until we get you set up with the proper anonymizing software. They have ways of tracing your connection." He was interrupted by a deep voice going "ARRRHHH!" Somebody in Nephi's circle had a Chewbacca ring tone. He grinned as he fished his phone out of his pocket. "I'll take it in the other room."

Joel tore into his breakfast. It was the first time in several days he'd actually been this hungry. *Guess being a fugitive catches up with you.* "Everything's *vunderbar*, Rosa. *Muy bien!*"

Rosa laughed. "Nothing special, just everyday cooking."

"So, Nephi tells me how Jack took an early retirement from the Marshall Service. Does he miss it, or does he like ranching better?"

Rosa's smile disappeared. "No, he actually resigned. Though he was vested in his pension plan, thank God. And to answer your question, he loves being out here, living off the land like his father did. But he sometimes misses the excitement of his former career, which is probably why he gets involved in things that maybe he shouldn't."

"Sorry, I hope I didn't hit any nerves there."

"No problem. I'm proud of Jack for wanting to help people, even if it does cause me a few sleepless nights. It's something he has to do; he's got a lot of remorse about some of the things he once did in the line of duty. Sure, he tracked down bank robbers and murderers, but in later years he had to arrest people who were totally harmless."

As Joel was about to ask another question, Nephi returned. "That was Enoch just now."

"Uh, weren't you just telling me they can track you through your cell phone?" Joel found the irony amusing. "To be perfectly honest, though, I'm surprised it works out here."

"It's satellite-enabled – expensive, but worth it. Besides, they're not looking for *me,* and if anybody thinks to investigate, I'm just visiting family."

"So what did your brother say?" Rosa asked.

"Joel had to abandon his truck back in Kingman. I sent Enoch an encrypted message to watch for it. He tows abandoned cars for the city. Somehow somebody found out where it was, because two guys with FBI badges showed up and impounded it. Wouldn't say anything except it was evidence. Technically E wasn't supposed to tell anyone about it, but... our codes are secure, how's anybody going to know? At least the Feds paid the towing bill."

"Well, I drove it 150 K, so I guess I got my money's worth. Better the truck than me." Joel grabbed a second piece of whole wheat toast, buttered it, and took a bite. "It's funny, though. Just when I was having second thoughts, like maybe I can cop some kind of a plea, this happens, and I say, 'No way!' They must want me pretty bad. I know Jack sounded really pessimistic, but I'm inclined to take my chances with the Canucks."

Nephi nodded. "I kind of had the feeling you weren't so sure. Seems weird to be saying this, but I'm glad you've decided not to turn yourself in. I hate to see an innocent guy get railroaded, and that's been happening way too often lately..."

"I can't tell you how much I appreciate your help. But you know what's been bothering me... let's say I go through all this bullshit– excuse my French– then get caught anyway. Am I making things worse for myself? How long can a person run from the law these days?"

"Sometimes a long time," said Rosa. "I have cousins from Sonora who've been here illegally for over ten years."

"I don't want to hear about any of this 'illegal' stuff," came a voice from the entryway. Jack entered the kitchen, grinning. He grabbed a cup, poured himself some coffee, added a splash of milk, and sat down. "You guys plotting some kind of commie insurrection?"

Joel laughed. "Not exactly. We were discussing where we should go from here. I'd still like to go to Canada, but from what you're saying it doesn't sound like a good idea."

Jack took a noisy sip of coffee and sat down next across from Joel. "I didn't mention it last night, because I consider this a last resort. I used to work with the Witness Protection Program, so I have a little knowledge of what it takes to disappear. It's not easy these days with all the databases and biometrics, but it is possible if you have the right connections."

"Really? I'm all ears!"

Joel looked at Rosa, saw her shoot a hard glance at Jack. Jack raised his eyebrows; it seemed they'd resolved some issue without a word. "As I said, I have some experience, though it's been a few years. Even so, it'd be risky for me, since I used to be in law enforcement. No doubt they're watching me. But I do know a guy back in the Midwest. Wasn't sure he was even still alive. This morning I was able to locate him; he might be able to help you."

"Wow, Jack, thank you, I don't know what to say!"

"Don't thank me yet. I called my friend from the store at the junction. Can't be too careful, but since there are so few pay phones left, except in the boonies like out here, the Feds don't pay too much attention to them. Anyway, the guy's number still works, it was his voice on the machine. Hell of a fellow, though definitely on the edge of the law. If he weren't an ex-cop, he'd have ended up in the pen by now. Don't know if he still works in freelance relocation, but it's worth a shot." He handed Joel a folded piece of paper with a number on it.

"I don't know what to say," Joel's eyes were starting to water, a condition he found highly embarrassing. "I mean, thank you, but the words seem inadequate for the risks you're taking."

"Think nothing of it! Besides, you know what the Arabs say," Jack grinned again, "The enemy of my enemy is my friend."

"So, Uncle, where's this old buddy of yours? Does he live near here?"

"Kenosha, Wisconsin. If he's still in business. He's quite cautious; you'll probably have to go there in person. He's got good reason to be suspicious of anyone needing his services."

"Kenosha, eh? My old stomping grounds!" Joel had actually grown up just across the Illinois line in Waukegan, but it was all still Greater Chicago.

"You can try calling from the junction. Another old pay phone, somehow never got the DHS biometric upgrade. The Feds can still record your call, but they can't trace your identity. It's about 20 miles north..." He rattled off directions, which Nephi entered in his Android phone.

Joel wiped up the remains of his eggs with a scrap of toast. "It's worth a try. Now I need to get an old junker car somehow, or even a motorcycle, without using my name."

Nephi smiled. "Too risky, Joel. I'll take you there, I'd like to meet this friend of Uncle Jack's. Plus I have an ulterior motive. I have a friend in North Dakota who's been working on the encryption project with me. Great guy, I met him at DEFCON a couple years back. Long as you don't mind the detour, I'm your ride. On the way, we'll keep an eye on things over the Net. There are things the authorities let slip into the media. I have Web bots searching for specific news items..."

"You watch that Internet!" snapped Jack, surprising them with his sudden vehemence.

"Come on, Uncle John!" Nephi seemed uncharacteristically annoyed. "You need to get with the twenty-first century."

"Now that's wishful thinking," Rosa laughed.

Joel pushed his chair back and stood up. Despite the danger, he was hopeful again. "It really was a great meal, Rosa! Thanks so much!" He excused himself to go outside to have a smoke. As he stood next to the porch railing, puffing away, Nephi appeared with his bags, and started fiddling with some of the equipment in the back of the van.

"Joel!" He spun around; Jack was behind him. I almost forgot– my friend's a bit paranoid, so when you call, you need to convince him you know me. Here, one of our pass-phrases."

Joel took the paper and read it. "This is mythological, isn't it? Sounds like a metaphor for our times."

Jack smiled. "Maybe just wishful thinking." He extended his hand. "Take care of yourself, friend. We'll be praying for you."

"Thanks," said Joel. The handshake was, as before, firm but not quite crushing. "For your help, and your hospitality, too." Seeing Nephi was ready to go, he took one more drag, then stubbed out the cigar.

Chapter 3 – The Griffin Project

"Stop it!"

"Huh?" Nephi was just getting out of the van, when he was startled by Joel's outburst. He stared at his friend, still reclined in the passenger seat.

"Stop it, Jasmine, that tickles!"

Nephi smiled and reddened a bit. Joel was talking in his sleep. Jasmine was the name of the cute barista at the Java he'd often seen him flirting with. It was downright embarrassing. Jaz was young enough to be Joel's daughter.

Nephi gently closed the door and headed for the red brick building. He'd been driving for several hours and needed a rest stop. He also had to call Uncle Jack's friend, since they hadn't been able to reach him yet. Griffin, Nephi's most recent open source hacker project, would have been ideal for this, had the friend been set up as well; he could have left the guy an encrypted voice mail. In a few years, this kind of privacy technology would be ubiquitous, like encryption was now, but it was unfortunately a bit early in the game.

For Joel, the clock was ticking. Nephi had been peeved when his friend fell asleep again, but he realized these last few days had been pretty exhausting for him. Luckily with satellite radio there was a lot to keep his mind occupied. He'd been streaming the 24-hour CNN news channel, and was surprised to hear Joel's name mentioned in the most recent update. Something about an alleged terror cell in Kingman, Arizona– "one-time home of Timothy McVeigh," the announcer had noted. Nephi's gut tightened, thinking of it. *So it's official now; Joel's a fugitive. The Albanians will have to stop hounding him, now that he's a fellow 'terrorist.'*

After emerging from the rest room, Nephi looked for a pay phone. Some of these remote areas still had them, and they could provide a relatively anonymous way to place a call. No such luck; they were quickly going the way of typewriters and fax machines. All the rest area had was one of those free 'emergency' phones that could only dial 9-1-1.

Back at the van, Joel was emerging from the passenger side door. "Hey," he said as he raised his glasses to rub the sleep from his eyes. "Where the heck are we at?"

"Idaho, fifty miles west of Idaho falls. By the way, they mentioned your name on the radio. Supposedly you're on the FBI website, though I haven't had a chance to look yet."

"Really? I hope they put a decent picture on there. My driver's license photo is pretty awful." His face went serious. "By the way, I need to send a message to my daughter, let her know I'm OK. Is there any way we can send it encrypted?"

Nephi frowned. "I understand how you feel Joel, family is very important to me. But it's quite risky. Maybe when we get to my friend's place in North Dakota, he has all the latest security tech. Out here we might be spotted at any moment. So quick, use the restroom, and get back in the van as soon as possible."

"Yes, sir!" Joel headed for the men's room at a brisk pace.

Nephi opened the side door and, ducking his head, crawled to the bench seats in back where he extended a tiny table. From the ceiling he folded down a flat panel monitor. He folded that down and grabbed the wireless keyboard and mouse from a cabinet. Then he hit a couple of keys and woke up the server from standby mode.

He sat for a moment as the system scanned the available options. No Wi-Fi here; in Arizona practically all the rest stops had it. That would have been the best bet, though by PATRIOT Act III; all providers were required to ask for the user's social security number. That could be defeated by entering any valid SSN; currently, there was no way to verify its user.

The scan showed two communications satellites on the horizon; that looked promising. The latest release of Griffin incorporated a tool for exploiting satellite Internet accounts. Nephi hated to do that because technically it was a theft of services, so for him it would be a last resort.

There was cell service here, but that was not a secure medium. It was bad enough to establish your location by making a call, but at least until now Nephi had only called family and coworkers. Jack's friend was another matter. Just in case, Nephi ran Griffin's UHF detector, which located not just the nearby towers but any phones in the vicinity. Since they were alone here, and his and Joel's phones were turned off, he didn't expect to see any.

But there was a stationary source– the emergency phone! Of course; why lay cable to a remote area like this? The Griffin suite included cell-phone-hacking tools, supplied by some radical Phone Phreaks from the West Coast. It might take a little while, but a pungent odor told him Joel was currently indulging his addiction, so he had some time to kill.

These public access phones, though hardened against vandalism, were vulnerable to a different kind of attack. Their firmware had a back door which accepted calls for service purposes. It didn't take long for Griffin to brute-force the access code and dial the number of Uncle Jack's friend. Nephi plugged his headset into his notebook's media jack, and waited nervously to the sound of a ringing phone.

Finally a voice answered. "Hello, Cook speaking."

Nephi had been ready to hang up; he was so surprised he forgot the pass phrase for a moment. Finally he got it out. "Sisyphus has reached the summit."

There was a pause on the other end. "So the old Snowman hasn't melted yet! Who am I talking to?"

"I shouldn't say," Nephi stammered.

"Don't worry," Cook replied. "I have security in place. Though nothing's foolproof, of course. I assume you're at a secure location yourself, so out with it."

Nephi's stomach churned with sudden fear. They may have obfuscated both ends of the connection, but there was no way to keep the NSA, or EID, as it was called these days, from monitoring the call and detecting significant words and phrases. He'd need to be very careful. "A friend of mine needs to relocate, and my, uh, friend Jack said you could help him."

"Relocate, eh?" The man chuckled, then coughed violently. "You picked a hell of a time! Our dear leader is talking about reactivating the TSA checkpoints on the highways."

"I realize it's bad timing, but..."

"Well..." The line crackled, obscuring the next few words. "...a while since I've helped anyone do that. For a while with all the biometrics and interlocking databases it was practically impossible. But the larger a system gets, the more vulnerable it is, and we now have 'technicians' who can take care of the paperwork, so to speak. But their services don't come cheap."

"I see," said Nephi with a sigh. It sounded promising, but he wondered if Joel could afford to pay for Cook's services. This whole trip might have been for nothing.

He thought back to that time when he'd been arrested for the 'crime' of photographing the police as they harassed a group of peaceful demonstrators. Joel, a total stranger, had come to his aid, deflecting the cops' attention. If not for that selfless act, Nephi might have been one of those unfortunates who were seriously injured that day. Nephi had been raised to believe in the American system. That day, his faith in America was seriously shaken.

"Are there any other options?"

"Your friend *could* try to go north, but I assume there's a reason he's not applying for refugee status, am I right?"

"Uh, yeah. Though Jack also mentioned the Caribbean or Central America."

There was another pause. "There are still a few places where a man can go to start over, but he stills need to have papers, so he can get on a plane or a boat. And right now, there's a lot of scrutiny of international travelers. Your friend would be wise to wait for things to blow over. Unless somebody wants him bad enough to send a team of 'specialists' after him."

"Probably not," Nephi answered quickly. Did the Feds seriously think Joel was a threat, or did they just need to have a suspect, make the public think they had things under control?

"I understand. Often they just want to make an example of someone."

"So what're the fees like, just a ballpark figure?"

"It used to run like 100K or more, but with the improvements in technology, that number has come down significantly, and some of our vendors are willing to haggle a bit. It's too complicated to work out over the phone, I'm afraid."

"Interesting," Nephi hoped Cook knew what he was talking about.

"Like I was saying, we can't do this remotely. You'll have to come out to my place."

"No, I understand the delicacy of the situation. As long you're sure it'll be safe."

"Everything in life has risk. Besides, I owe the Snowman my life, what's left of it, so I might consider giving your friend a substantial discount. Got something to write on?"

Nephi took some quick notes, thanked him, and hung up. Looking out the van's window, he saw they were no longer alone at the rest stop. A group of seven or eight bikers had appeared, wearing beat-up leathers, all without helmets, this being one of the few states where a person could legally do that. They seemed unlikely to be Federal spies. But these days, you never knew.

Nephi pulled off his headset and got out of the van. The sun was sinking below the mountains, and the photosensitive outdoor lights were flickering on. It was time to move on.

As Nephi approached the building housing the rest rooms, he smelled the familiar odor. He hated those stinky cigars, so much that he'd considered letting Joel sleep through their rest stop. On the other hand, he didn't relish the thought of driving with a grouch. Hopefully he was almost done. Nephi made a quick purchase at the soda machine, then rounded the building to the designated smoking area.

Nephi noticed a butt smoldering in the ashtray and shook his head. "Is that your second one? Well, don't be long, we need to get going." He forced a smile. "I'm glad you were able to rest up, get some sleep. It sounded like you were having quite a dream."

Joel took a long drag, blew out a stream of smoke, and grinned. "Was I babbling again? Used to get myself in trouble with the ex that way."

"You seemed to be enjoying it so much, I hated to wake you. But I was about to anyway, in case you had to use the rest room."

"Your infernal computer did that for you. I was rudely awakened by this voice saying, 'Security alert, security alert!'" He smiled. "At least you made it sound like a hot woman. Meanwhile, you scared me half to death, and I couldn't even get the monitor to come on."

"Don't worry Joel, it's not necessarily the end of the world. Could've been a number of things. I have a bot on the Internet checking the relevant websites and chat rooms 24/7. It looks for specific topics, like government alerts or law enforcement news. By the way, the system responds to voice commands. All you have to do is say. 'Monitor on.'"

Joel slapped his forehead with the palm of his hand. "What a *yutz* I am! I should have known it'd be something high tech like that. Oh, did you get in touch with your uncle's friend?"

"Yes. Good news is, he thinks he can help you. Bad news is, it'll be expensive, in the tens of thousands."

"Oy, that'll clean me out! Good thing I was able to retrieve certain collectibles from my house, or I'd be sunk. But to be honest, it's a relief, I was sure it'd be a lot more." He took one more drag, and stubbed the cigar on the brick wall of the lavatory. "Can't enjoy it anyway, with you and the disapproving look on your face. Like having a second mother."

"Thanks, I guess." Nephi headed back to the van, and Joel followed. "Before we go I need to check out that alert."

Once again Nephi climbed into the back of the van, and activated the monitor, keyboard, and mouse. Joel squeezed in behind him.

"It's an underground site, so you can't get on without a password." Nephi typed a couple of lines. "Holy cow! More bad news!"

"What do you mean *more*? I haven't even heard the other bad news!"

Nephi held up a hand to forestall answering Joel's question. "There's a major Federal dragnet in this area. Doesn't say who they're looking for, possibly a sweep for illegal aliens, but there's a checkpoint to the east, one to the west, and DHS helicopters have been spotted around Pocatello."

"Do you think they're looking for *me*?"

Nephi shrugged. "Earlier today there was an armed robbery in Idaho Falls. That might be the reason, but it doesn't matter. If they stop us and run your ID we're both in deep doo-doo."

"Well– what can we do?"

"Luckily, I've got detailed BLM maps in my Nav system." He typed furiously as he spoke. "Hopefully we can find a – yes! We can take the back roads all the way to Montana!"

"If the black helicopters don't see us, driving suspiciously out in the boondocks."

"We may have to go dark," Joel looked puzzled, so Nephi explained, "I never travel without my night vision gear. We should be able to drive without lights if we don't go too fast."

"Sounds *meshuggah* to me. Won't that make us even more suspicious?"

"Get in, I'll explain. You'll be navigating." He handed Joel a rectangular electronic device. "And you can have this, too."

Joel took the GPS, and the green and black can Nephi had been carrying. "Lightning bolt? You telling me this is LDS approved?"

"Not exactly. Vending machine was out of Pepsi. I was really worried about staying awake. Not anymore!"

"But – what about the other bad news?"

"Oh, I meant your making the FBI list. We'll have to be more careful from now on."

"At least we know. Besides, it's a bit of an honor, I'm famous."

Nephi glanced nervously at the bikers, who were sitting at the rest area's lone picnic table, laughing and joking, brazenly smoking cigarettes in a 'smoke free' zone. If any of them were informants, it was already too late. Joel would need a disguise. Already, though, a scruffy gray beard was coming in, making him look less like his clean-shaven on-line visage.

He started the engine. "Ready to rock and roll?" Joel nodded in response; they were off.

A few hours past sunset, the night was dark and moonless. They were on a dirt road, heading east into Wyoming. Nephi wore his low-light goggles as he drove. It had been quite confusing at first, but he'd quickly gotten used to the false-color scenery. Luckily, the van was old enough to have analog gages that could still be read with the lights off.

Joel was peering down at the GPS, currently the only light in the cabin. The backlight was pretty bright; he had it covered with his hat so it wouldn't mess up Nephi's vision. So far they'd encountered only one other car, and they'd pulled over until it had passed. It was a nerve wracking way to drive. He could only imagine how it was affecting Joel, who seemed prone to drama. Suddenly the air in the van became fetid. Nephi cracked open the window.

"Sorry," Joel muttered. "My intestines are doing back flips."

"Having any trouble with the GPS?"

"No, it's easy to read, even with my bad eyes. We're still on course. How you holding up?"

"Good, not tired at all. I wouldn't mind a little conversation though."

"OK. On the news earlier, did you hear anything about Wilton and the Canadians?"

"A fair bit. Our President met with the Canadian Prime Minister. She's still refusing to release the JFK Nine, which seems to me like political posturing. They may be Arabs, but they're also Canadian citizens." He exhaled in disgust. "It baffles me why people even voted for that woman, she was only a governor. She's got no foreign policy experience at all."

Joel laughed. "People used to find her outspokenness charming, at first. If only she'd shut her mouth for a while, the incident might just blow over. We don't have many friends left in the world, we don't have to alienate the Canadians, too."

"Canada's got its own problems with terrorism, you think we'd be working together. After that shooting at the CN Tower? I hear Thomas got a lot of heat for sticking up for those nine Egyptians, especially from the right wing parties in the western provinces."

"Imagine that, a politician with principles." Joel laughed. "Even if he does date the occasional stripper. I suppose if a person went on TV and acted sorry enough he could..."

"What?" Nephi glanced at him for a second and almost went off the edge of the road.

"Shh! Do you hear that? Sounds like some kind of aircraft!" He slowed way down and turned around. "Definitely an aircraft, something giving off heat coming this way!"

"Whoa, I better pull over. Man, why did it have to be when we were out in the open like this?" He looked around desperately, the optics half-blinding him with a flash when he looked toward Joel and the uncovered GPS. "Hey, a livestock shelter!"

"No!" Joel was adamant. "It's not safe! It could easily fall down on our heads. On the top of the hill, that oil rig. We can hide behind that."

"They might be scanning infrared..."

"Yeah, but it's pumping, so maybe the pump motor will mask our heat."

They waited nervously as the craft approached. Too small to have a pilot, it had to be an unmanned drone. It followed the road, playing its searchlights left and right. Just when it seemed to have passed, it circled back around.

Joel, who had been amazingly calm so far, was starting to crack. "We're dead meat; I'm sorry, Nephi!"

Nephi put a hand on his shoulder and half whispered, half growled. "Quiet! We need to be listening!"

They sat there, barely breathing, as the drone settled over the shelter and hovered. Nephi could just barely make out the twin rotors mounted atop the fuselage. *Amazing, didn't know they could do that.* There was a sudden flash from the bottom of the aircraft– some kind of rocket? No, just something round, which hit the roof, bounced, and landed back on it. Then there was an incredibly loud bang. When they opened their eyes, the structure had been flattened. The chopper was still above, hovering, probing the wreckage with its searchlight. All at once it turned the light off and flew away to the west.

"Whew!" Joel sighed. "Score one for me! If we'd been under there..."

Nephi was too relieved to feel foolish. "Good call, man. I was praying like crazy. I think that was a concussion grenade. Wonder if they meant to knock down the shelter, or if it was just that it was so old? We better wait here a while, in case it comes back again."

They sat there for twenty minutes or so, which seemed like an eternity. Once or twice Joel dozed off for a few seconds. Then, without a word, Nephi started the engine and got back on the road. "Still awake, Joel? Want to check the GPS? I need to know where we're at."

"Wyoming, a few miles south of Jackson. We're coming up on a highway pretty soon."

The GPS was correct. It was a state highway with the familiar cowboy number sign. "Should be past the danger zone, now." With a sigh of relief, Nephi pulled off the goggles and turned the van's lights on. "Joel, I'm pretty wiped out. Can you find us someplace to stop? National forest maybe, someplace with trees, where we can hide and get a little shuteye."

Joel consulted the GPS. "There's a primitive camping area fifty miles down the road. Can you make it that long?"

"Yep. We've got issues to discuss, anyway."

Siri moved her queen to king's bishop three. "Check."

A smile cracked Chiang Liang's weathered face. "That would be check-*mate*, my friend. I can't move my king because of your knight."

She shrugged. "I thought so, but I have this compulsion to double-check everything... if you'll pardon the pun. Would you like to play another?"

Chiang shook his head. "Sorry, I don't think my old brain cells are up for a rematch tonight. Nor do you seem to be, either. I can tell you're preoccupied."

Siri tried to feign innocence. "What makes you say that?"

"Despite your considerable skill, you made several foolish mistakes. I took your bishop and castle early in the game. At first I thought it a fiendishly clever ploy. But when you made your last move without realizing you'd won..." He shook his head.

"Guess I'm busted!" Siri forced a smile. "I was putting off telling you as long as I could, not that it makes it any easier..." She sighed. "I'm sorry, but I'm resigning from the University."

"I see. So soon after we hired you?" Chiang had advised Siri in her undergraduate days, so despite her short time on the faculty, he had known her for several years. "We'd hate to lose you. If it's a matter of pay, I'll speak to the chancellor on your behalf."

She shook her head. "No, it's my father. He just hasn't been the same since the heart attack. I'll be moving back to Madison after the end of the semester."

"I'm sorry to hear that. It was my impression that your father's attack was relatively mild, and that he was making good progress."

"He is, but with his diabetes, there's always the risk." Chiang was actually right. Siri's father had made an outstanding recovery, which his doctors attributed to his excellent fitness from a lifetime of yoga. His only vice was his excessive fondness for sweets.

Siri hated misleading her old friend, but she'd decided not to tell him the real reason for her resignation. After forcing herself to wait a few days, to make it appear she was giving it due consideration, she'd rejected the DHS offer of employment. Consequently, she'd had to discontinue her research–officially, at least. Agent Kudrmas had returned to supervise the removal of her files from the University computers, including all the backups.

They'd also inspected her personal Mac Book. It amazed her they hadn't searched her home. Even if they had, they probably wouldn't have checked the hard drive on her digital video recorder. The DVR's huge disk contained three downloaded seasons of *Star Trek – Alternate Time Line.* Hidden in the noise bits of all that video were the data she'd compiled for her thesis, and its continuation as a University research project.

Chiang put the chess pieces away in an ornate enameled box. His tiny apartment held few possessions. Since his wife's passing a few years earlier, he'd given most of them away.

"Tea?" He filled two handle-less cups and handed one to her. "We all have many reasons for what we do. As Master Lao said, 'He who does his duty as his own nature reveals it never sins.' I will miss our chess games, but I admire you for following your heart."

"You're very perceptive, Professor. I wasn't going to say anything, but you probably already know about ..."

Chiang nodded and put a finger to his lips.

For a second Siri was angry. *I could really use a sympathetic ear right now.* But she remembered Chiang's history; the decade he'd spent in prison in Mainland China. His refusal to discuss the matter was not from a lack of empathy.

Could it be he's not paranoid? If Chiang's apartment is bugged, mine is likely to be, too. She suppressed a shudder. She'd discussed the job offer with her father when she'd returned home the previous weekend. Hopefully the DHS hadn't thought to put surveillance on her family, at least not before she'd turned them down; unless they'd been expecting her negative response.

She'd have to be much more careful from now on.

★ ✪★ ★

Joel took a sip of warm Lightning Bolt, and grimaced. "Well, we survived the night. Don't know how you do it, with so little sleep."

"Guess I'm running on adrenaline now."

"No sh– no kidding. Next town we see, I'll buy you breakfast."

"OK, Joel, sounds like a plan."

"Speaking of plans... I know I've been waffling lately, but I've decided that getting a new identity from the Cook fellow is definitely the way to go, even if it costs every cent I have. Though I still feel awful about making you drive me there. You need to be getting back to work."

"Not a problem. It helps to be working for the family, makes things more flexible. Besides, I was planning to spend a week in Salt Lake. I felt bad blowing off my friends. Though I'm going to have some explaining to do if their folks talk to my folks."

"Too bad I can't just go to Canada. I love ice hockey and maple syrup; I even know a few words of French. We could head north and be there in a few hours."

"Sorry, no pancakes for you. I messaged Jon Larsen, encrypted, of course, and he said he'd be glad to have us to stop by. I've been wanting to see what he's been up to. We've been collaborating very heavily on the Griffin Project. His place is a bit out of our way, but we have good roads and good weather, so I consider it an opportunity."

"Say, how well do you really know this Larsen fellow? These days, the Feds have agents everywhere, inciting people to do something stupid and hang themselves."

"I am aware of the risk. One thing, though, I didn't join the Project until I'd met the man in person. It may sound like a cliché, but I think I can get a feel for a man's character by looking him in the eye. Also, I've read a lot about law enforcement, how they've infiltrated organized crime and so on. Larsen doesn't seem to be following any of those scripts."

Joel realized he still didn't really understand what the Griffin Project was supposed to do. Nephi had said something about protecting peoples' privacy against the government, but how a handful of computer geeks were supposed to prevail against the State and all its resources, he didn't know. He had enough trouble following that technical stuff at the best of times.

He took another sip of Bolt, and realized the can was empty. "So this Cook fellow says he can get me a new identity. Isn't there a way we could avoid going all that way?"

"If we want to use his services, no. For a connection we can trust, it'd be worth it."

Joel nodded. "Not to *kvetch*, but I'm starting to get a bit worried about the financial aspects. It doesn't leave much for me to live on, till I can find work."

"You probably won't find much better. I posted a query on the Motley Hacker website– you know, one of those numbered underground sites. According to them, the going rate for new ID, with documentation on the Federal database, starts at around thirty K.

Joel let out a long whistle. "Good thing I'm so paranoid. I've been slowly withdrawing my savings. Luckily I did it before the sh– I mean crap, hit the fan. But it's still a lot of money. Like I said, I've got collectibles that I could sell, much as I hate to."

"Uh huh." Nephi nodded in sympathy.

Joel noticed Nephi's eyelids starting to droop. After all the excitement, the lack of sleep was finally hitting him. "I can take over the driving, if you're getting tired."

"No, no, I'm fine."

"Then as long as you have a captive audience, why don't you tell me about this project of yours? You really think this thing could defeat the Establishment?"

Nephi chuckled. "Joel, your word choices are dating you." He rubbed his stubbly chin. "Last time I tried explaining, your eyes glazed over. So maybe I'd better show you instead."

"As long as it doesn't involve taking your hands off the steering wheel."

"No, but you'll have to go in back to check it out. I've got the latest version installed on my notebook. You can bring it up and play with it a bit."

"Sure, why not?" Joel reclined the seat all the way, and carefully climbed over.

The road they were driving was rough, so Joel swayed like a drunken sailor on the short walk to the back. Nephi's van was a camper conversion, though the mini-kitchen had been removed. Now it was packed with electronic equipment: servers, monitors, analyzers, tool chests, boxes of fiber optic cable. Joel opened a pantry and was surprised to see a fingerprint scanner and a bulky pair of VR goggles. "Where's your notebook?"

"Under the server rack. Wait – I have a better idea. Let's install it on *your* computer."

"Griffin runs on Windows? I thought you only used Linux."

"I do, but half the world is still on Microsoft. And we want as many people to use it as possible. Larsen helped port it to Windows, by the way."

Joel sat down at the table, slid his notebook out of its case and turned it on. "Now what?"

"Do a Wi-Fi connection and log on to my upgrade server. You remember how, right?"

"I'm not quite that senile," Joel growled. "OK, I'm there. What do I do now?"

"Look for an icon of a griffin, probably in the upper right hand corner, and click it."

"What's the significance of the griffin? You some kind of Harry Potter fanatic?"

Nephi laughed. "I wouldn't say *fanatic*. Actually, Griffin was the name of the Invisible Man in the H.G. Wells book. We thought it would make a perfect code name for the Project."

"It's been so long since I read that, I'd totally forgotten. OK, now what?"

"Install it on your machine. That should take just a minute or two."

Joel waited impatiently. He was starting to 'jones' for a cigar. The install completed quickly, providing him with a distraction. "OK, Griffin's running. Not much to see, is there?"

"There's a lot under the hood. Just a sec..." He spoke to a small mike mounted on the steering wheel. "Dish on, auto-track! Let's run a test. Go to 'mode' and select 'pass-through.' Then press the 'scan' button. It'll look for connections, like the Wi-Fi wizard on your PC."

"All I see is something called 'Netstar'. What is that, a satellite?"

"Yeah. Try clicking it."

"Hmm, progress bar – we're on already! So what can this baby do?"

"This should be interesting. Click the button that says 'Network Test.'

Joel did. A black box popped up in the middle of the notebook screen. It was instantly filled with white text, scrolling by too fast to read. "What the heck is this thing doing?" No sooner had Joel said that than the window disappeared, replaced with another pop-up.

"Did it finish?"

"Yes. There's a list of times and statistics and names of countries. China, Kazakhstan, Venezuela, Java, Nigeria – what's up with that? We're *at war* with some of those countries."

"That's where your test message was routed, through clandestine servers all over the world and back to you. I'm glad to hear China was still on the list. They keep trying to strengthen their firewall, but our proxy servers can learn and adapt to get the message through."

"Isn't it a little frivolous to hack through the firewalls of foreign countries just to do a demonstration for me?"

"Not at all. The more traffic we send, the more trouble for the authorities to sift through the haystack and find something important. And the more people will be encouraged to use it."

"Very interesting! I'm gonna come back up now, so we don't have to shout."

It was awkward getting back in the seat, while simultaneously holding the laptop. Once Joel was settled, he looked at Nephi, who was smiling smugly. "Let me ask you something, Neeph. When I logged onto Netstar just now, was that legit?"

It took him a few seconds to reply. "For the most part. We logged on Netstar legally, but to get onto the underground network, you need an open gateway. The governments have been shutting them down, so we move them around. But if people can't find them, they can't use them. So hide them right on servers belonging to multinational corporations."

"So we can't get on this network without doing a hack?"

"Yes. That's one of the things Griffin does. It automates the process, by making it easy to intercept and decrypt login sequences..."

"Nephi, I'm surprised at you! It's one thing to hack through the firewall of a dictatorship like China. It's another to impersonate the identities of legitimate users." It was difficult for Joel to keep a straight face, given the irony of lecturing his strait-laced friend on anything. "Don't give me that look. You're the one who's always going on about the sanctity of property rights."

Nephi sighed. "Honestly, Joel, I agonized about that for quite a while, and Larsen and I have had long discussions. It's not such a black and white issue. For one thing, we use so little bandwidth, the owners hardly notice. Besides, it's a good cause, we're helping people in oppressive countries. It uses a concept called 'onion routing,' which obscures a message's origin and destination info by adding layers, like an onion. The hard part is getting the user to the first server. Foreign governments– ours, too– have been arresting anybody who puts up a list."

Joel shook his head in mock outrage. "I'm still in shock. You were always such a law abiding person. With this particular exception, which I highly appreciate."

"I still follow the *real* laws like the US Constitution, the Ten Commandments. The Bible tells us to help people in need. We can't sit on our hands while people are killed, imprisoned and tortured. Especially where people are persecuted for their faith, like in China, Iran, or Cuba."

"You won't get any argument from me. What I don't understand is how did you and Larsen do all this? How did you get all those servers up overseas?"

"You give us too much credit! We're just part of a larger movement. The servers are there already, but until now only the most technically savvy have been using them.

"What Griffin does is tie these stealth technologies together, to make it easier for the average person to use. For example, we mask the illegal strong encryption we're using by encapsulating the message with encryption of legal strength. We use genetic algorithms– programs that learn, like living things– to find the best ways around blocks and firewalls, *and* hacking into corporate servers. The goal is to let people speak freely, even in China."

"We're starting to need that here in America, too," Joel added somberly.

Nephi nodded. "Even here. It *does* bother me." He popped a stick of gum in his mouth, and offered one to Joel. "But I don't see an alternative to hacking, 'til we can establish alternative channels of communication. Since anonymous Wi-Fi is illegal now, our users sometimes need to pretend to be somebody else. Anyway, most Wi-Fi accounts are flat rate, or free."

"Weird, me arguing on the side of 'law and order,' but there's another thing that worries me. This being an open-source project, there's no way you guys can restrict the technology. People could change the code, remove the safeguards, and use them to trick people."

"No way can we prevent that, unfortunately. Any technology is open to abuse. I've had that same argument with liberals about guns."

"Good point," Joel turned back to his notebook and checked out Griffin more closely. He began reading the background materials and the help files. Some of it was pretty technical, and it was starting to make him drowsy.

He glanced at Nephi, who was now gazing into the distance and humming along to an old Talking Heads tune on the radio. "Are you sure you don't need me to take over the driving?"

"No thanks," he said. "I've been up so long; I've gotten my second wind. Plus, I've got a lot on my mind to fret over and keep me from getting sleepy."

"In that case, I want to get myself up to speed on this Griffin stuff. I have a whole bunch of questions to ask you, so you definitely won't have the chance to get drowsy."

"Glad to hear it, fire away."

"You said Griffin was a collaboration, but in my experience there's always one person who gets things rolling. Whose idea was this Griffin thing in the first place?"

"Well it all grew out of the 'World of Transparency' website, the one started by that New Zealand guy who was publishing all those government leaks. If you remember, Finland offered him refuge, but then the US and Russia hit them with that embargo..."

"Son of a bitch!" Jon Larsen looked at his throbbing index finger, a small bead of red forming at the end. While twisting the end of the power cable, he'd encountered a sharp strand of copper. He looked around for the dispenser of disinfectant gel, which was buried somewhere on his cluttered workbench. He was ready to go to the house for a new one when he heard someone yelling.

"Hey Jon, you there?"

"In here, Dave!" Larsen found a shop rag with a clean spot to wipe his finger. "About time you got here!" His brother's heavy footsteps were punctuated by some choice curses.

"You need to park the machines farther apart. Ripped my new shirt on your combine."

Larsen laughed. "If you'd have been around to help, I wouldn't have had to hire the Johnson kid to help me with the harvest. Can't park straight to save his life."

"Sorry, Bro. I've been running all over hell and creation looking for a new diesel supplier. The way the price's been going up, people are hoarding it." After their parents retired and moved to town, the two boys inherited the family farm. Dave hated farm life, so he sold his share to Jon, and took over as the manager of the local Cenex. When grain prices shot up, Jon paid off that debt, before fuel prices rose and wiped out some of his neighbors who hadn't been as frugal.

Dave looked around. "What do you need me for today?"

"Same thing as last week." Jon pointed to the faded red Nissan pickup standing by the welder. "She's ready for her test drive. I need you behind the wheel while I monitor the sensors."

Dave grumbled. "The crazy things you get me into. You're going to find yourself in the pokey one of these days."

Jon shrugged. "Maybe. Least I'm not a summer soldier or a sunshine patriot."

After moving two tractors, a truck, and a combine, they were able to get the truck out of the big Quonset shed.

"It's the same piece of crap you drove all those years." Dave grinned. "But I like the new swivel gun. Am I gonna have to aim it while driving, or do I need a copilot?"

"Nope, it's totally automatic. I've trained it with images of the targets. All you need to control is the on-off switch. Folds down into the box when not in use."

"OK," he said, climbing in the cab. "So what do I do?"

"I've got three targets set up between here and the grain bins. I want you to drive west, turn around at the bin, and come around back. If all goes well, we can hit 'em from both sides."

Jon had recently added an awning to the side of the Quonset, and an extra, walk-in door to the workbench area, for those rare days when it was too nice to work indoors. Now it made the perfect place to sit with his monitoring gear and watch the show.

"OK, go!"

Dave took off, and passed the first target with no telemetry from the hardware. "Dumb ass, turn it on!" Jon muttered. He was double-checking the antenna when he saw a long shape rise out of the truck bed. As Dave passed the second target, it swiveled and fired. "God damn it, missed!" Then the third– a perfect hit as the blue paint splotch appeared on the glass fronted box.

Dave peeled around the far target, raising all sorts of dust, and sped up for the return. Jon checked the truck's speed data. *He's going too fast, it'll miss!* The next shot, as the truck accelerated, went wide. But the fourth and fifth hit dead on, and at 31 and 33 miles an hour!

"Sorry, I forget to turn it on at first," Dave mumbled as he got out.

"Hey, no problem!" Jon raised his hand for a high-five. "It's an even better test, when it has to handle adverse conditions. So what do ya think?"

Dave grinned. "Pretty cool, Bro, as long as nobody catches you at it. Hey, you missed a really great party at Ernie's the other night."

Jon raised his eyebrows. "You don't say. All the guys there?"

"Yup. Ernie's sister was up from the Cities, brought three of her friends. You should've seen the blonde!"

Jon slapped him on the back. "Davey, those big city babes are out of your league."

Dave flushed, for a second something like anger flashed across his face. "I don't see the women beating a path to *your* door. Jon, there's more to life than work and computers and politics. You gotta get out more. Hanging' with computer geeks is OK, but not enough females!"

"Speaking of computer people, I've got some friends coming up from Arizona if you wanna come by. We can have a few beers– no, one of em's a Mormon. Hope at least the other guy drinks."

"Close friends, if you don't know what religion they are." Dave watched as Jon tightened screws on the turret mount. "Amazes me, how you have time to do all this shit. Especially the software; you can't even program your satellite TV."

Jon flashed him a middle finger and laughed. "What do you mean 'can't?' I just refuse to screw around with a poorly designed user interface. I'd have done it totally different. As far as the Project goes, I've hired some of it out. You remember Bird from the U?"

"George Red Bird?" Dave shook his head. "I don't trust him, Bro."

"You hardly know the guy. You prejudiced or something'?"

"Nothing' to do with him being an Indian. I've just heard he's been involved in some shady business." He looked his brother in the eye. "I worry about you, Jon. The way you're going, you're gonna just disappear someday. And you know that'd just kill Mom and Dad."

"Don't worry Davey, I'm a big boy." He grabbed a ring off a hook and handed it to his brother. "Here's the keys. You put the combine back in; I'll get the tractors. Make sure we leave room to get the truck in and out. I'm hoping to use that baby soon."

After an hour or so of wading through Nephi's Griffin documents while simultaneously traveling on bumpy two-lane highways, Joel began to feel nauseous. "I shouldn't read in a car," he said. "How about I drive for a while?"

Nephi relented when they stopped for gas at the only store in Buffalo, South Dakota. There Joel paid for 'breakfast,' two microwave-warmed burritos, and filled his thermos bottle with coffee. Nephi was asleep before they hit the North Dakota line.

The sun was high over the prairie. A few scraggly clouds interrupted the intensely blue sky. The arid grasslands gave way to rolling pastures, morphing into fields of wheat and alfalfa as they continued east. Joel had not been in the Midwest since his childhood, and it brought back long dormant memories. Despite his precarious situation, he felt a mystical peace of mind.

It was strange how a random event could have a major effect on a person's life. Like that day two years ago in Phoenix. Senator Joseph Bishop was speaking at the Civic Plaza, a major campaign stop in his home state. The man had never met a war he didn't like. Joel was there with the Africa Action Coalition, which opposed the military action in Nigeria. The city had denied their parade permit, expecting them to protest five miles away, where nobody would see them.

The AAC didn't give in, and they had a new ally, the Smedley Butler Brigade. This group, named after the controversial Marine general, was founded by the equally controversial the Iraq War hero, Army Colonel 'Mac' MacGuiness. He was the last person Joel expected to see at a peace march. Mac had been discharged for roughing up a suspected insurgent in an interrogation about a bombing that killed three of his men. Now he'd taken up the cause of his fellow veterans, whom he believed had been betrayed by the their country. "We didn't risk our lives so we could protest in a cage."

It was late May, a sweltering day in the desert. Joel's gut tightened as the march began; he held his sign high to hide his fear. He chanted along with the crowd. "US OUT OF NIGERIA NOW!" Where were the TV cameras? Surely they had to be here for Bishop's speech.

There were plenty of cops: City of Phoenix, loaners from neighboring cities, plus the Maricopa County Sheriff's Department, out in full force. This protest was, after all, illegal, and they were expecting trouble. More likely, they knew how MacGuiness did things.

The tension was palpable as the police stood on the sidelines, allowing the demonstration to proceed, for now. How many marchers were there? Five thousand or maybe ten, according to the tweets. Joel looked over the crowd toward the Civic Plaza, hoping the Senator would be brave enough to show his face. People began pouring out of the auditorium. "What is that, some kind of church convention?" a woman wondered out loud.

"LDS," Joel replied. "Bishop's a member of that church; he's polling seventy percent for the Mormons."

"Traitors!" someone shouted across the street. "Go live in Iran if you hate America!"

Some of the peace marchers started to step off the curb. "Cool it, people, don't let them provoke you!" Joel, being one of the organizers of the Mojave County delegation, was charged with helping to keep the 'troops' in line. As plaza kept filled up, some of the assembled Mormons joined in an impromptu counter-protest.

There was some kind of commotion on the other side of the street. Joel craned his neck to see. Some kid with a camera? Cops these days were like the damned Soviets, treating people like criminals for taking pictures. *Like we don't have a right to record public events?* "You're in charge," he said to some young guy from Bullhead City, Jeff somebody-or-other, and handed him his sign. The rage welled within Joel as he pushed into the crowd. Three cops surrounded the kid, grabbed his camera, and threw him to the street. One had him in a choke hold.

"Hey, that's enough, he's down!" Joel shouted.

One of the cops whirled on him. "Get out of the street, sir! Or you'll be charged with interfering with an officer."

"You guys work for us taxpayers! I have the right as an American citizen to... ahh!" The stun gun hit him and he went down onto the street, just as the melee was beginning. He felt panic as he was kicked and jostled by dozens of feet. More shouting, screams, orders over bullhorns, a whiff of pepper spray. *Well, at least the media has got to cover it now...*

Later, at the infamous Tent City Jail, Joel sat slumped on a bunch, every part of his body aching. A long shadow fell over him and he heard an unfamiliar voice.

"Sir," the kid said, "I just wanted to say thank you, for sticking up for me. My name's Nephi." He extended a hand.

The guy had a firm, confident handshake. Joel was glad to see the man (too old to be a kid, he realized) was not badly hurt, just a few bruises. "Hey, we're all Americans, right? Gotta stick up for each other."

The two started talking, and discovered they were from the same town. Nephi had come with his family to hear the Bishop speech. While the two men waited to make their phone calls, their cells having been confiscated, the talk got around to politics. Despite their differences, their views actually had a lot in common. They'd been friends ever since.

And here I am, in my fifties, a fugitive from the law.

That 'fugitive' part was actually a bit exciting, if not for the possibility of being caught. Joel put it out of his mind and concentrated on driving. Following the instructions of Nephi's talking GPS, he avoided the Interstate and took two-lane highways in a zig-zag path through dozens of tiny towns. The roads were in reasonably good repair, and they made good time.

They stopped for a late lunch at a café in a small town called Harvey. Nephi hardly said a word through the meal, and didn't protest when Joel took the wheel again afterwards. The lack of sleep had finally caught up to him. His friend Larsen lived on a farm outside of Grand Forks, a few miles from the Minnesota border. As they traveled eastward, the rolling hills disappeared completely. It was the flattest country Joel had ever seen.

It was near dark when they rounded the last corner and saw the house, standing by itself in the middle of broad irrigated fields. Behind the house were more buildings: a garage and a large metal Quonset hut. On the side of the garage was a huge sign with the words, "Work Harder – Millions on Welfare Depend on You."

Chapter 4 – Homegrown Radicals

"This has got to be Larsen's place," Nephi said, chuckling to himself. "The sign certainly sounds like him."

Joel drove the van into the farmyard. "Impressive spread. Must be doing OK financially."

"Looks like it. Though you can never tell; lots of farmers are mortgaged to the hilt." They were about to get out when two huge dogs ran out, barking furiously between growls and snarls.

"Nice looking Doberman," Nephi commented. "And look at the size of that Rotty!"

"What's up with the Nazi dogs?" said Joel, with a straight face. "All your family and friends have them. Did you tell them I'm a Jew?" Nephi rolled his eyes; Joel laughed out loud.

A man emerged from the garage, wearing a baseball hat and oily coveralls. He was of average height and a bit stocky, almost chunky, with thick muscular arms. His face was covered with a bushy reddish-blond beard. He waved as he approached the van.

"Gerhard! Dietrich! Go lie down!" The dogs stopped barking and trotted obediently to their kennel, a wooden structure adjoining the house. The bearded man turned to his visitors and grinned. "OK, it's safe now."

Joel looked at Nephi and smirked. "Safe for Lutherans, maybe..."

The two men got out of the van. "Hello, Jon, good to see you again! This is Joel Walter, the friend I was telling you about."

Their host extended his hand, realized it was streaked with grease, then wiped it on his pants before offering it again. "It's JL, everybody calls me that." He offered his hand to Joel, who winced when he grasped it. "Good to meet you, Joel. Sorry, did I hurt your hand?"

"Yes, and you can expect to hear from my attorney." Joel laughed. "No, I just took the bandages off. I could tell you how I injured it, but you'd probably just scoff at me like Nephi."

The big man grinned. "Nothing wrong with being a skeptic." He left the obvious question unasked, and waved his hand toward the Quonset. "I was in the shop. Come on back, I'll show you my precious-ss." That last word came out in a breathy squeak, as he rubbed his hands together in Gollum-like glee.

They followed Larsen into the building, which resembled a giant soup can half buried in the earth. They slid past rows of tractors, trucks, and other equipment. On the far side of the building by a translucent fiberglass window was a workbench surrounded by jacks, hoists, and toolboxes. To one side stood a beat up red Nissan pickup.

"What specifically are we looking for?" Joel asked.

"Just a sec." Larsen opened the driver side door of the pickup, flicked a switch, and a long tubular object rose from the truck bed. The object swung back and forth, then with a 'pop', something spattered against a poster that had been tacked up next to the workbench. Joel hadn't noticed it before, but it appeared to be a glossy publicity photo of President Della Wilton.

"Simulated war vehicle?" Nephi asked.

"Nothing simulated about it! I assume you gentlemen are aware of the malignant evil of the traffic camera. Even our remote area has fallen prey to this affliction. But my little invention can blind the eyes of these modern day pirates."

"Awesome," said Nephi.

"Looks like a lot of work," Joel added. "How do you find the time, with farming and computers and everything?"

A brief flicker of anger crossed the Larsen's face. "Was gonna do some traveling this winter, but had to cancel my plans. I've got no livestock to tend, so I had to keep busy with something." He flicked the switch once more, and the tube sank back into the pickup bed. "Let me just put away these tools, get cleaned up a bit, and I'll show you my *other* project."

"You mean the Griffin Project? Nephi's been telling me all about that."

"Not exactly, that's more Nephi's baby. But it's definitely related."

In the short time they'd been in the Quonset, the skies had turned gray. The temperature had dropped by ten degrees– thunderstorm weather. At Larsen's insistence, Nephi moved the van inside. Joel was glad he'd brought his leather jacket. He lit a cigar and stared at the landscape. "I heard North Dakota was a like pancake, but I assumed they were exaggerating."

"They sure weren't! Least not about this part of the state. The whole Red River Valley was a lake in prehistoric times," Larsen explained. "At one time, it stretched into Canada and was bigger than Lake Superior."

Nephi emerged from the Quonset and pulled the door shut. "There wasn't much room in there. I had to squeeze it in next to a combine."

"It was nice of you to let us park it inside. But I don't think a little rain would've hurt it."

"It's not the rain I'm worried about." Larsen pointed at the sky. "There's government planes flying over, several times a day. Media says it's the DEA scanning for meth labs, but that's BS. Pseudoephedrine's gotten expensive; Mexican crank is cheap as dirt. So I hear, anyway."

Joel took a last puff before grinding out the stogie under his boot. "What do *you* think they're looking for?"

Larsen shrugged. "My neighbor– he used to be in the Midwest Militia– says they're using sensors to scan for 'suspicious' electronic activity. My lab's shielded, so I'm not worried about that. But I'd hate to have them photograph your license plate and run your records."

"Agreed," Nephi said.

"Anyway," JL headed for the door. "I need to put on some clean clothes. Come on in, I'll only be a minute. Anyone want a beer?"

"You won't need to twist my arm," said Joel. "As for our young friend here, I think not."

"Oh, that's right, he's one of those Mormon LSD fellows."

"LDS," Nephi corrected, then smiled, realizing Larsen's gaffe had been intentional. "Though I suppose it'd be kind of interesting if it was the other."

The side door opened on a short entryway to the kitchen. "Hope you don't mind domestic," said Larsen. "I drank all the good stuff last weekend. What about you, Nephi?"

Nephi chose a bottled water. They barely had time to open their drinks before their host returned wearing a clean shirt and jeans.

"This way, downstairs." Larsen's basement was unfinished; exposed rafters in the ceiling, a bare light bulb for illumination, and a gray painted cement floor. A wall of two-by-four studs divided off half of it into a laboratory that covered, floor and ceiling, with a fine wire mesh. In the middle was a bolt-together metal rack. Between the supports were dozens of green circuit boards arranged vertically like books on a shelf.

"Behold, the JL-9000," Larsen said with mock drama. "A homemade supercomputer for less than the cost of a mid-range Volvo."

"Amazing." Joel was no expert in electronics, but he expected that in the grand scheme of things, this computer was probably much more important than the paint ball cannon.

Nephi was silent for a moment, walking around the racks and looking at them from every side. "I've worked with a lot of high end servers, and I've never seen anything quite like *this*."

Larsen laughed. "If I used regular server hardware, I'd be spending a fortune in power bills; which might, incidentally, make the government think I'm growing weed. I bought a whole bunch of used PC's and stripped out the motherboards. Of course I had problems with heat, so I used liquid cooling, see all the tubing? Had to use special wrapping to prevent condensation."

This kind of tech talk usually made Joel's eyelids droop. But Larsen explained things simply enough so a non-techie could understand. Plus, the computer was a thing, visual and tactile. Joel found that much easier to grasp than the fuzzy abstractions of software.

Unfortunately, software was Nephi's next topic. "So these all run Linux?"

"You bet. To put Windows on each box would cost a fortune, assuming you did it legally of course. And wouldn't work as well. Plus there's so many great open source apps for Linux. You know the Gilgamesh Project?"

"Hmm, a mythological theme. Is it anything like Beowulf? I've used that."

"Gilgamesh is a successor to Beowulf. Though the name is a lot older. Let me show you the coolest part– the user interface. I wanted to put that upstairs, but there wasn't enough room."

Next to the server racks was a table with six flat panel monitors arranged in a semicircle. In the center was a multi-level ergonomic keyboard and a 3D wireless mouse. "Check this out. One seamless display space." Larsen picked up the mouse and waved it like a conductor's baton. The oversize cursor bounced between the six screens. "I can run a simulation of the weather for the next six months." He clicked an icon and the upper three screens filled with a real-time satellite map of the United States. "Now, we'll do a ten-to-one time speedup and–" He was interrupted by a chiming sound from a wall-mounted speaker. "What the hell? You guys stay here. Don't mess with anything!"

Larsen bounded up the stairs two at a time, surprisingly agile act for such a big man. Joel looked at Nephi. "I don't know much about computers, but it sure looks intimidating."

"I'm impressed," said Nephi. "This is what the Griffin Project needs: a high end development platform. With this baby we could crack almost any non-military security."

"Not very portable, though." Joel finished his beer and looked around for a place to toss the empty. Outside the lab door was a plastic garbage can, full to the top with aluminum. Joel stepped out and tossed in the can. "Hey, what's that?" He removed his vibrating cell phone from his pocket.

"Didn't you take the battery out like I told you?"

"Yeah, but it fell out of my duffel at Jack's place and I almost left it behind. I figured if I kept the switch off, what could it hurt?"

"Sorry, I should've been more specific. It's not just the built-in GPS that's the problem. There's actually a back door the Feds can use to remotely enable the phone and use it as a bug, and there's no way to tell it's doing that."

"Sorry, man! I'll pull it out again, but first I've got to see what this is." He flipped the phone open and opened the message. The sender was listed as 'Unidentified.'

Jewboy: U can run but u cant hide. If u talk we cut out ur tung. We will find u!

Nephi saw Joel's shocked reaction to the text. "What? Who was it?"

"My friends with the reptile fetish. Wishing me well. You were right, I think, about it being the Ahmedaj's. This is the first time they've specifically warned me not to talk. Before it was just vague crap about 'betrayal' and 'treachery.' Joel turned the phone off and removed the battery. "Feh! If the Albanians can track me, what about the Feds?" He glanced toward the stairs, "It could even be them at the door!"

For a few seconds, neither man breathed. Larsen's heavy footsteps upstairs were clearly audible. "I don't hear anybody talking up there. Probably a delivery, or a neighbor stopping by." Nephi looked back at Joel. "What was the date on the message?"

"Today, I think. Not sure. I was distracted by their kind offer to amputate my tongue."

"I wish you wouldn't have put the battery back in. It's partly my fault for not explaining it better."

"Don't beat yourself up. I'm the one who's technologically challenged."

From above came the sound of a door opening. "You guys behaving yourselves down here? Not messing with my stuff, are you?"

"We would've come up," Joel responded, "But you didn't say 'Simon says'."

"We didn't know who was at the door, either," Nephi added.

Larsen laughed. "Did you think it was the Feds? It was just my proximity alarm. I've gotta replace that sound, it's too much like the doorbell."

Joel followed Nephi up the stairs. "Proximity of what?"

"Like I told you," Larsen said as they returned to the kitchen, "there've been lots of over-flights. This one was real low, definitely DEA. Check it out." He pointed at an LCD TV mounted under the cupboard. It was playing a slow motion video of a plane crossing the darkening sky. The letters 'DEA' were clearly visible on the belly.

Joel snorted in surprise. "Marking their planes, clever. Won't that tip off the bad guys?"

"That's why I think it's cover for something more serious, like my neighbor said."

"It could just be PR, you know, security theater," Nephi suggested. "To make the voters think they're doing something about the drug problem."

"Whatever. They're up to *something*." Larsen opened the refrigerator and peered inside. "You guys hungry? Let's see what we've got!" He handed Joel another beer. "I'm sure I have some sodas in here somewhere."

"Can we help?" Nephi asked.

"No, sit! Joel, take the big chair, the place of honor. It's not often I have a Federal fugitive for a guest." He opened the freezer compartment. "Where were those steaks? Damn, guess I ate 'em. How's spaghetti sound?"

Hearing no objections, Larsen dug noisily through the cupboards. Eventually he produced a pot and a frying pan. He popped another beer, sipping and talking as he cooked.

"Hope you don't think I'm paranoid, but could the cops have tracked you guys here?"

"I haven't used any credit cards, if that's what you mean," Joel said.

"No, but he did forget to take the battery out of his cell phone," Nephi said. "Though it was in his suitcase in the back of his van, not in his pocket. It's an older model, so hopefully they haven't been able to trace our movements.

Larsen made an exaggerated show of rolling his eyes. "Don't you realize the FBI can turn your phone into a roving bug, even if the power is turned off?"

"I've heard people say that, but I kind of thought they were just being paranoid." Joel helped himself to another beer. "But Nephi has a cell phone, and I see yours on the counter, JL. If they're so bad, why do you guys have them?"

Larsen let out a guffaw. "What, be without a cell phone, and be disconnected?"

"Don't let him get to you, Joel," Nephi said. "Most people are blissfully unaware of the privacy implications of cell phones. But to answer your question, both of our phones are modded. My hacker group has figured out ways to disable the built-in GPS tracking device, and override any remote control of the microphone. You also have to fool the diagnostics, because technically the carriers are supposed to cancel your service if they detect a 'defective' phone."

Larsen stirred the boiling pasta. "It's the kind of thing used to keep me up at night. Every year, the government gets more power. More wiretaps, more cameras, more surveillance. Now, thanks to people like our young friend here, we can use technology to *protect* our privacy." The sauce spattered little drops of red all over the stove. He stirred it and turned down the heat. "We'll have to fix you up with a mod. Prepaid service, of course."

"If you techno-wizards can do that, I'd be eternally grateful." Joel hadn't realized how hungry he was. It was a simple meal, pasta with meat sauce and green beans on the side, and plain white bread and butter, "Before I forget," he said between mouthfuls," I need to get a message to my daughter in Arizona. How doable is that?"

"If she was set up with Griffin, I'd say yes," Larsen said. "But even then it'd be a risk, because the Feds will be watching her very carefully."

"Is this just a 'don't worry about me' message?" Nephi asked. "Though normally I believe in encrypting everything possible, we have to assume the FBI will intercept it. In that case, it may be better to send it in the clear, because they'll force her to give up the message anyway. So the answer is yes, if you're very careful to avoid specifics. We can use Griffin to obscure the origin of the message and make it very difficult to trace you."

"Don't let me forget, we'll do that right after dinner," Larsen said. "If not, first thing in the morning."

They finished their meal and continued talking. After his fourth beer, Joel was getting sleepy. Larsen seemed unaffected, except his voice was gradually getting louder. Nephi, sober as always, took it in stride, apparently glad he had someone to geek out with.

Joel gave up trying to follow their conversation. He was too distracted by his worries. He stood up, interrupting Larsen in mid-sentence. "Sorry, but I need a smoke. Is there a place I could go that's not totally wet?"

Larsen looked out the window. "Wow, didn't realize it was raining. No problem. The south porch is glassed in. If you open the door a crack, I don't mind if you smoke in there."

"Not even one of these?" Joel said, pulling a cigar from his pocket.

"If it's one of *those* I'll join you. Nephi, you can stay inside and save your virgin lungs from the evil second-hand smoke."

"It's not so much the smoke; it's chilly out there. I'm a thin-blooded desert dweller." But when Joel and Larsen got up, he put on his jacket and followed them.

Larsen took a puff, exhaled. "Not a bad smoke. Are these Cuban?"

"Dominican. Cubans are such a fad right now, they're totally overpriced."

In the distance, the thunder rumbled. The rain started falling harder. The cool air coming in through the propped-open door was refreshing.

Larsen sipped his beer. "So Joel, if you don't mind me asking, what's the plan?"

"Well, my first thought was to skip the country, but..."

"Good move. The Great White North is your best bet. First thing is to apply for asylum. That way Uncle Sam can't get you back without a special court hearing, and that can take *months*. If Nephi needs to get home, I can take you there. Not far at all from where we're at."

"I'd agree with you, if it was a regular 'political' offense, if I'd been arrested protesting the war, leaking government info or sending money to a Palestinian charity. But in my case, I don't think the Canadians will take me, even to spite the Wilton Administration."

"What?" The big man adopted a suspicious expression. "You didn't blow anything up, did you?"

"No, but..." Joel glanced at Nephi. "You didn't tell him about... you know?"

Nephi made a zipping motion over his lips.

"Actually, that's what they want me for, though I didn't do it, of course. You heard about the bomb in Phoenix, didn't you? The one that killed that Federal judge? Somebody planted some of my personal effects at the scene, and now the FBI's after me. With the PATRIOT Act and all the secret evidence they can use now, I don't think I have a prayer of getting a fair trial."

"Jesus H. Christ, I wouldn't want to be in your shoes."

"That's not all. Uncle Sam's not the only one after me. When I left Arizona, I was getting threatening mail from some former clients of mine, Albanian immigrants, who for some reason, think I informed on them. Remember how I winced when you shook my hand?" He held up his hand to show Larsen the scar. "Somebody put a rattler in my mailbox, probably them. I figured they'd be smart enough to let it drop, cause they're on the run now, too. But I just now got another message from them, and it wasn't friendly."

"Hmm, I'd still worry more about the Feds than a bunch of yahoos like that. You really think they could be tracking you here?"

"Maybe. They could easily have contacts in organized crime. I know our government's not much for legal niceties anymore, but they at least have to go through the motions. Not so with the Albanian Mob. I've heard they have operations north of the border, so why not in North Dakota?" He took a long drag, exhaled slowly. "Ideally I'd like to buy a citizenship in some South American country or maybe a Caribbean island, where I don't have to look over my shoulder, and my daughter can come and see me. But for now, I need some docs so I can stay underground. Nephi's uncle has a friend in Chicago who can supposedly help me with that."

"We've never actually met the guy," Nephi chimed in, "But I believe he's for real. Does this mean you've decided, Joel?"

"What choice do I have? Yes, let's see your uncle's friend."

"Hmm, Chicago. I could take you there," Larsen said.

101

"Thanks, JL," Nephi said. "But this guy's pretty paranoid, and he's expecting *me*. I'll just call my folks and tell them we have a few more things to work on up here."

Larsen raised his eyebrows. "They know you're here?

"Why not? They don't know Joel's with me, and we've got the Project as a cover story." He laughed. "I can always tell them I'm trying to convert you."

Larsen grinned. "Like that's gonna happen! Actually, I've been meaning to go there anyway. There's this guy I've been corresponding with at the U of Chicago; I wanted to discuss some of his ideas in person. Mind if I tag along with you guys? "

"Sure. Though you'll have to find your own ride home. I'm not coming back this way."

"There *is* a problem on my end," Joel said. "I need to pay Cook for the new paper, and still have enough to start over, wherever I end up. Also, I've been letting Nephi pay most of the travel expenses, and that's not right."

"Hey, Joel, you know it's OK," Nephi said. "Gives me an excuse to see the country, and visit my co-conspirator in the Project."

"No it's not OK, and not just because I feel guilty. I'm worried about you using your credit cards. You could be getting yourself in big trouble."

"That's true," Larsen agreed. "The DHS has computers scanning all the financial transactions in the country."

"Anyway, JL" Joel continued, "I've got something you might be interested in. I need to run out to Nephi's van and get it."

"Here." Larsen reached in his pocket, and tossed him a rubber John Deere key chain. "Brass one opens the Quonset. Don't get too wet out there."

The walk across the farmyard was enough to get him soaked. Just inside the Quonset was Nephi's van. Joel opened the back door and retrieved a large ASU Sun Devils duffel bag.

As Joel came back around the house to the porch, he heard Larsen and Nephi talking excitedly. He liked these guys, and he greatly admired their technological prowess. But he no longer shared their enthusiasm for political action. All of that was foolishness, like the political blog he'd recently abandoned. Even if Nephi's guess was wrong, and the Ahmedaj's, hadn't planted the bomb, it didn't make Joel feel any better. All it meant was that he'd made some powerful and ruthless enemies that were possibly gunning for him at this very moment.

Nephi and Larsen stopped talking when Joel came in through the screen door. He set the bag at Larsen's feet. "Such a deal I've got for you!" He unzipped the bag and pulled out a long shiny object.

"Holy shit! Is that what I think it is?"

It was a red and white Kramer electric guitar, gleaming in the light of the porch's fluorescent bulb. Across the bottom was a scrawled signature in black permanent marker. "Behold, Eddie Van Halen's personal autographed guitar."

"May I?" Joel nodded. Larsen took it in his hands reverently. He strummed a few barely audible chords. "His fingers touched this! How much you asking?"

"As much cash as you can spare," Joel said. "Lord knows it hurts to part with her."

"I'll give her a good home," Larsen said. "Would you take pre-65 silver coinage? I've got bags of the stuff!"

After some haggling, the guitar and the silver changed hands, much to Joel's regret. Larsen went to stash his acquisition in his gun safe. He returned to the porch a few minutes later. The conversation returned to politics and technology.

"By the way," said Nephi. "Your friend in Chicago, is he in the computer science department?"

"Mathematics. He's worked out the theory for a system of trusted anonymous economic transactions. I've been thinking, if we really want to stick it to Big Brother, we code the algorithms in software, and run it over Nephi's Griffin network, using a server like the JL-9000. We'd be free to exchange ideas and goods and services without Uncle Sam breathing down our neck. It'd be the biggest thing since the Boston Tea Party."

Nephi frowned. "Hey JL, don't take this wrong, but you aren't thinking about doing anything *illegal* with this technology, are you? Because, no offense, I really don't want to be involved in drug trafficking."

Larsen held up both hands. "No way! Dealing in contraband is not the point. Or even tax evasion. We just need a way to keep peoples' private dealings private, ya know."

"I totally agree," Joel added, "They say the Sixteenth Amendment was ratified illegally, which makes the income tax unconstitutional. I still pay my taxes, but only out of fear. Though I admit that as an accountant, I owe my job to Uncle Sam. Though I could always find something else to do."

Joel's cigar was getting short; he took another puff. "Anyway, I don't *encourage* people to cheat, because I wouldn't wish prison on anybody. But if they want to risk it, what can I say?"

"The possible applications of this technology are endless," Larsen said. Thus began an animated discussion of possible ways to foil government snoops. Occasionally Joel interrupted for an explanation of some technical concept. "I'm your litmus test. If you can get me to understand it, you can teach it to anybody."

Just then a gust of wind caught the porch door, which had been opened a crack for ventilation. It swung wide open, letting in a cascade of rainwater. Larsen had to struggle to get it closed. "It's a sign from God. Enough BS, time to get some shuteye. Oh, and we'll send that message for you, Joel."

"Sounds like a plan. I hope this lets up by tomorrow," Joel shouted over the wind. "We desert rats are not used to driving in this sort of crap."

★ ✪★ ★

As Emal returned from the rest room, he saw his brother quickly stick his cell phone in his pocket. "Egon, who were you texting just now?"

An evil grin spread across his face. "Making sure the Jew keeps running."

Emal put his hand on his brother's arm. Fighting his rage, he kept his voice low. "I told you to stop harassing that man. It's an unacceptable risk! The FBI can trace those messages!"

"Chill, big brother, these are black market phones, remember?" He backed away, stood in front of the driver's door. "I'll drive now."

Emal scowled, and walked around to the passenger side of the truck. He and his brother had always had their disagreements, but he could hardly take it anymore. The man had taken complete leave of his senses.

It was dangerous enough being fugitives, driving with fraudulent documents. They were also getting deeper into crime. Before they'd gone on the run, most of their work had been legit, or small-time contraband– counterfeit jeans, untaxed cigarettes. Never had they transported illegal drugs, until Egon and Enver cooked up the nefarious scheme behind his back. The Jew accountant noticed the irregularities and reported them to their sister Arjana. That was why at first they'd suspected he'd informed on them, but Emal now thought otherwise.

But that was in the past. Their father let Enver take the blame, also making a deal with 'The Corporation,' as the Albanian Mafia liked to call itself, to keep him safe in there. Of course, this deal came with a price.

Since then, drugs were the rule rather than the exception. Today they were on their way to Denver with a truckload of cheap Chinese furniture, obscuring a shrink-wrapped pallet of bags labeled as lawn gypsum, actually filled with pure Peruvian cocaine. Emal was sure he'd develop an ulcer from this new business. So far they'd made a dozen such trips without incident. Still, so many things could go wrong. As usual, they traveled on two-lane highways, avoiding I-25 with its cameras and RFID license scanners.

"Egon!" Emal had to shout above the rush of air past the open windows and the country western music blaring from the radio. "Don't drive so fast! We can't afford to get stopped!"

"I'm only ten miles over the limit," Egon grumbled. "If you let me take the Interstate, we could make better time; I wouldn't have to speed. We don't want to keep Arbnor waiting."

"Slow down," Emal repeated. "I mean it! No more than five miles over."

"You've really been touchy lately. Even talking back to Father. I thought the Prophet said to have respect for your elders."

"It does," Emal snapped. "But Father doesn't appreciate how much trouble we could get into. This is a very dangerous business. What will our families do, if we're put away for life?"

"The Corporation has good lawyers. Worst case, we'll be deported back to Albania."

Emal didn't believe that for a moment. Luckily (*Allah forgive me for the disrespect*) their father didn't have much time left. With Emal Senior gone, Emal Junior would be in charge, and the brothers would no longer accept these kinds of assignments. There were plenty of goods that were regulated enough to be profitable without carrying such a risk.

"Don't be so tough on Father," Egon said. "For years you've been harping on him to convert. Now that he has, you should be happy."

Emal considered for a moment. "You're right, I should be encouraging him. Our family was Muslim for generations. That cursed Hoxha tried to turn us into atheists. But is Father serious about his beliefs? What we're transporting is totally *haram* according to the Koran."

Egon shrugged. "Let the *kaffirs* have their poisons. Besides, your buddy Bin Laden and his mujahadeen sold opium to help them defeat the Soviet infidels."

Emal was about to say, for the hundredth time, that he despised Osama Bin Laden, but he knew his brother was trying to irritate him, so he ignored the jibe. "Not just that. He still drinks vodka and watches pornographic American movies. Do Friday prayers cancel that out?"

"Brother, I grew up hearing how religion was a tool of capitalist oppression. So I find it hard to share your faith. But Father doesn't have much time left; he needs comfort, even if he's not a perfect Muslim. Besides, his prayers seem to be helping. Things were very bad, but Allah smiles on us now. We have new identities, new homes, and new trucks. No Feds to bother us."

"Don't patronize me," Emal snapped. "And don't blaspheme by crediting Allah for the black market and the American infidels who run it."

Egon honked the air horn, made a quick dash around an old-model Chevy full of brown-skinned men. "Cursed wetbacks! Why can't they learn to drive?"

"Be careful, brother! This is a no-passing zone!"

"I'm not a child! Anyway, you have to admit what we're doing will help bring down this corrupt and decadent..." he glanced over at the mirror, switched to English. "Fucking shit! Smokey Bear's behind us!" Then back to Albanian. "Get some cash ready."

"You moron!" Emal snarled. "You can't bribe an American cop, not openly. They're too worried about getting caught."

Emal watched in the mirror as the trooper took a position behind them and followed. The lights came on. Cursing profusely, Egon pulled over.

Emal's scrotum tightened in fear. "Shit! Remain calm, or he'll suspect something's up."

Egon snarled. "Do I have to handle everything? Take the wheel. Answer his questions but volunteer nothing. And I am not here!" He got out of his seat and slipped behind the curtain into the sleeping compartment. Emal slid over, heart pounding. He was fastening his seat belt when the officer strode up.

"License and registration, please."

"Yes, sir." Struggling to remain calm, Emal removed the CDL and registration papers from the holder. They were forgeries, very expensive ones.

The cop looked at the documents, then back at Emal, squinting in the Colorado sun. "I saw you putting your belt on just now. I could write you a ticket, but I'll let you off with a warning this time."

"Thank you, sir," Emal would have gladly accepted the ticket just to get out of there.

"Another thing," the cop said, his dark brown forehead wrinkled in concentration, "I saw another man riding with you. What happened to him?"

"No, sir. Sometimes I – sometimes I play hip hop music and sort of bounce in my seat. It helps to keep me alert. So it might appear that– have I done something wrong?"

The patrolman suppressed a laugh. "You're not from around here, are you? Can I see your green card?"

"I'm a naturalized American citizen. Do you want to see my passport?" Emal instantly regretted saying that. The phony passport would pass a visual inspection, but if the cop decided to run a check on his computer...

The cop frowned. "Not today, Abdul. I need to see inside your trailer. Get out and open the back for me. Keep your hands where I can see them."

Maybe he wouldn't see the drugs. Maybe when he saw the trailer wasn't full of Mexicans, he'd let them go. The cop followed Emal around to the back. *Don't look at the patrol car,* he reminded himself. *There'll be a dash-cam.* He tried to keep his hands from shaking as he unlocked the back door.

"You see, officer? Just furniture." The cop nodded and motioned for him to enter. Emal squeezed between two dining room sets wrapped in plastic. To his horror, the cop's eyes went to the pallet up front.

He pointed. "Open one of those bags for me."

Emal tore open the plastic, then turned around. "I need a knife."

"Let me do it." As the cop stepped forward a dark shape appeared from behind. Egon was on him before he knew what was happening. The officer clutched frantically at his neck as the thin wire cut his throat. With a final gurgle, he slumped to the floor, blood oozing onto his collar.

Emal screamed. "Egon! Bastard son of an infidel dog!"

Egon sneered. "I just saved both our lives. We could have gotten life in prison, or even the death penalty. It was self-defense, Brother."

Emal pointed a finger in his brother's face. "Liar! What happened to 'worst thing that can happen is we'll be deported'?"

"Normally that would be true, but considering the value of this shipment..." He glanced at the palette of contraband. "Maybe you'd prefer to take that chance, but not me!" For a man who would slap his wife for being ten minutes late with dinner, Egon was being uncharacteristically, frighteningly calm about the situation.

It made Emal want to strangle him. "But, but... the radio, the dash-cam!"

"I'll handle that." Egon stuck a gloved hand into his jacket pocket and pulled out a ski mask. "Shove the body behind the dresser. Wear these gloves." He held out a pair of rubber gloves. "There's a foil bag behind the seat with a spare license plate, go get it."

Emal exited the trailer through the side door and entered the cab. He prayed the road would stay deserted. Quickly he found the pouch. He himself had suggested getting black market plates, just in case. He didn't know Egon had actually done it.

He came out the passenger side and joined Egon at the back. Grinning, his brother held up the cop car's dash cam and computer in his right hand, a bolt cutter and crowbar under his left arm. "Quickly, change the plate and we'll get out of here."

Despite shaking hands, Emal got the plate changed and was back in the cab in under a minute. Egon started the truck and slowly backed up into the cop car, pushing it off the road and into the ravine. Emal heard a muffled boom, saw smoke rising behind them, from down where the police car had gone. At least Egon was well prepared.

"Don't give me that look," Egon growled. "I wish I hadn't had to do that, it complicates things immensely. But it was necessary. Luckily he was just a deputy. It should take them a while to come after us."

"Yes, but the Holy Koran says..."

Egon sneered. "The Koran? The guy was just an infidel. We'll ditch the body. Then we'll drive the Interstate, where we should have been in the first place. Lose ourselves in traffic."

Emal struggled to slow his breathing. He felt like he'd pass out. "We'll be late."

"That can't be avoided. Call Arbnor and make up an excuse."

Emal stared at the man on his left, seeing not his brother but a monster. Even their sinful father never killed a man in cold blood. Surely this horrible, evil trap was Allah's punishment for the wicked business they were conducting. Once again he wondered if Egon had also been involved in the Phoenix bombing, despite his vehement denials. Would a man who could kill so casually not also lie to his brother?

As they drove on with a policeman's corpse in the trailer and blood on their hands, Emal made his decision. The longer he stayed with his brother, the longer he, Esma and the children were danger. He felt bad for Egon's wife and children, but there was nothing he could do for them. At the first opportunity, Emal would grab his wife and kids, and go. They needed to disappear from the family the same way the family had disappeared from the Feds.

Chapter 5 – Intersection of Fate

Joel found himself scratching his face for the tenth time that day. "JL, how do you stand having all that facial hair? This beard itches like crazy!"

"You'll get used to it. If not, shave it off." Larsen didn't look up from his keyboard. Like Nephi, he could type while talking, an ability Joel found disconcerting.

"It's not that easy. My face is on the FBI website now. It's not much of a disguise, but it's all I've got." The two men sat at the camping table in back of the van, leaving Nephi as chauffeur. Joel shuffled and dealt another hand of solitaire. He found handling the physical cards to be more relaxing than playing the electronic version.

"You could dye your hair. Get a tattoo. Or a nose job."

"Need I remind you how my people feel about tattoos? And you tell me to get rid of my big Hebrew *schnozzola*? You're treading on thin ice, pal."

Larsen laughed. "If the shoe fits... actually, I was thinking, the nose being the most prominent thing on a person's face, changing it could make you look significantly different."

"I don't know how much good that'd do you," Nephi interjected from the driver's seat. "The police are using facial recognition software that measures the distance between a person's eyes. That's impossible to modify, even with surgery."

Larsen smiled. "Give me a bottle of whiskey and some power tools, I'll do it."

Joel laughed. "I'd need a little stronger anesthetic than whiskey."

"What anesthesia? The whiskey's for me; the sight of blood makes me nauseous!"

"Another proud graduate of the Auschwitz school of cosmetic surgery!"

Larsen laughed and closed his computer. "Nephi, we there yet?"

"A few minutes away, assuming we have the right address. Everything looks so industrial." They were heading away from Lake Michigan, into the setting sun. To their left were rows of warehouses. To the right they saw factories with peeling paint and broken windows.

"Maybe your uncle gave you a bum steer," said Joel.

"Shut up, you'll make the kid feel bad. Nephi, it's all Joel's fault."

"You're both impossible." Nephi did his most annoying laugh, almost a giggle. "Here we are!" Beyond the warehouses stood a row of pastel tract houses. Nephi mad a left onto the narrow street. "Nice neighborhood."

"Seems appropriate for somebody in the underground," said Joel. "You wouldn't expect him to live in a mansion."

Most the houses were seriously in need of paint. One had a car up on blocks by the driveway. At least there was no graffiti or boarded-up windows. Their destination, Number 4556, was painted white. Its lawn was meticulously tidy compared to his neighbors' weedy front yards.

Joel jumped out and lit up a smoke, while Larsen and Nephi put their things away and locked up the van. They finished too quickly, forcing Joel to stub out the cigar and follow them. Nephi rang the bell. A couple minutes passed. He pushed it again, still no answer.

"Looks like Cook's not home," Joel said.

"Maybe," Nephi pulled out his phone and punched in a number.

This time, the door opened. A tall, skeletally thin black man appeared, bald except for a few tufts of white hair. He smiled. "Come on in, Gents. Sorry I didn't answer, but in this neighborhood it's either cops or robbers. I'm not sure anymore which is worse."

112

The three men waited while Cook bolted the door, then introduced themselves, and shook hands with their host. "So you're Jack's nephew," he said to Nephi. "I can see the resemblance. You've got the square jaw, the dimpled chin."

"So I've been told. You and Jack were in the MWM together?"

The old man laughed out loud. "You find that surprising? Didn't know there were people of color in with those Nazi militia boys?"

"Maybe. Sure you don't have any storm trooper boots in your closet?" Larsen laughed at his own joke, ignoring Joel's grimace.

Cook burst out laughing. "Larsen, you're OK!" He slapped JL on the back. "Sit down! What can I get you? I've got water and soda. There may be a beer in there, maybe not. I'm not supposed to be drinking. Got enough troubles with the AZT."

"Oh, we're sorry! Jack didn't say you had..." Joel stammered.

"That's OK. I don't like people feeling sorry for me." He grabbed a bottled water and twisted off the top. "Help yourself. I'm going to sit. I tire out quick these days."

Nephi opened the fridge, got himself a water and handed Joel a diet soda. Larsen hunted in the back and found a long-neglected can of beer.

Cook took a swig and continued. "You know, there's a bright side to everything, even being HIV-positive. I used to worry about going to prison, but now, who cares? I wouldn't be in there that long. Plus everybody would be afraid to molest me." To the awkward silence that followed, he added, "If you must know, I got stabbed by an addict with a dirty needle."

"So, how'd you get involved with..." Joel glanced around nervously.

"I've s bugs," said Cook, "but if you're paranoid, I understand. I can't guarantee the Feds haven't cooked up something undetectable."

A fluffy golden cat pranced in from the hallway and leaped onto Cook's lap. It purred loudly as he stroked its head. "As for the Midwest Militia, I got involved with those radicals in the Clinton years. My family liked Slick Willie, but I couldn't support a guy who was anti-gun. How are law abiding people supposed to defend themselves?"

"Call the cops and pray they get there in time," Larsen laughed uproariously, snorting beer out of both nostrils.

Cook chuckled. "I'm an ex-cop myself, so I know better. They kept us so busy with paperwork, busting people for dope and speeding, it's a miracle we caught any real crooks."

"I won't argue with you," said Nephi. "But we better get to business. What can you do for Joel, and what's it going to cost?"

"Things have gotten tricky lately. Like I told you on the phone, I've got to ask at least 50K. Medicare doesn't go very far these days. I'll take cash but I prefer gold or silver." The cat jumped off Cook's lap and meowed.

With some difficulty, Cook got out of his chair. "As I was saying, the identity biz is a challenge these days. Every document, every card's got holograms, micro-circuitry, biometrics. Luckily, the materials are available on the black market, if you know where to find them."

"What happens to our friend if he runs his card through a scanner?" Nephi asked. "They won't find anything in the government database to back them up."

"That's why my services are such a bargain. I've got hackers who can get into just about any system. Government data clerks are only human. Like they say, power breeds corruption. A lot of those government drones will help us out, for the right price." He poured food into the cat's bowl, then sat down. "If you're short of cash, we could kill you off, virtually speaking. That would get the cops off your tail for a while."

Joel shook his head. "I need to be able to work. Kinda hard for a dead guy. I'll need a new Social Slavery Number, employment history, and so on. The money I'll have left won't last me very long. How much more will this cost me?"

He shrugged. "Depends on what you're offering."

"US dollars, a few thousand Canadian, and some bags of junk silver."

Cook's eyes lit up. "Real money! And the Canuck bucks. Phony as they are, at least they're doing better than the US dollar or the Euro right now. Let's see..." He opened the freezer and pulled out a box labeled 'Omaha Steaks.' From this he pulled out three paper notebooks.

"'High tech' security. I write in code. When I'm gone, they'll be useless to anybody. Hmm." He rippled through pages of unintelligible symbols. "We send lots of clients to Florida. With all the drug trafficking, illegal immigration, the Feds have their hands full down there."

Perfect, Joel told himself. *A hop and a skip away from the Islands.*

"So how do we do this?" asked Joel. "Look for someone born around when I was, who died in infancy? I know it's silly, but I'd like to stay Jewish. It'd be easier to keep up the act."

"You always say you're not observant," said Nephi with a bemused smile. "Are spiritual matters more important to you than you admit?"

"It's an identity thing," Joel said seriously, "And I *can* fit in at the temple if need be."

"The dead-baby loophole's been closed off for some time now," Cook said, "But you're in luck. One of the best ways to go is becoming an immigrant. Israel's particularly good, 'cause when Hamas blew up the Social Security Center in Tel Aviv, a lot of records were lost. And since you're an officially recognized minority, it's risky for law enforcement to profile you..." He paused, as if he'd forgotten what he was saying.

"You OK, Mr. Cook?" Nephi asked.

Cook rested his head in his hands a moment. "I'll be fine. Let's move on, shall we? To be able to work, you'll need full Federal documentation..."

Within the hour, they' worked out the details of the transaction and haggled a price. Joel got to keep some of his US cash, but gave up all the Canadian paper and the silver coins he'd gotten from Larsen. It still hurt to think he'd sold the guitar. "What's next?"

"Go to this address tomorrow, between one and two PM," Cook said, "and ask for Ramone. The docs will be hidden in an item you purchase from him. Ramone's business is antiques, so it'll be something like me, tastefully old. Normally he gets only seven to ten percent for his services, so don't give him more than five K. Remember, it takes 48 to 72 hours to get your info into the system, so don't use the ID until then."

"But I don't even know my new name!"

"He'll have a memory stick with all the biographical information you need. Make sure you encrypt it and do a secure delete of the original."

"I don't know," Larsen objected. "No offense, but how do we know this is for real? How can we verify everything's cool?"

"I have a smart card reader in the van," said Nephi, "as well as a fingerprint reader, and a retina scanner. If there's any mismatch in the biometric data, we'll know."

"Biometrics!" Joel said. "Where do you keep all that equipment?"

"I was getting to that. Your driver's license, please." Cook glanced at it, looked back at Joel, and sighed. "Perhaps we need a new photo. Here, I have a setup in the next room."

They followed him to the living room, where an ancient computer sat on a battered desk. Nephi helped set up the backdrop. Cook snapped Joel's picture with a camera connected to the computer. He inserted the license into a slot below the video drive. A red LED came on, and then winked green. "Got it! Your physical data, decrypted, stripped of your name and address. We make small mods; an exact match raises a red flag. Still, it'll pass any biocard verification."

"I've been thinking," Joel said. "What if my appearance changes?"

"You'll have to hope whoever's checking it doesn't look too carefully. Or pay someone to get it updated. At the moment, the Feds don't archive the state driver's license pictures; they're not standardized enough to be useful. For now, they only get the birth date, sex, height and weight, and the digitized fingerprints."

Joel nodded. Cook had done a good job of improvising. He stepped up to shake the man's hand. Another hand he hardly felt worthy to shake. "Thank you, sir, you're a lifesaver! And it may sound cliché, but don't give up hope. They're getting close to a cure for AIDS."

"Not likely, not before I'm dead and buried. I appreciate the sentiment, but we've all got to go sometime." He smiled and shook the other men's hands. "Now, if you don't mind, I need to rest. Good luck, Joel. God bless you all. Keep up the good fight, for America's sake."

Nephi smiled. "We'll do our best."

★ ◎★ ★

It was well past noon as Nephi navigated the maze of south Chicago, looking for Washburn Street. Ramone's shop was in a tiny business district near some run-down apartments. He spent ten minutes circling, looking for a parking space. A shiny black Hummer pulled out suddenly, narrowly missing them. "Frack it all!" Nephi slammed on the brakes, sending the checker game Joel and JL had been playing crashing to the floor.

"You're too nice, kid," Larsen said. "I'd flip off the son of a bitch."

"So much for our game," said Joel. "Magnetic pieces don't help much when the board goes flying."

"I was kicking your ass anyway," Larsen snickered. He peered out the window. "I've been in some shit-holes before, but this place is one of the nicest I've ever seen."

Nephi parked in the Hummer's vacated spot. "Hurry, guys," he said. "We don't want to be here any longer than we need to." He wondered if the other two, Larsen in particular, appreciated the risks they were all taking. Sometimes he felt like the only grownup in the group.

Joel and Larsen followed him through the door of the tiny shop. An electronic beep announced their entry.

Behind the counter was a short, olive-skinned man with a shaved head and an enormous black mustache. He was busy showing a wooden mailbox to an elderly black woman. When the three men entered the shop he glanced over his shoulder at them. "Just a moment, ma'am."

"May I help you gentlemen?"

"Are you Ramone?" Joel asked.

He laughed "I'm the owner, so I must be!"

"I'm Emmanuel, this is Moe, and that's Jack," said Joel, using the code names Cook had given them. "We're looking for an antique Scottish lap desk."

"Mr. Emmanuel, I've been expecting you. One moment. Allow me to finish with my other customer." He turned to the lady, spoke quietly. Nephi heard him say "thirty percent off."

The woman smiled. "That's a good deal! I'll take it!"

The woman departed, beaming, with her prize. Ramone's smile and exhortation to "come back soon!" seemed a little forced. He watched through the window as she got into her car. Then he dead-bolted the door and turned the old fashioned 'Open For Business' sign to 'Closed.'

"Gentlemen." Ramone's expression was now a bit surly. "I have your package in the back. This way."

They followed him behind the counter and through a door paneled with a peeling oak veneer. The back room was even more cluttered than the sales floor. In one corner was a desk and a computer; the rest was shelving, filled to the ceiling with lamps, figurines, and assorted brick-a-brac.

"Just one minute." He unlocked a closet door at the back, disappeared within and returned with a walnut box about the size of a notebook computer, but several times thicker. "This item was hand made in Scotland, circa 1898."

"Very nice!" said Larsen. "What an amazing piece of work!" As he reached over to open the lid, Nephi shot him an accusatory look. He shrugged his shoulders and stepped back.

"OK." Joel removed a folded white envelope from his shirt pocket. He opened the envelope and removed a thick wad of multicolored bills. "Here you go, four thousand."

"I'm sorry. There must have been a misunderstanding. The price was seven."

"Seven thousand!" Larsen exclaimed. "Are you trying to screw us?"

"Uh, Ramone," Joel had a panicked look on his face. "We do have *some* leeway ..."

Good gracious, these two are going to blow the deal. Nephi said calmly, "We've been instructed we can go no higher than five thousand dollars for this piece." He looked into Ramone's eyes. The man's scowl softened, then turned into a smile.

"Young man, you drive a hard bargain!" he laughed. "Five thousand it is." Nephi nodded to Joel, who made a face, then reached into his wallet and pulled out a few more pink-and-gold hundred-dollar bills. Ramone flipped through them quickly to verify the amount, then pocketed the cash and scribbled out a receipt. "Shall I wrap your purchase?"

"Thank you, no." Nephi grabbed the box and headed for the door, before either of the others could say something foolish.

"Thank you, sirs, it's been a pleasure doing business with you!"

Once in the van, he handed the desk to Joel, who sat down in the back and eagerly opened the box. "Where is it?" he cried, a note of alarm in his voice.

"The bottom is a removable tray," said Larsen. "They stored pens and paper and ink bottles under here." He removed the inset, revealing a manila envelope. "Voila!"

Joel grabbed the envelope and ripped it open. Inside as promised, were the Florida driver's license, a Social Security card, and the thumb drive. "Samuel Steinberg, city of birth, Tel Aviv, naturalized US citizen, 2002. All right, I'm still Jewish!"

Nephi sighed in relief as he pulled out into traffic. He was still a bit worried Joel had wasted his life's savings on a pig in a poke. The ID would be fine for visual inspection, and a quick pass through Nephi's card reader verified that the encoded data matched what was printed. But for anything serious, like getting a job or opening a bank account, it would be worthless unless Cook's 'associates' had access, as the man claimed, to the proper government databases.

"All right, gentlemen," Joel said. "From now on, no more Joel, call me Sam, OK?"

"Let's go celebrate," said Larsen. "I know a great little place on Milwaukee Avenue."

As Nephi expected, Larsen's 'great little place' was a bar. What surprised him, as he pulled into the parking lot, was the neon sign of a curvaceous woman. "Is this a strip club?"

"Well, yes, Captain Obvious," Larsen smirked as he opened the van door.

"I don't mind going into a bar once in a while," Nephi continued. "As long as there's something else to do besides drinking alcohol. To watch a game or listen to music, maybe. But I'm totally uncomfortable going into this kind of place."

"Chill out, kid you're not going to be fucking them. You don't even have to look."

"That's not the point; if someone I knew saw me in a place like that..."

Joel put his hand on Larsen's shoulder. "JL, show some respect. If Nephi doesn't want to go here, we should find someplace else."

"It's OK, you guys go in. I'll go get a burger and pick you guys up later."

"Nephi, it'll be OK." There was aggravation in Larsen's voice. "There's two rooms. The side with food is a sports bar. We'll order lunch, then Joel and I can check out the ladies while you watch the game. I'll treat you guys to the best burgers in town. You don't have to look at all."

"Well, I suppose..." Nephi grumbled. *Good thing I don't know anyone in Chicago.*

Nephi regretted his acquiescence. First, the doorman asked for his ID, which was bad enough, but he also ran it through a scanner, probably capturing his personal data for marketing purposes. He then insisted on carding the two older men. "New Federal law," he said apologetically.

Joel doesn't dare use his, so at least I don't have to go in. No such luck.

"My friend is obviously of age," Larsen said, "though he forgot his ID at home. Oh here it is, an amazing likeness!" Larsen slipped the man a picture of U. S. Grant, and they were in.

Nephi grimaced. Larsen had not told him the only way to the restaurant was through the club. Nephi blushed as he caught a glimpse of the naked woman on the stage, plus three more girls performing at various tables. He sighed in relief when they got to the other room. Then their waitress arrived, a young black woman with triple-D breasts, in a translucent white top.

His traveling companions ordered beers. At least, as the designated driver, his Pepsi was on the house. Larsen ordered three "Chicago Fire Chili-burgers." Then Larsen and Joel ambled over to the other room. Nephi waited, trying to concentrate on the Cubs game on the big screen, and to quell his anger at Larsen. *That self-centered jerk.*

Joel and Larsen returned just as the food arrived. "Nephi, my boy, this place is wasted on you!" Larsen exclaimed. "Don't LDS guys like girls?"

"It's not that. It's a matter of having respect for women," Nephi replied sharply.

"Hell, I respect 'em! Just gave forty bucks worth of respect to a hot little redhead." Larsen drained his drink, and flagged down the waitress. She returned instantly with another round. "Damn! Forgot to call my friend! I need to step outside. I won't be able to hear in here."

"I'll come along," said Joel. "I need a stogie. These smoking ordinances suck!"

Several minutes went by. The waitress returned to their table. "What happened to the other two guys? They your uncles or something?"

"Just friends." Nephi struggled to keep his gaze above her neck as she set down another Pepsi. "Th-thanks," he stammered. He decided he should tip the girl. He fumbled in his wallet and put down a bill which he belatedly realized was a ten.

She smiled flirtatiously. "Thank you!" She stuffed the bill into her cleavage.

Joel returned in time to chuckle at Nephi's befuddlement. Larsen plopped down on the stool next to him, downed half his new beer in one gulp. "Hey, Neeph, you'll never guess what."

Nephi forced himself to smile. "Are we going to go see your friend?"

"Yes. Except he's actually a she."

Joel burst out laughing. "A *real good* friend, huh? Good thing she wasn't a casual acquaintance!"

"What can I say?" shrugged Larsen. "I'm an enlightened gender-neutral kind of guy."

Larsen insisted on paying, and Nephi didn't argue. The food wasn't that great anyway. He was still pretty steamed about Larsen's deception. Nephi was thankful *he* didn't need to view women sexually. It was pathetic, all the teasing, without even letting the men have what they wanted. Considering what Jesus said about lusting in the heart, prostitution didn't seem much worse.

It didn't take Nephi long to find the University. The greater difficulty was finding an available parking spot. Luckily he had some Reagan dollar coins for the meter.

"We going to your friend's office?" Joel asked.

"No, she says it's too small. We're meeting at a coffee shop nearby."

"Maybe she's not comfortable meeting a stranger on her own turf," said Joel. "I don't blame her. The Internet is a weird place. People are often not who we think they are." He grinned at Larsen, who ignored the jibe.

As they entered the shop, Nephi glanced around, expecting a plump middle-aged woman in a sari. All the tables had students in groups of two or three, except one. The woman seated there didn't look any older than the rest.

She had a slim, athletic build, with deep brown skin, dark eyes, and shiny black hair past her shoulders. In one hand, she held an iced drink; in the other, an obscure looking academic journal. To Nephi, there was a strange familiarity about her.

In her hair and complexion, she resembled Nephi's ex-girlfriend, Juanita, eldest daughter of a Hispanic LDS family from Texas. There the similarity ended. Juanita was short and busty, fond of low-rise jeans Nephi thought inappropriate for a religious woman. *This* woman wore a tailored blue suit that narrowed around her slim waist; under that, a crisp white shirt. On her nose sat a tiny pair of silver-rimmed glasses. But for those, she'd have seemed at home on a Manhattan runway. "JL, is that her?" he whispered.

"How would I know?" Larsen snapped. He was probably still annoyed from Joel's ribbing on the drive from the bar. He stared at the woman, who kept her nose buried in her journal.

Do I have to do everything? Though he'd always been awkward around the opposite sex, Nephi steeled himself to speak to her. To his immense relief,

Larsen strode up to her table, "Are you Sirimavo Jayasuriya?" Amazingly, he didn't stumble on the name. He held out a beefy hand. "Jon Larsen, glad to meet you!"

She put down her magazine, stood in one graceful motion, and took his hand in her delicate brown fingers. She smiled, her teeth like beacons between her dark lips. "I'm delighted to finally meet you, JL." She looked over at the others, holding Nephi's gaze for an instant too long. "I didn't realize you were bringing friends."

"That wasn't the only surprise... " Joel began, but Larsen gave him a scathing look. Joel grinned. "Just giving my friend a hard time. I'm– " he paused for a moment, "Samuel Steinberg. Call me Sam." Joel shook Siri's hand, his eyes briefly falling on her long, slender legs.

"And you are?"

Nephi felt himself blushing again. "Nephi Snow," he managed to blurt out. "I– uh– understand you're into computers." *Good gosh almighty, where did that come from?*

"Well, I've got an undergraduate degree in computational mathematics, but I still have trouble programming my cell phone." She laughed, like the song of some tropical bird.

Joel clapped him on the shoulder. "Nephi here can program anything, your cell phone, your VCR. He can get Angry Birds to play on your microwave oven."

"He's also very smooth with the ladies," Larsen added.

Nephi's earlier urge to punch Larsen in the face returned, with a vengeance.

"Gentlemen, we're blocking traffic," A line had formed at the counter of the café; they were standing in the middle of it. Siri gestured at the table. "Have a seat; I'll get you all coffee, or whatever you want to drink."

"What you're having looks good," said Nephi quickly.

Siri went to the counter to order. Larsen intercepted her and insisted on paying. They returned with two hot coffees and two iced drinks. "Thanks," Joel said.

Nephi took a sip. "This is good! What is it?" He raised the glass for another drink.

"You've never had iced chai before?" She gave him that smile again.

Oh, it was tea, that's why it didn't taste familiar! Nephi turned red, grabbed a napkin off the table and began coughing into it. Somehow this option seemed less embarrassing than admitting his mistake. Just drinking it was out, he'd sinned enough today by going into that horrible place. "Sorry, wrong pipe," he said, pushing the drink away.

Larsen raised his eyebrows. "You gonna live, kid?" His grin looked like a suppressed laugh. Mercifully he let the matter drop. "Siri and I have been discussing the advances in public key cryptography. On-line, that is. Chung He's new algorithm for multi-hundred-digit primes."

"Primes? The only prime I know is the prime rate of interest." Joel grinned.

"Don't you know *anything?* Large prime numbers are an essential element of strong encryption. I was going to use Chung's method in the 9000's security libraries, but Nephi already incorporated it in Griffin, so why reinvent the wheel? Of course," Larsen grinned, "it'll never be *certified.*" That meant DHS-approved, a legal requirement for all encryption software in the US.

"JL's been telling us about your scheme for anonymous barter." Joel sipped his coffee, made a face, and blew on the hot liquid. "I don't pretend I understand it. But I'm glad you're working on it. Because we need to protect what little privacy we still have."

"Well," Siri lowered her voice conspiratorially. "I'm not supposed to tell you this, and I'm probably already under surveillance..." She hesitated, looking at the three of them. "I recently received a visit from Homeland Security. They wanted to finance, and of course classify, my research. I politely declined, but of course that kills my chances for tenure here."

"So what did you do?" Nephi asked.

She shrugged. "I've submitted my resignation, effective at the end of the term. I couldn't really see myself developing new ways to spy on people."

They sat in silence for a moment, sipping their drinks. Joel, noticing Nephi's earlier predicament, went back to the counter and purchased a mineral water for him. Finally, Larsen said, "I didn't tell you about my new system. There's a portable version now; the JL-3000. I packed it up and brought it along in Nephi's van. I've been tinkering with it on the way."

Siri seemed relieved by the resumption in conversation. "How interesting! You must have solved the cooling problem, then. Are you running the new Linux kernel yet?"

"I'm still stuck on the previous release. But hey, maybe we should ease up on the tech talk. We don't want to bore everyone else to death."

"What do you mean bore us to death?" Nephi said. "Sam's the only non-computer guy here, and that's too bad, he's out-numbered."

"If Nephi would let me drive," Joel said with a laugh, "I wouldn't feel totally useless on this trip."

As the conversation went on, Nephi's shyness disappeared. He questioned Siri extensively about her research. Joel and Larsen listened, interjecting an occasional word into the discussion. The coffee shop emptied out and filled up again, as classes started and ended.

Siri glanced at her watch. "My goodness, the time! I need to get to my evening class!"

Nephi pulled out his Android. "Could you beam me some contact info?"

"Sorry, my phone is quite old and doesn't play well with the new protocols. How about a business card?" As she handed it to him, he noticed her perfectly manicured maroon nails, the tiny gold-and-jade ring on her right pinky, and the absence of any jewelry on her left. He dug through his pockets and produced a creased card proclaiming Snow Computer Services.

"It was wonderful meeting you in person, JL. You too, Sam, Nephi." Her eyes seemed to linger on Nephi as she said his name. She gave them a quick wave as she headed out the door.

Back the road again, Joel claimed the passenger seat. Rather than sitting back at the table, Larsen squatted behind.

"It's ironic. I'd actually been thinking about moving to Florida before this all happened," Joel said. "I hear companies are actually hiring people, you know, Latin American trade."

"Legal or illegal?" chuckled Larsen.

Joel ignored the joke. "The big deal is Cuba, since the Castro brothers are gone. Anyway, since I've got my papers, you can just drop me off at the bus station. You should be heading home, Nephi. You must be running out of excuses for your family."

"You remember what Cook said," Nephi cautioned. "Seventy-two hours. Greyhound would ask to see your ID. Anyway, I've always wanted to see Florida."

"You know what I'd like to see," Larsen said. "Our professor friend in a thong bikini. Holy shit, does she have a great body!"

"She certainly is an attractive woman." Joel added.

Nephi frowned. "Don't you guys ever get tired of treating women like sex objects?" He tried to say it jokingly, but couldn't keep the irritation out of his voice.

"Hey now, I know Siri is a great gal, and smart, too," said Larsen. "But that doesn't mean I can't appreciate the good looks God gave her."

"JL, I think there's a reason our young friend is being so sensitive," Joel said. "You see the way he looked at her? He's been struck by an arrow from the chubby little winged guy."

"A chance meeting, an intersection of fate that led to romance," Larsen intoned, in a fair imitation of the deep-voiced fellow who narrated all those movie trailers.

"Would you both just shut up!" Nephi roared. The two men stared at him, wide-eyed.

"We better give the kid a break, JL," Joel said. "He's gone way above and beyond, if you know what I mean."

"For Christ's sake, it was just a little good-natured ribbing," Larsen muttered. He went back to the camping table and sat, arms folded.

Nobody said anything at all for the next half hour.

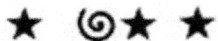

The next day was a quiet one. Joel could feel the tension between Nephi and Larsen. *I feel terrible I let JL railroad him like that. The kid risked his freedom to help me, and I let him down.* Nephi let Joel drive without any argument. The kid sat in back, working on his computer, occasionally making a hushed phone call. Meanwhile, Joel recruited Larsen to read Sam Steinberg's biography and quiz him on it.

"It's been a long time since I helped anybody with their homework," Larsen chuckled. "Father's name?"

"Moishe Itzak Steinberg."

"Christ, how Jewish can you get? Mother's name?"

"Sophia Ruth Perlman. Maiden name, of course."

"This says you grew up in Israel. Have you ever even been there?"

"Once, when I was in high school. The temple sponsored a trip. I mowed lawns all spring to earn money to go." The magnitude of this undertaking hit him. Joel Walter had spent three weeks in Jerusalem. Sam Steinberg had supposedly lived there for decades. No doubt he'd meet people in Florida who knew *a lot* about Israel. "Oy, I'll never remember all this!"

"Don't worry, you got your study buddy right here," Larsen grinned.

They stopped for the night in Chattanooga. At dinner, Nephi was still quiet, but he seemed to have mostly gotten over his anger. *He's a better sport than I'd be, if I were him,* Joel thought. Or maybe the kid really *had* been hit by Cupid's arrow.

The next morning Joel awoke with a pounding headache. After Nephi retired for the night, Joel and Larsen had stayed up late, having multiple rounds of drinks.

Larsen seemed unaffected. "I don't mind driving for a while."

"Thanks, JL," Nephi tossed him the keys. "You get any speeding tickets, you're paying." He retired once more to the back of the van and booted up his computer.

By evening they rolled into Tampa, Sam Steinberg's new home. The headache was gone; the pain was elsewhere. For the first time since Kingman, Joel had a knot in his stomach.

He had to take his new identity seriously, or suffer the consequences. With luck he'd escape the authorities long enough to establish a paper trail, and make the necessary contacts to start a new life south of the border. If he messed up and got caught, he'd be lucky if he'd ever get to speak to a lawyer. Running would get him classified as a terrorist for sure.

Though the odds were against him, he reminded himself that many criminals evaded capture for years. They hadn't caught 'Mac' MacGuiness yet, and they wanted him *bad*. After all he'd done for the country, fighting their stupid war in Iraq. Rumor had it he was underground, plotting rebellion, recruiting disaffected veterans to his cause. Joel hoped those rumors were true.

Joel checked into a long-term "executive suites" hotel near the airport using his new Steinberg driver's license and credit cards. After a gut-wrenching thirty-second wait, the card was approved. Nephi and Larsen helped him carry his luggage and boxes to the room.

"Before we go," said Nephi, "I'll update you to the latest rev of Griffin, so we can keep in touch without giving you away to the Feds." He booted Joel's computer and spent a few minutes installing software from a memory stick. He gave Joel a tutorial, while Larsen turned on the TV and watched a Marlins game already in progress.

Joel stood up. "I owe you guys a meal. I saw a steakhouse across the highway."

"Wish we could," Nephi said. "But we shouldn't be seen around town with you more than necessary. Security risk. I'll go get some steaks at the grocery store. We'll eat 'em here."

"My treat." Joel pulled out his wallet and handing him some bills. "As long as I can stay here and watch the ballgame."

Their lunch conversation was subdued, like a funeral reception. In a sense, it was the death of Joel's old identity. Finally, Nephi stood up. "We better get going," He held out his hand.

Overcome with emotion, Joel gave his young friend a hug. "Thanks for everything, Neeph!" The kid had become more like family to him than many of his blood relatives. It only seemed fair to also hug Larsen, who stiffened up and seemed relieved when it was over.

Larsen laughed and slapped Joel on the shoulder. "Good luck, you crazy radical bastard. Keep the faith. Some really exciting things will be happening soon."

Joel smiled and looked him in the eye. "Sounds like a Chinese curse. You and Nephi can carry the crazy torch for a while. I'll settle for safe and boring."

Chapter 6 – Deja Vu Again

It was great to be back in Madison. Siri loved the lakes, the trees, the diversity and openness of a college town. Though it seemed subtly different. There were street-mounted surveillance cameras, troops stationed around the state capitol complex, and police cruising slowly, in dark, unmarked cars. Just last week they'd used a SWAT teams to break up a noisy student house party. In most respects, life went on as usual, yet it seemed like a creeping paranoia was descending on the people.

One thing that hadn't changed was the Pita Paradise. In Siri's teenage years, it had been her favorite restaurant, a great place to hang out with friends. Now she worked just three blocks away. As she walked there one beautiful autumn day, she reflected on how lucky she was to have this job. Founded by UW-Madison alumni, the company was close to the campus, both physically and culturally.

As she neared her destination, she encountered a young man pacing the sidewalk, wearing a sandwich board reading "End US Imperialism in Nigeria." Judging by his very dark skin and unfashionable clothes, she guessed he had first-hand experience with his topic.

"Hello, Miss," he said, in a charming British Commonwealth accent, "will you take action to stop US atrocities in my home country? Here's a pamphlet. You can sign our petition on-line at Free Nigeria dot com."

She accepted the pamphlet and smiled. "I'll check it out. Good luck!"

Siri glanced at her watch, then quickened her pace. If she didn't hurry, she'd hit the noon rush, and probably be late getting back to work. Also, she was not dining alone today.

"Siri!" Her father got up, a bit unsteadily, from the bench in the Pita's entry way. "How's my girl doing?" He gave her a quick hug.

Siri grinned. "Hi, Dad! You're looking really good. Have you lost more weight?"

"Indeed I have. I'm getting stronger and fitter every day. Next week if I get my doctor's approval, I can go back to work. I never thought I'd miss it that much."

The hostess, a surly looking goth with a pierced nose, led them to their table, gracing them with the hint of a smile as she seated them.

Pradeep Jayasuriya sat down and caught his breath. He'd had a tough time since the heart attack, but he never complained about it. He regarded his daughter and beamed. "It's wonderful to have you back in town, Siriji. Your mother is always too busy to have lunch with me."

A waiter appeared, a tall, dark young man named Rajiv. "Hello Siri, how is work today?" When he started at the Pita a few months back, he'd hardly said a word to Siri, despite her flirtation. Now that he'd overcome his shyness; she was no longer interested. Still, Rajiv smiled hopefully as he took their orders; falafel for Siri, triple-cheese eggplant lasagna for her father.

"Don't tell your mother," her father said. "She doesn't allow me to eat this sort of thing."

Siri laughed. If an occasional indulgence kept him in good spirits, it was worth it. "Your secret's safe with me, Dad."

"Good. I already have my hands full, defending you." He switched abruptly to Sinhalese. "She accepts your decision, though she still thinks it was a mistake. As for me, I'm proud of you for sticking to your principles. But I'm also quite concerned."

Siri sipped her water. She'd spoken English almost exclusively since she'd left home for the University. It took her brain a few seconds to switch back to her native tongue. "Do you think I'd be better off if I had accepted their offer?"

Her father shrugged. "Financially, maybe. But as the Buddha says, 'Contentment is the greatest wealth.' Actually, your finances aren't my greatest worry. I know how stubborn you are. You won't give up your research project because two men in suits told you to."

The arrival of their food saved her from responding. That was another thing Siri loved about this place; quick service. "Ah this pasta looks wonderful," Pradeep said in English. Then, switching back to his native tongue: "I'm serious. Those people are not to be trifled with."

Siri leaned close to her father. Since her conversation with Professor Chiang, she worried about electronic eavesdroppers. Supposedly the government had made major strides in automated language translation, so Homeland Security might not need a Sinhalese speaker to understand them. "Dad, I'm very discreet. Besides, my dissertation is public knowledge. Other people are working on coding the algorithms. Mostly Dutch and Norwegian hackers."

"I hope you're not assisting them. As much as I'd like to see your ideas put into action, be very careful. Any of those people could be government agents trying to entrap you."

"I understand," Siri sighed. "But Nephi is familiar with most of them, and he's a pretty good judge of character."

A smile crossed Pradeep's lips. "Your young friend from Arizona. So he's the one who's putting you up to this!"

Siri laughed. "If anything, Nephi is a reluctant participant. He's a very principled young man, there's no way he's going to get into anything that's unethical."

Her father raised his eyebrows. Siri recognized that look as meaning, 'Yes, but...' As he was fond of saying, these days *ethical* and *legal* were often opposite things, a dangerous situation. To her relief, he changed the subject. "I have the feeling your relationship with this fellow has become more than intellectual."

"Dad, we're just friends..." She felt her face flush. "Though he's very sweet, and there's something about him, his old fashioned chivalry, that's very charming. He's a lot like Sanjeev; he can be very funny."

"You mean it's a brother-sister kind of thing? Your mother thinks otherwise. When you mention him, you light up. And you're always texting him."

Siri's mouth dropped open. "How could you possibly know that?"

Her father occupied himself adding Parmesan to his dish. "Your mother's been questioning your roommates. Janice has been quite talkative."

Siri shook her head and tried to keep a straight face. "That's why I didn't move back home. You and Mother have absolutely no respect for my privacy!"

Pradeep shrugged and went back to his pasta. "Don't look at me. I'm no snoop!"

A sudden noise interrupted their conversation. Outside the window, in the parking lot, they saw a tall black man (the same young fellow Siri had spoken to earlier) struggling in the grip of two black-uniformed Wisconsin State Police. "Release me, sirs! I know my rights!"

A third cop stood off to the side. "Stop resisting, now! You have the right to remain silent. Anything you say can and will be used against you in a court of law..."

"I'll sue for false arrest!" the Nigerian shouted.

The third cop calmly pulled a Taser from his belt, held it to the struggling man's thigh, and zapped him. The African convulsed and went limp. "Alright, I give up!"

Despite the prisoner's surrender, the cop shocked him two more times. Siri didn't want to look, but couldn't help herself. She saw the Taser-wielding officer laughing as his comrades carried the twitching Nigerian away.

Siri and her father finished their meal in silence. Rajiv brought the check, and Pradeep handed him his credit card. As they waited, he looked his daughter in the eye. "I have the greatest confidence in you, Siri. But I can't help worrying. Promise you'll be careful."

"I will, Dad." She smiled, took her father's hand. "You may not believe me, but I really value your opinion. I've been struggling with so many issues. Sometimes I feel overwhelmed. But talking with you really helps me put my life in perspective. I feel much more confident I can make the right decisions, discover my *dharma*."

"Decisions about what? Your friend from Arizona?"

"No, I mean my life goals and priorities. As far as Nephi and myself, we'll take that as it comes. He's been an indispensable ally, though probably he'll never be more than a friend."

"We'll see about that," her father said with a sly smile.

As Robert Plant sang the last few notes of 'Stairway to Heaven,' Joel was surprised to hear the announcer cut in. "This just in on the dramatic bank robbery in St. Petersburg. Police have identified the suspects as a man and woman in their early thirties, Caucasian, 6 feet and five foot seven in height respectively, said to be brother and sister. Suspects are armed and dangerous and may be suffering from post-traumatic stress disorder. They were last seen driving a late model green Ford minivan. If you have any information, please call Silent Witness..."

Since when did classic rock stations interrupt their programming with news bulletins? What bizarre times these were! Still, Joel had to chuckle. He could imagine robbing a bank with his sister. She'd complain about the lousy service, and periodically accuse the tellers of not listening to her. Once again, Joel reminded himself he no longer had a sister; Sam Steinberg was an only child. It was easier, having less phony personal history to remember.

Joel was so preoccupied, he almost missed the empty parking space. It was a tight one, but no problem for his Smart Car. He pulled in next to a gold Explorer. How could they afford the gas for that thing? As he emptied his pipe into the ashtray, he regretted his bright idea of switching from cigars. These days, it wasn't that easy to find pipe tobacco.

He unfolded himself from the driver's seat, got out, and looked in all directions. No bank robbers or Albanian gangsters in sight. Since he'd ditched the old cell phone he hadn't had any more messages from his snake-loving friends. Not that he wasn't still paranoid. If anybody was going to track him down and blow his cover, he'd bet money on the Mob before the Feds.

Thank God for Nephi's Griffin software. Every day he checked the Internet for gang activity. Florida had plenty of that, of course, but not so much here in Tampa. If he hadn't been able to cover his on-line tracks, the FBI's data miners would surely have noticed such an obsessive interest in crime. *Yes sir,* he imagined telling them, *I'm writing a crime novel.*

He had to wander around for a while before he saw the sign: 'Autumn Art Fair.' This was the place. Now he just had to find Serena Connelly.

Joel wasn't sure if she'd actually invited him, or had just mentioned it as part of her continuous chatter, as she dug through her box of receipts and bank statements. Her records were hell to straighten out, but he didn't mind. She was pleasant to look at, even if she wasn't his type. He normally wasn't interested in women who were tall, thin (that is, small breasted), or pale skinned. But he appreciated her abundant freckles.

She was close to his age, which inevitably led to thoughts about dating. In Joel's previous life, post-divorce, he'd had three serious girlfriends and numerous non-serious dates. By contrast, Sam Steinberg was in a long dry spell. It wasn't easy thinking of a good opening line when you were busy looking over your shoulder. Plus he had to stay focused and frugal, or he'd never save up enough money to make the next move to Aruba or Costa Rica or the Caymans. So even if he had an opportunity with Serena, he'd have to pass it up.

This was not, as he'd assumed, Serena's personal art show. There were at least twenty artists with booths in the parking lot, hawking their wares. It didn't take long to find her. She stood out, with her tie-dyed blouse, red bandanna, and the giant silver moon medallion around her neck. She eyed him blankly for a moment. Finally she said, "Sam! What a pleasant surprise!"

"Surprise? What's with the surprise?" He grinned. "Unless you didn't mean to invite me."

She looked sheepish. "Well, we artists have got to promote ourselves, so I tell everybody about the fair. But I don't actually invite *everybody*, only people I like." Her face reddened. "I mean people like you, who appreciate art."

"That's me." He gave her a reassuring smile. Next to the table was a box with a number of unframed canvases. He casually flipped through them. "What is this? Looks like something Andy Warhol might have done on acid."

Serena raised her eyebrows. "I'm a huge fan of Warhol, so I'll take that as a compliment.

It's an impressionistic view of the everglades, that is, not how they actually look *per se*, but a representation of the Spirit of the 'Glades. You know, alligator spirits, panther spirits and so on."

"Hey, you're all right," Joel chuckled. "I dissed your painting and you took it in stride. Actually, I love it, which might say a bit about my own strangeness." The painting was predominantly green, and the spirits had a rather cartoon-like quality. The panther's face resembled Della Wilton, and the alligator reminded him of Vice President Frommage– clever!

"See," she pointed, "There's a heron. And in this corner there's a Seminole warrior. And on the right side, by the edge, is the head of a panther."

"I saw that; it reminded me of my ex." Joel grinned. "How much?"

"Five hundred. I haven't gotten around to repricing my stuff, and with inflation, I really should." She laughed. "I could sell more if I painted the stuff the Midwestern tourists like. Every once in a while, I get someone, a New Yorker usually, who understands what I'm trying to say."

"I don't know..." Joel eyed her carefully. "It's not a bad price, but it's a bit more than I'm used to spending. Maybe if you threw in something extra, say dinner with me at Gino's?"

"Sorry, I couldn't afford that," Serena replied, then laughed. "Oh, you're asking me on a date? You're such a kidder!"

"Let's not call it a date," he countered, "just a chance to have some good food and good company. I haven't been in town all that long, don't know lot of people."

"Me neither. I moved here from Key West a few months ago. It was too freaking expensive there. And it's not all mellow like it used to be, with the INS looking for illegals, DEA road blocks on the causeway. Bring back the Conch Republic, I say!"

Joel laughed. This gal was OK, maybe even a bit of a radical like himself. He'd been wasting his time, hitting on his buxom Cuban neighbor, who always declined his invitations to coffee. That was the sort of woman Joel Walter would have pursued. As Sam Steinberg, it was time for his tastes to change.

Serena kept him there talking for nearly an hour. She ignored several sales prospects, as urban hipsters and gay couples wandered in, looked longingly at her abstracts, then drifted away. Instead Serena entertained Joel with humorous rants about her ex, now living in Miami with his young second wife. She also bragged about her granddaughter, whose finger painting was already showing artistic promise. When Joel left, he had something for his wall, and they'd set a date for the following weekend. It had been the only way he could get her to stop talking.

"Uh, Mario, you got a minute?"

"Sir?" Emal had been heading back to the truck to pick up another load of gravel. It always took him a moment to respond to his new identity. Albanians did somewhat resemble Italians; luckily Americans were too ignorant to know the difference.

Emal's supervisor, Chaz Robbin, looked like the archetypal cowboy: tall, sun browned and gangly, head topped with a black Peterbilt ball cap. He always had a wad of chew in his mouth. "Uh, yeah, step in my office please."

"Yes, sir." Emal could tell something was not right. "Beautiful weather today, isn't it?"

Robbin grunted agreement. "I'll cut to the chase. I've been getting complaints from the other workers about how many breaks you take."

It hit Emal like a punch to the gut. He knew what this was about. Somebody had observed him praying, despite his care to secure a private place. These days he worked long hours; often his shift included three of the five mandatory prayer times.

"Sir, I'm entitled to take breaks, and I always clock out. Some of the men take smoke breaks many times a day. I don't smoke; I only ask for two or three breaks each day."

"Yes, but..." Robbin fidgeted. "Damn, this is awkward. You ain't really Italian, are you?"

Emal looked him in the eye. "You know my situation. I need to work. Through no fault of my own, I must conceal my identity. I don't begrudge the percentage you take of my..."

"Christ, Mario, I told you never to mention that, understand? You've got to make a living, so do I. If anybody heard you say that, we'd both be in deep shit!"

Of course. They were both breaking the law. Emal was working under an assumed name and Robbin had filed false paperwork with the IRS. Most of Chaz's people were Hispanic, and many of them were no doubt undocumented as well. Yet one of them had fingered Emal as a Muslim. Someone who hated his kind enough to risk his job by making trouble for the boss.

"I'll level with you, Mario. You've been a good worker, better than most. You're never late, never come in smelling like whiskey or dope. If it were up to me, I'd promote you. But certain people ...." he paused to spit into a can on his desk, "think you're some kind of terrorist. I know that's bullshit. But with Homeland Security so touchy these days I can't afford to take chances." He cleared his throat. "I'm gonna have to let you go." He dug into his pocket, produced a wad of cash. "Here, take this. Consider it severance pay."

Emal nodded, took the money. "Thank you, Sir." He left the office without another word.

He walked dejectedly to his tiny Yang Chin pickup. It wasn't all bad, he told himself. Driving a ready-mix truck was too much stress; he greatly preferred a tractor trailer and the open road. And the pay had been horrible. His family used the word 'Jew' as a synonym for greedy, but Robbin, who was obviously one of them, made Jews look like Sufi ascetics. Emal's paycheck barely kept a roof over his family– but at least it was honest work.

What will I do now? I was hoping Esma could quit her job cleaning the kaffir's houses. How demeaning! Now we'll be lucky to survive on what she earns.

He pulled his phone out of his pocket, debating about when to call his wife. *This will be the first thing to go.* It was one of those pay-as-you-go phones. Expensive, but his only choice; he had no 'credit' for the corporate bandits to check.

"Hey Mario, where you going?" It was Rodrigo, one of the other drivers. "We're already short-handed today!"

"They let me go." Emal shrugged, as if to imply he had no idea what the reason could be.

"Man, that Robbin is such a hard ass," Rodrigo said. "I'll tell you what you do. Does your phone have Internet?"

Emal nodded. "Don't they all?"

"I'll give you the address for this underground website. I go there sometimes for jobs, day labor. I think they need drivers, too. Let me see." Rodrigo took the phone from Emal and punched in a long series of digits. "Check this out. Enter search term 'driver.' Here's one: Truck Driver, Billings–Seattle. You have your own truck tractor, don't you?"

Emal nodded again.

"Then what you doing here? Go check the site. Make sure to get the new code each day."

"Uh, thank you." Emal hoped it wasn't a trap. His situation left him no choice but to trust a man he barely knew. He turned back. "But why? Why did you help me?"

"You needed it." Rodrigo grinned, showing a missing tooth. "We immigrants need to stick together. Good luck, Mario."

As Joel drove home the following Friday, he was in high spirits, thinking of his impending date with Serena. Even when he passed a house surrounded by yellow tape and police cruisers, he kept a positive attitude. *At least there aren't any bodies out on the front lawn this time.* A few minutes later, when he stepped into his house, his mood sunk. As always, he was greeted by the smell of cat urine. He'd given up trying to eliminate that irritating reminder of the previous tenant's pets.

Despite Joel's best efforts to dress the place up with a couple of posters on the wall and a spider plant hanging over the kitchen table, it was still drab, empty and depressing. He missed being his own boss, and working from his tidy little home in Kingman. He missed the hotter, drier climate. Most of all, he missed his daughter Esther. The one thing that cheered him up was his ability to follow her life from afar. Before he even kicked off his shoes, he booted his computer, started up the Griffin client, and signed in.

He immediately went to Esther's social network sites. The pregnancy was going well. Her husband Jay had created a Facebook page for the upcoming arrival, complete with ultrasound scans and photos of the nursery. Seeing his daughter made Joel's heart ache. He thought of how they'd watched classic comedy together, and how she'd giggled at his dumb jokes. If only he'd known to set her up with the Griffin software, they'd still be able to communicate.

That reminded him that he hadn't checked his email. Nephi had set up a web-bot to scan the Internet for news of possible threats, especially concerning the Albanian Mob or crackdowns by Homeland Security. The bot's reports, along with all other Griffin-encrypted messages, went automatically into a hidden folder. To access them Joel placed his thumb on a biometric scanner.

Thankfully, there were no threat reports in the Griffin in-box. Not even the usual dirty joke from JL. To Joel, Larsen's obscene missives, albeit amusing, were a frivolous, unnecessary risk. JL refused to stop sending them, calling them "real world connectivity testing."

The lone message was from Nephi. "Sam– hope it's going better for you. Things here are getting really interesting. Been putting in lot of hours on new project (Son of Griffin.) Siri is amazing. The most complex math, she understands instantly, also good at explaining. I actually 'get it' now. Shame she doesn't live closer. You believe she's a Browncoat, too?"

Oy. "Firefly" fans were more fanatic than Trekkers. They'd petitioned the network, unsuccessfully, with tens of thousands of signatures to bring back the show. Joel had once met some guys who were filming sequels to the *Serenity* movie in their barn. He hoped Nephi never got that obsessive.

"Next month I'm flying to Milwaukee to do network roll out for the Xanadu, that casino ship in Lake Michigan. I'll definitely stop in Chicago to see Siri. We've got some issues with her Griffin plug-ins, much easier to work out face-to-face."

Joel had to laugh. If it was any *other* young guy he knew, it would be Griffin he'd be thinking about plugging in. If this thing between Nephi and Siri became more than platonic, how would the boy's family take it? Could love really conquer all?

He began his reply. "Glad to hear things are moving along. If the new project's anything like Griffin, the Feds are doomed. SJ is brilliant. I'm sure you have no other motives for your visit." Joel added a winking smiley face at the end.

A simple electronic melody interrupted Joel's train of thought. He reached in his pocket for his cell phone; nothing on the screen. The sound was actually coming from his computer speakers. *Damn, can't keep my ring tones straight.* It was a voice-over-IP call, routed through Griffin for maximum security. He dug out the old fashioned wired headset (wireless was not secure enough, Nephi insisted) from under a pile of papers and plugged it into the audio jack.

"Hello, Steinberg speaking." After several months living with the 'Samuel Steinberg' identity, he no longer hesitated when answering the phone.

"Sammy boy, how're they hangin'?"

"JL! I'm good, and you?" Until recently, the occasional call from an old friend was the most exciting part of his day. Not today. Joel glanced at the clock– it would have to be quick.

"So, how are things in the Great White North?"

"That would be Canada, though we're not that far off. Anyhoo, all the white stuff is melted, which suits me fine."

"I'm so glad you called. I have a technical question for you. I know I shouldn't be trying to contact family members, but if I were to post an anonymous notice to my..."

"I'll be happy to help you, Sam, but before we get off on personal stuff, I've got an important favor to ask you. Nephi tells me you're a personal friend of Commander MacGuiness. Since the guy is currently underground, do you think you could help me get in touch with him?"

Joel paused for a moment and let out a breath. Larsen always had some crazy project going, and every one of them was, at that moment, 'critically important.'

"I wouldn't say 'friend,' we're more like acquaintances. What I want to know is, do you think it's a good idea? He's on the DHS Top Ten list of domestic terror suspects. For all we know, he might be on the President's secret Termination List as well. You don't want the Feds to come knocking at your door, do you?"

"Sammy, my boy, don't be so paranoid! They'll never know I've contacted him. That's what the Griffin System is for. As for the 'why,' I want to offer my help to the Resistance. The Butler Brigade needs our help if they're going to survive the Feds' persecution."

"The Resistance? What is this, Vichy France? Any time you resort to violence it just leads to more oppression. Civil disobedience, like Martin Luther King, that's the way to do it. Honestly, I think Mac is a likable guy, a straight shooter, and it's totally unfair to call him a terrorist. That doesn't mean you should get involved. I'm sure they can figure out Griffin on their own."

"Well yeah, but right now Mac's got to be getting pretty paranoid. How does he know Griffin is the real deal, and not some kind of government trap? Plus the current release version doesn't scale up all that well. We need to get him the latest and greatest software, the stuff Neeph and I have been working on."

"And Nephi's OK with this?" Though their young friend despised the Wilton administration, he had said many times that he believed in the American system. Joel couldn't imagine the kid would support any kind of revolution.

"Absitively. Neeph's not as much of a libertarian purist as you are. To regain our freedom, we need allies outside our little political circle. In my book, Mac's a hero. He defied orders and took down that Afghan warlord who was selling little boys as sex slaves. Bastard deserved to die, even if he was technically on our side. They should've given Mac a medal, not a dishonorable discharge."

Joel sighed; this was a lost cause. Larsen could be a stubborn *eyzl* when he made up his mind. "Don't get me wrong, I think Mac is a decent man who made the best of a difficult situation. He claims that this Butler Brigade of his only wants to support the Constitution. But even with the purist of motives, anyone who tries for power gets corrupted, without exception."

"Well, there's a certain exceptional ex-congressman from Texas, but he's still under house arrest, and besides, he's too old to lead a rebellion. We can't sit around twiddling our thumbs, waiting for another Mr. Libertarian to come along. This country is going down the toilet. We need a man of action!"

Ouch. Joel felt bad enough about abandoning the struggle, without Larsen's snide comments. "OK, I'll try to contact MacGuiness, if you'll help me figure out the tech angle. If I mention certain details from when we worked together on the protests, maybe he'll trust me." The whole idea made Joel very uneasy. Though on the good side, he might be able to use the same method to contact Esther without alerting those goons in Homeland Security.

"You're the man, Sam. You won't regret it."

Joel put away the headset and returned to his unfinished reply to Nephi. Then he noticed the clock. He had to get ready for his date with Serena, quickly! Was there anything in his closet that didn't need ironing? At least he didn't need to dress up; she was definitely a casual woman. But it had to be quick. He didn't want to be late for his first date in months.

★ ◎★ ★

"Nephi, what a surprise to hear from you!" Siri appeared on the monitor with a bemused smile on her face. She stifled a yawn.

"Oh my gosh, did I wake you up? I keep forgetting about the time difference!"

"No, it's only an hour later here. I just fell asleep reading. I was up rather late last night."

"Doing what?" Nephi laughed, felt himself turning red. "That came out wrong, didn't it? Feel free to say, 'None of your business!'"

"OK, none of your business! Actually, I was on-line, working with Bjornsen on the software. He was having trouble implementing the 'exchange compatibility' piece."

"Sorry, I don't remember that part. Was that in the original paper?"

"Yes, but my dissertation barely touched on it. You remember the TV show M*A*S*H?"

"I've seen it in reruns."

"It's like the episode where they need supplies, and Corporal Klinger is trading this favor for that favor, and it gets tremendously complicated. In a system that can get scaled up to involve millions of people, we need to match up buyers and sellers in the most efficient manner. So we use a scoring system called 'compatibility factor', which helps the system find what people are looking for. Like a Google search, but with real tangible stuff."

Nephi grinned. "Gee, I might not have understood without the analogy. Oh by the way, I got an email from Krijk the other day. He was really impressed by your technical abilities."

Now it was Siri's turn to blush, though with her complexion it was difficult to detect. "Lars is a nice fellow. Did you hear he got caught up in the riots? It was lucky he didn't get hurt."

"I saw it on the news. Things have been crazy in Amsterdam lately."

"Nephi?" It was his mother's voice. Here in his parents' house, he'd always been able to hear footsteps coming up the stairs, but this time he'd been preoccupied. "We were wondering where you all were. We're having this party for you, and you disappear into the office."

"Uh, I've got to go, Siri. I'll talk to you tomorrow." He closed the program and spun around in his chair. "Sorry, Mom. Just had to check on my email, make a call."

Ariana Snow brushed a strand of her long black hair out of her face. Her stern expression disappeared. "It sounded like you were talking to your lady friend in Chicago."

Nephi got out of the chair and turned the monitor off. "Well, yes, we had some issues to discuss on the project we've been working on."

"You can discuss all that techie stuff later. We've got the whole family here to celebrate your new business. You know your father; he's threatening to start dinner without you."

On the way down the stairs the noise of conversation could be heard. Nephi could hear his brothers Jim and Enoch laughing, probably over some dumb political joke. His mother stopped walking in the middle of the stair. "Were the two of you really discussing computers?"

"Just what are you implying, Mom?"

"Oh, nothing. Just that you talk about Siri an awful lot. I'm thinking maybe your new company might have a position for someone as smart as you say she is."

"We're just friends, Mom."

"That's good, because you know, there's this new girl at church I'd really like you to meet. Then again, a person can always convert." She gave a sly smile; Ariana herself had been Roman Catholic before marrying William Snow.

"Cut it out, Mom," Nephi said with a grin, squeezing past her on the stair. "Enough talk, I'm starving!"

Chapter 7 – A Matter of Trust

Serena Connelly looked over the small pile of boxes in front of Joel's condo. "Christ, Sam, when you said you didn't have a lot of stuff to move, you weren't kidding."

"I believe in living the simple life," Joel replied. "Actually, my ex got most of my old possessions, but it turned out there were very few things I really missed. I promised myself that in the future I wouldn't be so hung up on material things." That was the cover story. In reality, he'd come to Florida with almost nothing and hadn't yet been able to afford all the necessities of modern life. Though in principle, he meant what he'd said.

Joel grinned and gave Serena a kiss on the lips. Inside his emotions were much more complicated. *I can't believe I'm moving in with her. Am I making a mistake?*

"I like your philosophy." She returned the kiss and gave him some tongue this time. "We'll make great roomies, Sammy. As long as you don't try to smoke that stinky pipe indoors."

"Yes, Ma'am." He put the last box in the back of Serena's VW. "That's it. Thanks for helping me, Babe. If I'd had to move all this stuff in my Smart Car, it would have taken forever."

She shut the back door and got in the driver's seat. "You know, if some guy called me 'babe' a few months ago, I would've bit his head off. But coming from you, it just seems right."

"Glad to hear it. As long as that remark doesn't indicate any Praying Mantis tendencies."

Serena laughed. "You're such a goof. See ya over there."

Joel got in his Smart Car, placing a shoe box on the passenger seat. This he was transporting personally; it contained childhood items with his real name on them. Could it be hidden in her attic? Serena was already on her way, so he started the car and followed.

Despite his misgivings, Joel was eager to move in with Serena. Over the last few months, her eccentricities had really grown on him. Their first date had turned into an all-night sex marathon. Joel hadn't expected to be able to perform multiple times in the same evening. He doubted he could keep that up every night, but he was willing to give it a try.

The problem was, there was also a big lump of guilt settling in his stomach. Serena didn't even know his real name. Joel didn't mind lying to strangers, or the government, but he wished he didn't need to lie to this wonderful woman. Yet it was all for a good cause. With the money he saved in rent, he'd be able to save up for the day he could relocate to the Caribbean. When that happened, she might just want to come along.

For now, though, she had to be kept completely in the dark. As they pulled up to Serena's place, he stashed the shoe box under the passenger seat. She was a late sleeper; he could easily bring it in and find a hiding place in the morning.

They couldn't have asked for a more beautiful day. An early morning rain had left the air smelling washed and clean. The two new house-mates walked back and forth between house and driveway, as they carried Joel's possessions into Serena's bungalow. "The neighborhood's not as nice as it it used to be, but it's tolerable. Besides, I couldn't afford to move even if I wanted to."

"What do you mean, 'not nice?' Are you talking about crime?" Joel's 'past life' experiences with the vengeful Albanian family had fostered an obsession with crime. It didn't help that the Albanian Mob was making inroads in Florida. Just last week there'd been a gruesome murder of two small time drug dealers dead in Orlando, throats cut and genitals mutilated. It happened all the time in Miami, but that was too close.

"Jeez, I didn't know you were such a wuss. No, not gun battles or anything, but we had a string of burglaries last month. That's why I wanted a *man* in the house."

"Just concerned for your safety." Once inside, Joel opened up a box of clothing. "I want to hang these up before everything gets wrinkled."

"You sure are anal," Serena laughed. "Not surprising, using your left brain all day. She put her hand on his, and assumed a stern expression. "Sir, step away from the box! There are better things to do on our first day as roomies. I declare an afternoon of celebration."

"I like the way you think, Girl." Joel began unbuttoning his jeans.

"Not just yet, Sam. I want to take the edge off first." She reached into her purse and pulled out a tiny wooden pipe. "Though if you want to smoke naked, it's totally fine with me."

Serena pulled the blinds closed. The two sat down on the beat up pink couch in the cluttered living room. Joel watched as she filled up the bowl and handed him the pipe. She dug a lighter out of her purse. "Newbie gets the first hit."

Joel grinned and took the first drag, then started coughing. He wasn't accustomed to inhaling smoke, at least not directly. It had been years since he'd smoked pot on a regular basis.

"You're such a wimp." She took the pipe from him and refilled the single-hit bowl. "You didn't even finish what I gave you."

"What's with you today? Is this some kind of Florida custom to haze the new roommate? You know how they say weed's gotten stronger over the years. Seems to me it's harsher as well. Which is OK, because it probably won't take much to get me off." Indeed, his head was already starting to feel funny. He accepted the pipe again, deciding he'd had enough. He didn't want to fall asleep in the middle of the upcoming festivities.

"Tell me something," he squeaked, trying to hold the smoke in his lungs. "Aren't you a little paranoid about buying illegal drugs these days, with the government so intrusive? And don't talk to me about medical marijuana, I know you're not on that list."

Serena took another hit and snickered as she tried to hold in the smoke. "I trust Ramon. Been buying from him from years."

"But you said you got this stuff somewhere else."

"Well, lately he'd been selling me some pretty skunky shit. A friend of mine turned me on to this new Internet thing, it's called 'e-Barter.' It's a completely anonymous, underground program that's like e-Bay and Craigslist combined. You don't even have to meet the person you're dealing with. You might leave the money in one place and pick up the stuff in another, like a bus station locker."

"Babe, that sounds too good to be true." She handed him the pipe; he shook his head and gave it back. "Definitely stronger than I'm used to. No, that Internet barter shit's a new one on me." This was another regrettably necessary lie. "It sounds like a great idea in principle, but I'm just too paranoid to try it." Despite the fact that he knew e-Barter's creators and considered them to be geniuses, Joel didn't quite trust it. Fine for normal folks, maybe, but not for someone hiding from the Feds *and* the Mob.

"You're right to be cautious. People do get busted sometimes. But now they have on-line tutorials, teaching you how to spot a cop. There's even an app that analyzes your on-line conversations and computes the probability that you're dealing with a narc."

Joel laughed. "How the hell do they do that?"

"You remember Guardian Angel? The program that analyzes kids' chat rooms for signs of predators in disguise? Well, it's based on that."

"I'm still skeptical," Joel said. "I suppose I might want to try it first for something a little less illegal. Like maybe get some tax free cigars."

"I thought you only smoked a pipe," she said, eying him suspiciously.

Joel racked his brains for a plausible explanation. "Um, only 'cause pipe tobacco is the cheapest way to go. Gotta economize in this crazy economy."

"I hear you." She rolled up the plastic bag and tapped the ash out of the pipe. "I've got cottonmouth something awful." She got up and went into the kitchen. "Want a glass of wine?" In a few moments, she returned with two glasses and a smirk. "I was talking to you, Bub, and you didn't answer. Are you totally baked already?"

My God, I'll give myself away if I'm not careful. Joel forced himself to laugh. "Guess so."

Serena handed Joel his glass of wine and sat down, grinning. "The guy said this shit was so good it'd make you forget your own name. Guess he was right."

It was one of those rare days when Siri was having trouble staying focused. She couldn't blame her work environment. Being one of the company's directors had its advantages. She had her own office, with a door and a nice sound system. She could plug in her iPod and play music all day–Mozart and Beethoven or Coltrane and Brubeck, depending on her mood.

Today's job was really tedious, fixing the user interface to payroll system. It was a major client, a popular casino on the Strip. Siri couldn't complain; someone had to do it, and she was the newest person here. The main business of Snow-Creche Systems was data security, but most customers wanted everything to interoperate– bookkeeping, payroll, employee records.

Nephi would have enjoyed this project. He saw each task as a challenge, a puzzle to be solved. To Siri, it had to be cutting-edge to be interesting. For example, her current project was a Bayesian analysis module, which the casinos used to help detect cheaters. The 'big brother' aspect bothered her, but as Nephi said, nobody forced a person to gamble.

Today Nephi was with Jeff, meeting with potential clients. Jeff Creche, a former BYU classmate of Nephi's, was a co-founder and the other half of the corporate name. Siri had been left alone to handle the payroll issue, which this particular customer saw as a crisis.

But her mind kept drifting back to her favorite extracurricular project. Bjornsen had asked her to help find a way to protect the Griffin 'web of trust' against government sting operations. Nephi would be angry if he found out that she was still involved. "You're already on the government watch list; let the Europeans take the risks now." But she found it hard to say no. When they'd integrated the e-Barter algorithms into Griffin, it had become as much her baby as Nephi's.

Griffin used statistical analysis routines, too, for the same reason the casinos did. Krijk, their Dutch hacker associate, had written them before he'd suddenly dropped out of the project. Their purpose was to flag the accounts of traders who acted dishonestly, so the system could delete them. A banned person could always start a new account, but this required earning the trust of the community all over again. The bigger problem was when someone was able to mimic an honest participant long enough to scam people– or worse, betray them to the authorities.

A hand on Siri's shoulder made her jump. "Time to go home, Busy Bee." It was Nephi, finally back from his meeting. He bent down, kissed her on the forehead. "Want to go get something to eat? I'm buying."

She narrowed her eyes. "Are you going to propose again?"

"No, I limit myself to one rejection per month." His serious expression gave way to his endearing childlike laugh.

Siri got up out of the chair, and grabbed his hand. "Don't think of a rejection, more of a postponement. You know how I feel about you; you're a wonderful man. But this is all going so quickly, I don't want to rush such an important decision."

"Understood. Right now I'm starving, and the payroll fix for the Treasure Chest can wait 'til Monday. I'll even let you choose the place."

"Sounds good." She smiled, but her emotions were in turmoil. Had it been a mistake to accept this position? It wasn't the job that caused her stress, it was the proximity to Nephi. From their first meeting she knew he was interested in her, and she couldn't help feeling attracted in return. He was so sweet, forthright, and handsome. But with their religious differences, could it possibly work out? His family was always polite, but she'd seen their appraising looks. Was she good enough for their Nephi? Was she willing to convert? Siri tried to put those thoughts aside.

He took her hand and led her out of the office, locking up on the way out. Everybody else was long gone. The parking lot was not quite empty, since Snow-Creche shared it with a couple of other businesses. Nephi's truck was off by itself on one side.

Nephi looked around the parking lot suspiciously.

"What's wrong, Nephi?"

"A couple minutes ago, I got a text from the security system in my truck. Somebody activated the motion sensor. I didn't want to alarm you..." He squinted at the display of his cell phone. "I got video of a some guy with a beard standing by the driver side door. He might have just been checking it out, you know how guys are. Don't see him actually touching it, but..."

Siri frowned. "What are we paying that security guard for, if he's not stopping random people from coming in our lot?"

"Easier said than done. There's always people coming and going from the slot repair place. It wouldn't be hard for bad guys to get in." Nephi took a device out of his pocket and started waving it over the truck. "Sorry I'm getting so paranoid."

"I don't blame you. These are crazy times. I don't like those slot people. Do you think they're in with the Mob?"

"Could be. Mob's been making a comeback in Vegas. In a weird way, that's a good thing; they've been wiping out the gangs, especially the crazies who've been doing the drive-by shooting. Those old fashioned Sicilian types at least have a code of honor."

He put the scanner back in his pocket and unlocked the doors. He started to get in, then turned back to Siri. "Speaking of Italian, how does that sound? I know I promised I'd cook you dinner sometime, but it seems like we always end up working so late."

"Don't worry about it, Nephi. I'm not fussy, as long as they have something without meat." Siri had cooked dinner for him several times, her native Sri Lankan dishes as well as American food. It was so sweet, the way he was trying to be a modern, well rounded male. She knew she should be appreciative, even though she felt pretty crabby, having skipped lunch. "I got a flier from a new Italian place downtown. It sounded interesting."

"Don't remember seeing anything like that, but then, I throw away most of my junk mail. Seems like it's all just bars and casinos."

Siri nodded. "I don't remember the name at the moment, but I'll Google it." She pulled her phone out of her purse. "Got it. Here's the directions."

"Great! You can drive your car home, and I'll pick you up there, OK?"

The drive home took only a few minutes. Siri liked her little house, it gave her a feeling of independence and control she needed badly these days. It was lucky that Nephi's religion forbade them to cohabitate without being married. If he asked, she would have had a hard time turning him down.

Siri put her car in the garage then climbed into Nephi's big Ford diesel pickup. As they drove in silence, she brooded about the suspicious guy with the beard. It could have been a Federal agent planting a tracking device; they didn't even need a warrant for that. Griffin was great, but it seemed to be making Nephi overconfident. *And he scolds me for being careless.*

Of course, she was just as likely to be the target. She'd already drawn the attention of Homeland Security's EID. If they'd planted the device, what would she do? Remove it and they'd know she was on to them; they'd need to be more intelligent in fooling the snoops.

Or it could be criminals; they were quickly adopting the government's surveillance technologies. If those Albanian hoodlums, for example, connected Nephi with Joel Walter a.k.a. Sam Steinberg, the two of them were in *deep* trouble. Though from what she'd heard, those guys didn't seem that bright. Siri had been using Griffin for all her communications, but it didn't stop her from worrying. That reminded her. "You heard from Sam lately?"

Being in Nephi's truck, she felt safe talking freely. Snow-Creche had developed an electronic-device detector they used to help the casinos detect high tech cheaters. Nephi used it to check his vehicle for bugs, almost on a daily basis.

"Yes, he sent a message just a couple days ago. He's doing well, no sign of his Albanian friends, but he seems terribly lonely. What a horrible thing to be cut off from your family! On the good side, he said he's met a lady artist around his age that he's interested in. I hope that works out. It's not good for a man to be alone." He glanced at Siri, eyebrows raised theatrically.

They arrived at the El Panda Loco, which was housed in a converted pizza parlor. The sign, shaped like a map of Italy, had been whitewashed and decorated with a black and white bear wearing a sombrero. "This ought to be interesting," Nephi said.

It was a charmingly offbeat place. Nephi ordered a *bulgogi* burrito, and Siri chose a rice bowl with fajita veggies. As they waited for their food, Nephi stared silently at the TV on the wall. Was he angry at her? Moodiness was no way to win a woman's heart. She smiled at him. "You're being very quiet tonight."

"Sorry, Seer, lot on my mind," Nephi said. "One of the clients inquired about Graham."

"Really?" Siri struggled to keep the fear out of her voice. 'Graham' was their code word for Griffin, one of many such terms they used when out in public. "What did you say?"

Nephi laughed nervously. "I had to act shocked. 'That would be illegal', I said. But that's not the funniest part. The guy looked me right in the eye and said, 'Rumor has it you know the guy wrote it.' I just laughed and said, 'Yeah, *right!*'"

"That's not funny! You know I'm already on *their* radar because of my doctoral thesis."

"I agree with you, it's funny strange, not funny ha-ha. Which reinforces what I've been saying about *your* project. I know it's hard to let go, but we've definitely done our part."

Siri sighed. The guilt hit her like a South Asian monsoon. "I know." The waitress arrived with their order, interrupting their conversation.

Nephi took a bite of his burrito. "Hmm, reminds me of a Mexican place I once visited in Seoul. Anyway, I felt bad having to lie to the guy. Graham would be perfect for them, and they have every right to want to protect their business's secrets. They use encryption, but anything that's legal is pretty easy for the bad guys to hack."

"You did the right thing, Nephi. It could have been a trap."

"That's what worries me. How long before 'doing the right thing' backs us into a corner we can't get out of?"

From across the table, she took his hand and squeezed it. "We're both reasonably intelligent people. We'll figure something out."

It was nearing dusk as the Larsen brothers entered the outskirts of Bemidiji, Minnesota.

"Wasn't much of a fishing trip, was it?" Dave said. "Nothing even big enough to keep."

Jon laughed. "You always say *I'm* too negative. We still had a pretty good time, Bro."

"Didn't say we didn't. As a getaway, it was great. As for the fishing, it sucked." At that moment Dave's cell phone interrupted with a snippet of the Temptations singing 'My Girl.'

"I'm amazed your girlfriend lets you out of her sight, the way she texts you all the time."

Dave read the message and smiled. "I like hearing from her. She cracks me up sometimes with the things she says." He typed in a few emoticons and hit SEND. "That's your problem Jon, you need a woman. Forget the crazy political conspiracy bullshit."

"I wouldn't mind getting out more, though I don't want to be tied down, either. It's just hard to think about dating when the country's going to hell. Take for example, the way the Feds are hunting MacGuiness like a dog. All because he speaks out for the rights of veterans."

Dave groaned. "Should have known you couldn't go a whole weekend without talking politics."

"You brought it up, Man."

"I did, didn't I?" Dave groaned. "As long as we're on that topic, it bugs me how one-sided you can be. I agree, the veterans got a bad break. But MacGuiness is sheltering deserters. What kind of war hero does that? Plus carrying automatic weapons and trafficking in drugs. I don't want to hear you complaining about searches and road blocks. Your buddy is the cause of it all."

"Man, you are so brainwashed. If it wasn't Mac, they'd find some other excuse. You expect him to run a background check on every guy he helps out? And he's not dealing drugs. He's supplying medicine for all the vets the government's abandoned. Half of 'em have PTSD and chronic pain and brain damage. Instead of taking care of our own people, the Feds bring in a bunch of foreigners for the Liberty Legion. We don't have enough jobs for our own people."

"Now that's a switch. Aren't you always the one who's defending illegal immigrants?"

"Hoist me on my own petard, huh? Well, defending's not the same as supporting all their actions. But MacGuiness deserves our support. That's why we've been re-engineering Griffin, so it would scale up for their organization. And we made damn sure they knew where to get it." Jon didn't know that for certain, since he'd received no response, but he wasn't about to admit that to his brother. "If it weren't for us, I'm sure the Feds would've caught him by now."

Dave's face was getting redder by the minute. "Don't get me started on that. It's bad enough you've been posting illegal software on the Net. Now you're brazenly aiding an official enemy combatant. And getting that Mormon kid involved. Plus, the fact that you're telling me all this shows how careless you are. You're messing with some pretty heavy shit, Jon."

"Are you saying I can't trust you, my own brother?"

"Of course you can trust me. Even so, I don't *want* to know about your illegal activities. It makes me a target for the Feds, too, and I'm not happy about that." He snorted. "Mark my words, Big Brother, you're gonna end up in a detention camp."

"Yeah right."

The brothers sat silently for a while, the truck's V8 rumbling as they waited for the light to change. It went green, then red, and the white Corolla in front of them didn't move an inch. Jon hit the steering wheel in frustration. "Sons of bitches!"

"What? What's wrong? We're not in that much of a hurry."

"Isn't it obvious? Why do you think the traffic stopped? Can't be an accident, check out the sign." Ahead of them, on the side of the road, a sign flashed 'Checkpoint Ahead, No U-Turn.'

Jon rummaged through the console between the seats. "Damn, where is it? You got your phone? Go to this website." He began rattling off a series of random letters and numbers.

"God damn it, Jon, slow down. I don't even have the browser open yet! What the hell kind of a site address is that?"

"Undernet, underground Internet. The URL is random; they change it every couple days."

"I'm not living in a cave, I've heard of the Undernet. OK, give me those numbers now."

Jon repeated the sequence. "You in now?"

"For crying out loud, what a cheesy website! Looks like something out of the 1990's. Now what?"

"Just type in Bemidji, MN."

Dave shook his head. "Doesn't sound good. It's definitely a Federal roadblock ahead. In fact, there's another sign with the Homeland Security logo." He sighed. "Jesus H. Christ, this sucks! We'll be in this for hours."

"Like hell we will! I'm turning around right now!"

"Dammit Jon, you can't do that! Evading a checkpoint is a Federal offense!"

"Don't be such a pussy!" Jon laughed, and made a sudden wide U-turn, causing some angry honking from drivers going the other way. "They're just trying to scare people. I can't take the chance they'll search the truck and see the JL-9000. These days they can copy all your data without a warrant. Once they saw it's encrypted they'd hold me hostage 'til I coughed up the key. My goose would be cooked."

"But they're not..." Dave looked down at his phone again. "Talk about a coincidence, they're looking for MacGuiness. Least that's what the commenters are saying. They say he was seen going this way, trying to get to Canada. So we should've just waited. That van on the other side of the road looked like a photo van. If they got your plates, you're really screwed."

"You're forgetting my 'special' license plate cover. When I flip the switch it goes dark; the numbers just look black. Go ahead, assholes, take my picture for all the good it'll do ya!"

"God damn it to Hell, Jon, I told you not to turn around!"

Jon glanced up; a highway patrol car was rapidly getting larger in the rear view mirror. "He's not after me; I'll pull over and he'll go right by– oh shit!" The patrolman had followed them to the side of the road and now had his lights flashing.

Dave was livid. "Jon, you stupid bastard, you've gotten us both in big trouble. You really think they'll believe you didn't know about the roadblock? They had the sign up plain as day." He buried his head in his hands. "What are we gonna tell our folks when we call from jail? If they even let us call?"

"Wrong again, Bro." Jon reached under the dash and flipped a switch. The door on the back of the topper opened slowly.

Dave looked back. "Jon, what are you doing? He's drawing his gun!"

"Keep your head down!" Despite his show of bravado, Jon's heart was pounding. The next two seconds seemed to take forever, but then he heard the familiar 'ping' of the rifle locking into place. *Bet that cop's really shitting his pants right now.* Jon heard the police car's engine gunning and its wheels spinning on loose gravel. *He thinks he's running for his life, but the jokes on him!* The gun went 'Pop! Pop! Pop!,' rotating on its turret to splatter three paint balls across the cruiser's windshield.

Now it was time for Jon to step on it. He peeled out, simultaneously cursing and praying as his old F-150 lurched into traffic, narrowly missing a big farm truck going the other way. The patrolman turned on his siren and followed Jon onto the highway, only to smash into a van that was right behind the truck Jon had narrowly avoided.

"Fuck!" Dave shrieked.

Jon kept his eyes on the road as he dodged around other vehicles, but out of the corner of his eye, it looked like his brother was about to explode, literally.

"Jon, you stupid fucking bastard, if that cop dies in the crash they can charge you with murder, don't you know that?"

"Yes, this being the Bizarro World where up is down and black is white." He laughed mirthlessly. "What kind of dumb ass pulls onto a busy highway when he can't see out his windshield?" Jon glanced in the mirror to verify that the paint ball rifle had returned to its stow position, then changed lanes and zipped around a slow semi-truck, narrowly missing a Corvette as he dashed back to the right side. "Maybe if we head back to the cabin..."

"Like hell we are," Dave snarled. "I won't have you leading them there to *my* property, and have them seize it. No, you're on your own. Let me out, I'll walk to the goddamn bus station and find my own way home." He threw up his hands. "*Now* what are you doing?"

"This mall's pretty busy. We can hide in the middle of all these cars." He pulled into an empty spot between a green Suburban and a blue Astrovan with peeling paint. The minute he switched off the ignition, he broke up laughing. "Woo-hoo, did you see the way the Moe-a-matic worked back there? Got that cop car good! Man, I regret not using it more than that one time. Even if the cops did almost get me in Sioux Falls..." Seeing that his brother was not laughing, Jon's smile disappeared, He sighed deeply.

"I know it's 'cause you're mad at me, but I agree you should take the bus. We shouldn't be seen together." Dave sat in silence, arms crossed. "I'll pay you back for the ticket." Still no response. "OK, Dave, I admit it; it's my fault. I shouldn't have brought the computer, but you know, fishing is not that exciting, and I can't stand sitting around doing nothing for very long."

"Here," Jon grabbed his phone from the center console. "I'll look up the bus station. We'll lay low here a while, then I'll drop you off a couple blocks away. If anybody back home asks what happens, tell 'em the truck broke down, and you had to be back to work on Monday."

"Don't bother. I know where the Greyhound station is. I'll walk from here." Dave got out, walked to the back of the truck and opened the topper. He reached over the stowed paint ball rifle, then unfastened the bungee cord that secured his bag to the side of the box. Bag in hand, he slammed the topper shut, and walked away without looking back.

Jon felt terrible as he watched his brother trudging angrily out of the parking lot. This wasn't the first fight they'd ever had, or even the biggest. Back in high school they'd slugged each other on several occasions. The apologies could wait; right now there were bigger fish to fry.

Now, how to escape the area without getting busted? Although the trooper couldn't have his plate number, he certainly got a good look at Larsen's truck, and the cruiser certainly had video. Still, ditching the truck was not an option; he had to get home somehow.

First thing was to get rid of the incriminating plate cover. He grabbed a socket driver from the console and quickly removed it, checking over his shoulder for possible witnesses. Next he'd change his looks. He grabbed his shaving kit from behind the seat. There was an Amoco station right next to the mall. Ten minutes later he emerged from its bathroom, clean-shaven from his chin to skull. *Maybe I got a little carried away.*

Nervously scanning the sky for police helicopters, Larsen returned to his truck. He unfastened the paint ball gun, wiped it down thoroughly and tossed it in a dumpster behind the mall. Then he looked up the local Goodwill store. At the drop-off point in the alley behind the store, he removed the topper and left it on the dock. Luckily, no one came out to check.

As he left the alley, Larsen passed a car wash and realized that his white truck was so dirty from the dirt road to Dave's cabin that it actually looked tan. Washing it would provide a quick change in appearance. He pulled up to the auto-wash lane and fed a bill into the slot.

As he sat watching the suds cascading down the truck's windshield, he pondered his options. Heading south on highway 71 would probably be safe; unlikely that they'd divert personnel from the search for MacGuiness. When he reached US 10 he'd head west to Fargo, and then back up north. He'd definitely needed to check the Undernet again, but his phone was showing zero bars inside this metal building.

Larsen felt a sudden chill down his back. There were sirens, loud enough to be audible hear over the sprayers, and getting closer. Could they possibly have followed him? Just then the water stopped, and the light above the exit turned green. He thought about trying to wait it out in there, but in the rear view mirror he saw a car pull in behind him.

As he exited the car wash in his newly shiny truck, the armpits of his shirt were soaked with sweat. Across the street in a bank parking lot were two police cars. A tall black man stood between them, hands behind this neck, as one of the cops patted him down. Judging by his tattered clothes, the suspect was probably homeless. Another look revealed that these were local cops wearing DHS arm-bands. Larsen sighed in relief; law enforcement ineptitude would save him. Though he hated to admit it, Dave was right. He had to be much more careful.

Larsen headed south and in a few minutes he had left the town behind him. No road blocks, and no black helicopters, thank God. On the one hand, he'd been reckless, but he'd also been too fearful to do what needed to be done. He needed to find a way to communicate with MacGuiness. Larsen's idea was to serve as a bridge between Mac's group and his own community of hackers, an alliance that would benefit both parties. If worse came to worst, and the Feds came after him, he could join the Butler Brigade and disappear. Though he wasn't a veteran they could surely use his high tech skills.

Whatever lay ahead of him, it certainly wouldn't be boring.

Chapter 8 – Unprecedented Events

Chandrika Jayasuriya pursed her lips and sighed. "I wish you'd have let me help you sooner."

Siri forced a smile. "I appreciate it, Mom, but there was nothing wrong with the other dress."

Chandrika grimaced. "Except for being five years out of style and not flattering. This is your wedding day, hopefully your one and only. So even if it's a bit extravagant to do this at the last moment, it'll be worth it."

Siri stepped onto the platform and looked at the salesperson. "Am I doing this right?"

"Hold your arms straight out like this." The woman demonstrated.

As Siri stood there, a red line ran down the length of her body. Assuming it was a laser, the power was quite low. She barely noticed the flash as it passed her eyes.

"This is the new technology the TSA is testing at JFK," the lady said. "It maps the body's contours without letting the agents see you nude. OK, all done. Now come over to the monitor. You can choose any dress in our collection, and we'll do the alterations overnight."

"Is there a guarantee?" Chandrika asked. "Because the wedding is tomorrow evening."

"On time or your money back. Minus the hundred dollar deposit, of course."

Siri tried to be patient as they browsed through the dresses, superimposed on her digital photo by the computer. They were all pretty, but she didn't see a lot of difference between them. Her mind drifted back to a stubborn problem in her latest network-based authentication scheme.

"So, dear, which do you like best?"

"Uh, number three. I liked the sleeves on that one." She didn't remember the sleeves at all, but she had to say *something.*

She was saved from her mother's interrogation by a phone call. She tapped her ear to activate the speaker.

Her mood improved instantly when she heard Nephi's voice. "Hi, Sweetie. Got bad news. Don't know how to tell you..."

"The Bishop won't marry us?"

"No. Wish it was that simple. The airline called. Your passport's been declined."

"What? Did they say why?"

"Only that you're on no-fly, and we'll have to take it up with Homeland Security. I can't believe they did this to us at the last minute. Probably they're confusing you with some terrorist."

Do those idiots think I'm a Tamil Tiger? She kept that comment to herself; it surely would have gotten her mother's attention. "So are they going to refund our money?"

"For your ticket, yes, the law requires them to. And we can cancel the hotel. But mine is totally non-refundable. We're just fragged, I guess."

"This is so wrong! What do they think this is, some kind of banana republic, where they can just mess up peoples' lives without any accountability? Even in Sri Lanka..."

"It's OK, Sweetie, we'll drive to Tahoe. I have a cousin at the Hilton who'll get us a really nice room. Mexico's gotten kind of dangerous lately, anyway."

She took a deep breath and gritted her teeth. "We should have gotten the trip insurance."

"Yeah, you were totally right about that and..."

"What's done is done, forget it!" Siri suddenly realized she'd been shouting. Everybody in the store was staring. She exhaled. "I'll be OK. Love you, Hon." She pressed the 'End' button.

Her mother pounced. "What was that about?"

"Uh, just a mix-up with the plane tickets. Nothing we can't work out." Siri hated to lie to her mother, but she didn't want to get into that business again. Her mother would blame it on her refusal to work for the Federal EID– and she'd probably be right.

Chandrika stared at her daughter. "Are you sure nothing else is bothering you?" She lowered her voice to a stage whisper. "I hope it's not the wrong time of the month. I don't know if Mormons have those ridiculous taboos, like the Muslims. It worries me a little. The two groups are so similar. Both have the history of polygamy..."

Siri's mouth dropped open. "Mother! You have no idea what you're talking about!"

Her mother shrugged and turned back to the clerk. "Could you show us Number Three one more time?"

Siri tried to keep a positive attitude, despite her mother's casual invasion of her privacy. She seemed obsessed about everything that could go wrong with this marriage – their different backgrounds, religions, and ages. All irrelevant. The last was especially silly; Siri was only four years older. Nephi was an exceptional man; she loved him, and they'd work it out.

But she *had* been worried, even before Nephi's call. This problem with the government was bad enough when it affected her alone, but when it involved other people, that changed the equation significantly. *Well, Nephi had worked on e-Barter, too.*

The trouble was, how much could you really know anybody? It all came down to trust, which had been a major factor in Siri's research. Trust was a valuable thing, the basis of any economic transaction, as E. I. Singh's Nobel-prize-winning research had shown.

That reminded her of her dissertation. She'd never been quite satisfied with the section on establishing secure credentials. It might be possible for an attacker to impersonate one of the parties to an economic transaction, provided he could simultaneously compromise all the...

Her mother stopped talking. Siri hadn't really been listening, but the silence caught her attention. Chandrika sighed deeply and put her hand on her daughter's arm. "Dear, you have got to make a decision. We have a lot more things to do before tomorrow."

"Sorry, Mom. I'm a bit frazzled with everything going on. I didn't sleep well last night."

"You can't afford to be tired, my darling." She squeezed her daughter's shoulder. The gesture seemed comical, since Siri was several inches taller than she was. "We're lucky Las Vegas has these high tech bridal shops."

"OK then, I like this one best." It was a white lie. Number six was just as good. She'd been preoccupied with her research as well as Nephi's bad news. But number three would do;

it was pretty without being ostentatious.

Her mother nodded. "I like that one, too." She flagged down the sales lady, who'd abandoned them in their indecision. "We'll take number three." She stepped up to the counter and paid. "Now, the reception. Should we serve tea, or will it offend the groom's family?"

As they drove back to the hotel, Chandrika was in a conciliatory mood. "I think your Nephi is a wonderful man, I really do. It worries me, how different your backgrounds are. But I believe you two can make it work."

170

"It bothered me too, at first," Siri admitted. "But I believe there are people who are a good match despite their upbringing. It's scary, in a way, how our interests, likes and dislikes mesh together. Marriage isn't as important to me as it is to him. But being with him is extremely important to me, and I also want children..."

Chandrika smiled and nodded. *That* definitely met with her approval.

Promptly at 6 PM, Siri's three bridesmaids showed up at her hotel room door, determined to take her out on the town. She was happy to see her friends, but not at all in the mood to party. The whole excursion turned into a fiasco. First there was all the teasing about her becoming "a good Mormon housewife, barefoot and pregnant." Then they announced they were taking her to an all-male revue, to "stuff dollar bills in the G-strings of well-hung strippers." Not something she wanted to do, either. As luck would have it, Cherisse over-indulged at the bar and dashed to the bathroom to be sick. Siri drove them all back to the hotel.

When she crept into the suite, her parents were asleep in the other room. She could hear her father snoring. She dialed Nephi's number, hoping she wasn't waking anybody. He'd just started moving in to their new house in Henderson, boxes everywhere. Half his immediate family (at least 15 people) was staying there, camped out in sleeping bags on the floor.

He was awake, of course. "Hey Sweetie, how was your bachelorette party?"

"Never mind that, how about yours?" teased Siri. "Did your brothers get you a stripper?"

"My family?" He laughed, his endearing childlike giggle. "You must be joking! We spent the day playing paint ball. I've still got red stuff in my ear. You and the girls have a good time?"

"It was OK, but I miss you. I'd have rather been discussing secure crypto-systems, or even grading papers."

"I'm sorry; tomorrow night we won't be doing that!"

Siri laughed. She'd never before had a serious boyfriend who'd refused sex, in the technical sense, anyway. It was ironic they'd been more intimate over the telephone, in their separate homes, than they'd been in person. Not that they'd planned that. Siri doubted premarital phone sex was LDS-approved. It was something that just happened after they were engaged, when he'd been trying to cheer her up, when the stress was getting to her.

"You're still upset about the honeymoon, aren't you?"

"It's not so much that, it's– before today, it didn't seem real. Even with the DHS agents; sure, they sounded threatening, but I still had a choice, I could still turn down their offer. Now it seems like my choices are disappearing."

"Let's not worry about it now. After we get back from Tahoe, we'll rethink our priorities, decide how much risk we can live with. Right now, I only want you to think good thoughts. Focus on the wonderful day we're going to have tomorrow."

"Tell me what you have planned for me, tomorrow *night*."

"The first thing is to kiss you, starting on the lips. Then I'll kiss your ears and your chin and your neck, and move downward."

"What kind of places would you like to visit?" As Nephi described his inspirations, she pulled off her slacks and slipped under the covers.

The next thing she knew, the sun was streaming in through the window, and her mother's face was gazing down at her. "Get up, dear! It's your wedding day! Goodness, have you started sleeping with that phone thing in your ear?"

She laughed. "No, I was drowsy last night. The girls talked me into having some wine."

He mother frowned. "I certainly hope you didn't make yourself sick."

"Don't worry, Mom. I only had two glasses. My God, what time is it?"

"Plenty of time to get something to eat before the chapel. Come on, get dressed. You know your father and his blood sugar. He'll be irritable if he doesn't eat."

As a girl, Siri had fantasized about her wedding day, but never foresaw all the worries and problems. Yet when the moment came, it all melted away. Her excitement overcame the previous day's dark mood. Walking down the aisle with her father was like a beautiful dream.

At least one of her worries had not come to pass. Nephi had said some of his relatives didn't approve of his marrying a Gentile who was *not* converting. This meant the wedding could not be in the Temple; a particular disappointment for Nephi's mother. Yet his family had shown up in force regardless; the groom's side of the room was quite full.

Siri's mother had been more vocal about her own concerns. "Why does it automatically have to be a *Christian* wedding?" But Siri thought the compromise was reasonable. This was a non-denominational wedding chapel ('Maryam's Garden of Love') and they'd arranged a blessing by a Buddhist priest, which would be done while they stood on the traditional Sri Lankan *Poruwa* platform. It stood off to one side of the altar like a miniature gazebo. Seeing that reminded her of her brother's recent wedding, and she felt jittery for the first time.

The ceremony went quickly. They went through the Christian wedding first; a gospel reading, a brief sermon and two hymns. Then they performed a shortened version of the *Poruwa* ceremony; they fed each other sweetmeats, and received the blessing. At the end, the Bishop pronounced them 'man and wife.' The kiss was disappointingly quick.

The rest of the evening was a blur. The reception line stretched on forever. Nephi's family was huge, with brothers, sisters, aunts, uncles and cousins to meet and greet. Siri's extended family was also well represented; they'd flown in from all over the country. Her maternal grandparents had come all the way from Colombo.

Near the end of the line were two big ruddy-faced fellows she didn't recognize. One of them grabbed Nephi's hand and pumped it enthusiastically. "Nephi, you old son of a– uh, gun!"

"Good to see you!" Nephi smiled broadly, but he stiffened a little as they shook.

"Siri!" The big man stepped up and gave her a huge hug. There was a hint of beer on his breath which somehow got past his overpowering aftershave.

"JL, I didn't know it was you without your beard! I'm so glad you could make it!"

Larsen laughed. "Got to look respectable these days. Siri, Nephi, this is my little brother David." The resemblance was obvious, but the man was anything but little.

Siri was glad she'd invited him, despite the unexplained tiff between him and Nephi. After all, if it hadn't been for Jon Larsen, she and Nephi never would have met.

"Uh, just a sec, JL," Nephi said, holding up the rest of the line. He lowered his voice. "What happened to the other two guys, the ones sitting in the pew next to you?"

Larsen knitted his brow. "The guys in the expensive suits? Haven't a clue. I figured they were overflow from your side." He glanced back at the line behind him. "We'll talk later." JL slapped Nephi on the shoulder and the brothers disappeared into the crowd.

Siri looked at Nephi, puzzled. "What was that about, Hon?"

"Oh, nothing." He smiled. "Hopefully. Tell you later."

The clock on the bedside table said 2 AM. Joel lay in bed staring at the ceiling, listening to Serena snoring softly beside him. For some reason, he hadn't been able to sleep, despite the pot they'd smoked and the exhausting sex afterwards. His mind raced, keeping him awake with random thoughts and worries.

By now, Nephi and Siri would be on their honeymoon. Joel felt a pang of regret he'd missed the wedding, though not as bad as when he'd missed his daughter, as well as the birth of his first grandchild. It was depressing. Even if he could avoid arrest, he'd never again be really free. There was so much he couldn't do, so much of his life the authorities had stolen from him.

Joel sighed. If he couldn't sleep, he might as well do something productive. Earlier in the day, he'd once again been agonizing over that same issue. Should he try again to contact Esther? He'd only done it once, and then to let her know, in vague generalities, that he was alright. He'd given her no means of contacting him.

Months later, after Nephi and Siri's improvements in Griffin, he'd thought about doing it again, this time with the goal of two-way communication. Larsen had talked him out of it, saying it would be a risk to his daughter's safety. What a hypocrite! He was the most careless of all of them. Esther was a smart young lady. Surely there was a way to accomplish this.

What clinched it was the picture she'd posted on her Facebook page. Mom stood in the nursery, holding the sleeping baby, next to a lamp with a familiar lion insignia from the Harry Potter movies. It reminded him that Harry's house was called 'Gryffindor', which Joel chose to interpret as a hidden message. She was inviting him to contact her using the Griffin system.

But what to say? Once he'd decided to send the message, its content became the sticking point. How to atone for what he'd done, suddenly disappearing from her life? And what, if any, details of his current life were safe to tell her? Maybe he needed another look at her page.

He got up, put on a robe, and took his notebook out to the Florida room. It was warm and muggy, typical for this time of year. He lit a cigar, inhaled, and sighed. He had a good air cleaner in his study, but Serena was finicky and the smoke, being the 'wrong' kind, was likely to wake her. Here he could indulge himself, and access the Internet via his heavily encrypted Wi-Fi.

When the PC finished booting, a message window appeared, beeping insistently. "Urgent", the title bar said. Underneath, the message: "Call me, I'll be up late – JL." *Now there's a surprise.* Chuckling dryly, Joel clicked the button to connect.

A video window opened up, showing Jon Larsen, eyelids heavy, an absent look on his face. "Hey, you're still awake!" Somebody said something off-camera, and Larsen disappeared; for the next two minutes, there was a still image of a generic hotel room wall. He returned, grinning. "Sorry, had to piss. So Joel, you old bastard, how's life treatin' ya?"

"I should ask who this Joel person is? Is this one of those crank video calls?"

"Oops, forgot your cover. Call's encrypted anyhow. If they break that we're in deep shit."

Joel didn't feel like arguing. "So where are you? You look like you've hoisted a few."

"Vegas! Me and my brother were just at Nephi and Siri's wedding. Well, that was a couple hours ago, just got back from the titty bar. Anyway, thought you'd like a report."

"So how *was* the titty bar?"

Larsen snorted. "On the wedding, asshole! Too bad you couldn't be here; it was a real nice wedding, even if there was no booze at the reception."

"Very moving," said a slurred voice from the background.

"Yeah, everything went smooth. Families got along quite well. Siri's dad and Nephi's dad were talking investments and financial modeling, made my eyes glaze over. But it was cool. Too bad about the honeymoon, though."

"What? You didn't play any pranks on their hotel room, did you?"

"Hell, no! Too much else to do in Vegas. No, they had to cancel their trip to Mexico. Neeph said the airline kicked back Siri's passport. The TSA put her on no-fly."

"*Oy*, that's awful! I tried to warn Nephi about that. Integrating her algorithms into Griffin, it was too much too soon. Even if the Norwegians were actually doing the coding, it'd get the government's attention. Young people, they don't listen."

"You know the Feds, it might be a screw-up," Larsen countered. "Know what else? There were two dudes in dark suits at the wedding. Real serious-looking, Dave and I thought they were Nephi's people. But nobody knew 'em. They didn't stay for the reception, but it bothered me."

"What? You think they were Feds? Why would they be so obvious?"

"Maybe they weren't Feds. Real expensive threads, you should've seen the gold watches. Guys looked kind of Mediterranean. Sound like anybody you know, Joel, I mean Sam?"

"Who's that?" Serena's voice almost made him jump out of his seat.

Larsen grinned; he must have got a glimpse on the web cam. "Uh, yeah, better let you go, *Sam*. Keep in touch, Sam!" The window disappeared.

Damn, Joel told himself. *I should have worn my headphones.*

Serena stood with crossed arms and a knitted brow. "Who were you talking to just now?"

Keep cool. Don't act suspicious. "Old friend, guy I used to work with."

"Why'd he call you Joel?"

"Just a nickname. After... uh, Billy Joel, my favorite singer!"

Serena frowned, crossed her arms over her chest. "You like Billy Joel? The other day in the car, and you changed the station the instant 'Piano Man' came on."

"When I said 'favorite', I meant it sarcastically." He did 'air quotes' with both hands.

"Sam, don't give me that bullshit! I can tell when someone's lying to me!"

She couldn't be *that* perceptive; he'd been lying to her for months. Not that he was proud of it. "Actually it's something kind of embarrassing from my past that I don't want to talk about."

Serena's face reddened. "My ass! You're getting yourself in deeper! You know what's funny? Your accent, the way it fades in and out. I told myself, no big deal; all these years away from Boston, I never totally lost my accent either." She paused. "Are you even *from* Israel?"

"Would I lie about a thing like that?"

"Who was the first Israeli group to win the Eurovision song contest?"

Joel threw up his hands. "What? How would I know that?"

"Dana International. If you were really Israeli, you'd follow stuff like that."

"Feh! I hate European pop music!"

"As much as Billy Joel? Sam, or whoever you are, I hate being lied to! My ex did it all the time. How can I trust you? You might be some kind of a narc!" She stormed into the house.

He got up and followed her. "Narc? Are you crazy, woman? If I was a narc would I waste my time on small potatoes like you?"

"Oh, so now I'm small potatoes? Is that some kind of Irish joke?"

"No, I meant that in a *good* way. That you're not some kind of drug kingpin."

"So now you're on me for my smoking? You always partake when I offer it!"

Joel raised a finger in triumph. "Which means I'm not a narc, right?"

Serena didn't answer. She went to the closet and began pulling out Joel's clothes, willy-nilly, throwing them on the bed. "I want you out of my house this instant!"

"Come on, Serena, I can explain!" He stood in front of the closet, blocking her progress.

"Get out of my way," she snarled. "I'm not some helpless chickie you can push around. I have a Taser in my purse, and I'm not afraid to use it!"

Joel stood his ground. *The woman's totally paranoid! Can't hardly blame her, with the Feds and their spies everywhere. Damn, I might regret this, but I have to do something.* "Hear me out for a minute. Check this out." He held out his right hand. "These scars here..."

"What, so that story about the terrorist attack was another lie?"

"I'm sorry. It wasn't a nail bomb; the real story's a lot crazier. Now Serena, I'm trusting you. Just listen, that's all I ask. And please don't repeat to anybody what I'm about to tell you."

Joel took a deep breath and began. "One day I was opening my mailbox, when..." He told her a condensed version of the events of recent months, leaving out names, exact locations and other pertinent details, just in case. She stood there silently, as if entranced, as he spoke.

Finally he finished. She sat down on the bed, and looked at him with a furrowed brow. "Am I supposed to believe that bullshit story?"

"Sometimes you've got to trust your heart. That's what I'm doing now. I've spent the last few months on the run, and I've managed to stay a step ahead of the Feds. If you choose to inform on me, I'm as good as caught. You're not the one taking the risk. Think about it. If I was DEA, why would I pick on *you?*"

She gave him a wounded look. "I still don't know how I can trust you." She moved a bit closer. "A friend of mine got busted, down in Key West. That's the main reason I left."

"What happened to your friend?

"I never found out. Don't know if they deported her, or gave her a trial. They might still be holding her. She's Canadian, so they could declare her an 'enemy alien.' You see why I'm paranoid?"

"You? I'm the one who should be paranoid. For all I know, *you* could be a Fed."

"Now *that's* crazy!" She moved close to him, a half smile on her face. "Does a Fed kiss like this?" She gave him two smacks on the lip. The third kiss turned passionate. Joel put his arms around her for another. Soon she pulled off his robe and pushed him into bed.

Afterwards, Joel felt so wired, he wondered if he'd sleep at all. But the warmth of Serena's body felt too good for him to leave the bed. So he pondered the day's events. Those mysterious guys at the wedding worried him. Though if they'd been mobsters, and tried to pull something, they'd have gotten a nasty surprise. He doubted Nephi was the only one in the family with a concealed-carry permit.

As for Serena, had he made the right decision? Obviously the 'fugitive' thing excited her, the way some women were into bikers. He was afraid he'd put her at risk, but excessive caution was what kept people apart, defenseless against the state. He needed an ally, not just a video stream over the Internet. Forging alliances was necessarily a risky business.

Sometimes you just have to throw security to the winds and trust somebody.

Emal rolled up to the truck stop, just in time for afternoon prayers. He was hungry, tired and depressed. It had been nine long days since he'd seen Esma and the children. *Don't be ungrateful,* he chastised himself. Allah had blessed him. Against all odds, he was still a free man. He had plenty of work, even if he didn't get to spend enough time at home. Getting fired by Chaz had been a blessing in many ways, least of all which was being free of that arrogant *kaffir*.

The life of an independent trucker was hard, especially in these times of economic hardship. As a fugitive from the law, Emal had lost his commercial drivers' license, and could not work legally. Yet, the economic crisis was his salvation. Taxes, restrictive regulations, and soaring interest rates had driven many businesses underground. Each day Emal visited the Undernet, looking for jobs that, for one reason or another, needed to be done under the government's radar.

He chose carefully, avoiding high profit, high risk loads such as weapons and illegal drugs. To play it safe was a salve to his conscience as well. Let the infidels have their poisons, he wanted no part of it. Instead, he hauled gray-market merchandise, not legal but also not particularly criminal: unregistered computers, counterfeit watches, incandescent light bulbs.

Today the cargo was counterfeit blue jeans. He'd picked up a load in Salt Lake City (such commodities tended to move north from Mexico) and was due to deliver them in Kansas City. Since his trailer had some empty space near the back, he went inside and spread out his prayer rug, checking his smart phone app for the direction of Mecca. Someday Islam would be accepted in America, but for the time being, he didn't dare to draw attention to himself.

Usually after prayers he felt uplifted, but today, as he headed east on I-80, Emal felt a strange melancholy. He couldn't shake the feeling of foreboding, though it was pointless to obsess about a future that only God could foretell.

About half an hour past the Nebraska line, he saw the flashing electric sign with the Homeland Security logo: 'TSA checkpoint, all trucks must exit.' Emal groaned; this would certainly wreck his schedule. For a moment he considered ignoring it, but there was a police car idling by the side of the road just beyond. It left him no choice; he signaled and took the exit, ambiguously labeled 'Ranch Road.'

Please, Emal prayed, let this be a routine 'drugs and weapons' checks. He was carrying neither. His documents, though forgeries, were good ones, purchased via the Undernet from corrupt civil servants. If he didn't act nervous, he'd most likely get through without incident.

He pulled up behind another tractor-trailer. The checkpoint had an improvised look, with the trucks stopped in a line along a trampled strip of prairie south of a dirt road. A trailer with the Homeland Security logo was parked on the side of the road, probably a portable office. It was flanked by two dark SUV's. Men in uniforms were walking up and down with dogs. Emal shuddered; he'd never liked the animals, especially the vicious breeds preferred by the police.

A man approached Emal's truck wearing full riot gear. Strangely, the chest armor was military cammo, while the pants were black. The helmet's visor was down; his face was difficult to see through the tint. He stopped a few yards away and shouted, "Step out of your vehicle, Sir. Keep your hands where I can see them. Leave your cell phone on the console." His speech had a distinct Hispanic accent, which Emal supposed was not surprising.

Emal got out of the truck, cautiously, his hands raised on either side of his head. As he stepped out he realized that there were only six vehicles here being screened. Despite the sign's generalized message, they'd selected only Emal and the handful of others for this 'security check.'

This couldn't be a general screening, or they'd have collected fifty trucks in five minutes. If only he'd taken the back roads, like he and Egon had done when they carried serious contraband...

It was too late for second-guessing; if your goats were eaten, the color of the wolf didn't matter. Emal marched ahead of the officer with his hands up, which reminded him of the time as a teenager back in Kosovo when he'd been detained by Serbian militiamen. He had expected to be shot that day; why they had not done so still mystified him.

They hustled him into the trailer he'd noticed earlier. "You wait here." The officer left without further explanation. The waiting room was empty except for three chairs and a coffee table with some car magazines. Emal fretted about his possible fate, and wondered where the other drivers were. At one point, he poked his head out the door; a guard pointed his rifle at him, so he returned to his seat. Without a way to tell time, the wait seemed to take forever.

In Emal's limited experience with these checkpoints, this wasn't the usual procedure. They had the dogs, but he'd seen none of the portable X-ray scanners the Feds used to look for weapons. Perhaps they were looking for tobacco and liquor in vehicles without the BATF's hologram tax sticker.

They'll find none of that in my trailer. Emal hoped they'd lack the expertise to recognize counterfeit jeans. The big worry was, would they run a full check on his identity? There were records in the Federal license database matching his alias, plus recent tax records, but nothing more than five years back. He hadn't been able to pay the scammers for a complete life history.

"Julio Estevez?" The DHS officer stood at the door with narrowed eyes, as if pondering whether Emal was actually Hispanic. Judging by his hair and complexion, this man was Latino himself. He wore black uniform of the Federal police, but without a name badge or rank insignia.

"That's me. Is there a problem, Sir?"

The cop motioned for him to follow. Emal's heart beat faster, though he tried to reassure himself. Maybe they were just making him sweat, before letting him go on his way.

They walked a few yards down the road to an impromptu inspection table. Emal's gut tightened. Right in the middle was a carton of ersatz 'Denim Republic' jeans from his truck.

"Is this from your cargo?" the man asked.

Emal hesitated "Possibly." The box was open; they could have planted drugs in it.

"We've run a check on the serial numbers on the carton. These jeans are stolen property. By US Code chapter 113 we're impounding the cargo, and the vehicle as well."

"What?" Emal was flabbergasted. "These trousers cannot possibly be stolen!" His mind was racing. Was this for real, or an elaborate setup? Telling the truth might make the situation worse. He had to keep his mouth shut, or lose all hope of getting his truck back.

The man scowled "There's a procedure to contest the seizure. You need to file a report with the FTC and request an appeal. I'd advise you to obtain legal counsel. Making false statements on the form is punishable by a term of up to five years in Federal prison."

"So..." Emal said weakly, "Am I under arrest?"

"No, you're free to go. Though we may contact you within the next few months."

"May I retrieve my personal luggage?" Emal was too stunned to ask any other questions.

"Yes. Sergeant Mellis will escort you to the truck, and then give you a ride to the nearest rest stop, where you may use your cell phone to call for a ride."

Emal felt sick as he grabbed his suitcase. The sergeant gave him a funny look as he rolled up his prayer mat, but made no comment. Emal's cell phone was where he left it; probably they'd copied the data. Good thing his encrypted list of contacts was concealed inside a ten minute video of romping kittens. The authorities considered any use of encryption to be suspicious.

The ride to the rest area was a short one. The sergeant's car was unmarked. Inside, it looked like a civilian vehicle, with no barrier in front of the passenger area, and no built-in computer by the driver's seat. It seemed slightly off, like everything else about this place.

Emal was immensely relieved when they arrived at the rest area; he'd half expected to be taken to some secret site to be tortured. Wearily he trudged to the picnic area and sat down at a table. He dreaded calling Esma. Not that she could blame him; his work was inherently risky, and no one could have predicted the surprise checkpoint. Which begged the question: why had they accused him of the wrong crime? Why was he not arrested? By now he realized the whole point of the operation was to seize his truck and his cargo, a simple case of corruption.

Corruption or incompetence, it didn't matter. As a fugitive, he had no good options. Picking up his bag, he walked out past the pet exercise area, away from potential eavesdroppers. He entered the access codes for Griffin and dialed Esma's number.

"Emal? I'm so glad you called. When you didn't call, I was worried you were in trouble."

"I'm alright, Dear, but you were correct about the trouble." He explained the situation, while his wife maintained on ominous silence on the other end of the line.

When she spoke, there was panic in your voice. "Oh heavens, what will we do? How can you earn a living without your truck?"

"Calm down, dear, we'll get through it. Allah will provide." He could hardly stand the sound of her weeping. "I hate to suggest this, but are you still in contact with Sjellmira?"

"Why?" Esma sniffled. "You aren't thinking of going to the Corporation for help?"

"No, and her husband must not know. You can trust her, right? She seems to have a lot of contacts. Perhaps she knows of some kind of legal assistance."

"Yes, though I don't know how that would help. We're fugitives, after all. But I'll try."

He went back to the table and waited, even more depressed. His Esma was his pillar of strength; if the pressure was too much even for her, what on earth would they do?

In less than ten minutes, Esma's text arrived. "Call Islamic Aid Society," followed by a number. *Islamic Aid Society? Hadn't the government shut them down*? "They'll send a ride, no cost." Emal's anger turned to fear. How could they know it wasn't an FBI trap? If not, what would this group want in return?

"IAS," said the voice that answered. It sounded like a woman, which Emal found quite surprising. He gave her his current location and a brief summary of his predicament.

Emal waited. As he calmed down, he was even more mystified about what had happened. Why had he not been arrested? Were these men really TSA agents at all? He'd heard rumors about fraudulent government agents seizing vehicles, but they'd seemed so *official.*

Over an hour went by; he was about to give up hope when a green and gold truck labeled 'Trans American Towing' rolled up to the picnic area. The driver, a black man wearing a dark jumpsuit and a green and gold cap, got out and walked toward him across the grass. "Mister Estevez? I'm Willie from the IAS. Need a lift?"

An American! Probably a follower of Elijah Mohammad, a man Emal had never considered a true Muslim. But he would not question his rescuer's faith. "Yes, thank you, Sir."

Emal got in, stowing his bag behind the passenger's seat. The driver wasted no time getting back on I-80 eastbound.

"If I may ask," Emal said, "How did you become involved with the Society?"

Willie Mohammad smiled. "It's a long story. The pay is lousy– actually it's nothing– but as the Hadith says, 'That which you want for yourself, seek for mankind.' But you first, *Julio*." He raised his eyebrows as he said the name. "What's the scoop?"

Emal related the story in detail. Normally he'd never share his business with a stranger, but the government already knew what had happened, so what was the harm?

When Emal had finished, Willie shook his head. "Man, I had this feeling your situation was not what it seemed, and I was right! The Armero boys are at it again."

"What do you mean?"

"Brother, the men who stopped you were not Feds. Being short on manpower, the DHS started hiring 'contractors' here in the boondocks. No pay, just a share of the proceeds. Then the gangs got involved. These guys split off from one of the Colombian drug cartels. I don't think the government knows or cares what they're up to, long as it helps keep the sheep in line."

"It *did* seem suspicious. But the uniforms, the vehicles! Where'd they get those?"

"Black market. Or they make their own. They figure, folks are so afraid of the government they won't call them on their scam. Especially people of color, or anybody foreign. They've got spies at the truck stops who pick out victims, people who consider themselves lucky they're not arrested. I've got to call my contact! But first, what does your truck look like?"

Willie pulled his cap up off his right ear and tapped a wireless device inserted there. For commercial drivers, cell calls were illegal even with a headset, but the ban was unenforceable.

"Ahmed? This is W. We may have a twenty on the Armeros. Someone's seizing trucks on I-80 in Nebraska just east of the Wyoming line. Can you check the cameras for me? Look for a white Peterbilt with red trailer, no logo. We need to take these bastards out."

Willie listened for a while, nodding. "Good, let me know. Salaam, out." To Emal, he said, "Security on the highway cameras is a freaking joke, especially here in the boondocks. We get the same video feeds the cops do."

A few minutes later, Willie received a brief return call. He man grinned. "Allah's smiling on you, my friend. We found the bastards in Kansas, going south. Probably headed for the border where they can fence their loot. I can't go along but, we'll arrange a ride for you to meet them."

"Why? What do I need to do? Is it safe?"

"As safe as anything else in these troubled times. Brother, we take care of our own. Since the Society went underground, we armed ourselves. Besides, if you want your truck, you have to go there, because that's where it is. Finally, we need you to witness against the perpetrators. Have to follow the Koran, after all. Here's the the drop-off point. I know it looks like nowhere, but I promise you, your ride will be along real soon."

It was the off-ramp to a minor state road. "Go with God, Brother."

Emal thanked the man, grabbed his bag and went to sit on a rotting hay bale near the side of the road. Except for the highways, the landscape was empty prairie to the horizon.

He sat there nervously, brooding over the possibility he'd been abandoned, or more likely, that a patrolman would happen by and arrest him on suspicion. But Willie was true to his word. After another excruciating hour-plus wait, a green Mustang pulled over to the side of the road.

The window rolled down and the driver, a skinny olive-complexioned man with a thick black beard, leaned over toward the passenger side window. "Get in, Brother,"

"Thank you so much. I'm Julio." Emal decided to maintain his cover, just in case.

"Call me Mahmoud. Buckle up, we need to haul butt to catch them."

Loud instrumental music blared from the car's stereo; a saxophone played an impossibly complicated solo. Seeing Emal's expression, Mahmoud turned down the volume. "Farzad Esfahani, king of Persian Be-Bop. If it offends you, I'll turn it off."

"No, it's tolerable at this volume." Having been misled at first by the beard, Emal was surprised at the driver's youth. He appeared to be barely out of his teens. "You're Iranian?"

"American; my parents came here from Tehran. And yes, I'm Shia. The Society is non-sectarian. In America, we can't afford to fight each other. We need to band together and protect the community of believers."

Emal nodded. "I totally agree. We all have a common enemy." He glanced at the instrument panel. The digital speedometer flickered between 99 and 102. "I don't mean to be critical, but you're driving very fast. What if we're arrested?"

Mahmoud laughed. "Don't worry, I have high tech anti-radar paint. Also a direct line to Society HQ; they'll notify me of any speed traps or police aircraft."

"Please don't take offense, but I'm curious how the Society stays in business despite the ban. There has to be money involved. How do they get funding with the government monitoring the banking system?"

"We have wealthy friends abroad. And we avoid the banking system entirely. Couldn't do that before the Griffin software made anonymous bartering possible."

Emal cleared his throat. "I hope this doesn't involve any violence against innocents." He immediately regretted his candor; if they were indeed terrorists, he might be a dead man.

"Of course not! That sort of thing is *haram*. If America is ever to become Islamic, as it's been prophesied, it'll be through reason and persuasion, not violence."

They crossed the line into Kansas, zooming south toward the town of Hays. Shortly thereafter, Mahmoud received a call in his ear piece. "Good," he said. "We're almost there."

According to the GPS on Emal's phone, they were 10 miles north of Hays. His heart leapt when he saw his truck on the side of the road. A second truck, a tri-axle, was parked nearby.

"That's our mobile interrogation unit. The thieving assholes are inside. Come on, Julio."

Mahmoud led him to the back of the truck and raised the rear door. They entered, closing it again behind them. The mostly empty interior was lit by battery powered lights mounted on the walls. Three armed men stood guard; two had swarthy complexions and Semitic features; the third was tall, thin and very dark. Two prisoners sat cross-legged on the floor, blindfolded, wrists tied behind their backs. Emal recognized one as the phony DHS police officer from the checkpoint. The other had a familiar build, but he couldn't be certain.

He turned to Mahmoud. "Can you have the man on the right say something?"

The Iranian gestured to one of the Semitic-looking men. He nodded in response, then said something in Arabic to the tall black man, who kicked the unidentified prisoner in the side.

"Filthy dog!" The black man's accent was thick, probably Somali. "Your victim is here. What do you have to say to him?"

"I don't know what you're talking about! This was a licensed DHS operation!"

"Liar!" The Arabic-speaking man held up what looked like a holographic badge. "This is definitely fake!" He turned to Emal. "Were these the men?"

"Yes, I'm certain now; I know the first one by sight and I recognize the second man's voice. What will you do to them?"

"We have our own dispensation of Islamic justice. If they'll admit their guilt, we'll be merciful. If not, the punishment will be more severe."

"OK, I admit it!" the phony policeman shouted. "We were only following El Jefe's orders. They threatened the lives of our families."

"Me, too," the second prisoner added. "The government would have done the same thing, seizing those trucks. It's not like we killed anyone."

"We commend you for confessing," the Arab said. "Yet your excuses are no help. You chose a sinful path, and you must pay for your crimes. Bring the man here and prepare him."

They pulled the prisoner to his feet, removed his bindings and blindfold. He grunted in protest as they tied the dirty cloth around his face and another around his wrist, very tightly.

The Arab smiled, showing coffee-stained teeth. "You see the guns pointed at your chest. If you make any sudden moves, you'll die. Ahmet, administer the punishment."

"Yes, Commandant." The second Arab picked up a pair of garden shears. The Somali grabbed the prisoner's arm and placed the prisoner's pinky finger in between the blades.

Emal looked away. He heard the muffled scream, then looked back to see blood dribbling from the man's hand and a severed finger on the floor.

"You will survive," the Commandant said. The Colombian clutched his wrist, writhing in agony on the floor. "Remember this lesson, and serve as an example to others." He turned to the Somali. "Now the other prisoner."

"You don't look well," Mahmoud said to Emal. "I'll take you to your truck, so you can be on your way."

"Thank you." Despite being a bit nauseous, Emal was overwhelmed with emotion. These men were risking their lives to protect the community, and asking nothing in return.

When they reached his truck, Emal had to blink back the tears. It was intact, and in the trailer, his cargo appeared to be all in place. *They've given me back my life, my livelihood.*

The Commandant approached them as Emal stashed his bag in the cab. "We're glad you came to us, Brother. Those dogs preyed on the innocent, and the government did nothing."

"On WhistleBlower-dot-com," Mahmoud added, "there was a document that said the Feds were intentionally turning a blind eye. A way to discourage the underground economy."

"What will happen to those men now?" Emal asked.

"We'll bind their wounds and drop them off somewhere, perhaps Kansas City or Denver. We warned them the consequences of informing on us will be lethal. But they can say what they did. We want people to know what happens to those who wrong our people."

The Iranian shook Emal's hand, and the Arab gave him the traditional double kiss, which he returned awkwardly.

"I want to thank you again," Emal said. "I can see the need for this organization. We have the right to defend ourselves, as long as innocents are not harmed."

The Arab laughed. "We've made many changes since the government branded us as terrorists, but that's something we will never do. The Prophet forbids it."

Emal smiled. "Then may God smile upon you and your struggle. Here's my Griffin contact code. If the Society needs anything, please contact me."

Mahmoud nodded. "We will."

Chapter 9 – Bullets and Betrayals

Sam Steinberg was dreaming he was a guy named Joel. He was married to a woman named Joan, an attorney for a major law firm in Phoenix. She had just made partner, and her new position was the impetus for another one of their knock-down, drag-out arguments.

"Why do you insist on embarrassing me? Your blog makes you look like a crazy person, with all the wild conspiracy theories. I can only imagine what our clients think when they find out you're my husband. Some of them have a close relationship with the government!"

"Your clients' sex lives are no concern of mine. They think the politicians will respect them in the morning? More likely the warm feeling is a golden shower."

"You're incorrigible. Rotting your mind, reading this rubbish all day!" She picked up a stack of his books off the desk, meaning to pitch them at the wall. He stepped in the way to save his prized possessions and was hit in the face by Friedrich Hayek's *Road to Serfdom*.

Joel woke up rubbing his jaw. *Oy vey, it hurts! No wonder I'm reliving past miseries.* The toothache was bad enough to feel in his sleep. And he could only *get* to sleep by taking black-market Tylenol 3. That settled it. If it was going to make him dream about his ex-wife, he had to go to the dentist. Trouble was, he didn't have any dental insurance. In his situation, he could hardly apply for government aid, even if he'd been inclined to do so.

He looked at the clock, 2 AM. Serena was snoring softly beside him. It was too soon for more narcotics, so he took ibuprofen, and went to the study to check his email. Half an hour later, the pain had hardly subsided. Maybe a bit of Serena's weed would help. He went in the bathroom and turned on the fan. He loaded Serena's bong and did a couple of quick hits.

The pain was still there, somehow more distant. Despite the pot, he was now wide awake. He decided to check his daily web scans; he'd gotten behind on that. For all he knew, the Albanians could be closing in on him this very moment. He sat down at his desk, opened his laptop and booted it up.

"Hey, Babe, what're you doing?" Serena stood naked in the doorway to his study. It was a distracting image, but it didn't necessarily mean she was coming on to him, because that was how she always slept. "Having trouble sleeping?"

"I *am* asleep; you're in my dream." He laughed. "Actually, this toothache is killing me."

"Could I do something to get your mind off it?" She had a mischievous grin on her face. She knelt beside him and started licking his ear.

"That's a tempting offer." He reached down and playfully patted her bottom. "But even your overwhelming hotness can't compete with this pain."

"Poor baby! We need to get you to a dentist!"

"That's the problem. How am I going to afford it? I'm barely scraping by."

"Well," she plopped down in the office chair next to him. "I have this friend who's an 'underground' dentist. He's really reasonable."

"What's the catch? Doesn't use anesthetic, makes you meditate to dull the pain?"

"No, it's just he's lost his license." Seeing his alarmed look, she laughed. "For an anti-government radical, you're sure a stick in the mud. He lost his license 'cause he couldn't pay his child support, which was unreasonably high. His ex wasn't even letting him see the kids, and she was the one who cheated on him in the first place."

She paused to yawn broadly. "He works out of the back of a warehouse in Miami. Charges half the normal rates. You pay cash, he gets tax-free income."

"That's a heck of a drive to get my teeth fixed. And I can't even afford half that price. If only I could put it on my Visa card."

"Are you forgetting e-Barter? That's the only payment he takes, that or tangible assets, gold or silver coins. Baby, I know you're trying to keep a low profile, but millions of people are already using the system, it's got to be pretty safe."

The idea made his stomach queasy, but she was right. He didn't have a choice. "OK, I'll look into it in the morning."

"I'll email him right now." To his shocked expression, she added, "Don't worry, I have encryption, too." She pulled her phone out of her purse and scrolled through the contacts. "I need to figure out how to upload this to my computer. Silly random addresses, it's easy to screw them up. That's B-seven-three-nine..."

"Thanks, Babe. I think my meds are finally kicking in. I need some sleep." Joel got up and headed for the bedroom. He hoped he *could* get to sleep, with this new thing to worry about.

"Hey, I've got a response already! Must be automated. He's got an opening on Thursday morning. You're lucky you have a flexible schedule. We'll keep you doped up 'til then."

Joel got up early on Thursday. Just as he was ready to walk out of the door, Serena came shuffling out of the bedroom. He appreciated the gesture. For her, it was an obscenely early hour. She grabbed him in a hug and gave him a long kiss on the lips. "Be careful, Love."

"What was that for? Since you moved in you're my keeper?" He grinned. "Not that I'm complaining." He kissed her again.

"I'm serious. I mean, I'm glad you decided to trust me with your secrets, but now I have to worry about more than car wrecks or random crime. You might get arrested and taken to some secret detention facility. Or maybe those Albanian guys..."

He laughed. "They haven't found me yet." He kissed her once more, and was off.

Joel headed east across the peninsula, and then south on I-95, to a decaying industrial park on the edge of Miami. This particular building was not so well maintained, but at least it was free of graffiti. The sign in front said Mondo Nuevo Industries.

He looked around nervously as he walked through the parking lot. According to the "Crime Net" website, this area was an orange zone, which meant moderate risk. If only he dared bring a weapon, but that could be disastrous if a cop stopped him. He didn't have a carry permit, and forgeries of the required biometric smart-card were difficult to come by.

At the door of a huge warehouse, he showed the guard a bar-coded pass on a sheet of printer paper, and went inside. At the heart of the building, between racks of microwaves, computers and TV's, was a cluster of improvised walled offices. The doors were marked with numbers, no names, and he had to consult the printout of the dentist's email to find it.

The door had no name, just a number. Inside was a tiny foyer with one chair. A dark-haired young woman sat behind a pane of glass with a circular hole. Joel introduced himself (as Sam, of course), careful to maintain eye contact, as the girl was quite well busty. He presented his thumb drive, letting her copy his public key. She glanced at his printouts and yelled, "Dad!"

"Come on back, Sam!" came a voice from within. He was momentarily surprised at the familiarity, but of course he hadn't given the doctor his last name. The e-Barter system ran on a first-name basis, like an AA meeting.

It looked like a normal dentist's office. Doctor Bernard was a slight, thin man with hair balding at the crown and graying at the temples. He looked at Joel through wire-rimmed glasses. "So you've got a toothache?"

"That's right. Even on codeine it's throbbing pain."

"Let's have a look," The doctor slipped on a pair of latex gloves. He shone a light into Joel's mouth, and prodded around a bit. "Hmm. Looks like some decay under the crown, but we'll need to take some pictures." He pressed the intercom button. "Melissa, we need an X-ray."

"Be right there," answered the speaker.

"Your daughter is a lovely young lady."

"Yes indeed. She wants to follow in her old man's footsteps." He sighed. "It was an ugly divorce, but we kept in touch, despite her mother's unfortunate attitude. After high school she moved in with me. Now she goes to college and helps me out in her spare time."

Melissa appeared with the lead apron, but none of the sharp-edged in-mouth film squares Joel had hated so much in his younger days. This guy had a state-of-the-art digital imaging system. When they were finished, the doctor said, "I'm going to check on another patient while Melissa prints out the pics." He gestured to a rack on the wall. "We have magazines."

"Thanks." Joel grabbed a recent *Newsweek*. He hadn't read a mainstream publication for months. The cover featured a cartoon of a tattered Uncle Sam with empty inside-out pockets. The headline screamed, "The Federal Revenue Crisis." Joel opened it to page 20, chuckling at the irony. The doctor was, like the people being demonized in the article, a tax-dodging scofflaw.

Half an hour later, Joel's fears were confirmed: he needed a root canal.

"You're from out of town, aren't you?" Bernard smiled. "Don't worry, lucky guess. We can adjust our hours a bit and save you a return trip. How's six AM tomorrow?"

"Uh, sure," said Joel, a bit unnerved by the fluidity of Bernard's schedule. *Is his daughter the only other employee?* he wondered.

A few minutes later, he was in his car, dialing Serena's number. Joel's smart phone digitized his voice, encrypted it with her personal key and embedded it in an innocuous data stream. (Any eavesdropper would see a You Tube video of frolicking cats.) "I'm going to have to spend another day up here, Sweetie." He told her about the root canal.

"Oh damn, Baby, I had a special night planned to celebrate your homecoming. Oh well, you've got to get it done. Good thing I got some new Dura-charge batteries." They said their good-byes and Joel reached in the glove box for a stogie.

A sudden noise made him jump; the metallic crunch of one vehicle hitting another. It sounded close; had somebody been drag-racing in the parking lot? Then, a much louder noise– the crack of a gunshot and shouting. It wasn't English. Not Spanish, either; Joel understood a fair bit of that. Yet the words and cadence seemed oddly familiar.

He crouched low in his seat, knowing the thin metal of the doors wouldn't offer much protection against an errant bullet. The cigar was still clamped between his teeth. Half of it had broken off in his dive for cover.

There were more shots and shouts, this time in English. "Over there!" "Die, bitch! This is for Hector!" Somebody yelled in Spanish, though Joel couldn't comprehend the invectives that followed. *Just my luck! I'll die from a stray bullet in a gang battle.* Serena did say "be careful," but he hadn't expected anything like this.

Joel crouched on the floor under the steering wheel, flinching each time he heard another shot. With some difficulty he pulled his cell phone out of his pocket. *I should call Serena, so she knows where to find my body.*

Then he remembered Bernard and Melissa. They probably didn't have a clue what was happening out here. As if on cue, there was the sound of approaching helicopters.

He did have the doctor's phone number (actually an underground answering service, rerouted through the Caymans), so he sent a quick message to the obscure address Serena had given him: **Warning, gang battle outside ofc. Cops coming.**

The chopper sound was getting louder. Joel panicked. Everybody in the vicinity would be dragged in and interrogated. Carefully he raised his head and peeked out the window. Couldn't see anybody, so he quickly got up and started the car.

There was only one exit from the lot. He slouched down in his seat as he rounded the corner, expecting to be hit at any second. One of the gangs had already fled. A group of swarthy men with guns, dressed in blue jeans and work shirts, were piling into a panel van. At the back, two guys were lifting what looked like a body into the cargo area.

Joel looked just a second too long. As he turned onto the street, he caught the eye of the last man getting in. There was a ski mask on the guy's head, but it was pulled up. For a moment Joel's heart nearly stopped. Was that Egon Ahmedaj? No, it couldn't be. The odds against it were astronomical. But it certainly wouldn't have surprised him if his old clients from Green Star Trucking had graduated from snakes in mailboxes to parking-lot shootouts.

As he got on the freeway, fear rose in the of Joel's stomach. He knew now why their speech had seemed familiar; when he met with the family in his office, they'd often conferred in their own language. Was there any chance someone had recognized him as Joel Walter? He had a beard now, he was coloring his hair– gray to blond, ha ha– but he was no master of disguise. He was already paranoid enough every time he saw a police car.

Joel looked at his hands on the steering wheel; they were literally shaking. Should he stick around and keep the appointment, or should he head back to Tampa? He pulled into a Denny's parking lot, lit a new cigar, and made an encrypted call to Serena. She was frantic when he told her about the shootout.

"Was it the Albanians? I'm worried sick, Hon. From what you said about those guys, they don't give up on a grudge. You've got to come home; if they find you, they'll kill you!"

"No, I'm sure it wasn't those same guys." Damn, the woman was psychic, he hadn't mentioned the Albanians in ages. "Even if it was my old friends, they're a bunch of *schlemiels*. The Gang Who Couldn't Shoot Straight."

"I should never have sent you to Miami. It's a war zone, with the drug trade and all."

"Don't blame yourself, how could you know? Maybe the gangs are getting desperate, with people getting their drugs on the Undernet." He took another drag and blew the smoke out the window. "I feel better already, hearing your voice. Wish I could come home, but with the price of gas, I don't want to make this drive twice. I'll text the doc, and if the morning appointment still stands, I'll get a hotel."

"Just be careful," she said.

"Don't worry. I have an app on my phone with crime stats for each area. I promise I'll be home by tomorrow noon. Love you, Babe." *Did I really say that?*

"Love you, too," she said without hesitation.

After they hung up, he sent a text to Bernard, then realized the food smell from the restaurant was making him really hungry. *It's a crazy world, but a man's got to eat.*

★ ◎★ ★

"I'm not the doctor, so I'm not supposed to say anything, but to me, everything looks fine. Your baby is developing right on schedule."

"That's wonderful!" Siri wished she could get up. The gel on her stomach was still cold.

"Cindy, is that what I think it is?" Nephi was staring at the monitor, which was impossible to see from Siri's vantage point.

"It sure is, Nephi," the young blond woman said with a grin. "You're going to have a son!" The ultrasound technician just happened to be Nephi's cousin. His family was huge; it seems they ran into Snows everywhere.

Siri could hardly contain her excitement. Not that she wouldn't have been just as happy with a girl, but it was amazing to know at such an early stage. "May I see?"

"I'll print it out." Cindy pressed a button and a piece of paper issued from the slot.

Siri's heart raced as she took the picture. They'd known about the pregnancy for several weeks now, but somehow, seeing the baby inside her made it real.

On the way home, Nephi was surprisingly quiet. Siri put her hand on his shoulder. "What's wrong, Sweetie? A little while ago, you were totally excited about the baby."

"I'm still excited. Just a little worried. "It's such a messed-up world to bring a child into."

Siri laughed. "That's a very un-Mormon thing to say. You should be keeping that positive attitude. Besides, you've always wanted a family, right?"

"Of course, but..." Nephi's expression turned dark.

"What is it, Hon?"

"See that black car in the mirror? The guy's following us."

"Are you sure?" She glanced back; it was too dark to get a good look at the driver. "Could it be an unmarked police car?"

"Wouldn't be surprised; he's sure been matching our speed. Maybe he's trying to figure out why he can't read my chip."

Siri shook her head. "I told you it was a mistake to do that." Nephi had used an EM pulse generator to zap the remotely readable radio frequency ID chip (a recent Federal mandate) on his license plate.

"Better to get a ticket than to get carjacked." Recently there'd been a spate of robbers using plate-chip-scanners to target their victims. "The IC's are unreliable anyway; about 10 percent of them just stop working on their own."

"Nephi, is there anything you're not telling me? I know how you don't want to worry me, but if there's a problem, I have a right to know, too!"

"Well, maybe..." He signaled, made a left turn at the stop sign. The mysterious car did not follow. He sighed. "It might be nothing, but... you know, Bob from church? He had a brother in Phoenix a lot like Uncle John, former law enforcement guy who went over to the militias and the Second Amendment groups. Last week he just disappeared. It's kinda got me paranoid."

"Well, it could have been a random kidnapping. But..." *Not likely, the guy could certainly defend himself.* Siri bit her lip and blinked back the tears. She didn't want to be one of those hysterical pregnant women. "What are we going to do, Nephi? It's getting as bad as Sri Lanka before the partition. Pretty soon they'll start shooting people in the streets!" Her voice rose in volume. "I lost my sister; I don't want to lose anybody else! Nephi, we have to do something!"

He put his hand on hers. "Ssh, ssh, chill, Hon, everything will be all right."

The instant they pulled in the garage, Nephi popped the hood and checked the truck's engine. This was another of Nephi's obsessions. He was always worried about tampering. Siri trudged in to get ready for bed. As excited as she'd been earlier, she now felt totally exhausted.

By the time she had her PJ's on he was still not in the house. She went back downstairs and poked her head out the laundry room door into the garage. "I'm going to bed, Sweetie."

Now he had the van's hood open. "Uh huh," he answered distractedly. "Get some rest."

She was dreaming about Daksha again when she heard an urgent voice. "Siri! Get up!"

She knew something was wrong. He almost always called her 'Hon' or 'Sweetie.' He called her by her name either when they were arguing (their fights were mild, compared to her parents' shouting matches) or he was upset.

He was still dressed, another bad sign. "We got a call from JL. He says the Feds are doing a major roundup, starting tonight, anybody who's anybody in the underground economy."

"What?" She rubbed her eyes. As bad as her dreams had been, she just wanted to go back to sleep. "How can he be sure? He's been talking gloom and doom for ages now."

"He's got very specific information. A guy he knows in the hacker community, very reliable. JL believes him, 'cause he's been data-mining the news, and all the signs are there. The red-light terrorism alerts, the moratorium on gun permits, the backlog on passports."

"OK, I just have to get a couple things." Her heart pounded as she packed her bag. She realized Nephi had changed from his work clothes to jeans and a t-shirt.

"I've got all the important stuff in the van. You've got ten minutes, Hon!"

In just seven minutes, she was in the garage with her suitcase. Nephi was at the back of the van, trying to squeeze in one more toolbox. Before he could object, Siri slid in behind the wheel. "I'll drive. It'll help me not be nauseous. You probably need to make some calls anyway."

"I hate to wake them up, but... hope Mom answers, not Dad." Nephi's father was, like most of the family, upset about the current political situation, but he hadn't yet lost faith in the American system. His mother had grown up out East; even after all those years in the family she was a relatively liberal Democrat. Nephi expected her to be a bit more sympathetic.

As Siri drove up the on-ramp to the freeway, she heard Nephi talking in hushed tones with his mother. Thank God he'd put encryption on their smart phones.

"Mom's upset," Nephi said, "but she understands. She'll contact Uncle John for us. Now, let's go over our cover story."

"It's simple," Siri said. "We're going to San Francisco to make a proposal to the city. Totally believable." All the city's computers had been taken down by hackers just weeks before. If anybody needed to beef up their security... which reminded her. "Nephi, could you please check the home security?" In truth, she dreaded what they might discover.

Their home had some pretty sophisticated electronic surveillance. Like their vehicles, it was set up to broadcast video, albeit low-bandwidth, to Nephi's modified Android.

"OK, got it. My gosh, we're lucky we got out when we did! They're in already."

"Who? What? They've broken into our HOUSE? How dare they!"

"Calm down, Siri, do you want me to take the wheel? We don't wanna crash on the way out!" He looked back at the tiny screen. "Four guys – no, five in SWAT gear, automatic weapons. Going through our dressers, the closet. And downstairs..."

Siri's clenched her teeth. "Don't say another word. I can't deal with it now. I can understand how my people felt, when the British took over the country."

Nephi grabbed her hand and squeezed it. "Thank the Lord for friends and family. If I ever lost you to those goons, I could never forgive myself."

She squeezed his hand back. "Same goes for me, Love, double."

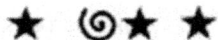

Jon Larsen opened his eyes and blinked painfully. "Somebody turn off the God-damn light!" Then he realized it was morning; he'd forgotten to close the blinds. His head was throbbing. To top it off, nature was calling. *Might as well get up.*

He rolled out of bed and landed loudly on the wood floor. "Hey!" somebody mumbled. The sight made his headache go away– Andrea, the cute red-headed bartender from the Sportsman's Lounge, naked, sheets around her ankles.

For months he'd been chasing Andrea, and she'd always shot him down. Now that he was planning to leave town, she was suddenly in his life, in his bed. Things had gotten complicated.

When he called to warn Nephi and Siri, he'd known he was at risk, too. Any day now, somebody would come and bash the door in. This farm had given him financial independence, but it was also his ball and chain. How he'd hated to sell the family homestead, but realistically, it was either that, or have the government seize it when they arrested him.

Larsen put on a robe and shuffled off to the kitchen. Might as well earn some brownie points with his overnight guest.

Lately he'd done a lot of soul-searching. His parents were happily retired; they wouldn't want the land back. His brother never wanted to farm in the first place. So Larsen put it up for sale, all but the southwest quarter, where the house buildings stood. That he deeded to Dave, who agreed to let him live there rent-free until he made his move. The proceeds from the sale would be very helpful, if he could find a discreet way to withdraw it as cash. Taking it all at once would be a serious red flag for the authorities.

That was why he'd been at the Sportsman's, celebrating the sale of those 960 acres. Drinks all around– how many times? He'd lost count. His memory of the rest of the night was fuzzy; but considering the evening's end, it had been well worth it.

By the time Andrea got out of bed, modestly wearing one of his shirts, as if there were anybody else in or near his house, Larsen had eggs frying, bread toasting, and coffee brewing. She looked at him through bloodshot blue eyes and smiled. "Mornin', JL."

He grinned, gave her a quick peck on the lips. "Sorry I woke you up so early. Being a morning person is a hard habit to break. And I'm not used to having overnight guests." The last comment was unfortunately true. Dave was right, there was a *lot* more to life than politics.

"No problem. Your bed was a little hard for me." She grinned. "Not that's an entirely bad thing." She was rummaging through her purse. "Uh, food smells great, but I need a smoke."

"Sit over here." He moved a chair to the other side of the table. "I'll throw open the window, you can blow the smoke outside." This was something he'd never let his other friends do, but hell, there was a first time for everything.

Breakfast was not the uncomfortable affair he'd expected. It was like nothing had changed. They still made jokes and laughed at each other. Except now he could kiss her without getting punched. As they ate, Larsen considered the situation. Didn't women like guys who were unpredictable and spontaneous? Hadn't she said she really liked Canada? Problem was, they didn't know each other all that well. If only this had happened just a few months earlier.

"I suppose it's time for me to take you home. I'd love to hang around with you, but ..."

"Take me home?" she laughed. "Very funny! We have to get your truck, which you left at the bar. Darn good thing, too, you were pretty wasted."

"Oh shit! I have to see this guy in Minnesota. Sorry, we have to leave *now* or I'll be late!"

Another girl might have been irritated, but Andrea took it in stride. "OK, let's go. Can I put on some clothes first?"

It took ten minutes to get to the Sportsman's, where Larsen's truck sat alone in the lot. "Man, it looks like I spent the night!" He jumped out of the car, then leaned back in to kiss her.

"Call me," she said.

"You got it!"

Larsen whistled happily as he crossed the river on his way to Red Lake. It had been years since he'd been to the Rez. Not that he didn't like Indians; but it was a depressing place. It was, though, a good spot to meet with George Red Bird to make the transaction. Larsen had promised himself, after this last deal, he would disappear *and* lay low. Joel was already on his case to be more careful. But he just couldn't pass up this opportunity.

Bird had grown up in Red Lake, so to meet him there wouldn't seem suspicious. It saved Larsen the trouble of meeting him at his place in Minneapolis. Also, the tribal police were crooked enough that if he got into trouble, all he had to do was grease the right palm. Suddenly he heard David Lee Roth sing, "Panama! Pana-ma-ma!." Larsen flipped open his cell phone.

"Hey, JL," said a familiar voice, "It's Bird."

"Yeah, Bird, what's up?"

"Sorry, something came up. We have to postpone 'til four. That OK?"

"Yeah, sure." Bird was lucky he'd caught him in a good mood. Also that Larsen badly wanted what he was selling– a proverbial informational gold mine, like one of those giant data dumps from the dearly departed Wikileaks. "I just now crossed the river."

"Good, you haven't gone too far. See you at four."

Larsen was about to turn around when he saw the sign for the Fighting Sioux Cafe. It was one of many places that adopted the University's old team name when the NCAA forced them to drop the 'insensitive' nickname. Jon and his brother had become instant loyal customers. Better stop now, who knew when he'd be back?

207

He strolled in, intending to just order coffee, but the caramel rolls looked too good to pass up. As he smeared butter over the gooey treat, he hoped everything was OK with Bird. Contrary to the stereotype, the guy was pretty punctual.

Bird had sounded strangely subdued on the phone. He wasn't the most talkative guy, but he always spoke clearly enough. Only on the two occasions when Larsen had drinks with him had Bird become soft-spoken– and he'd sounded lucid enough on the phone.

Larsen finished up and realized he still had another hour to kill. *Hardly worth heading home now.* He was contemplating calling someone when the phone rang with the opening drum solo from 'Hot For Teacher.' Instead of a name, the display said 'SECURE CALL'. That meant the call had been secured through Griffin.

He was pretty sure who'd be on the other line. "Sam?"

"Speaking," It was Joel's voice, a bit distorted by the encryption. "What's up, JL? Haven't heard from you for ages. Thought maybe you got killed driving that rolling deathtrap of yours."

"Good to hear from you," Larsen said sardonically. "Maybe I won't pick it up next time."

Joel laughed. "You know I can't resist laying the Jewish guilt trip on you. Actually, I *was* worried. I was hoping you were on your way north by now."

"No, I'm still at large and in charge. Just a sec, let me pay my bill and get out to my truck, where we can have some privacy."

"I'm glad you called," Larsen continued as he got into the cab. "I've got good news." *Besides my social life.* "Remember our talk about taking Griffin to the next level? Anonymity is great, but for a lot of things you need ID, and black market ID's aren't all that safe."

"Agreed, but shouldn't you be making yourself scarce? Didn't you hear about our friends? They just escaped the Blue Meanies by the proverbial skin of their teeth."

"Really? Thank God for that. It's OK, Sam, I'm a big boy. Anyway, I know a guy who's worked for EDR Enterprises, you know, the place that did the software for the Real ID program? He's sneaking me the source for the whole verification system. We'll merge it into Griffin and host the upgrades on the JL-10K. We'll be one more step ahead of Big Brother."

Joel cleared his throat. "What'd you do, take pictures of him diddling little boys?"

"Ha! Between you and me, the guy had some problems in his consulting business, and he's got to leave the USA, but no way to get a passport, because of issues with the Infernal Robbery Syndicate. So I'm helping facilitate his illegal *emigration* to Mexico."

"That's a switch," Joel said. "I'd say it's a bargain, if he's crazy enough to go south right now. Doesn't he realize he could get a phony passport for only a few tens of kilobucks?"

Larsen laughed. "True, but he's short on cash, so he needs to barter. He's got a really nice car, but he doesn't want to part with it. Normally I'd be against stealing intellectual property, but these EDR guys got paid with my tax dollars to put an end to my privacy. So I say, screw 'em!"

"Sounds our discussions have had an impact on you."

"Don't give yourself too much credit, old man. I was a card-carrying Libertarian when you were doing door-hangers for the Dems. Not that I could hate the gov'mint much more than I already do. By the way, you hear any more about those attacks on the IRS computers in Ogden? It's weird nobody's claimed responsibility."

"That's all they're talking about on the Undernet," Joel said. "But you have to dig through the mountains of bullshit to find the diamonds." He laughed.

"Hopefully they'll do it again." He paused, as if choosing his words carefully. "You have any other plans for the ID software?"

"I meet a lot of people who want to enhance their privacy," Larsen answered, "which is not easy, considering the biometric crap they put in driver's licenses and passports these days."

"A worthwhile goal, but risky. The Feds came after you-know-who and they can easily get you. I can't understand why they don't have you already. Be careful, JL. I don't want you to end up in one of those detention camps everyone's talking about. In case the rumors are true."

"Somebody has to do it!" Larsen was trying, unsuccessfully, to keep his anger in check. If there was anything he resented, it was being treated like a child. His parents had been like that, overprotective. They didn't let him have a motorcycle, or go to rock concerts in the Cities.

Joel sighed. "Of course. I hope *somebody* does it. But it doesn't need to be *you*, and I don't say that just 'cause you're my friend. JL, you're a leader in the Movement. There's a reason they don't send generals to the front lines. It's because they're most effective where they're at. You're the genius who puts together technological solutions that will save freedom for all of us."

"I appreciate the vote of confidence. But nobody's indispensable."

"True. Be careful anyway, OK?"

Larsen smiled. "OK, *Dad*, I'll be careful. You too. I've heard about that young lady of yours. Don't let her give you a heart attack or anything."

Joel laughed. "She's actually only three years younger than I am. But she *is* young at heart." He winked as he said that, the gesture barely visible on the phone's stuttering video.

They said their goodbyes and Larsen headed for Red Lake again. His earlier good mood had become a mild melancholy. It was hard having to worry about your friends being arrested. He envied his parents, who had been antiwar protesters back in their youth. There were plenty of problems then, but at least you could criticize the government without fear.

Larsen found the designated meeting place without trouble. Bird's email directions were thorough. Usually he just sent GPS coordinates and expected him to MapQuest the address. Even so, Larsen remembered they'd met here before, long ago. Maybe Bird had forgotten that.

It was a dairy once owned by the tribe, now abandoned. The paint on the building was peeling, and the windows were busted. Bird's shiny red Mazda sat by the loading dock. There he stood, sipping an energy drink and glancing around nervously. Larsen pulled up next to him, got out of the truck, and made a quick visual survey of the place. Bird's nervousness was contagious.

"JL, how's it hangin'?" Bird took a last swig of Red Bull and crushed the can under foot.

"Pretty good." Larsen grinned. "Hey, what a surprise meeting you here!"

"Yeah. Hey, good job winning that thing the other day. The trophy, you know?"

"You mean the shooting tournament? Yeah, I did OK. I prefer handguns, but I could never get the accuracy. High-powered rifles, that's the way to go."

"Right." Bird turned to rummage in his car. "Here you go." He handed him a DVD-ROM in a clear plastic sleeve. The man's breath had a faint medicine smell. Had the Red Bull had a little something extra? If so, Larsen couldn't blame him; what he was doing really took balls.

Larsen handed him a key. "Your docs are in a locker in the Grand Forks bus station. Don't use 'em 'til the first of the month. It takes time to get all the data entered in the system."

"OK, thanks." Bird gave him a sullen look.

"Sure." Larsen knew his friend would be unhappy about the delay, which he'd actually arranged on purpose. It gave him a few days to check the code, make sure it was all there, before Bird could make his getaway. He didn't think

George would try to pull a fast one on him, but in this business you could never be too careful.

"Take care, Bird." Larsen extended a hand. Bird just stood there, staring at his feet.

Suddenly there was a blinding light. "Freeze! Federal agents! Hands on your head!"

Larsen stared uncomprehendingly at the helmeted, armored men surrounding him, then at Red Bird. His erstwhile friend also had his hands on his head, but didn't look the slightest bit surprised. Bird lowered his eyes and exhaled loudly.

"And I actually thought you were getting the short end of the deal," Larsen said quietly, as the men in Homeland Security vests closed in.

"Yeah, ironic, isn't it?" Bird lowered his hands as the agents pulled Larsen's arms behind his back and cuffed him.

Chapter 10 – It Ain't Bound For Glory

Antonio Cordoba Pool Supply was just off the freeway, along the eastbound side toward Orlando. As Joel drove in, he sized up the place. The lot was almost empty, but the building looked clean and well-maintained.

The door chime sounded as Joel walked through it. He smiled at the pretty young Latina standing behind the counter. "Hello Miss, I'm Sam Steinberg, here to see Mr. Cordoba."

She returned the smile half-heartedly. "I'm sorry, he's not in yet."

Joel glanced at his watch. Eleven AM on the dot. "That's strange; we had an appointment. When are you expecting him?"

The girl frowned. "Actually, he should be here already, but I haven't heard from him. I tried calling his cell and his land-line. I'll try again." She dialed the phone and waited. "Sorry."

"Maybe he got held up in traffic. Mind if I hang out here a while?" He pulled a business card from his shirt pocket. "I'm his new accountant."

"Sure, Mr. Steinberg, he told me to expect you. Help yourself to some coffee if you like." She pointed to a table in the corner with an air-pump coffeepot, paper cups, and sugar packets.

"Thanks." He grabbed a cup and poured some coffee. It was weak, and the creamer was the powdered non-diary kind. *Feh!* He drank it anyway.

"Hope your boss is OK. He wouldn't stand me up, would he?" Joel grinned to show he was joking. He didn't want to sound like a whiner.

"Oh no, he's very punctual."

Joel sighed. Bad enough to waste his time, when he was already worried about finding enough work. Was it the recession, or growing black market? Not much demand for tax accountants with everybody doing business under the table.

Speaking of underground... He turned back to the young woman, who was staring at a tablet computer. "I'll be right back," he said. He went out and to the side of the building where he punched in the code to set his cell to Griffin mode. As he waited for the connection, he lit a cigar. He hated to smell too smoky for a first meeting, but the guy was *late*.

Joel's private directory appeared. The contacts were represented by icons instead of names. He clicked a John Deere tractor to call Jon Larsen. Nobody answered, so he sent a text. "Did u get those source files? Call me."

That wasn't the real reason Joel called; the tech stuff was over his head. He hadn't heard from JL in days, and he was worried. Would Nephi know anything? Hard to say, since he and Siri were hiding in the mountains. They had satellite Internet, but their outbound connection was packet radio, a dinosaur technology. Joel wrote a quick email, asking how Siri was doing (he worried about her, pregnant and away from modern medicine) and whether they'd heard from JL. It might be days before they could respond.

Joel sighed. *I drive to the far side of Tampa and the schmuck stands me up.* He paced back and forth as he puffed on the cigar. When he'd finished, he went back inside.

"No news yet, Mr. Steinberg," the girl said.

"It's OK. Just have him call me, please."

Joel got back on I-4 and off again at one of the downtown exits. Since Serena was out today, teaching an art class at the community college, he decided to stop for a nosh at Zandar's Deli. If Cordoba *did* show, he wouldn't have to drive all the way back from St. Pete.

The place, he recalled, was by the Verizon design facility. No, it closed years ago; the company had shipped all their engineering to China. If he wasn't mistaken, the government had converted the building to a law enforcement 'Fusion Center.'

The traffic was unusually heavy. Pulling up to a stoplight, Joel discovered why. They'd closed down the entire street by the Fusion Center (the road signs indicated he'd been correct about that), forcing him to head south toward the bay. What was up? Car accident? Terrorist incident? Angry about the unexpected detour, Joel decided against his lunch stop.

At that moment his cell phone buzzed. The words 'URGENT ALERT' appeared on the screen. *Better pull over for this one.*

It was an Undernet site that sent updates via Griffin about government activities. The headlines screamed, "IRS Crackdown on Barter Economy. Thousands Arrested." Joel felt sick. Was this the cause of the roadblock? Had Cordoba been arrested? Were JL, Nephi and Siri still free?

Are Serena and I at risk? He wanted badly to call her, but she wouldn't answer during class. The panicky feeling said 'Do something,' but what? He didn't have JL's chutzpah, Siri's genius, or Nephi's religious faith. He wasn't a leader like MacGuiness. Joel's political blog, mostly *kvetching* about local government corruption and police abuses, had ended when he assumed the Steinberg identity. Thomas Paine would have called him a 'sunshine patriot.'

Joel was about to squeeze back into the re-routed traffic when another text arrived, marked as being from 'NS.' It was too soon to be an answer to his previous message. "What's up? Undernet full of rumors of mass arrests? Maybe JL? Please answer."

"I'm OK, more later," Joel replied quickly. That settled it, he had to take action. Maybe a blog, maybe an Undernet news digest, but *something.* As long as he could remain anonymous.

It couldn't be just opinion, it needed to be useful to its readers. He'd always had a knack for gathering and interpreting information, so maybe some kind of news analysis. In any case, it would be risky for a fugitive like himself, much more so than the brief messages he now exchanged with Esther. "Love you, Dad," her last response had ended. "Take care of yourself." Becoming political again would endanger that tentative contact.

Though the Griffin software could mask his location and hide his identity, the Feds had other tools. Nephi said they now had software that analyzed anonymous web posts for clues to their authors. Any little detail could give away your location, age, gender and profession. Yet removing all details would make his writing bland, something nobody would want to read.

Even without this threat, it would be challenging. Americans were a jaded and apathetic lot. On his previous blog, Joel had joked that there were more government agents in his audience than actual readers. To get people's attention, he'd need to be entertaining, bring laughter as well as information. He needed a persona, a shtick, something he'd ponder on the way home.

When he reached home, his mind was still devoid of ideas. For a time in his youth he'd done stand-up comedy, a typical routine about his dysfunctional personal life. That kind of detail would certainly put the Feds on his tail. A fictional character, then? It seemed counter-intuitive to tell truth through a fantasy, but that's what Ayn Rand did with John Galt. More to think about.

It still stung him, remembering the time Esther said he was "turning into a crazy person." What had happened to him? Life had happened– but knowing that didn't help the cause.

Oh Lord, what would you have me do?

The prayer came into his mind unbidden. Though Joel wasn't an observant Jew, it seemed wrong to pray bare-headed. Guilty, too; he had not been to Temple since he'd left Arizona. Yet he wasn't sure the God of Abraham, Isaac and Jacob existed. How could such a God allow the good people to suffer and die while the evil prospered? Still, a little prayer, what could it hurt?

He went to the closet for his box of childhood mementos. Since coming clean with Serena, he no longer had to hide it. He opened it and found the *kippah* his mother had lovingly decorated for his Bar Mitzvah. He put it on, bowed his head, and began, "*Baruch atah Adonai...*"

As he prayed, he was transported back to his childhood. He saw himself on stage, taking bows at the conclusion of the Central High production of *Merchant of Venice.* The scene shifted; he was with his family at China Doll, the restaurant where they'd gone to celebrate.

His father, ever the drama critic, said, "My only complaint was that you played the role with a bit too much schmaltz,"

"Don't listen to him!" his mother countered. "You were just like Dustin Hoffman!"

Joel's uncle was uncharacteristically quiet. "Did you like the play, Uncle Isaac?"

"I think," the old man replied slowly, "You're a fine young actor. But you should not have played that role!"

So that *was* it! "I'm sorry if I offended you, Uncle. But Shylock is a complex character. Which is why I played the part *satirically*, to mock the stereotype."

"We have such a brilliant son," his mother said. "Did you hear all the laughs he got?"

"And at the curtain call, the loudest applause of all," his father added.

Joel's eyes snapped open. That was it! His humor didn't need to be specific. It would start with his ethnicity, why try to hide it? Most of his fellow Jews were liberally inclined and, like him, disturbed about what was happening to this country. *My people have suffered through enough tyranny to know it when they see it.*

The Jews hadn't survived for millenia among enemies without being able to laugh. He thought of the great Jewish comics; the list was practically endless. Yet his favorite act from his early childhood (and his father's time as well) was the Three Stooges. Larry, Moe, and... well, if you knew your Stooge history, there were three other Stooges besides Curly Joe. *I could be the seventh Stooge!* Inappropriate and low-brow, perhaps, but it was a start. *Nyuk! Nyuk!*

Joel smiled. *If there was a God, considering that He'd created the human race, He had to have a sense of humor.*

The air in the train car was stifling. Tiny lights along the edges of the aisles provided the only illumination. Larsen sat between two really fat guys. He'd never been thin himself, but he looked pretty good next to these two hippos. Their snores made him envious; how could they possibly sleep? They smelled like a duffel of sweaty gym socks with a dead cat or two inside.

Larsen had no idea where the train was going. Nobody he asked knew either, though one wiseacre said 'Guantanamo.' If they were indeed going to Cuba, at least they couldn't go the whole way on this damned train.

A particular song was stuck in his head: "Riding on a train, and it ain't bound for Glory." If there were a train to Hell, this one would have been a good candidate.

He wished he could open a window. The car's occupants, himself included, had gotten progressively smellier. Or was it night? The windows were blacked out, as if they were being shipped to a top-secret location. Or maybe the lack of scenery was part of the punishment.

With some effort, he looked over his shoulder. All seats were full, plus people sitting in the aisles. The passengers were a cross-section of America: male, female, young, old, black, white, brown. No young children, thank God.

That would have been torture for everyone, though several appeared to be teenagers.

Suddenly there was shouting. "No! My wife needs those crackers for her blood sugar!"

"Shut up, Wetback, you got food, so share it!"

The little old man wasn't about to do that, even if the two bullies were much younger and stronger. He shoved the closer one, causing the other to fall back into the aisle.

Another man yelled, "Ow, my foot!" Ignoring the complaint, the young man got back up and slugged the old guy in the jaw. A woman behind them screamed. The passengers tried, like one organism, to back away from the altercation.

"You punks!" Larsen shouted. "Cut it out!" He squeezed past his obese neighbor, stumbled on the man's enormous feet, and almost landed on some poor kid.

"Excuse me, sorry." Larsen shoved his way back through the people-choked aisle, where the two hooligans were dividing the stolen snack.

With a deadly calm voice, Larsen stared down the taller of the two hoodlums. "This is what's going to happen: First you give back the crackers. Then, you apologize to these people!"

The kid spat; the gob landed on Larsen's shoe. "Who died and made you king of the train, Chunk-o?"

In an amazingly quick move, Larsen grabbed the kid's collar, yanked him downward, and slammed his head on the back of the seat in front of them.

"Shit!" the kid yelled. "That hurt!"

"Don't be an asshole and it won't happen again." Larsen took the remaining broken-up crackers from the smaller of the two guys; the kid's face went pale.

"You two out!" Larsen gestured with his thumb toward the packed aisle. "I'm sitting here now!" With some effort, the two young men stood up and squeezed out through the crowd.

"Here you go." Larsen handed the crackers to their owner. "Sorry, they're broken up." He smiled. "You'd think with these first-class accommodations, they'd at least give us some peanuts."

"Thank you so much! We tried to reason with them!" the woman said.

"I could've taken those punks," said her husband, "but I've got a heart condition, and the DHS agents took my nitroglycerin."

"Assholes! By the way, my name's Jon Larsen. Where you folks from?"

"I'm Hernando, this is Maria. We're from Topeka. Do you know where we're going?"

Larsen shook his head. "It's getting hotter so I assume it's south. Hmm... 'scuse me a minute, I need to use the facilities." There was no rest room on this car, just a couple of chemical toilets behind a flimsy curtain at the back. After so many hours cooped up in here, he could no longer avoid the inevitable.

Hernando shook his head and grimaced. "Good luck, man. I was back there two hours ago and they were both already full."

"Good Lord, no wonder it stinks so bad. How can you stand it, sitting here in the back?"

Maria smiled weakly. "We were hoping it'd keep the bad folks away."

Larsen shrugged. "Not that they can go very far. Besides, punks like them have to be used to stench, or they couldn't stand themselves." Reluctantly he forced his way through the aisle to the back. Some innovative soul had found a plastic bucket (at least it had a lid) to supplement the toilets. It was an experience he hoped he wouldn't need to repeat.

Larsen returned to his new seat by Maria and Hernando. "So if you don't mind me asking, what are two nice people like you doing on a train full of Uncle Sam's rejects?"

"I'm not sure," Hernando said. "But I've been doing a lot of work for barter lately. Otherwise it's hard to make ends meet, with gas and food and taxes so high. I clean somebody's carpet, and they fix my truck, or fix Maria's hair, or spray our house for bugs."

"Sounds like a good deal. If only the IRS didn't think they deserved a cut, eh?"

"Yes. I started bartering last year, but only for two or three small jobs. This year I did mostly barter. I thought about filing the IRS barter forms; Maria was worried." He glanced at his wife. "But we were going to lose the house. Since all those millionaires got bailed out by the government, we thought we deserved a break. Besides, everybody else was doing it. I figured the Feds would be too busy to go after small fry like us. When we got arrested, it was a total shock."

"So what was the charge, failure to report income?"

"They wouldn't say *what* it was, but probably that," said Maria. "And if you wonder, we *are* citizens. Our family's been here since Guadalupe-Hidalgo."

Larsen gave her a quizzical look.

Hernando laughed. "You know, the treaty where the US took half of Mexico. Our ancestors came along with the territory. So," he eyed Larsen suspiciously, "why are *you* here?"

"Pretty much the same reason, I think. I'd wager I was into the underground economy a bit deeper than you were."

At this point, Larsen decided he'd better play it safe; he steered the conversation to neutral topics like family and the weather. Eventually they ran out of things to say. He crossed his arms, closed his eyes, and miraculously, he was able to sleep fitfully in his narrow seat.

He dreamed over and over about his arrest. Each time something surreal would happen. One time he escaped and ran through the fields. But it was winter and the snow got deeper until he couldn't walk. Another time his parents were the arresting officers. In the third dream, he smarted off to the Feds. The agents raised their weapons and pumped him full of bullets.

Larsen awoke, sweating profusely. He was embarrassed to discover he'd been resting his head on Hernando's shoulder. Minutes later, the train came screeching to a halt.

It wasn't easy to walk after riding cramped for so long. He was hungry and thirsty; he reminded himself that everyone was in the same predicament. Everybody was silent as they walked out, as if they were actors in some old black and white Holocaust movie.

The sunlight blinded Larsen as he stepped onto the platform. Judging by the vegetation, they were in the desert Southwest. Some good-sized mountains lined the horizon. In front of him, rows of identical buildings, surrounded by a ten-foot fence topped with razor wire. Prominently displayed above the platform was a huge logo; a slanted red "H" merged with an aerodynamic "D", the logo of HalDyne, a major government contractor. *Great, now they're privatizing the concentration camps.*

"Well, Toto," he muttered to himself, "We're not in Kansas anymore."

As they gathered on the platform, several grim-looking soldiers, armed with automatic weapons, eyed their every move. A pair of huge signs commanded "ALL PASSENGERS THIS WAY" in English and Spanish, and pointed down the stairs from the platform.

A few yards further on, another group of soldiers greeted them. They were mostly swarthy Middle Eastern types, probably the Kurdish, Tajik and Uzbek fighters the US took in after the wars in their homelands went bad. Their uniforms were a shade of khaki Larsen had never seen on US troops. *Must be from HalDyne's private army.* A beefy man with sergeant's stripes stepped forward, and shouted, "Everyone must line up at the office to be processed!" His accent was very thick, and some of the detainees looked puzzled. "Line up, NOW!" The soldiers beside him started to raise their weapons. The stragglers hurried to join the line.

In his youth, Larsen had experienced run-ins with the police, but this was nothing like those times. The guards were not just arrogant, they stared at the detainees like they were cockroaches. Larsen recognized one of the hoodlums who'd been bothering Maria and Hernando. The kid had the temerity to ask the sergeant to repeat an order, and got smacked in the face with a rifle-butt. When he fell to the ground, they kicked him until he got up. The mercenaries laughed and pointed at his bloodied face as he staggered away like a drunk.

Despite his intense dislike for this punk, Larsen felt his blood heat up. These foreigners– whomever they were– were abusing his fellow Americans on their own soil. Heroics on his part, though, would have been pointless.

The detainees were allowed to use the rest room, then sent to the mess hall. The food was undercooked macaroni coated with an orange substance that vaguely resembled cheese. As noxious as it tasted, Larsen devoured his portion, and chugged his paper cup of warm water.

His stomach was beginning to rebel when another group of soldiers, with pale-skinned, stubbly faces, and Slavic accents, ordered them out of the mess hall. Though the sun was high in the sky, Larsen felt totally spent, as if it were 3 AM after a night of carousing. He wasn't the only one moving slowly. The soldiers separated the prisoners by gender, and assigned them to barracks on either side of the camp. Tears were shed as couples and families were separated.

As Larsen walked with the men, he considered his options. He doubted he'd be allowed a phone call to a lawyer. At least he'd taken the trouble to disassemble the JL-9000 and archive the data. He hoped Dave would realize he was gone, and come get the dogs. It pained him to think of his canine friends starving to death.

Escape didn't look like an option. Larsen doubted the HalDyne guards would hesitate to fill an escapee full of holes.

Having no realistic alternatives, he fantasized about women (specifically Andrea), beer, and coffee. Especially coffee. He'd had a headache all day. He was startled to hear a voice behind him calling his name.

"Jon Larsen!" The speaker had yet another different foreign accent.

He whirled around to see a pair of olive-skinned men with thick mustaches in those same khaki uniforms. "Who wants to know?" He was supremely irritated and too tired to care.

The closest of the soldiers slapped him on the side of the head, hard. He let out a yelp of surprise, and he saw flashes of light in front of his eyes.

"OK, don't get your skivs in a wad." Larsen got up off the ground, staggering from the blow. The two soldiers flanked him as they passed through a gate and a fenced corridor to another building. This building was not a modular metal unit like the mess hall and barracks. It was constructed from cinder block, painted drab gray-brown. As they entered the armored door, a blast of cool air hit him. Unlike the train and the barracks, it had *air conditioning*.

They brought him into a small windowless room, where two men sat waiting. One looked like the archetypal retired Marine– tall and muscular with a gray crew cut, wearing an olive-drab t-shirt and pants. The other was a short, somewhat pudgy fellow with dark hair and Italian features. He wore a white dress shirt and tie, like some corporate marketing director. "Jon Larsen," the dark-haired fellow said. "We have a few questions we'd like to ask you."

Larsen stood as straight as he could, despite his back, which ached from the long, cramped train ride. "I know my rights. I don't have to answer any questions." He kept his face expressionless, struggling not to show the terror he felt.

"Rights!" growled the Marine. "You don't have any God-damned rights in here, you traitorous tax-dodging scum!"

"I wasn't aware that the Bill of Rights had been repealed," Larsen set his jaw and looked Sergeant Crew Cut straight in the eye, despite the pounding of his heart.

Mr. Marketing folded his hands, looked up slowly and sighed. "Regrettably, due to the current crisis, our President has temporarily suspended the right of habeas corpus," he said calmly. "These extraordinary detentions have been ordered by President Wilton herself and approved by Congress. I assure you this is completely legal. My advice is that you cooperate with the questioning, and things will be much easier for you."

"Do you expect me to incriminate myself?"

The Sergeant jumped over the table, grabbed Larsen by the collar and slammed him against the wall. "We expect answers. You have a problem with that, Asshole?"

"Mr. Harris," said the other man reproachfully. "There's no need to resort to that kind of violence. I'm sure Mr. Larsen will listen to reason." With obvious reluctance, Harris released him and returned to his seat.

"First, let's verify some background data," said Mr. Marketing. "Your address is 13500 Agassiz Road, Grand Forks, North Dakota. Is that correct?"

"You *know* it is," Larsen replied. Harris glared at him.

"A simple yes or no will suffice." Mr. Marketing smiled. He continued with innocuous questions: parents, school, occupation, and so forth. Then he dropped the bomb shell.

"Are you familiar with a woman named Sirimavo Jayasuriya?"

Larsen hesitated. "No."

"Liar!" shouted Harris.

"If you know the answer, why bother asking?" Larsen glared at Harris and his colleague.

Mr. Marketing clucked his tongue like a disappointed parent. Larsen lifted his chest and gave them his best look of defiance. Out of the corner of his eye he saw Harris pull something out of a desk drawer. It looked similar to a TV remote control, but with a hefty power cord hanging out the back. Harris plugged it in, pointed it at Larsen, and pressed a button.

Instantly Larsen doubled over in agony. His stomach felt like it was on fire. "What the hell is that thing?" he growled through clenched teeth.

Mr. Marketing got up from behind the desk and calmly walked to where Larsen crouched in a fetal position. "The device emits directed high-frequency microwaves. It's designed to cause discomfort without causing permanent damage."

"At least, that's what the manufacturer claims," Harris gave an unpleasant grin.

"We regret having to cause you pain, but we require your cooperation. Harris, let's give Mr. Larsen a break for a minute." Harris removed his finger from the button and put the remote down. All at once, the pain stopped. Larsen felt a flood of relief, almost a rush.

"So," continued the nameless Good Cop. "Are you ready to cooperate? I hope so, because then Mr. Harris won't be able to use his device."

"I'm gonna enjoy myself either way," Harris growled.

"We have another name," his colleague continued, "William Nephi Snow. Our records show you began exchanging emails with him approximately three years ago. After that, you used illegal message-laundering tactics to conceal your communication. Is this correct?"

Larsen took a breath and stared at his interrogators. "I do have a name for you. He's a real low-life, a threat to the country. His name's George Red Bird."

Good Cop motioned to Harris, who raised the remote again and pushed the button. The searing pain returned, all over Larsen's body. "Don't insult our intelligence, Mr. Larsen. Red Bird works for us now. There's nothing you can tell us about him that we don't already know."

Larsen dry-heaved a couple times before he managed to look up. "I'm sorry. Unless it's about Red Bird, I'm not talking."

"You shouldn't be so hard on your friend," said Harris. "We used enhanced interrogation techniques for at least eight hours before he cracked, and you will, too. You'd be wise to save yourself the trouble." He released the button and lowered the device. Larsen un-clenched his teeth, took a deep breath, then collapsed to the floor.

"OK," said the Good Cop. "They say you rural folks are made of stern stuff, and it appears they were right. I think we need to handle this a little differently." He picked up a phone. "Lugetti here. Red Team report to Interrogation C."

Through the back door came two burly black men in white orderlies' garb, followed by a chubby white nurse with a needle. The men grabbed Larsen by his arms and held him while the nurse lowered his pants and jabbed the hypodermic into his right butt cheek. After the previous ordeal, Larsen's brain didn't even register it as pain.

"This is an experimental drug called Arachniol, derived from black widow venom," Lugetti explained. "The neurotoxin will take it only a few minutes to reach your brain. You'll feel about eight hours of intense pain, which we'll be able to stop at any time when you're ready to tell us about Mr. Snow and his little Indian girlfriend."

Larsen opened his mouth to correct him, but thought better of it, and closed it again.

"Would you help Mr. Larsen out, please?" Lugetti asked the orderlies. "And Jon, I'd advise you to be someplace safe when the venom takes effect. There are some nasty people in this camp, not just tax evaders like you, but violent criminals. They won't hesitate to harm someone who can't fight back. We wouldn't want anything to happen to you."

The men dragged Larsen out the door of the interrogation room, down the hall, out the front door, and into the main yard of the camp. Without a word, they released him and locked the gate behind themselves, leaving Larsen to collapse into the dirt.

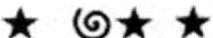

Emal was famished. He'd been driving for many hours, longer than he should have been or wanted to. Underground truckers could evade some of the taxes and fees, but there were still disadvantages compared to legitimate businesses. Though he collected half his fee up front, clients did not always pay the remainder, sometimes sticking him with a cargo that wasn't easy to sell. There was the constant risk of arrest. At any time they might be stopped by the authorities, which necessitated some very good (and expensive) fake ID and an 'alternate' set of logs.

If criss-crossing the nation wasn't enough, Emal now had another job. His new role was to help his people as a volunteer for the Islamic Aid Society. Until now, the tasks had been infrequent: give rides to stranded brethren, or transport guns and ammunition for their self-defense. One duty was constant: to watch for any government or criminal activities of that might be a threat. Today, for the first time, he had a mission to gather specific intelligence.

Luckily, he didn't need to leave his planned route. According to his contact, an Albanian café in Omaha was rumored to have connections to the Mob. Sources said 'the Corporation' was planning something major, possibly a treaty between criminal organizations. True, it was the government's responsibility to protect its citizens, but that didn't seem to be a high priority, particularly for Muslims. Emal's assignment was simple: stop there and eat, watch and listen. It was unlikely to pay off, but with operatives throughout the country, surely the Society would discover *something.*

Just off I-80, Emal found a truck stop, where he filled his tank with diesel, then parked the truck in the lot. Because it was difficult to be unobtrusive in a semi, he carried a 350 Yamaha in the trailer. He brought out the bike, donned a jacket and helmet, and was on his way.

As he rode, he worried, was he headed into peril? Praise the Prophet, he hadn't crossed the Corporation directly, but if word got back to his brother Egon, it wouldn't just endanger Emal, but his wife and children as well.

Since the brothers' falling out, their wives had secretly kept in contact. It was easy, with the 'underground' security technology that was available. Egon and his wife lived in Miami, where they were in the 'import/export' business. Hah! In Florida, there were scores of former Kosovo Liberation Army partisans, running a brisk trade in illegal drugs. The mainstream news had stories of gun battles between the Albanians and rival Colombian gangs. Egon would come to a bad end and, considering his many crimes, that would be Allah's just punishment.

Logically, Emal told himself, the chances he'd be recognized today were quite slim. Courtesy of the IAS, Emal abandoned his earlier Italian-American cover identity and 'became' Hispanic. At first he worried about *La Migra,* but the government tended to ignore illegals, as long as they weren't involved in black market barter. Though Emal was in pretty deep, he had the benefit of experience, and an occupation that made him a moving target. Even his family was mobile, living in a recreational vehicle and moving frequently. That allowed Emal to see Esma and the kids more often.

Though they kept a close eye on the mobsters of 'the Corporation,' the IAS was not mainly a vigilante group. Its primary purpose was to defend the Islamic community in America. The ethnic mafias preyed heavily on minorities, especially Muslims, who garnered little public sympathy.

The café, located near the university, was called Tirana. Emal parked his bike two blocks away and walked. The storefront was unremarkable, the inside shabby but clean. Emal walked to the counter and picked up the one-page laminated menu. Past the open counter was a view into the kitchen. Emal glanced up when he heard a man and woman standing by the ovens, arguing quietly but heatedly in the native tongue. *Just like home.*

It was before noon, so there was no line at the counter. Emal stepped up to the register and ordered lamb souvlaki, intentionally mispronouncing the name. The clean-shaven young man behind the counter was polite, but in his face there was no recognition of a countryman. Good, Emal thought, *the accent is working,* or maybe it was the thin mustache and goatee, the working class clothes, and the fake 'bleeding heart of Jesus' tattoo on his arm.

Emal took a quick look around the restaurant. Most of the clientèle appeared to be young white Midwesterners. He filled his cup at the soda station then took a seat in an open booth near the counter. His order took only a few minutes. The lamb and rice dish smelled delicious. *Eat slowly*, he reminded himself. He needed time to check out the employees, see if he recognized any faces from the IAS report on suspected government collaborators.

As Emal waited, a fiftyish guy with a thick mustache emerged from the kitchen and motioned to the young man at the counter. In turn, he beckoned to the woman from the earlier argument, who came up to take his place. The two men moved to the back of the kitchen, past the loud fans where there conversation would not be audible.

Except to someone with the right equipment. Emal reached up to his ear and adjusted the slider on what appeared to be a hearing aid. It was actually a high tech listening device provided by the Society. Not only did it amplify and filter speech directionally; it also sent a wireless signal to a recorder concealed on his person.

The device worked. The men's voices were as clear as if they'd been in the next booth. The younger said, in Albanian, "Have you heard from the Boss?"

"Not yet," replied the mustachioed man. "Arvid is convinced the answer will be yes."

Emal risked a glance in their direction, saw the young man shake his head. "I thought the Boss would be smarter than that. How does he know we can believe the government? The way they supported our home country and then betrayed it..."

The older man laughed. "We have the word of the President herself. Not that we trust the bitch. As long as we get to keep our guns, we don't have to." He pulled a package from his pocket, removed a cigarette, and placed it behind his ear. "The opportunity is too good for the Corporation to pass up. We only need to do this one operation, then we get blanket amnesty, and guaranteed employment in the Federal Police."

At that, Emal dropped his fork, which clattered off the table and onto the floor. With the eavesdropping device turned all the way up, the sound was momentarily deafening. Some of the other diners stared at him, but the two Albanians were still absorbed in their conversation.

The young man shook his head, lowered his voice. "That last part I definitely don't believe. The American people won't accept it; there will be widespread protests and rioting. When that happens, the government will use us as convenient scapegoats."

"You are wrong, the President needs us. Unemployment, rising prices, and mass arrests, those things have angered the people. Wilton has no choice, because the troops are overseas. She doesn't trust the police, especially in rural areas. Many of them are right wingers with ties to the 'gun culture.'" He said that phrase in English. "It's our job to save America from anarchy."

"They could just as well use the Russians or the Colombians, or the Asian Syndicate."

"Those idiots? We're the only group clever enough to pull this off. We will make a co-ordinated attack on September 11th ceremonies in several cities.

After all the false warnings, we'll have the element of surprise. There will be conspiracy stories, but most people won't believe their government would betray them. They will welcome martial law."

"Do you have particulars? What sort of attacks? Who will co-ordinate the operation?"

The old man looked over at the plates of food waiting behind the counter. "We can discuss this tonight after closing. You have customers to serve."

Emal's appetite was now gone. He forced himself to finish the lamb and most of the rice. He left a tip on the table and got up to leave.

Emal got on his motorcycle and headed back for the truck stop. He wanted to call Esma and tell her, but he didn't dare, not yet. She worried enough already, and there was a chance she'd accidentally say something to Sjellmira. Emal would report only to Mohammad, his contact at the Society. Would they even believe him? Just a few months until the Albanian Mob staged a phony terrorist attack? That would be a disaster, not just for Muslims, but for the entire country.

Ideally, the IAS should release this information. Certainly Americans had a right know, but there were great risks. If it came out too soon, it might bring the IAS to the attention of Homeland Security. At present, they seemed unaware that the Society was still active, or at least not of its rapid growth. For now, let them concentrate on known enemies like the Butler Brigade and the new right wing militias that were popping up everywhere.

Even if they could conceal the story's origin, there were other problems. The best 'alternative' news sites were closed, and their owners in custody. The Undernet had hundreds of uncensored news sites, but gossip, rumors and half-truths ran rampant. If only there were a good place to publish, a source people trusted. Certainly, Emal mused, they would not trust Muslims.

Chapter 11 – Missing Persons

"Where could that guy have gone?" Joel muttered. It had been weeks since he'd last heard from JL. He'd tried calling and sent at least ten messages. No answer. Larsen had sold the farm, and was talking about skipping the country, but Joel doubted he'd gotten that far. Supposedly Jon's brother Dave was also set up on Griffin, but the emails Joel sent him all bounced.

It didn't add up. Larsen was a resourceful guy. He'd have found a way to communicate. If he'd had an accident, it should have appeared somewhere in the media. Joel had set up a search-bot to comb the Net 24/7 for any mention of the name. That hadn't been helpful, considering all the thousands of Larsen's in the USA.

A pair of hands on his shoulders startled him. "What's wrong, Stud Muffin?"

He swiveled the chair around, and Serena planted a kiss on his lips. Her long red hair, with its intermingled threads of gray, tickled his chest. She raised her eyebrows, puzzled by the lack of his usual enthusiastic response. "You must be really upset."

"Still haven't heard from JL. I just know something bad's happened to him. I warned him not to mess around with that Federal ID software!"

Serena pulled up a chair and sat down. She was an excellent listener (at least by comparison to his self-absorbed ex-wife.) Joel didn't regret revealing his true identity to her. It was a lot less stressful, having someone he could confide in. Though for the first few days, he'd worried she might leave him, or worse, turn him in to the Feds.

His fears had been unfounded. He felt ashamed he'd had so little faith in her loyalty. Her discretion was another matter; she'd started calling him Joel. "Keep calling me Sam," he said, "so you don't slip and call me Joel out in public." She stopped using either name, instead calling him 'Hon' or some other term of endearment.

Serena reached out her hands to rub Joel's neck. "I sensed a negative force this morning while I was mediating. I just knew something had happened to someone close to you. I should have said something then, but I didn't want to upset you, in case my hunch was wrong."

"I appreciate the thought, but there's nothing I could've done about it," he said. "JL was– is– too stubborn to listen to my advice anyway."

"You've got to stop being so obsessive. No use making yourself sick. The brain needs rest to work properly. Let's go to the beach, relax. Get our minds off of it for a while."

"Oy, Serena, I'm not in the mood." In the end, she prevailed. They got in her blue Vee Dub and headed for the beach.

It was hard to relax, but the sand, the gentle waves, and Serena's natural goofiness got him to smile. They swam for a while, then lay on the sand. Still, he couldn't stop his mind from worrying, not just about JL, but the political situation. His new blog had made him feel better, but what good could it possibly accomplish?

When they returned home, Joel went directly to the office and got on the Undernet. Serena, who'd had other plans, let out a snort of disgust and went out to work in her herb garden.

The first thing he did was open the Kachina high security email program. Not much in his personal in-box. There was one message from Nephi (*Siri doing fine, still no word from JL*), one from a guy he'd been debating in his Financial Planning chat group (should we expect deflation or hyperinflation?), and five spams. *How the hell did they spam a secure address? If we could harness that genius in the cause of good, we'd already have a cure for cancer.*

The blog was a different matter. His original concept sucked, Joel decided, but Serena loved it, so he kept the "Stooge" theme. He rejected her suggestion that he count the three actors from the recent remake, keeping the title of Seventh Stooge rather than Tenth. Its content was political satire in the tradition of Jonathon Swift and Stephen Colbert. To his immense surprise, it caught on.

This morning, there were 872 responses, added to the tens of thousands he'd previously received. How awesome to be overwhelmed by success! Luckily, Kachina included an AI-based statistical filter, created by a Chilean friend of Siri's. It weeded out the 90% of the emails that matched two predominant patterns: fawning compliment or fuming hate bomb. Sadly, it couldn't sift out the third biggest type: rants about readers' favorite conspiracy theories. Joel was forced to scan the rest manually, because in these he'd sometimes find useful information.

Even so, reading through the 80-odd remaining emails was tiresome. Roswell, Kennedy, 9/11 – delete, delete, delete. The official story was usually a lie, he agreed with that, but he'd heard all these stories before. He resisted the temptation to delete them all. *If I finish scanning them, I'll feel like I've accomplished something.*

He was about to quit and play a game or two of solitaire when a subject header caught his eye: ALBANIAN MOB PLANNING NEW 9/11. Probably crap, but intriguing nonetheless.

"Dear Mr. Stooge: You probably won't believe me, but I am writing about a matter of utmost importance. I chose your blog because you have a large following, and this information needs to be spread as widely as possible. This is important to me, because as an immigrant, I know how miserable life can become when people are not free.

"There is a grave danger to America. I have discovered that Homeland Security is hiring

a gang of criminals to stage a phony terrorist attack on this coming September 11th. I don't have many details, but I believe it involves 9/11 memorial ceremonies. The President will then declare martial law. Afterward, the members of this same gang will then be hired by the DHS to oppress us.

"I encountered this plot as a member of a religious group banned by the government as terrorists, despite being completely innocent. We have gone underground, where we collect intelligence to protect our people. Please respond so we may discuss this issue further."

Joel's first response was disbelief. Yet another paranoid rant about a government conspiracy. Not that he doubted that Wilton and her minions would stoop that low, but could they pull it off? And the banned religious group, what else could it be but Islamic? It didn't incline him to trust the man's world. Still, it was too important to ignore, just in case it *was* true.

He felt hands on his shoulders again. "Serena?" he said, swiveling around on the chair.

"So are you going to be fighting the revolution all evening?"

Joel smiled. For a fifty-year-old chick, she looked pretty darn good naked. "No, I think I'm ready to take a break."

Larsen awoke with a groan. His shoulders, back, arms and legs all ached, but especially his jaw. That had bothered him since the guy hit him on his first day here. The effects of the pain ray were short-lived, but the spider toxin injection caused several hours of agony. Why? It didn't make sense to kill him before the next interrogation. When the painful delirium ended, he realized he'd been brutally grinding his teeth. Two were cracked so badly they were loose.

What a nightmare! Larsen promised himself if he survived this ordeal, he'd never again complain about trivial problems.

The government goons had at least tried not to cause him any permanent injury. His fellow prisoners hadn't been so careful. He remembered Joel's paranoia about anti-Semitic skinheads; here he'd met some of them. The ringleader's name was Dietrich, same as Larsen's dog. Once again, he hoped Mom, Dad or Dave had thought to check on his 'boys.'

Damn that Dietrich! Sharing the name was an insult to his beloved rottweiler. Larsen supposed it was his blue eyes and fair skin that made those bozos think he'd accept their racist bullshit. In retrospect, it was a mistake to say, "Hitler was a gay, vegetarian socialist!"

At the moment, Larsen lay in the gravel behind Barracks G. With great effort he stood, using the building for support. He rubbed his jaw again. A third molar was loose, on the other side of his mouth. If he stayed here much longer, he'd need dentures. Slowly he headed back to Barracks E.

In an effort to get his mind off the pain, he returned to the unanswered question: where the hell was this place? Somebody had said New Mexico, but that was a big state. There were some large cacti in the distance, but not saguaros like in Arizona. There were also gnarled, stunted trees. He didn't know enough geography to pin it down closer.

He limped along, still rubbing his jaw, wondering how to get the authorities to let him make a phone call. As if he needed more pain, somebody jabbed him the ribs.

"Oye! Ten cuidado, puto!"

Larsen never learned that in high school Spanish, but he understood. *"Perdoneme, señor."*

The guy was short, muscular, and brown-skinned, with the stubbly beard on his chin. He looked surprised to see a sunburned gringo speaking Spanish.

In English, he said, "No problem. But watch your step. Lotsa guys got blades. Look at 'em funny, they'll cut you."

Larsen laughed, then groaned again. "As you can see, I've already had problems with some of our fellow inmates."

"Man, they worked you over good. If it'd been Los Locos, you'd be dead." He looked toward the far side of the camp. "This sun is brutal. Come on, we got shade by Barracks C."

"Sounds like a plan." Larsen appreciated the offer, but was wary of the guy's motivations. "I hoped the weather would be cooling off by now."

"Stays hot a little longer every year." The guy turned and started towards 'C'. Larsen walked beside him, hoping he wasn't heading into an ambush.

"So, what they get you for?"

"A tax thing," Larsen was deliberately vague. He hadn't endured the 'pain ray' and spider venom to get careless now.

"I hear you, there's lotsa folks here for that. So am I, sort of. I was making *mucho dinero*, running cockfights in Colorado. That Undernet is great, you can promote an event, do everything anonymous, and the Man is none the wiser."

Larsen nodded in response. He'd never witnessed a cockfight, and expected he'd find it revolting, but he realized that many would view his hunting and fishing activities in a similar way. "How'd they catch you?"

"One of the breeders got busted bartering for a new truck. Undernet stuff is hard to track, but the Feds lucked out. They leaned on him, got him to spill a few names. Mine's Raimondo, by the way." He offered a hand for Jon to shake.

"Jon Larsen. People call me JL."

"You're not from around here."

"Nope. North Dakota." There was no harm telling him what the Feds already knew.

Behind Barracks C stood a group of seven Hispanic men in their twenties or early thirties. Raimondo introduced him, and JL tried to memorize their names, despite the palpable feeling of hostility. Luis, the tall skinny fellow, remarked, "Were you the dude who helped the Garcia's?"

"Excuse me?"

"The Latino couple, in the train when them two punks were hasslin' them, stealin' their food? Man, you're OK by me."

Larsen shrugged. "It was the right thing to do." Luis slapped him on the back and suddenly he was *in*. What luck that he'd bumped into Raimondo, and that he'd been crazy enough to stick his neck out for a stranger. *Sometimes karma works like they say it does.*

He tried to follow the conversation, as best he could in his rusty Spanish. They discussed the various power groups in the camp, particularly White Cross. Larsen asked, "You know a tall, skinny guy with the scar on his left cheek?"

"That Nazi asshole? He one of your amigos?" the fat guy said.

Larsen laughed. "He beat the shit out of me. I got in a couple of good swings, but his buddies held me down."

"And they let you live!" said Raimondo. "Dude, they must have a *special* evening planned for you. Those guys are the biggest fags in the camp." Everyone laughed, even Larsen.

"Speaking of tail," said Luis, "the female kind, of course— I heard the guards have a deal going. You get 'em some money, you get your pick from the ladies' side of the camp."

"What do the women have to say about that?" Larsen winced at the implications of Luis' statement, but he didn't want to get on the wrong side of these *chollos*.

"Nothing, if they're smart!" said the big guy. Once again, everybody laughed. Larsen forced a chuckle. *Don't be stupid*, he told himself.

Concentrate on keeping yourself alive, and handle the moral dilemmas when they arise.

The guys continued talking; Larsen followed the conversation as best he could. Raimondo mentioned one of their comrades who'd been sent to "the Hellbox."

Since the camp had been designed not as a prison, but as temporary disaster housing, it had no cells, except for the so-called Disciplinary Center, located next to Barracks H. It had earned its devilish nickname not because it was necessarily hot inside, but because it was designed to apply maximum psychological punishment. "They know how to make you totally crazy," Raimondo explained. The infractions that landed a person there were mysterious. Some guys went to the Box for mouthing off to the guards, while others beat or molested their fellow inmates yet remained in the general population. Larsen had so far escaped the experience.

I've gotta get out of here, or I'll get myself killed. If the guards were as corrupt as the Locos claimed, there might be a chance. The gang would know which ones could be bribed. If certain guards would just look the other way, perhaps they could escape. Larsen had always believed that with enough brains and determination, a man could accomplish anything. So far the camp had not beat that optimism out of him.

The Locos were tough; with Larsen's ingenuity they might all get out, and flee across the border. Compared to life in the camp, even the drug wars in Mexico seemed attractive. With some hair dye and a fake tan sprayed on his fair Nordic skin, he could pass as a native. The Undernet was spreading to Mexico; Larsen was confident he could make a living there.

Joel paced back and forth on the apartment balcony, puffing furiously on a cigar. In these finicky times, he was probably breaking some kind of rule.

There were lots of stogie-smoking Cubans in the complex, so maybe they didn't enforce those 'smoke free rental housing' laws.

His mind quickly returned to other matters. *I must be insane, Why'd I let Soozie talk me into this?* It was bad enough for a wanted fugitive like himself to have a political blog at all, even an anonymous one on the Undernet. He had frequent nightmares about a gang of uniformed goons bashing in the door of Serena's house at three AM.

Soozie was a close friend of Serena's, a poet, musician, and self-published author. The weird spelling of her name was a tribute to her Bohemian personality. Short and busty, she had numerous tattoos and bleached blond spiky hair. She called herself a lesbian, but after a couple of rum-fueled *menages a trois*, Joel knew that wasn't exactly true. He'd allowed Serena to tell her about his blog; but not his real name, only the Sam Steinberg identity.

Soozie's politics were somewhere to the left of Noam Chomsky. She disagreed strongly with about half of Joel's on-line rantings, but she loved the central premise: humor as a subversive activity. "If you're going to get the audience you deserve," she'd told him one day out on the balcony, "you need to do a pod-cast."

"But it's risky enough as it is, without putting my voice out there."

Soozie took a long drag on her cigarette. "I've got some good voice distortion software. Used it for the Zaynab project, to protect my actors." *Zaynab* (a rock opera she had written, produced and directed) was about the Jewish woman who, according to Islamic tradition, had poisoned the Prophet Mohammad. Not that Soozie had any particular animus against Muslims, but she loved the idea of a woman striking back against a patriarchal system.

So it was ironic that Joel's first interview was with a Muslim. But not nearly as strange as his being someone from Joel's own past. Despite the corny alias– Yusef Islam, *the guy must love Cat Stevens*– and an obviously phony accent, Joel was not fooled. He could never forget that voice. It was Emal

Ahmedaj, one of the clients who had threatened him back in Arizona. If the Albanian suspected the 'Seventh Stooge' was his old nemesis, he hadn't let on.

Luckily, they didn't have to meet physically, Having witnessed a shootout involving Albanian gangsters here in Florida, Joel was paranoid already. He was highly skeptical about the reason Emal gave for contacting him, as well as the man's alleged religious conversion.

"Sam!" came Soozie's voice over the speaker. "Ten minutes to air time!"

"I hear you!" he snapped. He felt bad for grousing at her, but he was very nervous. This pod-cast would be streamed on the Undernet, 'almost' live, with a time delay for the sake of security. Still, the urgency of this news, assuming it was real, left little time for editing.

Soozie's studio was in the spare bedroom of her apartment. It was tiny and the feeling was positively claustrophobic. As Joel was going over his notes one last time, he was interrupted by Belinda Torres, their audio engineer. "*Hola, Señor Sam!* Just doing a quick sound check!"

"Check away." He adjusted the microphone on his lapel. "Number nine, number nine..." He tried not to stare at Belinda's bosom as she bent over the mixer board. She was Soozie's 'domestic partner' and the reason the threesomes with Sam and Serena had ended. Joel's mind ran to fantasies of a foursome. *Cut it out, old-timer,* he scolded himself, *you've broken enough Commandments already. Besides, this girl's younger than Esther.* Like her lover, Belinda knew nothing about Joel's true identity. As Serena put it, "Safer for all concerned."

"You're good!" Belinda sashayed out of the studio, her round tush prompting another sequence of naughty thoughts.

"Sam," came Soozie's voice. "Five minutes to air. Mister Y would like a word with you."

"Put him on." Joel tried to sound confident despite his growing paranoia. He braced himself for a hateful Islamist tirade, or maybe more of those threats of bodily mutilation he remembered so fondly. His fears were unfounded.

"Mr. Stooge, thank you for the chance to tell my story on your show."

"No problem. You're the one who deserves thanks, for having the guts to blow the whistle. The name's an alias, right? I don't want to put you or your family in danger."

"Yes, of course it's an alias. One more thing. A confession."

Joel's gut tightened. "Let's save it for later... we go on in four minutes..."

"A quick one. I have many regrets, but one of the worst is the hateful things I've said and done to one of your fellow Jews. I want to apologize on behalf of my whole family."

"Uh, thanks!" Joel was stunned. "Though I bet you say that to all the infidels." The guy had no idea how appropriate the apology was. "Hold on, we'll be back to you after the intro."

Soozie cut in. "Boss, you're on in five, four, three..." She held up two fingers, then one.

"Hello America, this is Surly Moe, the Seventh Stooge, broadcasting from somewhere in America, in the belly of the Beast." The new tagline was Soozie's brainchild, though she hadn't yet gotten him to change the blog's 'ridiculous' name. "In honor of our first-ever audio pod-cast, we have a guest who's pure dynamite. In fact, we decided to digitally obscure his voice to protect him from all the dirty rats who'd like to bump him off. My voice, too, by the way."

"We'll call him Yusef Islam, but he won't be singing 'Moon Shadow.' He's a member of that religion that thinks women only look good in basic black. But he's a swell guy, I promise you. In fact, he's come on to warn us about an evil gov-a-mint plot. So Yusef, what's shaking?"

"Mr. Stooge, I was hesitant to come forward, for the reason you mentioned. First, the conspirators would want to silence me any way they can. Secondly, my own people are opposed because this story would bring us unwanted attention."

"Hold it, Yusef, are you saying there's an evil conspiracy and you guys want to keep it under wraps? What kind of Americans are you, anyway? I want to see your birth certificate!"

Emal cleared his throat. "Please don't judge my religious brethren. The persecution we've endured in America has made us fearful. It's because of my mistakes, my sins and hateful actions, that I've come forward, as a way to atone to God and my fellow Americans. Believe me, I love my adopted country, and I'm very afraid for its survival."

"I apologize, Yusef, for being such a wise guy. Please continue."

"I'll try to be brief. The President is in trouble, and needs the people's support, and what better way to get that support than if the country suffers another terrorist attack similar to 9/11. In order to keep her hands clean, she has engaged the services of the Albanian Mafia. If the attack succeeds, they are to be rewarded by lucrative positions within the national security apparatus. If anything goes wrong, we expect that these criminals will serve as convenient scapegoats."

Though Joel was still quite skeptical, he wasn't inclined to dismiss the man's allegations out of hand. "You're serious about this? If I went to the major media with a story like this, they'd have men waiting outside for me with a white coat and butterfly nets. How can we believe such a crazy story?"

"Unfortunately I don't have any proof I can share with your listeners, but I do have details of the operation. Possibly the plotters will change their plans, and I'll appear to be a liar, but if the attacks are prevented, that will be worthwhile."

244

"OK, give us the details, and if your trousers undergo spontaneous combustion, we'll take that into account."

"They intend to plant bombs at 9/11 memorial ceremonies in ten major cities. The explosives will be hidden in speakers brought in for the public address systems. Part of the festivities will be the simultaneous playing of the 'Star Spangled Banner,' and the bombs will be rigged to detonate on the final bars of the anthem. The bombings are planned for the cities of Washington, New York, Los Angeles, Chicago, Houston, Miami, Denver, Philadelphia, Salt Lake City, and Honolulu."

"Honolulu? Those rotten creeps are going to blow up Pearl Harbor again?"

"Not the harbor, the Civic Center, at Honolulu Hale."

"That's pronounced Hah-lay, but we'll forgive you, being a alien foreigner and all. One thing doesn't add up. There'll certainly be politicians and other big-wigs at the ceremonies. They don't want to blow themselves up, do they?"

"No, the explosions will be directed toward the crowd. Also, none of them are supposed to know about it. This is a top level operation between the President and her senior advisors."

"And a whole gang of crooks?"

"That knowledge was supposedly for their leaders only. Fortunately for us, they became arrogant and careless, and didn't expect to encounter others who spoke their language."

The interview went on for about thirty minutes, in which Joel tried to draw out more details of the plot. The more specifics they had, the more likely someone could confirm or disprove this story. Joel wished he dared question Emal on his sources. How the hell did a lowly truck driver come across this information? As much grief as this guy had given him, Joel didn't want to endanger his life; especially not that of his family.

"One more question. If the government is in such trouble, why would the gangsters cozy up to them? Don't they make more dough selling drugs and loose women? And how can they trust the authorities not to do the old Benedict Arnold on them?"

"I don't know the answer to that. I do know that lately the gangs have been battling among themselves. Even if the government is weak, an alliance with Homeland Security would be a great advantage."

"I think you're on to something," Joel said, "The bad guys are in trouble, too. The Undernet lets folks cut out the middleman and buy their happy pills right from the source. Like my college professor used to say, if drugs are outlawed, only outlaws will have drugs..."

Emal surprised him by interrupting. "Mr. Stooge," The frustration was evident in his voice. "May I say something else?"

"Uh, certainly," Joel was embarrassed. The scoop of the century, and he had to ham it up.

"I have noticed a lot of hate against immigrants these days. I don't want people to think we're all that way. Most of us are hard-working, law abiding people with families."

"Fair enough. Yusef, you sound like a real *mensch*! Our peoples may not get along real well, but deep down inside, we all pretty much want the same things."

Joel glanced at the clock on the monitor; time was almost up. Just as well; he could tell Emal had no more to say, or had at least said as much as he was willing. It was a very brave thing he'd done, assuming this wasn't some kind of sneaky Islamic red herring (was fish *halal*?)

Emal said a few more words about redemption, how he prayed for the innocents who'd lost their lives in America's recent conflicts. Behind the monitor, Soozie signaled Joel to wrap it up. Not that they were on a schedule, but she insisted people liked their podcasts in predictable chunks. Just as well; as sincere as this guy seemed, Joel didn't want his show used to proselytize for a competing religion. *Lots more of them than us, we have to keep on our toes.*

"That's all the time we have. Thanks for joining us, Yusef. You're a brave man. I intend to check out your amazing story, and I urge all of you listeners to do the same. Be skeptical, you knuckleheads! Next time you hear politicians say they care, ask yourself if they'll still respect us in the morning. This is Surly Moe, the Seventh Stooge, signing out."

Soozie grinned and gave Joel a thumb's up. She clicked a button on the computer to play a recorded message. The door swung open and Serena burst in. "Great show, Hon!" She listened for a moment and grinned. "Hey, that's me!"

It was Serena's electronically modified voice reading the promo. "Jeff the Auto Merchant has a huge selection of used cars at bargain prices. He has locations all over the USA for secure, anonymous barter transactions. For an additional fee, he will scan for, and disable, any government tracking devices. See his up-to-date inventory at AB657398..."

"Sam?" Soozie said. "Mr. I is still on the other line."

"Thanks, Sooz." Joel un-muted his headset. "Yes, Mr. Islam?"

"I want to thank you again for the opportunity to share my message. Like you said, our faiths have had a lot of historical animosity between them. But we have more in common than differences. After all, we're both Peoples of the Book. Peace be unto you, Mr. Lox."

Joel couldn't help but smile. "Shalom to you, Yusef Islam."

What the hell time is it? It really bothered Larsen not to know. He supposed it was the Protestant work ethic of his upbringing. He'd been trapped for days in this tiny windowless cell, and the idleness was driving him crazy.

Not that leaving this place would necessarily be an improvement. During the most recent interrogation, the always-sadistic Harris had presided over at least a dozen 'simulated' drownings. The near-death character of those experiences had felt quite real. If Larsen ever had to argue with some right winger about 'enhanced interrogations', he'd have an informed opinion.

Larsen's stomach rumbled. It had been a while since he'd eaten, and that had been some stale bread. He supposed he could pat himself on the back for not having cracked under the pressure. He refused to answer their questions about Nephi and Siri, their activities or whereabouts. When they asked about Joel Walter, he denied even knowing the guy.

A few days back (or was it weeks?), when he fell in with Los Locos, Larsen thanked his lucky stars for the promise of protection. No more beatings by the skinheads from Barracks E. In return, Larsen helped the Locos build stuff, like an improvised stun gun made from stolen batteries. The Locos had access to drugs, and on one blessed occasion, a bottle of tequila. Larsen's Spanish improved exponentially. Despite the hell of being here, the camaraderie and the secret collusion made things exciting at times.

Of course, Los Locos couldn't protect him when the guards grabbed him on the way to the mess hall. They trussed his hands behind his back and dragged him to the interrogation center. As torturers went, Larsen's captors were fairly 'civilized'. They stopped short of pulling fingernails or impromptu dental surgery. Nothing they did left a mark, except a few burns from the electric shocks. Yet his captors didn't figure on his Scandinavian bullheadedness. The abuse made him more determined to resist.

This last time, they didn't dump him in the yard and let him to crawl back to the barracks. Instead, they threw him in solitary confinement and kept him there. Since then he hadn't slept at all; they kept bright lights on 24/7, freezing cold air alternated with sweltering heat, random sprays of water. Nowhere to lie down but the concrete floor. No doubt somebody was watching him, though the camera was too small to see. Every time he'd start to drift off, there'd be a loud noise (usually death metal music, which he'd never much cared for) and sleep would elude him again. He was exhausted beyond belief.

He'd done enough illegal stimulants in his youth to know what it was like to be awake for extended periods, though never this long. After a few days the hallucinations started, which were a definite improvement. Many of these waking dreams featured his parents, Dave, or his friends from the Sportsman's, especially Andrea.

Then he started hearing Joel Walter's voice. "It's OK, JL, you're going to get through this." Strange, he never knew the guy that well; since the trip to Florida, all contact had been on-line. Though those memories were relatively recent.

Larsen was sitting on the bare floor, arms around his knees, shivering, (at the moment the A/C was on full blast) when he heard the voice again. "JL, can you hear me?"

He laughed. "Yeah, right! You're in my imagination. I'm not actually hearing this."

"Get serious, man, it may only be a few minutes before they break the link."

"But how is that even possible? Not even Nephi could..." He realized what he was saying and stopped himself.

"JL, you've got to help. Nephi's gone missing. Poor Siri is crazy with worry." Definitely Joel's voice. What a realistic dream!

"Bullshit!" Larsen sneered. "This is some kind of trick, I just know it."

"You want I should jump through a bunch of hoops before you'll talk to me? This from the man who had the good taste to buy Eddie Van Halen's guitar from me?"

"Joel – but how?" Larsen's heart was hammering. "I don't understand. What do you want from me?"

There was a brief pause. "I'm trying to gather information about the conditions in the prison camps. The people have a right to now. And to get you out of here, too, of course."

"You're doing your blog again? That's awesome! I thought for sure they would have shut you down by now!"

Another pause. "No, of course not. So tell me, old friend, how are they treating you?"

The sun was sinking over the river in the west. Nephi swung out of the saddle and hopped to the ground under the shelter of a grove of scraggly trees. He was getting pretty good at this cowboy stuff. "Good girl." He patted the horse on its shoulder. He understood why Roy Rogers had been so found of his famous palomino, Trigger. Sadie had been a lifesaver for them these last few weeks. Now where was Bobby? He was running late.

Nephi thought about Siri, sitting in the cabin, working on her economic analyses. He checked his walkie-talkie; were the batteries still good? It was a police-only model that encrypted all its communications. Another useful thing he'd gotten through the e-Barter system.

Finally he saw Bobby coming up the trail in his four-wheel-drive pickup, raising dust all the way. His ranching cousins seldom rode horses, except as recreations. Machines were the work horses now, except maybe for trips to the roughest summer pastures.

"Hey, Nephi," said his cousin as he pulled up. "Got your supplies here."

"Thanks a million, Bobby. I'll put some extra credits on your account to cover your gas." Nephi started loading the groceries from behind the truck's seat to the saddle bags. "Oh good, you got salt— and toilet paper, we were almost out."

Bobby frowned, pulled off his cowboy hat and scratched his head. "Nephi, there's been a problem. The barter system has been down for four days, so we haven't able to use your credits."

"You had to cover it for me? Gee, Bobby, I feel bad about that. I have a bag of silver quarters back at the cabin, I'll bring some along next time."

"It's OK; we don't mind carrying you for a while. I'm sure the barter-net will be back up soon. After all," he grinned, "you invented the thing."

"Actually, it was Siri's creation, though I did help a bit," Without her barter algorithms, the Griffin system would never have been so useful to the general public. And just when they needed it most; unemployment at 30 percent, monthly inflation in double digits. The downside was, Nephi felt an enormous burden. People would go hungry if the system was down for long. "We need to figure out what's wrong with it. What exactly were the symptoms?"

"I wrote it down." He fished a slip of paper out of his pocket. "When I log on through the Undernet, it says 'Unable to contact nameserver proxy.' Whatever the heck that means."

"Hmm, not good. I apologize for the techno jargon, but it made sense when I wrote it." Nephi laughed weakly. "Possibly the Feds have figured out how to disrupt the bots that dynamically generate the directories of the roaming site servers."

"Not surprising," Bobby nodded as if he understood. "Another thing. You've heard about the random disappearances? It's gotten worse. All of a sudden lots of people are gone, whole families, no word from the police."

"The Rapture?" Nephi grinned, then worried he might have offended Bobby. Despite the fact that the pre-tribulation Rapture was not part of LDS theology, some of the family followed the *Left Behind* Internet TV series religiously (so to speak.)

"Not unless the Lord takes people away in black vans with Federal license plates."

Nephi sighed. "Why did I think they'd stop with me and Siri?" He forced a smile and clapped his cousin on the shoulder. "Thanks, man! I'll look into those network problems pronto. And I'll bring along some silver coins next week to make up for these groceries."

Bobby started the truck. "Save 'em for an emergency. We know you're good for it."

Nephi thanked his cousin again, checked the saddle bags and swung himself back up on Sadie. "C'mon girl, let's go home."

Nephi prodded Sadie and headed up the trail. His stomach was in a knot. A new electronic economy had grown up around the application he and Siri had developed. Neither of them had expected things to go so far, or happen so fast. If the Feds were after the small fish, no wonder he and Siri were number-one Enemies of the State.

He had to stop fretting about things he couldn't control, or he'd make himself sick. Instead he tried to focus on the beauty of God's creation. This was surely among the most majestic places on earth; arid, rocky and forbidding, but that added character. With places, like people, it was the flaws that made them more interesting.

Speaking of attractive– Siri was wearing a loose pink dress, hanging the wash on the clothesline they'd strung between the cabin and a pine tree. Her long black hair hung in a braid down her back. She had a clothespin in her mouth; her face had the same look of concentration she had when studying complex mathematical systems. In her simple garments, she shone like a Hindu fertility goddess in one of those brightly-colored Hare Krishna books.

She looked up as he rode Sadie into the yard. "Hi, Hon!" she called. She walked toward him, slowly and awkwardly, smiling nonetheless.

He leaned down to kiss her, losing his cowboy hat in the process. They both laughed. He swung down off the horse. After giving Siri another kiss, he unloaded the groceries from the saddle bags to the weathered picnic table. He pulled off the saddle and bridle and patted the horse on the rump. Sadie walked a few yards to the other side of the cabin, and began to graze.

Siri rustled through the plastic bags. "No cherry tomatoes? I was hoping we could get some." She had plants in pots indoors, but it would be a while before they were mature.

"Sorry, Sweetheart. Bobby must have forgotten. Anyway, we're restricted to what we can fit in the saddle bags."

"I've been a pretty good sport." Siri's voice took on a harsh tone. "Eating fish every day. That wasn't easy to get used to, but the baby needs protein, and it's not easy to get that out here."

"I know," Nephi carried the groceries to the cabin. "Sorry to have to put you through this. But it beats the alternative. Bobby says the Feds are rounding people up like crazy."

"Oh no!" She gave a heartfelt sigh. "I should have known this would happen. I don't know why, but I didn't expect people to abuse it so much the way they have." She sighed again and sat down heavily in the cabin's only padded chair.

"I don't consider it abuse. If the Treasury and the Federal Reserve hadn't wrecked the economy, spending so much and printing money like crazy..."

"I know! I was joking, dear. Tough to pull it off when everything is such an effort!" Her smile looked a bit like a grimace. "The government is definitely the abusive party. You *could* make a rational argument for taxing people who participate in their monetary system, a kind of convenience charge. But when they force their funny money monopoly on everybody, it's not fair– but I'm preaching to the choir, aren't I?"

"I haven't told you the biggest news yet. Bobby said the Undernet is down. They just can't get onto any of the barter sites."

"Oh, no! With the above-ground economy so wrecked, people depend on e-Barter. I almost wish we hadn't developed it," she paused to catch her breath, "I feel like I have to play mother to half the country."

"You worry too much. Not good for the baby. Anyway, I set up a 'bot to monitor the remote servers; have you been checking the reports?"

"You can check it as well as I can, Nephi. I haven't been feeling very energetic lately."

Nephi glanced at Siri's enlarged belly. "Sorry, Sweetie. I've been preoccupied the last couple days, between fixing the water pump, scrounging for food, and keeping our Undernet connection alive. I'll run some diagnostics, but I've got to get something to eat, or I won't be able to think straight." He squeezed his wife's shoulder on the way to the 'kitchen.' He opened the tiny cupboard. "Yeah, a quick peanut butter sandwich. I'll make you one, too."

"No thanks, I'm not hungry right now." Siri sat down in front of the computer. "So what is it, the directory servers?" She looked at Nephi, who nodded in response. "I thought so. I know you assume the Feds brought them down, but we need to be sure. It's possible it might not be them. Maybe with it scaled up to a billion transactions a day, we've run into a latent defect."

"This is no software bug." Nephi said between bites. "Don't worry about it, you rest, I'll check it out as soon as I've finished my sandwich. If the packet transponders are still up."

"They *were* up earlier today. We got a Griffin message from Joel, and I was able to reply. So hopefully they're still functional."

Nephi and Siri had a small satellite dish on the roof of their cabin, which brought them news of the outside world. Communicating the other way was more difficult. They'd mounted a fifteen foot antenna on top of a nearby tree. This connected to a series of solar powered packet radio transmitters, painted green and brown and affixed to more trees. These propagated the encrypted outbound signals to reach the county's rural Wi-Fi network. Nephi worried that the signal, low powered as it was, would be detected; but so far, so good.

"So what did Joel say?" Nephi asked. "Has he heard from JL at all?"

"Still no word. I think JL's disappearance is connected to those mass arrests, though he might have been a special target, like us. By the way, I've been doing some more analysis this morning. Check this out." She leaned back in her chair and typed some commands on her wireless keyboard. The PC's monitor lit up with a brightly colored display. She stroked the trackball attached to the keyboard, and moved the cursor down to select a bar graph.

"These are government revenues over the previous two fiscal years. Now, here are the figures for this year. They haven't been officially released, but I got those from that Treasury website you hacked into."

"Wow, they're dropping every month! No wonder the Feds are freaking out. Still, it serves them right. They're the ones destroying the economy." He looked back at Siri and sighed. "First thing, let's contact Bjornsen and Van Pelt and have 'em set up some new Griffin servers in Europe. These days, it doesn't matter where they're located."

Siri shook her head. "The Feds will find them and pressure the EU to shut them down. We need to find our vulnerability and fix it. I have some ideas, but I'll need your help. I'd like to get this stuff done before the baby– oh!" She dropped they keyboard and clutched her side.

Nephi's mouth dropped open. "What's wrong? Do you need– should I– what?"

"Don't panic. I don't know how close together the contractions are yet, because that was the first one. To be on the safe side, call Rosa's niece. What's her name again?"

"Juanita." They were lucky to have a midwife in the family. He grabbed the keyboard off the floor and frantically punched keys until the instant-messaging window appeared on the monitor. He had to try three times before he got Juanita's IM handle spelled correctly. By the time he'd gotten through, Siri had experienced two more contractions.

Nephi typed, "Siri having labor pains, can you come soon?" He looked over at Siri in a panic. "OK, what do we do now?"

She smiled weakly. "Don't panic, Hon. It might be false labor. We need to time the– oh!"

"Another one?"

"Yeah. I'll go lie down a while." She struggled to get up. Nephi jumped to help. He led her to the cot in the cabin's other room, then rushed back to the PC to check for a response. Juanita should have gotten the text; she always carried her cell. Why wasn't she responding?

Nephi paced between the rooms, alternately checking on Siri and the computer. The subsequent contractions came faster, so he held her hand while she did her deep breathing. "Too bad we only got to go to one Lamaze lesson," he laughed. Siri could only grimace.

He looked at his watch. Amazingly, it had only been 45 minutes. It was bad enough, seeing Siri in such pain, but to experience it... that was hard to imagine. How long could this go on? Nephi's mother had been in labor for twenty two hours with him, steadfastly refusing a C-section until the doctor had no choice. What would happen to Siri and the baby if there were complications? He'd seen video of a doctor reaching in and turning a baby that was coming out breech. That Nephi would attempt, if it came to that. Beyond that, there wouldn't be much he could do but hope and pray.

The minutes went by, and still no message. The birth was well underway. It went quickly, thankfully without complications. The computer chimed as Nephi was rummaging around in the kitchen for a clean towel. Juanita had finally responded. "Sorry it took so long– assisting on a difficult birth– get the web cam, I'll coach remotely." Before Nephi could respond, Siri let out a scream from the other room.

The baby's head was visible, and the rest was coming quickly. Living in the mountains, with their limited diet, the baby had not gained excessive weight, which would make for an easier delivery. Still, 'easy' was not a word he'd use to describe the birth process. Siri grabbed his hand; she was practically crushing his fingers. "I can't stand it! Get me something for the pain!"

"Flip it, Siri, we don't have anything stronger than Tylenol! Just breathe!"

She didn't have time for further complaints. The baby was on the fast track to the outside. All poor Siri could do was grunt, moan and push. Nephi glanced at his watch again; two hours so far, and all body parts pointed in the right direction. Exactly what he'd been praying for.

When the baby had emerged completely, there was a loud cry. Nephi took the slippery newborn and carefully set it on his wife's stomach. He found his fishing knife, sterilized it with rubbing alcohol, and cut the cord.

"He's beautiful!" Siri said weakly. They'd known the baby's sex since the initial ultrasound, and had already decided to name him both his grandfathers– William Pradeep.

Nephi stood up, thinking, *I need to clean up this mess.* But the panic and adrenaline had finally let go, and the significance of the event finally hit him. "I love you so much!" He kissed his wife's sweat-soaked lips, then sank to the floor beside them, staring at them both, big tears dripping out of his eyes.

The next few weeks would be very challenging, but for the moment, there were only two other people in the world who mattered.

Chapter 12 – The Wrath of Sting

"Hey Muchacho, get up! The big break out! It's happening!"

Jon Larsen moaned and rolled over. "Leave me alone!" Maybe if he ignored the irritant, it would go away. No use; the intruder started shaking the bed.

"Cut it out!" Larsen sat up and rubbed his eyes. A golden light poured in the window; was it morning or afternoon? "Bad enough you're keeping me prisoner. Go, leave me in peace!"

"What the hell you talkin' about? The others *vamosed*, do you wanna get left here?" A frown crossed the oddly familiar face. "Man, get your shit together and get your doped-up ass out of bed. I was gonna cut you off, anyway. We all done stuff we're not proud of. You don't see us layin' round getting wasted all day."

"Return to Hell, foul creature!" Larsen shut his eyes and lay back down.

"And they call *us* loco! OK, I tried. "Stay there, you crazy *cabrón*, we'll be long gone."

Larsen watched out of half open eyes as his assailant stormed out. He lay back down, his mind filled with scenes imagined or half-remembered; dear friends and comrades being dragged away by inhuman thugs. He felt responsible for their plight. In his weakness, he had betrayed the people he cared about to achieve respite from his torments.

Now I'll never get back to sleep. He pulled off the scratchy gray blanket, found a tiny brown bottle by his elbow, and twisted it open. *Only one left.* He swallowed the pill dry, and lay back down.

Larsen was drifting off again when he heard thunderclaps, three in a row. They seemed very close. In this hostile land, danger was everywhere. He sat bolt upright on the hard bunk, confused and disoriented. It seemed that his recent experiences were nothing but a dream. Somehow he'd forgotten his true identity and his duty to destroy the Ring and save Middle Earth.

A panic overtook him. *Where am I? Where's Sam?*

There was a loud 'whoom', a crash, and a tinkle of glass as the nearest window shattered. Startled, Jon rolled out of bed and hit the floor. He scanned the dismal surroundings of his prison in Sauron's tower. The sound could not have been thunder; the sky outside was clear. *It must be Legolas and Gimli, firing explosive arrows in an effort to free me. But where's Samwise?*

He pulled on a foul smelling shirt that was much too large for him. Under his bunk lay a pair of shoes, but he ignored them. Being a hobbit, he didn't need them. He rushed outside in bare feet.

Outside, all was chaos, yet fortune was with him. Not fifty yards from the Tower he encountered his comrades from the Fellowship, accompanied by the others from Rivendell. "Strider! Legolas! And brave Gimli!" He clapped a hand on the stout fellow's shoulder. "We must hurry. We have to rescue Samwise!"

It was not a warm reception. Gimli scowled; though his manner was normally gruff, he seemed to be offended. "Homeboy, you're trippin'! How come I got to be the dwarf?"

"Who else but you, Chico?" laughed Strider, whom Jon now realized was the intruder who'd tried to rescue him from the tower. Jon followed without comment. His friends seemed to be speaking nonsense, perhaps due to some evil spell. All around were signs of a recent battle. The corpses of warriors from both sides lay where they'd fallen.

"Shit, it's trouble!" It was uncharacteristic for Legolas to use profanity, but these were desperate times. They were near the frontiers of Mordor, where they came face to face with a band of renegade elves. These outlaws had allied with the Dark Lord, and shorn their elfin locks in rejection of the society that bore them. They were well along in the transformation to orc.

"Well, if it's not our spic friends," jeered their leader. Jon recalled the vile creature was called Dietrich. "You going back to your shithole country, or should we send you to Hell instead?"

"Ignore these bastards," Strider warned, speaking Elfish, a tongue in which Jon had recently become fluent. "We need to get out of here, not start a rumble!" He led the way, giving wide berth to the malodorous servants of Sauron. Jon followed with the rest of the Fellowship.

"What's wrong, you pansy-assed dick-smoking faggots afraid to fight?" Dietrich adopted a lisp and pantomimed a limp wrist. The others in his party howled with laughter.

"I warn you orcs; do not insult these brave warriors!" Jon bellowed. "Take back your evil words, or feel the wrath of Sting!" He brandished his 'weapon', a gift from Strider: a wondrous implement with a silvery surface and a pitch black point, which could not only slay one's enemies but could also inscribe messages on any material.

"Shut your hole, Butt Boy," sneered another of the dark elves. His visage was marred by a misshapen nose that had likely been broken in battle. "You're no better than the wetbacks."

There was dead silence between the two camps. Jon looked back at his companions, who seemed to be reconsidering their plans for a quick escape.

"You asked for it," Strider growled, advancing slowly. He reached into the waistband of his bright orange traveling cloak and produced a tiny dagger. Rivendell steel had not the beauty of an elfish sword or dwarfish ax, but in the right hands, it could be just as deadly.

Jon unsheathed Sting and tensed for battle. A booming voice startled them all.

"Yo, all of you!" came a shout from beyond the Dark Lord's fortress. "Hands up, everybody, and back off, slowly! I've had enough killing for one day, but I'm in a real bad mood, so don't fuck with me!" The man's accomplices brandished exotic weapons, crossbows of unusual design.

Jon stood unmoving, hands at his sides, and regarded the four newcomers. They wore elfin colors, brown and black like the woods themselves, but carelessly intermixed, as if painted by a drunken troll. Their leader was a dark skinned man from the regions south of Gondor. He wore a hat with the brim bent upwards on one side, confirming his foreign origin. Though perhaps it was another illusion. Had their wizard friend transformed his appearance again?

Jon bowed to the visitor. "Hail, great wizard! Is it now Gandalf the Black?"

"You drugged-out race traitor," muttered the broken nosed elf, under his breath. Though his hands were still above his head, he glanced around nervously, as if expecting something to happen. "No self-respecting white man would bow down to a god damned spade."

"You have slandered my noblest friend and comrade! Die, foul creature!" With a blood curdling yell, Jon charged the offending elf, his 'blade' leveled as if for a deadly thrust. Not daring to lower his hands, the man took Jon's charge directly in the stomach.

There was another thunderclap. Jon saw flashes before his eyes as he was struck in the head by a cowardly blow from behind. He fell into the dust at his feet and lost consciousness.

Larsen awoke to find himself lying on a vibrating metal floor. His head pounded as if he'd spent a wild night partying. Dimly he remembered a really crazy dream. Perhaps the long stretch in solitary had given him hallucinations. As he lay there, too tired to get up, scenes from the dream returned to him in vivid flashes of sound and color.

He remembered pulling himself up from the gravel, a taste blood of in his mouth. Ahead of him was the prison camp's main entrance. The gates, diamond-patterned steel mesh topped with razor wire, hung at a weird angle, partially ripped off their hinges. The blue and red "HD" logo, painted on a metal placard four feet square, lay on the gravel, dented and riddled with bullet holes. Smoke and flames issued from the warden's office and the interrogation center.

Troops in desert-cammo fatigues stood before them. In Larsen's mind's eye they looked like regular army, except for the red "BB" insignia on their helmets. Their leader, a tall black man, stood over the corpse of a gaunt fellow in a prison guard's uniform. Somewhere there was gunfire and shouting, but the sounds were muted, like a television with the volume turned down.

"Awake already, Mister Barbarian? Or maybe with that red beard, you're more of a Viking," the big man guffawed. "Running around barefoot on hot gravel, you must be tougher than nails."

That was when, to his great embarrassment, Larsen remembered the day's previous events. It hadn't been a dream, he'd actually been convinced he was the hero of the *Lord of the Rings*. He felt like a complete idiot. For lack of a better plan, he stayed in character, raising his hand in a gesture of friendship. "Hail, brave warriors!"

Those images faded. Slowly Larsen sat up; his whole body ached. He was in the cargo area of a military vehicle, lying between boxes of ammunition and medical supplies. Two men sat up front, speaking in low voices, occasionally talking to a third, crackly voice on the radio.

"Jesus Christ, that was *real*?" Larsen muttered out loud.

A dark face turned to look back at him from the passenger seat. It was the big man from his 'dream.' "Lieutenant, I think Sleeping Beauty's awake again." He chuckled. "You made it all the way to the truck and passed out."

"Uh, yeah. So... what happened? Where the hell am I?" He stared at the fellow who'd spoken. "Man, I know this sounds lame, but you're somebody famous, aren't you?"

"Show some respect," barked the driver. "You're speaking to Commander 'Mac' MacGuiness of the Smedley Butler Brigade. The man who's going to save this country from the God-awful mess you people have made of it."

Of course! Jesus, was I out of it! No wonder the face looked familiar; Larsen had seen it a hundred times on TV, the Internet, and on posters in the Post Office. "Holy shit, it *is* you. Man, if I disrespected you back at the camp, I totally apologize. I was in a really screwed-up mental state at the time. Actually, I'm a big supporter of yours."

The big man busted out in a hearty laugh. "See, Lieutenant, I told you he was one of the good guys." He turned back to face Larsen again. "Actually, you saved my life. When you went all bat-shit and attacked that skinhead, I stepped back, and somebody fired a full auto at the spot where I'd just been standing. Those Haldyne assholes had a sniper on the roof, but we got him."

Larsen managed a sheepish grin. "Glad I could be of assistance. Even if I didn't know what I was doing at the time."

"I'm glad you realize that," the Commander chuckled. "I was afraid you might freak when I told you we're not in Middle Earth." He laughed again; this time the lieutenant joined in.

Feeling foolish, Larsen declined to respond. Instead, he looked out the window. They were traveling on a gravel road through the desert. Funny, there were no vehicles ahead of or behind them. "Where are we going? And what happened to the Los Locos guys?"

"You're lucky you were hangin' with the Locos," said the lieutenant said in a Hispanic accent. "At first we thought you was with White Cross, you being kind of pale for a Latino."

"No way would I be with those skinhead sons of bitches." Larsen considered his words for a moment. "Commander, am I still a prisoner, or am I free to go?"

The Commander turned back to face him again. "If you'd like to go back to the camp, we'd be happy to oblige."

Larsen turned red, nothing was coming out right today. "Oh, I really appreciate the rescue, Commander. I've been following your blog on the Undernet..."

"Good, just don't start trippin' again and decide we're the Dark Lord's henchmen."

"I'll behave myself from now on. They had me in solitary, and they were doing all the bright lights and loud noises. I feel like I was awake for weeks." He decided not to mention all the drugs he'd taken afterwards, in a failed attempt to forget.

"First of all, don't worry about your amigos. They're the reason we hit the camp at Ruidoso, because Lieutenant Hernandez here was convinced we could recruit them to our cause. White Cross, those dumb shits, we left 'em locked up for Uncle to take care of. But you don't seem to fit in with anybody. What's your name, Hobbit boy, and where you hail from?"

"Larsen, Jon Larsen, of Grand Forks, North Dakota." He stopped short of mentioning his role in the Griffin Project. He'd heard that the Butler Brigade used Griffin extensively for its secure communications, but he wondered what the Commander really thought of it. To someone in authority, an unbreakable form of encryption might be a threat. MacGuiness seemed like a good man, but power had a way of corrupting people.

The Commander laughed. "North Dakota, eh? Cold up there! Good to meet you, Mr. Larsen. I hope your brain's not too fucked up to remember a few things. Because it's obvious that Uncle is very interested in you, and we need to know why."

"I'm just a farmer who dabbles in technology. Call me JL, all my friends do."

"And you can call me Mac. Except in front of the troops, it's 'Commander,' OK?"

"Yes, Sir, I mean Commander. May I ask a question? What happened to everyone else?"

"Security," explained the Lieutenant. "We split up to keep from drawing undue attention. We'll all meet at the rendezvous point in less than an hour."

"Not to sound ungrateful, but what's the point of all this? Won't the Feds just recapture everybody?"

"Not necessarily. There *are* a few safe places in the country; of course, safety's a relative thing. Long as you don't mind living in the ghetto, the barrio, or on the Res. The Man doesn't give a shit about those folks in those places, so that's where we hang."

They turned off the gravel road onto a trail that consisted of two wheel ruts in the desert. Hernandez slowed down the Hummer as the jarring increased exponentially. Larsen's stomach began to turn. To keep his mind off of it, he kept talking. "So where's the rendezvous point?"

"If I told you I'd have to kill you," Mac laughed again. "Actually, it's an abandoned mine in the Sangre de Cristos. The Feds will try to track us from the air, so we have to blend in with the local yokels."

A sudden excitement drove the nausea from Larsen's mind. "How many men we talking about? Does this mean the revolution's starting?"

"No," Mac said. "We've got a long way to go. This is guerrilla war; the victory goes to the side that's the most patient."

"But we can't afford to lay low much longer," Hernandez chimed in. "With the Feds putting all those people in camps, and plotting with the Mob to take out their enemies. Did you hear about the new 9/11 plot? Sons of bitches almost got away with it."

"Is that for his benefit or mine? Don't forget, I'm still in charge here." There was a hardness in Mac's voice; until then, Larsen wasn't convinced these guys were serious. "As for you, Mr. Larsen, if you're at all good at computers, you can take the blood oath and join us"– he paused a moment to let Larsen know he was not joking– "'cause we sure could use your talents."

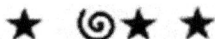

"It'll be a quick stop," Serena said to Joel as they got into her old Beetle. "I just need to drop off this painting for Soozie."

Joel grimaced. "Can't it wait 'til tomorrow? I'm beat tonight. I was looking forward to a nice hot meal, a glass of wine, and a long hot shower, preferably not alone."

"If you want company in the shower, you can't be *that* tired." She gave him a playful pinch. "You've been down on Soozie ever since she hooked up with Belinda, haven't you?"

"Who, me? If the woman prefers tacos to tube steak, that's none of my business. I owe her big time for all her help with my pod-casts. But it's a long drive, and with all the checkpoint nonsense, who knows when we'll get home?"

Joel wasn't that tired, just grouchy . The threat of arrest, which had nearly given him ulcers a few months back, seemed distant now. The cop-finder app on his Android gave a pretty reliable warning of road blocks. Still, getting around them was a damned nuisance.

"Then let's get it over with, before it gets too late in the evening."

There was no arguing with her. Fortunately, traffic was light and the TSA was busy oppressing people in other places. They reached Soozie's complex just after dark.

Serena got out, opened the trunk, and removed a flat package wrapped in paper. "You don't have to come along, I'll just drop this off and be right back."

"Are you kidding? It's my manly duty to protect you." He grinned at her irritated reaction. "Besides, you don't let me smoke in the car, so I have to get out anyway." *And if Soozie offered Serena weed, it could take much longer.*

It only took a couple minutes to reach the other side of the complex, where Soozie and Belinda shared a second floor apartment. No light shone from their window.

"Oh, hell! She said they'd be here! Did we make this trip for nothing?" Serena grabbed her phone out of her purse and angrily began to punch in Soozie's number.

"No!" Joel grabbed her arm, dropping his freshly lit cigar on the pavement. He lowered his voice to a hoarse whisper. "Don't you see the yellow tape? Come on, this way!"

There were voices and shuffling sounds coming from the building's outdoor stairwell. Joel was glad he'd scoped the place out; they retraced their steps without being spotted. Back at the car, he got out the night-vision binoculars he'd gotten in trade from a client. A man and woman, wearing dark suits unusual for this climate, stood in front of Soozie's door. "What did I tell you? That was a close one!"

Joel's hands were shaking as he pulled the car out of the apartment parking lot. It was difficult for him to drive cautiously, but to be stopped for speeding would have been a disaster.

"Where are we going, Hon? I'm really worried about Soozie and Belinda, isn't there something we can do?"

"There's nothing we can do, at the moment. I'm afraid we might be in danger, too. If they got your friend, it's only a matter of time before they get us. Soon as we get a chance we'll check with her connections. Maybe they were able to get away ."

"Do you mean we can't go home? I don't have a change of clothes, or even a toothbrush!"

"Me neither. My love, I'm afraid we may need to leave the state altogether."

"What? But... my clothes, my paintings, my art supplies! I can't just leave them!"

"We'll do what we can, Babe. Tomorrow, if it looks like it's safe, we may be able to grab a few essentials from the house before we make our getaway."

They found a place the Undernet's 'Anonymous Traveler' website declared to be safe: the Notel Motel, located in a run-down commercial district near the Airport. It was the kind of place that inspired you to scratch at imaginary bedbugs for days afterward.

When they got to the room, Serena sent a message to Soozie on Griffin. No response. She made an encrypted call to Belinda, who claimed to know nothing; they'd broken up a few days before. "Just don't go to her apartment," Serena warned her. "It's crawling with cops."

The news made Joel's stomach hurt. "I never trusted that little bitch. For all we know, her phone was tapped. Good thing Griffin calls aren't traceable– we hope."

"Bullshit! Belinda would never narc on Soozie."

"Chill, Sweetie, I'm not saying she did. But just to be safe, we need to get new identities and move, right away." He paused a moment to gauge her reaction. "How about Texas? They're talking again about seceding from the Union. If they do, it'd be a great place to start over."

Serena surprised him with her vehemence. "Texas? That redneck backwater? No way! If we have to move, there are a lot better options than that. But I like your idea. If you and I can't leave the country, we can do the next best thing, go to a place that's likely to break away."

"Where? Vermont? Alaska? No way, you hate cold weather!"

"California, silly! Haven't you heard how the new governor's fighting with Wilton over tax and spending policy?"

Joel was surprised; he'd thought she didn't follow the news. "*Feh!* I spent a couple years in LA in the 1990's. When I moved back to Arizona, I promised myself, never again."

"Don't be so negative, it's changing! They have to, the state's broke. Governor Lopez talks like you. He wants to get government off everybody's backs so the economy can recover."

He regarded her skeptically. "OK, Serena, what's your angle?"

"Didn't you hear? They legalized pot, not just medical purposes, but for *all* adults. You can go live in Alaska if you want, but I'm heading to California."

Joel couldn't help laughing. "OK, I'll think about it."

Her mind made up, Serena's panic subsided. Over Joel's objections, she smoked a couple of bong hits in the bathroom, then went to bed and was soon snoring.

Joel lay awake next to her, playing scenes of potential disaster over and over in his head. By one AM he'd had enough. "Get up, Sweetie, we're going to the house."

"Huh? It morning already?"

Serena was very groggy, but he harangued her until she was dressed and got in the car. It was a short drive to the house. To Joel's great relief, it appeared to be undisturbed, and his car was where he'd left it in the garage. He hated to make Serena drive, but they couldn't afford to abandon either vehicle. "You go in and pack, Babe; I'll start out here." Quickly he gathered up his tools, motor oil, and emergency supplies.

Inside, Serena was moving at a sloth's pace. "Come on, hurry!" he scolded. They boxed up the dishes and non-perishable food, then their clothes and personal effects. Finally they were on their way.

"Put your ear piece in, so it'll be easy to call me if you need to," Joel said. Half a mile from the house, they already had their first crisis. "Joel, I forgot my paintings!"

"I'll go get them, I'll meet you back at the hotel."

He drove back as fast as he dared. *"Scheisse!"* His irritation turned to horror as he turned onto Serena's street. There were three vehicles in front of Serena's house, one of them a van. At that very moment, a squad of men in helmets and black uniforms were kicking down the door. Joel made a U-turn; thank God no one followed.

Back at the hotel, Joel filled her in on what had happened.

"Assholes! I loved that place. I always wished I could afford to buy it, not just rent."

"That's just as well, considering the bank would have ended up getting it back."

She ignored his attempt to console her. "Our first home together. It's like losing a friend."

"Not to mention your cleaning deposit."

★ ◎★ ★

"But I–" Emal sputtered into the headset, "You could've reminded me! Or you could've bought a present for him from me. You know I'm on the road so much lately."

"Which should give you plenty of time to think, and not forget things like your children's birthdays," Esma said icily. "Ylli hardly gets to see you. When you sent the toy car from Daytona, it meant the world to him..."

"I'll try, but out here it's mostly nothing," Through his windshield, he saw just that– miles of dry, barren plains. "Maybe a cowboy hat. Couldn't you just get something for me?"

"Your son's not stupid; he'll know if I buy the gift." Esma sighed. "Listen, Emal, I'm sorry I got so angry. It doesn't matter what you get. At your next stop, find something to make it up to him. It would really mean a lot."

"OK. I will. Love you, bye." His hand brushed the 'off' button.

Emal did feel terrible, but he'd been preoccupied by other issues. He fretted about his decision to leave the Islamic Aid Society, and to go public with the story of the new 9/11 plot. The group's leadership had been adamantly opposed, "It will endanger our organization," Ahmed said. "We will deal with this when the time is right."

But would they? Emal suspected there were those in the IAS who would take advantage of the chaos that would have ensued. He was convinced he'd done the right thing, because of the crackdown on the Corporation that quickly followed his revelation. Still, he had disobeyed his superiors, and he wondered what the IAS would have done to him if he'd stuck around.

A sign ahead said 'Casper – 5 miles.' He was almost to his destination, which made him feel somewhat better. After his delivery at Casper, the trailer would be empty. He'd spend the night there, and hopefully be able to find a good gift for his son.

Today his cargo was Chinese electronics, which had become very expensive due to the precipitous drop in the US dollar. No wonder his clients turned to smuggling. On top of that, the 'carbon fees' the authorities tacked onto imported goods made legitimate products unaffordable.

Emal checked the in-dash navigation system. According to the map display, the drop off point, one of those gigantic warehouse stores, was located at the edge of town. He was surprised to be delivering to a major retail chain, because they didn't often deal in electronic contraband. Maybe they were feeling pressure from the out-of-state e-warehouses.

He pulled up to the loading dock. A lanky guy in jeans, a cowboy hat, and the store's official orange vest came up to the window. He was rather dark complexioned, probably Hispanic. "Manifest?" he said, giving Emal no more than a bored glance.

"Here you go, man," Emal said, handing him a sheet of paper. The cowboy nodded, none of the thinly-veiled hostility Emal had encountered in some places, especially down South. If the fellow mistook him for a compadre, that was good.

"It'll be a few minutes," said the cowboy. "Come in, have some coffee."

"Thanks." Emal followed him inside to a tiny nook with government employment posters, a water cooler, and a coffee pot. He grabbed a Styrofoam cup and sipped coffee while he watched the workers unload his cargo.

Minutes later, the brown-skinned cowboy returned. "Got your tablet?"

Emal nodded. Best to avoid unnecessary conversation. He logged on with his smart phone while the cowboy poked a few buttons on the touch screen monitor.

Emal brought up the balance sheet and checked the accounts receivable. *Cursed computers! Why can't they ever work right?* "I don't see my credits. Can you try it again?

The cowboy shook his head. "Better wait a minute, our Wi-Fi is slow. We don't want to pay you twice. Oh, could you please move your truck? We got another delivery coming in."

"OK, but I can't leave until we get this straightened out." Emal winced as the words came out. Under stress, his Albanian accent was reasserting itself. Keys in hand, he went back out to the dock. He hoped they weren't trying to cheat him. Surprisingly, that rarely happened to him.

He was more worried about being attacked by some anti-immigrant bigot. It might have been his imagination, but it seemed worse since he'd done the pod-cast. Two weeks ago in Biloxi he'd feared for his life from some drunken fans from a monster truck rally at a convenience store. Only the clerk's threat to call the cops had saved him from a nasty beating.

Emal was surprised to see three men coming up the steps. The first two were dressed like office workers, in jackets, Polo shirts, and Dockers; the third wore a dark suit.

"It's him!" cried one of the Polo shirt guys. It took a second for Emal to realize he was speaking Albanian. The dark-suited man reached into his jacket, jerked out a handgun, and fired. Despite the silencer, it was surprisingly loud in the enclosed space of the loading dock.

The bullet struck Emal in the chest, knocking him off his feet. He slammed his head on the concrete and closed his eyes, almost losing consciousness. Through slitted eyelids, he saw a pair of shiny brown shoes approaching, and a voice asking "Is he dead?"

As the shoes got closer, Emal heard the squeak of a door, and the cowboy's voice. "I tell you, I heard something – shit, he's got a gun!"

Emal jumped up and ran for his life. The Kevlar vest had saved him, but it wouldn't protect him from the next bullet, which would surely be to his head. One of the thugs pounded on the metal back door, while the other two took off after him. Luckily Emal had a head start of several seconds. As he rounded the corner of the building he could think of only one course of action. He slowed to a walk, and entered the store's front door as calmly as possible .

Briskly Emal headed toward the back. There was a sign saying 'Rest Rooms,' he could hide in there. He wanted to run but was afraid to draw attention to himself. When he was almost to the door, someone shouted, in heavily accented English. "Stop that man! He's a terrorist!"

Involuntarily, Emal whirled around to see his fellow Albanians storming up the aisle past the big TV's. At that same moment, he felt a painful grip on his arm.

"Stop right there!" It was the store security guard, a big muscular black man, wearing a gun. From the man's swagger, and the authority in his voice, Emal guessed he wasn't some two bit security grunt, but an off-duty cop.

"You can call the police," Emal panted as the guard patted him down him, "but keep those men away from me." He raised his voice so everyone in the store could hear him. "They're not cops, they're gangsters! They tried to kill me, see?" Emal gestured with a nod of his head toward the bullet hole in his shirt.

The guard eyed the two men suspiciously as they approached. The store was dead quiet except for the cheerful background music, an instrumental version of Green Day's 'American Idiot.' A middle-aged woman risked a quick glance around a row of shelving.

"I tell you, they're criminals! Illegal immigrants! They can't even speak good English!" Emal was painfully aware of his own accent, reasserting itself under stress.

"Put your gun away, sir," the guard said to the man in the suit, one hand reaching for his own holster. "I have the suspect under control. May I see your identification?"

The Albanian lowered his gun. To his colleague, he said, "Show your badge."

The second man flashed a wallet with something glittery in it, and just as quickly put it away. He grinned maliciously, showing tobacco-stained teeth. "Homeland security."

"It's fake! That's not even a real hologram!" Emal shouted. "It was on CNN last week, crooks posing as Federal agents!" Though if the *Seventh Stooge* pod-cast hadn't derailed the President's conspiracy, they could easily have been both.

"Hold it right there!" Another voice came from the next aisle; it was a chubby fellow in a ball cap and a pro wrestling t-shirt. "How do we know you're not those mafia guys who were plotting those terrorist attacks? If this rent-a-cop here won't take you in, I'm gonna have to make a citizen's arrest." He held up a shiny revolver, a .357.

"Put away the gun, sir!" The security guard drew his own Glock; a barely-suppressed rage in his voice. "I *am* a police officer, I have the situation under control, and we have a 'no weapons' sign posted clearly on the door."

The civilian interloper stood there petrified, except for his panic-stricken eyes, which darted back and forth between the crooks he was targeting and the guard who had his own weapon trained on him. "Hey, not me, the bad guys are over there!"

"Drop it now! There are innocent people..."

He was interrupted by the chirp of a silenced weapon, as the dark-suited foreigner shot the fat man in the chest. The customers' stares gave way to screams as the would-be vigilante tumbled to the floor, spattering blood everywhere.

The guard whirled around to face the shooter. "Put down your weapon, slowly! And you, hands up!" With a look of bored indifference the gangsters complied. The dark suited man lowered his arms and gently dropped his gun to the floor.

Glancing over his shoulder, the guard yelled to some unseen employee. "Marie! Are you there? Bob, Jennifer, somebody, call 9-1-1!"

Emal, who had been edging away from the security guard as soon as he'd been released from the man's grip, suddenly turned and dashed out the exit.

"Get him!" shouted the dark suited gangster. They both ran for the door, the Polo shirt guy stopping briefly to pull a small gun from a holster in his jacket.

"Stop right there or I'll shoot!" The guard bellowed. His gun followed the two gangsters, but he didn't pull the trigger. There were too many people in the line of fire. He lowered his gun and took off running after them. The Polo shirt thug turned and fired, missing his pursuer but shattering a display case full of the latest smart phones.

The commotion gave Emal the head start he needed. He sprinted through the parking lot in a mindless terror. As he neared his truck, he unlocked the door with the remote and scrambled into the cab. The third gangster was standing on the loading dock, smoking a cigarette. He looked up in shock when he heard the diesel engine start up.

"Infidel dogs!" The gangsters' black Lincoln was blocking Emal's escape. *No problem.* He threw the truck in gear and slammed into the vehicle, smashing the driver's side and pushing it, sideways, several yards through the mostly-empty parking lot. Throwing it in reverse, he narrowly missed running down the two men who'd been pursuing him on foot. *Maybe next time.*

Emal peeled out of the parking lot as they riddled his trailer with bullets. Heading down the highway, he heard sirens approaching from the other direction. He took a really deep breath and tried to calm himself.

An hour later, Emal pulled off onto a secluded side road to check the damage. There were eight small, neat holes in the back door. As his fear gave way to anger, he wondered how these men had found him, when the mighty Federal government had not. On a hunch, he inspected the underside of the tractor portion of his rig, where he found a small black plastic box attached magnetically to the frame near the passenger side door. Now he knew for certain there was a turn-coat in the Society. Only by Allah's mercy had he survived this one.

Despite their best efforts, Joel and Serena were unable to find out what had happened to Soozie. After the crackdown on the black market a few months earlier, someone created an Undernet wiki site where people posted names of the disappeared, which others would cross-reference with possible sightings. No mention of Soozie, by her alias or her real name, Susan Sherupsky. Nor did any mutual friends know why she'd been arrested. Possibly one of her controversial theatrical works had drawn the ire of someone in Homeland Security.

Over Joel's objections, he and Serena ended up in California. If politics made strange bedfellows, a good bedfellow could also compromise one's politics. *Look at the bright side,* Joel told himself. To a journalist, even an amateur like himself, it was a rare opportunity. Now he could see first-hand whether California had the *cojones* to break free, even after Texas had chickened out.

Serena lived in the here and now, oblivious to such weighty issues. She soon overcame her romantic notions of life as a fugitive. Both of them adopted new identities. That was still an expensive proposition, but the existence of the Undernet made it much more convenient. All of Joel's accumulated e-Barter credits, plus his Smart Car and several of Serena's paintings served as payment in that deal.

The first meltdown occurred a few days later when Serena realized the ramifications of their situation. "You mean I can't see my kids, or my granddaughter ever again? That's horrible!" Her loud sobs earned her a grimace rather than sympathy from Joel. "How do you stand it? Being cut off from your family?"

"In a word, it sucks. I've never even met my only grandson. I keep telling myself it's temporary, someday the nightmare will be over."

Serena's response was a poisonous glare.

"No, I'm not including you in that. Without your love and support I'd be a basket case."

Despite her occasional tearful episodes, Serena could be strong when she needed to be. She was good at finding humor in misfortune, the silver lining in every cloud. The new identities excited her, like a girl in her first school play. The new names were Ed and Beverly Zigurdregy. It amused Serena that they were now married. "If I have to divorce you, I'll get half your stuff."

Joel chuckled. "Put those ideas out of your head, *Bev*. I know how much you made on your last couple paintings, and I'll get half your profits."

After the move to California, Joel didn't even try to restart his tax business. Instead, he focused on another of his skills. Most small businesses used financial software of one form or another, and Joel had experience with all the major packages. He became a sort of computer consultant, despite his claims that he was "not technical."

Meanwhile, the Seventh Stooge blog and pod-cast had become far more successful than he ever expected. As with everything else, the eighty-twenty rule applied. He put a vast amount of work into it and received a pittance, mostly e-Barter points given as donations. It wasn't money, but you could use it to get stuff, even food, if you avoided grocery stores and went to farmers' markets.

The blog was great fun, but it became more difficult as time went by. Joel felt compelled to broaden his subject matter beyond simply making fun of the government. There were other people, issues and movements that desperately needed lampooning. Sometimes he wrote on trivial matters such as the latest hit movie, but he always returned to the Resistance movement.

People spoke of the Resistance in hushed tones, either with hatred or admiration, but Joel found the whole thing ridiculous. They all took themselves too seriously. Even the Butler Brigade, though Joel had once met its leader, MacGuiness, and he seemed sincere. Most of the other groups had far less integrity.

Joel hoped his readers wouldn't think he had any fondness for the government. Still, he wanted to be at least somewhat impartial, or his reputation as an irreverent goof ball would be shot. Considering Joel's cynical, typically Jewish sense of humor, an endorsement of any group would seem phony. He wanted people to think for themselves, not follow.

Anyone who spends time on the Internet will eventually learn these great truths: (a) pornography is the driving force of all technological progress, and (b) all human knowledge can be expressed in list form. Because no one in their right minds would want to see my naked keester, I've continued with the latter theme by making yet another list.

The new list builds on the brilliance of the previous two: 'Federal agents Classified by Smell,' and 'The Ten Kinds of Snitches.' This week's topic is rebel groups, who they are and what they'd like to do to, oops, I mean for us. Consider it a scorecard of all those wise guys with the *chutzpah* to stick it to the Feds.

10. Free Speech Alliance. Technically I shouldn't include these fellas because they've got more foreigners than Americans. No hankering for power, just unlimited network bandwidth. The biggest gathering of nerds since Comic Con.

9. La Solidaridad. A lefty-pinko Chicano rights group left over from the 1960's. Worst thing to happen to them was the new Latino majority and all those Spanish-speaking Republicans. Love the catering at their rallies, though, even if the tamales give me heartburn.

8. New Africa Resistance. They want to split off five states exclusively for people of darker color. Sounds like segregation to me;s Lester Maddox would have been proud. Let's give 'em Jersey.

7. Deseret Militia. The Mormons are restless, who'da thunk it? Maybe because Wilton supports gay marriage. The Prez is right, let them marry. Why should just us straights suffer?

6. Pledge Keepers. Not the manly Jesus club, but a bunch of cops and soldiers who promise not to violate the Constitution. They're pretty tame, but they scare the Establishment silly.

5. Native American Movement. I've been rooting for the Red Man even since I saw the movie 'Dances with Coyotes.' Besides, Joseph Smith says we're cousins. Down with White Eyes!

4. Texas Patriots. These guys believe Texas should be a separate country. Now there's an idea that's about 180 years overdue.

3. Islamic Aid Society. Nothing about STD's. The scapegoats of 9/11, those intrepid followers of the Prophet Mo, have created their own militia.

Can't say I blame them. They say they're non-sectarian but let's keep an eye on 'em. I enjoy bacon way too much to risk Sharia law.

2. Raptor Group. Holy flashback, Batman! Remember the Militia Movement of the late Twentieth? They're back and badder than ever. The Group is several regional militias joined together, headed by a schlub named John Tole. His group is almost as lily white as in the old days, except they let Asians in now. Which is good, in case they need any math problems solved.

1. Smedley Butler Brigade: Why would anyone name their kid Smedley? He was a bona fide historical war hero who got all disenchanted and cynical. "War is a racket," he said, who can argue? The real schnook behind the Brigade is a modern-day war hero, "Mac" MacGuiness. He's done right by his fellow vets, and his group is popular with folks of color (my favorite is purple, by the way.) How would he govern the country, given the chance? Hopefully to a reggae beat.

Then again, what do I know? I'm only a Stooge.

It's not exactly a knee slapper, Joel mused. *But it helps to have a good catch-phrase.*

Chapter 13 – Extraordinary Renditions

As a child, Jon Larsen had expected he'd always live in the country. The urban jungle he'd seen on TV seemed like another planet. Yet here he was in East Saint Louis, in a tenement that was currently the headquarters of the Butler Brigade. As a blond red-bearded Swede, he felt painfully out of place. But it was a hell of a lot better than the Camp.

Despite their squalid surroundings, the Brigade possessed all the latest technology. MacGuiness recognized Larsen's talent and made him network admin of the entire organization, which was formerly DeLane's responsibility. Larsen was reluctant to take the job away from the Commander's son. "You're welcome to it. " DeLane told him. "I hate that Mickey Mouse shit."

Larsen had never done admin work professionally, but it didn't take him long to come up to speed. He'd spent many hours messing with computers during the long North Dakota winters. Plus he'd done various jobs for friends and family: data recovery, virus removal, and network troubleshooting, all free of charge.

His work here at HQ was not particularly challenging, there was just a lot to do. The first thing Larsen tackled was a complete overhaul of the group's network security. The Brigade was no longer a radicalized community outreach group. Since they'd defied the government's order to disband and taken up arms, the stakes were now much higher. Larsen was amazed they'd made it this far without revealing their personnel and movements to the enemy.

Despite the long hours and the urgency of the tasks, Larsen hadn't felt much stress, until today. Mac's new mission was to find common ground with all the other rebel groups, and somehow organize the Resistance. He wanted a summit meeting of the various leaders, but with the Feds cracking down on travel and public gatherings, it was dangerous to meet physically. A virtual meeting seemed less risky, considering the recent advances in Undernet technology. It was Larsen's task to ensure that all their equipment worked, and everything was secure.

In principle, that should have been simple, because all the groundwork had been provided by the existence of Griffin servers and the Undernet. Though in practice there were a million things that could go wrong. Larsen had spent the preceding two days checking and re-checking, looking for any hardware or software that might have been compromised. The morning of that day he was still at it, testing the vicinity of the telephone closet with a radio frequency monitor. Beads of sweat rolled down Larsen's forehead as he ran diagnostics on the server. Mac had taken his lectures on security to heart, and refused to let him access it via Wi-Fi, which meant he had to use the hard-wired terminal in this hot, cramped space.

"Yo, JL!" Mac's booming voice caused him to bang his head on a junction box. "How's my tech genius doing? We going to be ready in time for the conference?"

Larsen nodded and rubbed the sore spot on his head. "Hopefully. Original installation was a total shit job." For a moment he panicked. Was he dissing DeLane's handiwork?

Mac laughed. "What did you expect? Government housing project. My people don't expect to get high-end service. But I have faith you can do it, JL!"

"Glad to hear it. We're just about ready. Have you done a virtual meeting before?"

"Of course. In Afghanistan we did them all the time; it was a lot safer than venturing out into Injun Country, as we called it."

"Well... this is probably a lot different. We're using a virtual reality system, because it lets us mask details like locations and people's faces in case the connection is compromised– not that I'm expecting that. You should try it out; don't want to be fumbling around in the conference."

He helped the Commander strap on the VR goggles, then handed him the ear buds. "Damn!" Mac complained. "It's black as the inside of a cat's ass."

"I wouldn't admit you know what that's like." Larsen laughed nervously. Mac didn't respond; maybe he hadn't heard under all that gear.

"Here we go." Larsen flicked the switch.

"Holy shit!" Mac exclaimed. "This is better than magic mushrooms! Not that I'd know anything about that, either." His grin was visible below the visor.

Larsen looked up from his monitor and saw DeLane standing in the doorway watching quietly. "Perfect timing, Lieutenant. We're running tests on the VR hardware. The conference will start in..." he glanced at his watch, "holy crap, just twenty minutes."

"I've got the data gloves," DeLane said, holding them up.

"Good." He held out goggles and ear buds. "Put these on and sit down. I'll join you in a sec." Mac was groping around like a blind man, so Larsen flipped a switch to turn on the local camera, then spoke into the mike. "Commander, find a seat before you trip over something."

Larsen felt a sense of deja vu as he put on the headset. He'd done this countless times gaming. He blinked as a new, bright world appeared before him. His desk morphed into a large round conference table. To his right sat Mac and DeLane, appearing as they did in real life. To his left and also across the table sat four people he hadn't met before. In this particular interface, if you looked at someone and blinked three times, and it showed you all their relevant stats, in this case, name or handle, organization and public key certificate.

Beside him on his left sat Mary Standing Bear of the Native American Movement, on the FBI's most-wanted list for seven years. On the other side of her was Ahmed 'X' (no last name given) of the Islamic Aid Society, a volunteer organization which the Feds had banned five years before. Then Captain Roe (another alias) of the Pledge Keepers, an organization of cops and military, both active duty and part time, who'd sworn to support the Constitution, refusing any illegal orders from superiors. As Roe was officially 'not here,' his image was an avatar, a character from the VR game Minutemen 1776.

'General' John Tole sat across the table and a bit to the right. Larsen had never met the guy, but he'd heard plenty about him from Brigade members, most of it derogatory. Tole didn't bother to hide his face; it was posted prominently on the FBI website. The man's body looked buff, which was surprising, since Mac liked to call him 'that fat poser.' Larsen chuckled when he realized that Tole's 'body' was a rendering from the Desert Warfare video game.

The people on both sides of Tole had blanked-out names on their status displays, but Mac had briefed Larsen about them. The woman with flame red hair and a sour expression was from the Texas Patriots; supposedly a close friend of the Governor, though he vehemently denied any involvement with the Resistance. The other was a balding man in a white shirt and tie, from the Deseret Militia. Each had a digital 'mask' obscuring their upper faces.

"Mr. MacGuiness, good to see you again," Tole said with unctuous courtesy. "I see you've altered your appearance since last we met. I must say it's an improvement."

"Thank you." Mac now had dreads and a beard, which made him look like Burning Spear, the reggae singer. "I trust you've been *busy* in the meantime." No doubt Tole knew what Mac was implying. There had recently been kidnappings of three Federal judges, and the bombing of an IRS data center in Atlanta that killed two and injured seven. Nobody had taken credit for these acts, but the media was happy to blame the Brigade. Mac's denials went unpublished.

Tole grimaced; he was about to reply when Captain Roe interrupted. "I suggest we skip the social niceties and get to business. One thing, though, I don't know if it's a malfunction, but I'm not seeing any stats for the fearsome warrior on my right."

In real life, Larsen's cheeks burned. The VR software he was using was from his on-line gaming days. Thank God he'd archived his best programs and schematics in that offshore backup in the Caymans. This program altered his image to give him the swarthy skin, dark hair, and ridged forehead of a Klingon. He'd forgotten to turn off this feature, yet it was appropriate, since it obscured his identity. It was unnecessary, though; like Tole and MacGuiness, his face was also on the FBI website.

MacGuiness laughed. "My IT guy. Please excuse his appearance, he got exposed to toxic waste and mutated." The other conferees laughed, except Tole, who gave a patronizing smile.

"*tlhIngan maH!*" Larsen cried, raising his fist in greeting. The software translated his grin as a grimace. "Forgive my oversight; I forgot to add my security certificate." The data magically appeared in a box in front of him. "We're using gaming software on this end, which is the reason for my unusual appearance."

"Which some folks would consider an improvement," Mac added.

Tole joined in the laughter this time. "Now," he began in a haughty voice, "Shall we get down to business, gentlemen and ladies? The first issue is..."

"Excuse me, sir," said Mac, "I move we choose a chair democratically. I nominate the distinguished lady sitting to my left." A brief glimmer of a smile crossed Standing Bear's face.

"Second!" DeLane added quickly.

Roe moved the question; it was 6 to 3. Tole scowled and surrendered his virtual gavel.

"Alright, um, everyone," Though Standing Bear was clearly unaccustomed to public speaking, she surprised Larsen by taking charge immediately. "Now, the agenda. As you know, everybody sent a list of concerns. I will select the first item from each list in no particular order."

"Objection," said Tole. "The chair has no authority to arbitrarily set the agenda."

"Madame chair?" Mac interjected. "I move we accept the chair's recommendations as to agenda." Despite Tole's silent grimace, the motion was seconded and carried, again 6 to 3.

"Our first item is immediate threats. This was not my own group's submission but it's also a big concern for the NAM. Were the 9/11 bomb rumors for real? Are we in danger of some other false flag operation? Opinions, anyone?"

"Of course the threat was real," Ahmed snapped. "It was our group that discovered the plot, and it was we who stopped it by revealing it to the public."

"With all due respect, Mr. X," said the Deseret guy (whose name, Larsen recalled, was either Smith or Schmidt), "we've heard that the IAS opposed the release of this information, and that one of your members blew the whistle regardless."

"It doesn't matter," said MacGuiness, "because in the end the story *was* leaked. We at the Brigade believe the threat was real, and that the high-profile arrests of members of the Albanian Mob was how Wilton covered her tracks. As for any continuing threat, I wouldn't expect the Feds to try that same angle. It would be something else next time."

"Unless that's what they want us to think," said Roe with a smirk on his virtual face. "I move we table this issue until someone comes forward with concrete evidence one way or the other." The motion passed, this time unanimously.

"Next item is strategy," Mary looked at her virtual notes and read, "Resolved, we should combine forces to move against the unconstitutional and despotic Wilton Administration. In light of recent attempts to lock down the Internet, we should move within the next thirty days, while we can still communicate securely."

Larsen watched Tole as Standing Bear spoke. From the man's smirk it was evident this was his submission.

"There's no way!" The speaker was Carlos of *La Solidaridad*, a Latino group that Mac had invited to join the alliance, over the objections of the more conservative participants. "We're not ready! The Feds would slaughter us and the media would pretend like it didn't happen."

"You're wrong!" Tole exclaimed. "If we wait, we're dead for certain. If we fight now, at least we have a chance." He looked at the red-headed Texan who had supported him so far.

"I'd first have to consult with my constituency," the woman said. "There's a very real chance that Congress will pass the ammunition ban proposed by Homeland Security. That would be extremely unpopular in Texas, which may cause our secession proposal to succeed. At the present time we abstain."

"For once I agree with the man," said Delbert Geary of New Africa Resistance, another of the radical groups that Tole's right wingers despised. "I move we form an action committee to organize a direct assault on Washington and other centers of Federal power before the end of the year. With all their pathetic security measures, they won't be expecting us."

Tole seconded it, though his expression looked like he'd been sucking a lemon.

"Let's discuss this. Carlos is right," Mac said. "There is no way we can be ready by that time. Which is not to deny the urgency of our situation. You've heard the rumors that several active guard units are considering changing sides. We need more time to make that happen."

Tole jumped to his feet and pounded a fist on the virtual table. "That is just plain foot-dragging cowardice. Someone has to make the first move, to encourage others to do the same. If we as a group don't agree to act, some of us will take manners into our own hands."

"And they'd be fools!" DeLane said suddenly. Everyone stared; since the start of the meeting, he hadn't said two words. "It's braver to wait for the right time, not go off half-cocked!"

It was difficult for Larsen to restrain himself; he wanted to jump up and applaud. Though he knew such a display would only antagonize the others.

Tole showed his crocodile smile. "Esteemed colleagues, it will only take one more incident to make the enemy shut down the Internet entirely. Sure it'll wreck the economy but they'll claim an 'emergency.' Then they'll destroy us all, one by one. Better to go out fighting!"

"At what cost?" asked Roe. "Our actions determine the character of the Rebellion. We don't want to replace the current government with something worse. We need strict rules of engagement so civilians aren't harmed. Violence must only be used in self-defense."

"I object to your simplistic views," Ahmed interrupted. "There are certainly situations that merit retaliation for crimes against people and property. Currently the government is too busy trying to put down the rebellion to protect its citizens from criminal exploitation."

"Can everyone please stop talking all at once?" Standing Bear's outburst caused everyone to fall silent. "If we can't stay on topic I'm going to enforce strict rules of order. The discussion has gone beyond the scope of this meeting. If we need to define rules of engagement, we can assign a committee. Right now we have more important issues."

"I concur," said the elder MacGuiness. "As for the timing of any collective action against the regime in Washington, we need better intelligence. The sky is filled with drones and attack helicopters. We don't dare move until we have a plan to neutralize these threats."

"Hypocrite!" roared Tole. "You and your people took attacked three major FEMA camps and released a whole bunch of Federal detainees, and the rest of us are supposed to sit on our hands. I'm out of here!" Without a sound, his image disappeared from the conference table, followed shortly by the representatives from Texas, Deseret, and New Africa.

"Well, that was a fiasco," Larsen said. "So much for unity. The resistance movement seems to be going the way of the country."

"Not at all," Mac argued. "If those of us remaining can come to an understanding, we'll have accomplished quite a bit."

After that, the meeting was civil; they were able to discuss, though not resolve, the remaining agenda items. Larsen would probably have nodded off, if not for his lingering anger at the Raptor leader. When he finally pulled of the VR helmet, he was seriously in need of a drink.

"You were right about Tole," he said to Mac as he held out his glass for a refill. "I was trying to keep an open mind, but the guy is a real asshole."

Mac poured him a generous shot of whiskey. "Just like M-O-M." Seeing Larsen's quizzical look, he added, "Militia of Missouri, Tole's original group. Bunch of poseurs and weekend warriors. Too radical for the Tea Parties, too inexperienced to be a *real* militia."

"I first met him at a Free Acadia rally in Louisiana," DeLane said. "The guy couldn't tell a .38 from a 9 mil. He worked at a bank for 15 years, played a few war games in the woods and decided to become a revolutionary." He laughed. "He tried to speak French to the Cajuns; didn't know the local dialect at all."

"Biggest problem I have with the Raptors," Mac said, "which is actually like nine or ten local groups joined together, is their tactics. They're like the 1960's Weather Underground; bank robberies, fire bombings. Tole keeps out of the messy details, but doesn't actually discourage any of the violent shit. It's an old CIA tactic, get it done, don't tell us how. Plausible deniability."

"What about these Pledge Keepers? I never heard much about them before I got this gig."

Mac finished his drink and refilled it, emptying the bottle in the process. "Those guys actually have principles. That's why the group was founded; they were tired of being used to violate the Constitution."

"You think they have much support among the rank and file police?"

"We don't know for sure," DeLane said. "I haven't heard many cases of cops refusing to arrest protesters, or insisting on their suspects' habeas rights."

"Well," Larsen said, "I never thought I'd hear myself say this, but I have a lot of respect for the IAS. The Muslims have had a real bum rap. Don't get me wrong, though," his eyes flashed from father to son and back, "I still don't trust 'em."

Mac let out a mighty guffaw. "Suspect everyone, that's my motto. We'll cross that bridge later. What pisses me off is we didn't get to the big issue, which is the Guard."

"What's the problem? The Vermonters refuse to go to Nigeria, and volunteer to join the Resistance, that's awesome!"

"Yes, but if we need to make sure they join *our* alliance, not Tole's. We're vets, they're military, we've got to have a unified command structure."

"Meaning you, right?" DeLane grinned. He took a swig of his drink, grimaced, and topped it off with Coke.

"Whoever. All I can say is we gotta keep a close eye on Tole and the Raptors. They could be big trouble, maybe worse than the Feds."

Larsen raised his drink for a toast. "To the Brigade! We'll show 'em who's boss!" As he drained the glass, he was already wondering if the rogue guard units would take orders from Mac. The man was as controversial as he was charismatic. As for Tole, he wasn't as ignorant as he'd originally seemed. He could give Mac a run for his money.

The rain started just as Joel pulled up to the gas pump. Getting out of the car, he was pelted with big fat raindrops. *Waiting for me, weren't you?* Though he had no reason to *kvetch*. The weather had been perfect earlier, on the two half mile treks between his car and Mrs. Johnson's craft store. He could've driven right up to her door, but all the government surveillance made him paranoid. His feet were getting blisters on the corns on the bunions, but at least he wasn't sitting on his tuchis all day.

I'm reaping the whirlwind, he chuckled to himself. Who knew that by running from the Feds, he'd bring together the people who could pull down the temple, metaphorically speaking? The work of Nephi, Siri and JL had strengthened the black market and undermined the demand for tax accountants. The continuing recession wasn't helping the situation, either.

A man had to support himself, though. Joel's day job had gone away, and writing anonymous political diatribes wouldn't put food on the table. If only 'the wife' could sell a few paintings– but she was a fugitive, too.

Necessity, though not always the mother of invention, was definitely a mother of some sort. Joel had fallen into his new vocation accidentally. In his time as Sam Steinberg, tinkering with computers, messing with Griffin and the e-Barter app (brilliant stuff, though sometimes a bit quirky) some tech knowledge had rubbed off on him. He'd turned geek without realizing it.

Now he got paid to fix people's computers. Nothing too difficult, but he could remove viruses and reinstall Windows, cheaply and no questions asked.

He didn't have any of the licenses California required. The talk of independence hadn't lessened the state's greed, so he couldn't advertise or maintain a store front. He found clients by word-of-mouth, and always made house calls.

Another plus on Joel's ledger was the fact that he'd finished work early today. He had time to stop by Serena's class, an opportunity to atone for his sins. When she'd first mentioned her idea about teaching art at the community college, he'd gotten furious. "Why don't you just take out an ad in the *Sacramento Bee*, and publish our real identities?"

She'd started to cry. "How can I stop being myself? I feel like I'm already in jail!"

Joel withdrew his objections, and she'd taken the gig, Tuesday and Thursday afternoons. Adult classes, so there weren't the invasive background checks the authorities demanded every time someone got within fondling distance of a minor. Joel had to admit Serena was much easier to live with, now that she was reunited with her first love, a guy named Art.

Tonight he planned to stop by the college, meet Serena at her class, and take her to dinner. He looked at his watch– half an hour to spare. Time to replenish his cigar supply. That was getting more difficult; you couldn't buy tobacco in grocery stores anymore. Thankfully, convenience stores were still exempt from that nanny state foolishness.

He found a parking spot and walked a half block to the Quickie-Go Mart. There was a paunchy bald-headed white guy behind the corner. *For this kind of place, it should count as a minority-run business,* he mused. A huge poster advertised specials on soda. He decided he could afford the calories today, so he filled a bucket with Dr. Pepper and strolled to the counter. "I'll take a pack of Antonio Y Cleopatra's, the long ones."

"That'll be fifty-five bucks, plus five for the drink."

Like Weimar Germany, tomorrow maybe they'll be sixty. Joel checked his wallet; to his dismay, he realized Mrs. Johnson had paid him in hundreds. Retailers hated them, but with prices so high, the Quickie-Go could hardly object.

The clerk grabbed the bill and held it up to the light. He daubed it with a special marker. Still frowning, he inserted it into a slot next to the cash register. A red light flashed.

"Sorry sir, it's counterfeit. I'll need your photo and fingerprints."

"No way! I'm the one who got cheated. I'm out a hundred bucks!"

The clerk scowled. "It's the law, sir. If you're clean, you got nothing to worry about. You want to catch the people who do this, don't you?"

"Not if it means being treated me like a criminal." Joel turned; he heard the front door lock electronically.

"Turn around, sir. If I don't get your picture, I'm calling the cops."

Without thinking, Joel looked back, was blinded by a flash. *Oh shit, if that new biometric crap is for real... can they match my face, even with my beard, my dyed hair, my nose job?* His fear turned to anger. "This is unlawful detention! I demand you release me!"

Looking at the computer terminal, a broad grin formed on the clerk's face. "That's not gonna happen, Mr. Walter! Nothing personal, but there's a 500 K reward; though surely you know that. That's several months' rent, even with the dollar as worthless as it is..."

Joel reached into his pocket. "I have a gun!"

"No you don't; I've got a metal detector in the doorway." The clerk produced a shiny object from the pocket of his smock. "You familiar with the new Air Taser? I can hit you with 50 thousand volts from across the store."

Without thinking, Joel popped the lid off the drink and tossed it in the man's face, just as the guy was raising the weapon. Time seemed to pause as the clerk, not expecting the liquid attack, failed to stop himself from squeezing the trigger. There was a loud ZAP and the man fell to the floor, twitching.

Joel remembered that the new wireless Tasers worked by emitting a stream of particles to ionize the air. His improvised attack had short-circuited it. For a panicky moment he thought the guy was dead. But the man's fingers released their grip and it shut off; he lay there, gasping.

Gotta get outta here. Joel hopped over the half-door next to the counter and searched for the door button, studiously avoiding stepping in the brown puddle. There it was! The door gave a satisfying click. Pausing to grab a few packs of smokes, Joel ran for the door, discovering that though the lock had been disabled, the alarm hadn't.

As the siren screeched, he dashed down the street, hopped in his car, and drove away unmolested. *Nobody expects a Jewish guy who's pushing sixty to rob the corner store.* He drove through unknown streets until he reached a small park, where he stopped under a tree, heart pounding. *Get a grip, they don't know my current name, address, or job. But they do know what I look like now.* He texted Serena: **Sorry babe sprained ankle pls get home ASAP.**

An hour later, he heard the front door open. He stood behind the bathroom door and held his breath until he heard the familiar voice. "Joel, what happened?" By the loudness of her voice, he could tell she was on the verge of panic. "Are the Feds coming to get us or did you really hurt your ankle?" She saw him and let out a shriek. "Oh, it's you!"

"Sorry, didn't mean to startle you. Yes, it was our secret code phrase, not a real sprain. Somebody ID'ed me, so I figured I better change my looks, *schnell.*"

"Somebody recognized you? You don't look anything like your FBI picture now."

"It was one of those networked government cameras. They measure things you can't change, like the spacing between the eyes."

She looked puzzled. "There are cameras everywhere. They never recognized you before."

He shrugged. "I went to buy smokes, accidentally gave the guy a counterfeit hundred. Got it from one of my clients, little old lady, totally clueless. When they get a bad bill they're supposed to take your photograph. Computer sent my picture to the FBI. Guy tried to tase me so he could get the reward, but I got him with a Big Gulp."

"Christ, Baby, that's awful! Thank God they don't know your new name." She sat on the arm of his easy chair and gave him a kiss. "I worry about you so much. You sure you're OK?"

"I'm fine! I've been through worse stuff than a scuffle with a dickhead store clerk."

She kissed him again, this time nibbling his ear a bit. "Well, if you need stress relief, I'm available." Suddenly she brightened. "Oh, I was gonna tell you before you startled me, one of my students won the California On-line Art Challenge. I'm so proud of her!" She shifted herself onto Joel's lap and ran her fingers over his bald scalp. "This is gonna take a little getting used to. Guess I'll pretend I'm balling Kojack." She kissed him on the head. "It'll all be OK."

"No, it won't! Don't get up, I'm not mad at you. The FBI will send out a bulletin saying I've been sighted in the Bay Area. Landlord knows what I look like, what if she turns me in? At the very least, we've got to move."

"God damn it, Sam– Joel– Ed– whatever your name is now!" She jumped off his lap. "I'm fed up to my eyeballs with running! I'm sick to death of it! I can't sell my paintings, can't have any friends..."

"I never said you can't have friends, as long as you're discreet! And I wish you *could* sell your art, but if they catch us, we're liable to end up in the Gulag. No big whoop for me, but I can't stand the thought of you in prison."

"I can't take it anymore!" she wailed. "You've done enough, you don't have to save the world all by yourself! We could be happy together, I know we could. Tell you what, you give up this political stuff and let's skip the country while our phony passports are still good. I hear Costa Rica's nice. We should be safe there. Let the people save themselves; nobody drafted us to save America. I'll be happy as long as I can have my art, even just to teach."

Joel slumped off the chair to the floor, put his head in his hands. "All this time I said I'd do that soon as I saved up the credits, but now that I can almost afford it, I don't know anymore. I threw my lot in with the Resistance, I just don't know if I can let go." He exhaled loudly.

"And I don't know if I'm that strong! I need time to sort this out." She disappeared into the bedroom and slammed the door.

She was sobbing in there. He tried the door– locked! "Come on, Bev, er Serena, open up, let's talk!" No answer. So he went to his office, turned on the air cleaner, and lit one of his ill-gotten stogies. *The guy owed me that much, for trying to rat me out. Why is everything always so damned difficult? I'd be safer on my own, but Lord help me, I love that crazy shiksa.*

For lack of anything better to do, he worked on his blog a while. The Stooge hadn't posted for days. He had a hundred emails from people worrying he'd been 'disappeared.' After an hour he'd written a rant about video surveillance. *It's probably a bad idea for me to publish this, but what the hell.* It was quite late, and Serena still hadn't emerged from the bedroom. There was nothing to eat in the fridge, so he drank a beer, then crashed out on the couch.

When he awoke everything was dead quiet. Serena had covered him with an afghan. He eased open the bedroom door and gazed at her in the pale illumination from the streetlight in the window. Had she decided he was worth keeping, despite the cost? How he wished he could crawl into bed with her, pretend nothing had happened.

He knew what he had to do: disappear from yet another loved one's life. Once again he regretted having broken off contact with Esther when they'd fled Florida. *Does she hate me? I'd love to talk with her now, but it's just too dangerous.* No doubt the Feds were watching her.

He looked at Serena again. It was breaking his heart, but she'd be safer without him. He wrote a note; it was a pretty poor expression of what was feeling. "You're a wonderful woman. These last few months have been some of the happiest in my life. But I can't give up the fight, and I can't continue putting you in danger." He stared at the paper for a few minutes, then ended with, "Stay out of trouble. Yours forever, Joel."

Holy cow. Nephi took the last bite of his steak sandwich and pushed himself away from the table. As much as Nephi loved the outdoor life, it was great to be back in civilization, with microwave ovens, running water, and flush toilets.

Today, Will had gone down easily for his nap for a change. It gave Nephi time for a rare, leisurely lunch. He wished the meat could have been cooked over charcoal, but Siri forbade it. Not because of her reversion to vegetarianism; rather, barbecuing steaks would blow their cover. He and Siri were posing (with lots of makeup, in Nephi's case) as Indian immigrants.

It was a good time to check his email, yet another luxury he'd missed. The cabin's satellite reception was intermittent at best. Downloading was bad enough, but sending anything out was excruciatingly slow. Their real reason for leaving the mountains, however, was Will's persistent colic. Both parents agreed, modern medical care was worth the risk of returning to the city.

Nephi typed in today's pass-phrase and waited for the system to establish an untraceable path to a secure message server located in some foreign country. The clock icon stayed on-screen, its tiny hands spinning round the dial. Why was it taking so long?

Often the authorities in other countries would succumb to US pressure and shut down any Undernet servers they found, reducing the number of available connections. So Nephi typed in the address of the e-Barter support page, the most reliable on the Undernet, then went to the kitchen for a dish of ice cream. When he returned, the browser said: '404 Error Page Not Found.'

A few more tries produced the same result. Nephi scratched his head. There had to be something wrong with the connection. To double check, he started up Foxbat, a popular pre-Undernet browser. The animated fruit bat icon flapped furiously but never got out of its cave.

Now it said, "Unable to connect to Network." *Oh, shucks!* He'd hoped to get some stuff done while Will was asleep. Now he'd have to break out the network analyzer. By the time he got it fixed, the little guy would be ready to play. So went the life of a stay-at-home dad.

This, too, proved to be frustrating. He'd expected that either the modem or the router was malfunctioning, but everything checked out fine. To top it off, there was a wail from the next room. How long had the baby been crying? Nephi peeked through the door. The poor kid was kicking at the bars of the crib like a miniature kangaroo.

"Hey, why so much noise?" He picked up the baby and sighed. How could somebody you loved so much drive you crazy? "Ssh, ssh", he cooed, rocking gently. "Good gosh, now I know why you're up. Pee-yew!"

Nephi was no stranger to diaper changing. As a kid, he'd helped out with his youngest two siblings. He had the dirty diaper off and the new one installed in under a minute, without getting sprayed. "You're wide awake now, aren't you little buddy? Guess it's play time."

He placed Will in the middle of the living room rug, and dumped the box of colored blocks. Will ignored them, and crawled toward the easy chair, where he saw his favorite toy, a white stuffed rabbit. He leaned on the chair sleepily, chewing the bunny's ear.

Feeling restless and frustrated, Nephi switched on the TV and sat on the floor next to his son. He was surprised to see President Wilton, in the middle of an unscheduled broadcast.

"The Internet, which has become an essential part of our lives, is also our latest peril. The illegal use of anonymous communication endangers us all. This vile technology enables hate speech, child pornography, and terrorism. Therefore, we will institute a system of compulsory ID verification for all Internet users. We regret the inconvenience to law-abiding Americans."

Nephi grinned. He'd heard that fairy tale before. The European Union had instituted a similar rule ten years ago, and hackers widely bypassed it. Even in places like China, Russia, and Iran, the Undernet was becoming a household word. How the flip did Wilton think her administration could succeed where more oppressive regimes had failed?

He was about to switch it off, when he heard the word 'biometric.' As the President described the plan, Nephi felt a lump in his stomach. "This tamper-proof device reads the print on the right index finger to authorize Internet access. These will be provided free of charge to each American fourteen years of age and older. To prevent any disruption of Internet commerce, we will allow unverified access to trusted sites such as schools, banks, government agencies and major corporations for the next 30 days. For that same period, unverified users may still send email, but only without encryption or attachments, through the Postal Service's free portal."

Maybe there's a silver lining here. How would people react to the loss of their Twitter, Facebook, and on-line gaming accounts? Nephi imagined crowds with torches and baseball bats converging on the White House.

The President continued, "Since most adult Americans already have their prints in the FBI database, due to military service and occupational licensing, this will be no more than a temporary inconvenience for most citizens. For those not yet registered, we have set up fingerprinting stations at Post Offices across the country."

"Yeah, what about cell phones?" Nephi wasn't normally one to talk back to the television. Hearing the anger in his father's voice, little Will looked up from his bunny rabbit in alarm.

As if she'd heard him, Wilton explained, "Internet phones and other mobile devices provide a special challenge. For this reason the Verifier, as the device is called, supports wireless protocols such as Blue and Purple Tooth with the installation of an optional watch battery. In the meantime, we are working to make retinal analysis more reliable, so mobile users can be freed from this inconvenience."

Nephi's heart pounded in his chest. The measure was drastic, even for Wilton. They'd tried to eliminate Griffin and e-Barter before, by shutting down servers and arresting developers. This time they just might lock them out completely. He picked up his cell, but hesitated, wondering if the DHS had somehow found a way to circumvent his built-in bug scanner. *No matter.* He clicked the contact from the top of his list; a familiar voice answered.

"Ameritech Data Security, Samaria speaking."

It jarred him to hear Siri say that, though they'd been using these identities for months. "Hello, Love. We have a situation."

"What?" Her voice sounded panicky. "Is little Benir all right?"

"He's got a major case of the poops. And I'm feeling pretty ill myself."

"Oh!" The relief in her voice was obvious. "Nothing a visit to the doctor can't fix. Hold on, dear. Love you." She hung up. The code phrase had been Siri's idea. Her employer had generous family leave policies, so a phony illness would provide a good cover.

When Siri arrived twenty minutes later, Nephi was feeding Will strained peas. "Hi, Honey," he said. "I think Billy Deep's got more food on him than in him."

She bent down so her face was level with Will's. "He's just as handsome when he's a mess." She pressed a finger to the end of his nose; the little boy giggled. She turned to her husband. "So what's the emergency? Is everyone OK?"

Nephi was incredulous. "You haven't heard?"

"You mean the Internet thing? That's your emergency? Nephi, we agreed you'd say 'sick' if there was a situation, and I should leave work early, if possible. The word 'ill' we reserved for emergencies. Clearly you've overreacted!"

Nephi moistened a cloth and wiped the baby's face, "But Honey, if they lock down the Internet, the Undernet is blocked. Millions of people will be left high and dry." He sighed. "I knew this was coming, but I didn't want to believe it would actually happen." He stood up, tossed the washcloth in the sink.

"And why is that our responsibility?" She picked up Will and rocked him in her arms, looking at the baby rather than Nephi. "People knew it was a risk when they started using barter to avoid taxes. It's not our fault the government pushed back!"

"That's true," said Nephi. "But the Undernet is more than barter, it's our source of intelligence. Without it, we're sitting ducks."

"But what can we do? We're fugitives. We don't dare draw attention to ourselves."

"Don't look at me. I'm not the math nerd who conquered the world's most advanced economy." He grinned at her reaction. "But you didn't do it alone, people all over the world helped implement it. Which is why we need to reach out to the hacker community for help."

"It's not the same thing," Siri said. "We built our system on top of the Internet, how can we communicate without it?"

"Well, there's always the telephone. Before the Internet, there was the BBS. They can't shut down the cell networks; almost nobody has a land line anymore."

"But they're certainly monitoring all phone traffic. How do we know we haven't already been compromised?"

"Risk is part of life." Nephi pulled his cell phone out of his pocket. "Good thing we have our own social network." He held the phone to his ear. "What in the world?"

"What's wrong?" Siri's voice cracked a bit.

"I can't dial out. It says 'No Service.'" Nephi stared in disbelief at the phone in his hand. "But I just called you half an hour ago."

"Let me try mine." She touched her iPhone and held it to her ear. "Same thing. Nephi, I'm worried." She rushed to the window and peered out. "This could mean we're about to be arrested. We should never have returned to the city!"

"Calm down, Dear, I doubt it's just us. Probably everybody's flipping out over the speech, tying up all the cells." He thought for a moment. "It's got to be worse here in the middle of the city. If I drive a few miles, I might get a connection." He opened a closet and grabbed his jacket.

"Wait! You're not leaving me with the baby while you go out and get yourself arrested! I did not agree to this, Nephi Snow."

"I'm sorry, but we have to do something. I'll head north to the suburbs; that's a wealthy area, good coverage. When I get a signal I'll stop and contact as many people as I can."

"What if the Feds shut down the whole network, like in Egypt during the Arab Summer? How do we maintain contact?"

"Snail mail and Captain Crunch decoder rings. Whatever it takes."

"It's *you* I'm worried about contacting. What if you're arrested? How will I know where you are, what's happened to you?"

"I'll be careful."

"Wait, Nephi, or I should say *Anil,*" Siri was obsessive about their new identities, "have you looked in the mirror?"

"What? Is it my hair? The spray tan?" He looked into the mirror by the entryway. "Oh, man!" He headed for the bathroom.

"A blue-eyed Indian is very suspicious," Siri said. "You should wear the contacts all the time."

"Sorry, Hon, my eyes get itchy, even with soft ones. There. Non-suspicious brown eyes."

He kissed Siri and Will, who giggled at his father's fuzzy mustache. "When I go back to my real self, our little guy won't know me."

Siri's right to be paranoid, Nephi realized as he started the car. Still, one of them had to do it, and he preferred to be the risk taker.

It was strange to be in Atlanta; Nephi had never lived east of the Rockies. He wasn't used to all the trees and the winding roads. Still, northern Georgia had its own beauty.

He took US 19 north, surprised that the traffic seemed so normal. Now and then he glanced at his phone, which he'd programmed to dial Siri's number once a minute. If it got through, he'd know the problem was over and return home. If he got the "not available" message, he'd know he'd made a connection. It occurred to him that even if that happened, there was no guarantee he'd reach anyone. The Europeans, perhaps, but there it was the middle of the night.

As he passed through the suburbs, the 'fast busy' tone went away and the phone began ringing. "We are sorry..." Nephi sighed in relief. One down in the long list of worries. He took the nearest exit, which happened to have a sign for the Big Trees hiking trail. *Perfect.*

Nephi parked in the nearly-empty lot, put his headset in his ear, and started walking. In this inter-connected age, no one would question a grown man talking to himself on a nature trail.

His first two tries were lucky ones. First he spoke to Janusz Zlotnick, the convicted system cracker whose parole barred him from using any electronic communications. He'd returned to his devious ways, thanks to the Undernet, and was distressed about the prospect of losing it. The second guy was Jeng Shen, the fallen security guru, busted a few years ago in a teen prostitution sting. As vile as Nephi found that vice, he felt sorry for the man. Jeng insisted he'd believed the girl was of age, and the FBI was notorious for using entrapment. Both men volunteered to help.

The next several tries were failures. "We are sorry..." Nephi wished he could punch the disembodied voice. Discouraged, he sat on a big rock beside the trail. He realized he was really thirsty, and he'd gone hiking without any water. *What a moron I've been.*

The thought made him think of Joel's 'Stooge' pod-casts. Nephi didn't care for his friend's vulgar sense of humor, but he enjoyed the impressions, particularly of Bugs Bunny. "What a maroon," he'd say, usually about some blowhard politician. Amazingly, the guy had become an Undernet celebrity; too bad it might be ending soon.

Nephi chastised himself for not trying Joel right away. True, the guy wasn't a techie, but he had connections. When he clicked Joel's entry, it rang immediately, numerous times. He was about to give up when he heard the voice. "Affordable PC Repair, Ed speaking."

"Hey *Ed.* I hope I'm not taking you away from a client, but we're trying to get some people together to tackle this Internet problem."

"You sure you have the right number?" It was Joel all right. "To whom am I speaking?"

"Brigham Young," he said, using the annoying alias Joel had assigned him. "Stop kidding around."

"BY, great to hear from you! I knew it was you, but you can't be too careful these days."

"How are things out west? Around here, they're overloading the cell towers. I'm amazed I got through."

"Well, Bev and I... no, never mind, not relevant. Things are a bit different here. The Governor went on TV right after Wilton. He issued a counter-order that the ISP's out here *may not* restrict access. There's a huge demonstration downtown in support of him and against Wilton. Social media, no doubt."

"And the National Guard isn't putting them down? Wilton threatened to call out all units."

"Not yet." There was the sound of an inhale and exhale. "*Oy*, I knew this was coming. There were lots of rumors. Haven't you read Slash-dot lately? The Chinese rolled out a similar system. It's got their black market in chaos; prices on the official economy have skyrocketed."

"You're reading Slash-dot? I'm impressed! Just a sec." He waited while a family of hikers passed by, then got up and walked behind them at a discreet distance.

"The way I see it, there are two challenges," Nephi said, breathing heavier as the trail sloped upward. "Our goal is to find a way to spoof the authentication device. But that may take a while. For the time being, we need to find a way to keep the Undernet going. Millions of people depend on it now. If they have to go to the government for help, the bad guys have won."

"True. Wouldn't it be cool to use the prints of the big wigs? President, senators, generals, Federal reserve bankers. Let them explain that to their cohorts at the next Bilderberg summit. Unfortunately, I'm not the engineer here. I'll spread the word, do whatever I can."

After they'd hung up, Nephi mulled over the ideas they'd discussed. The *real* goal would be to bypass the elite-controlled networks entirely, maybe put their own satellite into orbit. Until then, what? *God, please help us save America*, he prayed silently. Nephi believed that the Lord would provide, but He wasn't required to make the way easy for His servants.

Tired and discouraged, Nephi headed back toward the trailhead. A chime in his ear startled him; he glanced at his phone but didn't recognize the number. "Hello?"

"Hey, Neeph, it's JL!"

A grin spread over Nephi's face. "No way! I thought you were... where the heck are you?"

"Not in a FEMA camp, if that's what you're thinking. Thanks to a certain rebel leader who's been in the news a lot lately. Didn't you hear about the ruckus in northern New Mexico?"

"On the Undernet. Nothing on the MSM, of course. What're you doing now?"

"Since my liberation I've been working for the Mac and the Butler boys. They needed an IT guy pretty badly. Anyway, I heard you were asking around."

"What? Who told you?"

"When Wilton gave her 'Up yours, America' speech today, I called a mutual friend of ours. I should have contacted you guys a lot earlier, but, security protocol and all that BS. In the Brigade we've been working on this very problem. MacGuiness is a fanatic about free speech. We're proposing a joint effort with the hacker community."

"That's great! But what about the short term? What can we do without the Undernet?"

"It's simple. The Undernet runs on the Internet, and the government has the support of the companies that own the backbone. We just need to bypass it."

"Now I get to call *you* Captain Obvious. Easier said than done. There's packet radio, for example, but that's way too slow."

"That's the idea, sort of. We're the jellyfish, we don't need no stinking backbone. We'll use the cell network, hop from one phone to another, just like normal video calls, but with our data hidden in the noise bits."

"Smart phones as mobile data routers, very clever. But how could we possibly get enough volunteers?"

"We could pay them with e-Barter credits. Your lovely wife can work out the details."

Nephi stopped and scratched his chin. "Totally crazy, but it just might work. JL, I can't tell you how much I appreciate your call. Not just because we were worried about you, but because Siri and I were getting pretty frustrated."

"What, the eternal optimist getting discouraged? Inconceivable! Don't despair, I've been talking with Bjornsen in Norway and he's convinced the idea is feasible."

"OK, then. I've got to hurry to get back to the car, they'll be closing the park soon. I'll explain some other time."

With everything on his mind, Nephi found it hard to concentrate on his driving. Good thing the traffic was light. He fought the urge to speed. *Almost home now!* Five miles from his exit, he saw the red lights in his mirror. As he pulled over and the patrolman came up behind him, he prayed, *Lord please let me get through this*. It was all he could do to maintain calm.

The police car sat there for a few harrowing minutes; the cop was apparently talking to someone. Suddenly he put his lights back on, pulled around Nephi's vehicle, and zoomed on down the freeway. However it happened, his prayer had been answered.

Emotionally exhausted, Nephi pulled into his parking space and trudged up the stairs to their apartment. Siri almost tackled him at the door with a crushing hug. "Praise the Buddhas you're alright! I was so worried when I couldn't reach you."

"What a greeting! Is everything OK? Is there a problem with Will?"

"He's fine, sound asleep. No, I heard on the news there were riots downtown. Several people were shot, they claimed there were 'racist attacks on foreigners.' It's horrible to have to depend on the television. Who knows what you can believe?" She gave him a long kiss. "I guess we better go inside." She shut the door behind them. "How did it go? Did you reach anyone?"

"Yes, it was tough going at first, but at the very least, we'll go down fighting. Did Willy give you any trouble?"

"Not at all. I shouldn't have let him go down so early, he'll be up half the night. I guess he got bored. I was going over the old Griffin design docs, trying to find a workaround. Nothing yet, but we'll keep trying. Before I forget, your brother called on Griffin, voice only. I tried to take a message but he insisted he had to tell you in person. I guess he meant first person."

Nephi shook his head. "Sounds like Enoch. Anyway, like I said, it was really frustrating at first. I finally reached Joel, or Ed, or whatever his name is now. He was pretty encouraging. You'll never guess who else I talked to!" He paused as she stared at him expectantly. "JL! He escaped from detention and he's working for the Butler Brigade!"

"Butler Brigade!" She wrinkled her nose. "I'm glad he's free, but I don't trust that MacGuiness guy. Sometimes I think he wants to take over the country for himself."

"Well, I think– wait, this must be him." The ring-tone was a snippet of an old Garth Brooks song. "Enoch! So good to hear from you!"

"Nephi," his brother's familiar voice responded. "Thank gosh I got through. I was afraid Wilton might shut down the cell networks, too." He paused. "Is this app still secure?"

"Pretty much. They're not likely to break the encryption. My only worry is if they trace the call. Griffin's safer over the Undernet, but that's out of commission for a while."

"Then I'll keep it short. I never was good with this kind of thing anyway." Enoch paused, and his voice cracked as he continued. "Uncle John's passed away."

"What! When? How?"

Siri's face mirrored the stricken look on his own. "What happened, Nephi? Are your mom and dad OK? Is it—"

Nephi held up a hand for silence. "Was it something.... medical?"

"Homeland Security agents ambushed him at the ranch last Tuesday night. Battered down the door. He thought it was a robbery, shot two of them in the face. So they backed off, regrouped, and set fire to the house with him in it. Absolutely no respect for human life."

"Oh my Lord." He glanced at Siri, who was looking like she was ready to burst from anxiety. "And Aunt Rosa?"

"She got away. Remember that secret tunnel to the horse barn? The Feds didn't see her on Esmeralda's back when the horses got loose; they must've thought she was in the house, too."

"And we thought Uncle Jack was paranoid," Nephi shook his head. "Why didn't he go, too?"

"He told her he'd be right along. Probably he wanted to distract the Feds so she could escape. But he never made it. She called us from Colorado; she's hiding out with her family. She's doing well, considering everything that just happened."

After a brief discussion of the family's reaction to the incident, they said their good-byes. Nephi sent his love to his parents and other siblings, then hung up.

Siri embraced him. "Oh, Nephi! I've heard about this kind of thing but can't believe it actually happened to your uncle. He was a retired US Marshall, wasn't he?"

"Yes. I can't believe they turned on one of their own like that. If he did violate the law, it would have been for a good reason. There's no way he would have intentionally hurt anyone."

"I'm so sorry." Siri hugged him tighter. "You two were close, weren't you?"

Nephi just nodded, tears streaming down his face. Inside, he felt a rage he'd never felt before. *It's true then; the bad guys are totally in control. I never wanted to sink to their level, but this time they've gone too far. I can no longer pretend I haven't taken sides. This means war.*

Chapter 14 – Enhanced Interrogations

Larsen glanced at his watch and sighed. He hated it when people were late. It reminded him of a certain occasion at Red Lake. Plus, he had much higher priorities at the moment. The President's Chinese-style Internet clampdown had turned Larsen's world upside down. The Brigade's communications had been severely hampered; he had to find a workaround. On top of it all, the public was about to break into open rebellion.

The Raptors insisted, though, that this was a critical mission. In an effort to repair the cracks in the Rebellion, MacGuiness had promised them the Brigade's support. Then at the last moment, he decided he could only spare the Brigades least military member.

The mission did sound intriguing. Supposedly John Tole himself had acquired a high level Federal defector. Larsen appreciated Mac's vote of confidence, but he felt totally unqualified to participate in a debriefing. DeLane would have been way better at this.

His phone rang. He answered immediately. "Hello."

"Look alive, Loki! We'll be there with the subject in five minutes," Larsen didn't care for the stupid code name. Even worse was the man's arrogance. Did Tole think the Butlers were going to flake out on this one? *He'd* been here on time, after all.

"Roger, Thor." Larsen sighed again. At first, he'd supported this alliance. Like Ben Franklin said, they needed to hang together or hang separately. Unfortunately, the Raptors had a tendency toward recklessness and unnecessary violence. They were weekend worriers, not like the Butler

Brigade. Mac's people were mostly combat veterans who'd seen their share of killing, and regarded the Rebellion with the seriousness it deserved.

Larsen got up and stretched. The rendezvous point was a conference room in a repossessed office building. The table was gone and the chairs were arranged in the middle. The sole window opened on an interior hallway.

The door burst open. Two guys in camouflage rushed in, dragging a person with a cloth bag over his head. Larsen recognized them as Tole's personal bodyguards, Smith and Jones.

"Sorry about the wait, Loki." Tole stood in the doorway, a smug smile on his face. "But it was worth it. We got an IRS regional manager."

"This is a kidnapping?" Larsen's gut tightened. "I thought it was a defection."

"What did you expect?" Tole held out a pair of mirrored sunglasses. "Put these on, so she can't ID us later."

Jones pulled the hood off the prisoner's head, and removed the gag. She was fair skinned and portly, probably mid-fifties, with graying black hair. Her eyes were wide with fear.

Larsen fought the impulse to mock her plight. This woman was part of the Machine, the Federal leviathan that imprisoned and tortured him. *Ain't payback a bitch?* Yet he hated to see her mistreated. Enemy or not, she was probably somebody's wife and mother.

Tole cleared his throat. "Geri Lynn Simpson, you are accused of crimes against...."

"I don't talk to terrorists!" The prisoner's expression had changed to icy fury. "You're nothing but a bunch of murdering cowards."

Larsen exhaled deeply. What was his role in this? He didn't want to be here, but they obviously needed a more tactful approach. "Ma'am, nobody's gonna kill anyone. We just need a little information." They hadn't discussed beforehand what they were trying to accomplish, so he'd have to improvise. Christ, he needed a drink. Tole handed him a three by five note card.

Larsen glanced at the card and continued. "Ms. Simpson, the Federal government has arrested a lot of people," *like me,* he wanted to add, "and is holding them without due process. Some of the names have been made public," *no thanks to you,* "but most of them haven't. We need to get those names, and the locations where those people are being held."

"I don't have to tell you traitors anything. This country is in a state of emergency. Besides, how would I know any names? You think I keep that information in my head?"

"We have the right to know, and as a director, you must have access.." Larsen's guilt and pity had morphed into anger. "We just want that information and you can go free."

Tole shot him a look that said, *Just tell her what she wants to hear.*

"I know your game. He's bad cop, you're good cop. Well, I won't fall for your bullshit. You're a big fat fake just like your friend over there."

Larsen snorted. "Gee, Ms. Simpson, no reason to get personal!"

"Fuck off, red-beard. You smell like alcohol. In Washington, they yank drunks like you off the street and put them in rehab. And if you don't stay sober we send you to prison. What do you think of that, drunkie?"

"That would take care of Congress, wouldn't it?" Larsen shook his head and clucked his tongue. "I wasn't aware it was illegal to have a beer at lunchtime."

"Simpson, you will treat my colleague with the proper respect." Tole signaled to Smith, who stepped forward and slapped the woman's face with his open hand.

She let out a shriek "How dare you!" Tears streamed down her face. The dread returned to her eyes. Smith looked at Tole as if eager to continue. Larsen exhaled through clenched teeth. He didn't like where this was going.

"Can I talk to you for a minute?" Larsen whispered to Tole.

Tole grimaced. "Not in front of... her. Let's step out for a sec." He turned to their captive, and chuckled. "Don't go anywhere, Ms. Simpson!"

Outside the room, Tole frowned. "Loki, I don't appreciate you undermining me."

"*John*, with all due respect, you shouldn't be mistreating the prisoner. Take it from me, it doesn't work. First they get pissed and refuse to cooperate. If you keep at it 'til they crack, they start babbling, saying anything they think you wanna hear."

"Is that how the Feds broke *you*?" Tole grinned evilly.

Larsen ignored the jibe. "I'm just saying if you'd been through that kind of thing, you'd understand. MacGuiness doesn't allow mistreatment of prisoners, and I agree with him."

"Man up, JL. Wouldn't you love to hit this bitch? I could hear it in your voice, after she insulted you. They even hate her at the IRS. One of her own underlings gave us her address. Besides, this is war, and as far as I'm concerned, the IRS and its employees are the Enemy."

"You don't beat up somebody who can't hit back. 'Especially not a woman."

"This is not the Butler Brigade, JL. I'm calling the shots here, and I consider this insubordination. Now get back in there, and no more of this bleeding heart bullshit!"

Larsen shook his head.

"I'll deal with you later, Jack-off!" Tole stormed into the conference room and slammed the door.

Larsen tried the knob; locked. Probably for the better. Though he carried a Ruger SR9 in his shoulder holster, he didn't want to play quick draw with Tole's goons. Now what? *Should I get out of here? Call the Brigade?* By the time they could send backup, Simpson might be dead. Should he create a disturbance? The conference room had a window, currently covered with newspaper. He pounded on the glass. His fist just bounced off.

If I had some heavy furniture... Larsen headed down the hall. The first two doors were locked, but the third opened into a dimly lit room with a large desk in the middle. Behind it sat a slender young man with olive skin and a thick black beard. He glanced up from a computer screen when Larsen entered.

"*Now* what do you want?" he snapped. His voice had a slight Middle Eastern accent.

Larsen instinctively felt for his gun, but he realized this guy might be an ally. "I'm not in the Raptor Group; I'm with the Butler Brigade."

The thin man laughed dryly "I heard we were cooperating, but I know that's a sham. You should hear what they say about you guys. I know, I run all the security."

"So you're the IT guy? Cool, I'm into that myself."

The man didn't respond. Larsen looked around the room. Monitors on the left and right were filled with simulated strip charts that looked like medical displays. In the center was a video feed from the conference room. Simpson's left eye was swollen shut. A trickle of blood ran down from her mouth. "My God!"

"Yes, they're a bunch of animals. I regret that I fell in with them." He gave Larsen an appraising look that made the big man nervous. "They know I don't approve of what they're doing. Not that they care what I say, as long as I don't try to leave."

"Would they try to stop you?"

He shrugged. "Probably not, but I once saw Tole's goons shoot a government informer."

"That's seriously fucked up, almost as bad as the government. In the Brigade, we're mostly vets. Not me, but I appreciate their service. They've

don't need to prove their manhood. By the way, I'm Jon Larsen; my friends call me JL."

"My name's Mahmoud." He kept his hands on his keyboard. "Are you a local? You sound like one."

Larsen shook his head. "Midwest. The accent's pretty similar, though. Why do you ask?"

"I'd like to get the heck out of here, but I don't have a car, and I don't know the area. And they took my phone, so I don't have a GPS."

Larsen nodded. "Me too; I've seen enough of Tole's methods. But I hate to leave Mrs. Simpson to his tender mercies. Can you control the lights with this setup?"

The man laughed. "You watch too many movies. Circuit breakers are in the closet."

"Good. I've got a flashlight in my pocket. We'll have the element of surprise."

The computer guy began shutting down the computer. "What am I doing? I can't take these along." He yanked the cables from the box, then hurled it to the floor.

Larsen gasped; to him, computers were like family. "I'll get the breakers, then we'll go."

"And what about the prisoner?"

"Maybe I was a little hasty just now. I'd like to stop them, but we're kind of out-gunned."

"I thought you Butler Brigade guys were better than that."

Larsen sighed. "OK, but if you get me killed I'm coming back from the afterlife to kick your ass!"

Mahmoud laughed, pushed past him and flipped the breaker. The building was plunged into darkness. Larsen drew his pistol and handed Mahmoud his flashlight.

As they came down the hallway, they heard muffled shouting from the conference room. "The window's tempered glass, but probably not bulletproof. If I shoot near the top..."

"No! It's too risky! If we both hit the door at once and..." Before Mahmoud could finish his sentence, the door flew open and Tole burst out.

"Freeze!" Larsen pointed his gun at Tole, hoping to God he didn't have to use it. To his surprise, the skinny IT guy give the militia leader a snap kick to the stomach. Tole fell to the floor, retching, whereupon Mahmoud relieved him of his pistol.

Smith and Jones were close behind. "Drop your weapons!" Larsen bellowed. To his immense relief, the men complied. "Phones, too. Now, untie the prisoner."

"You'll never get by our men at the front door," Jones growled.

"Not your problem then, is it?"

Simpson whimpered as Larsen helped her out of the chair. God, she was a mess! "Come on, Ma'am." He backed out of the room with her, pausing to pick up the phones.

Larsen set the dazed woman on the floor, but she immediately jumped up and delivered a fierce kick to Tole's crotch. "Aagh!" All the man could do was gurgle as he kicked.

"Stop that!" Larsen pulled her away. "Now you two, back in the room. Take your fearless leader with you." Larsen handed Mahmoud the pistol so he could keep them covered, then ran to the computer room. He returned in a moment with a big piece of glass substrate from one of the broken LCD monitors. It was thin enough to jam under the door, which would make it pretty difficult to open. "That should buy us a few minutes."

They ran down the hall, half-dragging the woman between them. Passing the door to the reception area, they came to the end of the corridor, which ended with an exterior window. Mahmoud gave it another fierce kick. Nothing happened. "You want to use the gun now?"

"You got it." Larsen raised his pistol and aimed downward, hoping the bullet would lodge safely in the ground. The blast echoed through the hallway. A small hole appeared, surrounded by a sunburst of fracture lines.

"Good enough." Mahmoud kicked again and the glass fell out. From behind they heard wood fracturing and then shouting, getting nearer.

"Hold this!" Larsen handed him the gun, picked up the dazed Simpson and lowered her out the window.

Mahmoud hopped out behind them. "You have a vehicle, I hope."

"This way!" As they ran, Larsen carried Simpson on his shoulder. He unlocked the doors with the remote, and they piled in. Since the pickup had only two seats, he shoved over some toolboxes to make room for Simpson in the cargo area in the back of the cab. "You behave yourself, or we'll give you back to your friends." He started the truck and peeled out, just as Smith and Jones, followed by the front door guards, dashed out after them.

"I don't have a seat belt," Simpson complained.

"Be glad you don't have to ride in the box." Larsen said. "And if you don't stop whining, I'll give you another kind of belt."

"What are you going to do with me?"

"Let you go, of course. If I wanted to be a god-damned kidnapper, I'd go work for the Feds." *Or the Raptors*, but he kept that thought to himself. Larsen headed through a residential neighborhood, then four-wheeled it through a city park.

"Are you trying to get us arrested?" Mahmoud put his hand on the handle above the door.

"I think we've lost 'em," Larsen said. "Let's get the hell out of Dodge, take the back roads. There's a GPS in the glove box."

"That's something, at least. It makes me feel naked, to not have my smart phone."

"You promised you'd let me go," In the rear-view mirror, the woman looked frightful. Her left cheek was swelling; tears were streaming from her right eye.

"We will. We'll even give you a phone."

"I suppose I should thank you, assuming this isn't some kind of trick. But I warn you, you could both be sent to death row for abducting a Federal official."

Larsen laughed. "I'm sure they could fry us both a dozen times over by now."

Mahmoud rolled his eyes. "Speak for yourself."

Thirty minutes later, they stopped, ten miles down a National Forest road. Larsen pulled out Smith's stolen phone. "It's showing a couple bars; you should be OK. But first," he handed a silver roll to Mahmoud, "put this duct tape over our plate until we get out of sight."

Before pulling onto the highway, they stopped again to remove the tape. Mahmoud was back in a second, rolling the silver stuff into a neat ball.

"Jesus H. Christ, I can't believe we did that! My hands are shaking." Larsen fumbled in his jacket pocket, removed a metal flask. He took a swig, ignored Mahmoud's evil glance, then put it back. "Medicinal, OK? Would you like a swig?"

Mahmoud shook his head. "It's against my religion. Though maybe I should start; I'm probably bound for Hell anyway."

"You sound like my kind of guy. How'd you end up with a bunch of SOB's like the Raptors?"

"First of all, don't make assumptions. And second, I had to go somewhere, after I got kicked out of my previous organization. They aren't terribly fond of homosexuals."

Larsen let out a laugh, then stifled it. "Sorry, I don't mean to minimize your pain. I'm just surprised the Raptors let you in. I guess John Tole's not as big of a douche bag as I thought."

"No, he's not a homophobe at least. His bodyguard Jones is definitely gay, and I have my suspicions about Smith. But they don't know I'm a Muslim. I said I was from India, not Iran."

Larsen laughed again. "I've got no problem with either of your identities. I've even got a gay cousin; I'd introduce you to him, but we haven't exactly kept in touch. He likes the exotic types."

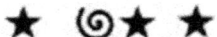

"On the road again..." Willie Nelson's familiar nasal voice blared from the radio.

Siri exhaled loudly and rubbed her temples. This morning her head ached as much as her back, although, praise Buddha, she was several weeks past the morning sickness. She took a deep breath and tried to calm herself. She wasn't going to miss Atlanta, but the song reminded her just how impermanent her life had been lately.

"Sorry, Sweetie, forgot you hate country music! I'll change it."

"No, Nephi, I don't *hate* it, I just don't care for it, and I've got a terrible headache."

"Oh. Are you still ticked off about us not contacting your parents?"

"I'm disappointed. I worry about them; I wish we could take them along, get them out of harm's way. At least we could let them know where we're going, so they don't worry. But you're right, we can't risk it. Not after what happened to your Uncle John. If it was just you and me, it wouldn't be so bad, but..." She glanced back at little Will in his car seat.

Nephi grimaced, never taking his eyes off the road. "Yeah, it stinks. Can't visit family or friends, and Will's never even met his grandparents. All because of that megalomaniac in the White House."

"Bad as she is, you can't blame it all on the President. Things were already pretty awful when she took office. And she had a lot of help from the crooks in Congress." She looked at her husband, gave him her best pleading look. "I know we don't dare risk a direct contact, but the Secure Message Board just got a security upgrade. If we posted there, *somebody* in our families, especially yours, would see it. We could let them know we're OK."

"I'll think about it." He tried to avoid eye contact, knowing what she could do with those big brown eyes. "We should be grateful we could do secure video calls before Wilton's Internet crackdown. At least our parents got to see Will a few times. We'll get the Undernet back up and running eventually. Until then, they'll understand, because they know our situation."

Siri sniffled. "Sorry I'm so emotional, but I can't help thinking that if the government can keep us separated from the ones we love, then they've won."

"We were really lucky at that last checkpoint," Nephi was anxious to change the subject. "I'm proud of you, you played your part well."

"I can't take the credit. We were fortunate the contractors were Russian. I don't like to stereotype, but they were so apathetic, they were just happy to take the bribe. If they'd been from the Third World, they'd have shaken us down for everything we had. Or worse."

"It's time we Americans stop taking crap from those Homeland Security goons. I would've killed them both if they'd done anything to harm either of you."

"Shh! We don't need any crazy talk!" She gave him a withering look. He knew what she was thinking; she'd said it a hundred times. *We have to be better than them.* She looked back over her shoulder, "Good, still sleeping. Will's been such a good traveler!" The little boy's head lolled back against his car seat. They'd hung a flat screen on the back of the seat, and kept him quiet with Big Blue House videos, though she hated to pacify him with TV at such a young age.

They reached Memphis around dusk. "Hon, do you still have JL's text on your phone?"

Siri smiled. "Amazing! A man who's not afraid to ask directions."

She pulled the phone out of her purse, and with her right eye, stared directly into its camera. This was one of Krijk's applications, a personal retinal scanner that worked on any e-Phone with the enhanced camera. That was her high security login. If the phone detected fiddling by unauthorized persons, would short the battery and fry the device's memory.

The map and directions flashed up on the screen. "Take highway 300 west, get off on US 51 northbound. Then turn left on Frayser Boulevard."

It didn't take long to get there. Nephi was glad he was still wearing his dark makeup; he would have been very conspicuous without it. "Interesting place." The area was dominated by pawn shops, adult movie theaters and seedy bars. Many stores were closed, with windows boarded up. Here and there the walls were defaced with gang tags.

Siri wrinkled her nose in disgust. "In Jaffna, even our poor neighborhoods were better."

When they arrived at the Frayser Heights Apartments, Nephi let out a low whistle. "I hope it's safe to park here." The building looked even more dilapidated than its surroundings.

"Nephi!" Two young black men approached, wearing Titans jackets, gold chains, and blue kerchiefs. In her years in Chicago, Siri had become wary of young men in matching outfits.

Nephi hesitated, then rolled the window down a crack. One of the men bent down to peer in the window. "Anil and Samaria?" His accent was reminiscent of white suburbia. "I'm Jared Harris, this is Taylor. The Commander is expecting you. I'll open the gate; there's parking in back."

Nephi thanked him and drove in. After parking in the walled lot, they followed Harris and his comrade through the grungy back doorway. Nephi

322

handed her the diaper bag and picked up young William Pradeep. Siri was grateful; her own weight was plenty to carry these days.

Inside, it was different. The walls were freshly painted. The floor, though cracked in places, has been mopped clean. None of the light fixtures matched, but all of them worked. Anticipating Siri's question, Taylor said, "We'd like to fix up the outside as well, but the Commander feels it's best to blend into the area. People think it's gang turf and stay away."

"What about the police?" asked Nephi.

"A few bribes take care of them. We let 'em think we're drug traffickers."

Harris knocked at a door marked 33. Hearing no answer, he slowly pushed it open. "Sir?"

"Yes, Private? Oh, it's the Snows! Come in!"

Their escort nodded and left, and they entered the personal office of America's Most Wanted Terrorist. It was a modest apartment without decoration, dominated by a large desk to the right. In the center of the otherwise-neat room was an oasis of clutter – a table strewn with cards, empty glasses, and a half empty bag of pork rinds.

The commander got up and extended a hand to shake. He was not, as he invariably did in photographs, wearing a uniform. His white t-shirt and sweat pants were typical inner-city dress. "Welcome to Butler Brigade Headquarters, for the moment anyway. We've been playing musical ghettos for some time how." He looked over his shoulder. "Rise and shine, JL, your friends are here."

Larsen was stretched out on a worn green couch on the far side of the room. He wore a seriously wrinkled Rams jersey. He saw Nephi and burst out laughing. "Who the hell are you? We were expecting some white Mormon guy."

"And I'd have expected to see you in purple, not blue and gold," Nephi said with a grin.

"I know. The sacrifices I have to make working for this guy! Nephi and Siri, I assume you've already met Commander Eldridge MacGuiness, better known as Mac. And this must be little Will. Oh man, how he's grown!"

The little boy regarded Larsen with wide eyes, then hid his face in his father's shoulder.

"Excuse the mess," MacGuiness grinned. "Last night we were engaging in a little R and R. Your friend ended up bunking here." He stacked up the empty glasses and tossed a depleted whiskey bottle into the trash.

Larsen grimaced. "You forgot to mention I just drove halfway across the country. They'll think I'm a total lush. Come on, I'll give you guys the nickel tour."

They followed Larsen out the apartment door, where he stopped suddenly and faced them. "I'm so glad you guys made it!" He hugged Siri, awkwardly due to her expanded waistline, then Nephi, who smiled in embarrassment. They headed down the hallway, Nephi carrying little Will in his arms.

"I'm glad you guys finally decided to join us. I know you had reservations about the para-military thing, but in times like this we have to compromise sometimes. Anyway, Mac's a rarity, a revolutionary who's actually a good guy. You won't regret it."

"We won't," Nephi said. Siri shot him a dirty look that Larsen didn't seem to notice.

"You two had good timing. We just finished some major repairs. We've been acquiring real estate in depressed areas around the country, using aliases generated through Griffin. Good thing we did that before they took down the Undernet." Siri and Nephi followed without comment, down to the basement.

"Here's where you two will be working. The IT department." Larsen opened a door to what looked like a storage area. The room was filled with rack-mounted computers, and desks with keyboards and monitors.

"Never thought I'd have *you* for a boss," Nephi laughed.

"And you won't. I'm not in charge of IT anymore, thank God. Nowadays I do security: surveillance and perimeter defense. Your new boss is a guy named Jeng Shen; I'm sure you've heard of him. We, or should I say the Brigade, busted him out of one of those FEMA camps. Currently he's in the field, working on our mobile-router Undernet fix. That'll be you're first job, helping him." Nephi had expected that. Anonymous communication was once again possible, but not yet reliable. The underground economy was still seriously hobbled.

"We were doing that already" Siri had sat down on an office chairs and began rubbing her own ankles. "Sorry, I'm really so stiff from the long drive."

"No, I'm sorry. I'm an asshole, not offering a pregnant lady a seat. And that's just a small part of the job. You and Neeph will be making sure our communications, procurement, and personnel movements stay hidden from Uncle Snoop. Until recently, we've done that all through your e-Barter app, by the way. I've had to make some proprietary enhancements, but in general, it's been amazingly scalable."

"My wife, the genius," grinned Nephi.

"You're so embarrassing! All I did was the secure barter protocols. E-Barter would never have been possible without the Griffin system."

"Ma!" Little Will looked expectantly at his mother.

"My little man is hungry," Siri reached into her bag for a jar of food, then looked at Larsen. "Is there a good place to feed him? He'll be pretty grumpy if we make him wait."

"Right here." He swept the books papers on the desk into a stack and set them on top of a rack enclosure. "Just try not to get any strained carrots in the server."

Nephi handed the little boy to Siri. "I wish it was a better environment for the baby."

"No problem. The Commander's daughter lives here; she's got three kids. The youngest is Will's age." He leaned down to look at the baby. "Somebody to play with. Cool, huh?"

It only took a couple of days for Nephi and Siri to settle in. The Brigade assigned them a modest apartment. Will spent most afternoons with Mac's daughter Marva and her three kids. Sadly, the kids seldom got to play outdoors, except in the apartment's tiny courtyard.

On rare occasions, Marva would take her kids to a park, zoo, or museum, accompanied by some of Mac's best men in plain clothes. For the first few weeks, Siri refused to let Will go along, until Marva convinced her it was no more hazardous than remaining in HQ. Still, Siri insisted either she or Nephi accompany them.

One afternoon Siri had just laid down for a brief nap. It was a rare opportunity, and being late in her pregnancy, she was exhausted. Still, she wondered if she could sleep knowing Nephi and Will were out on one of their field trips. Just then the phone rang. It was Marva. "We're back!" Siri thanked her and lay down again. Nephi could enjoy his 'dad' time a little longer.

She was just drifting off when she was startled by the fire alarm. She'd gotten so used to sirens and gunshots, she wondered if it was real.

"Nephi?" No answer. *Were they with Marva?* Still groggy, she dialed the woman's number; no answer. The moment she hung up the phone, it rang. There was a recorded message in DeLane's voice. "Emergency! All personnel prepare to evacuate!"

Siri burst out of the bedroom. Nephi sat in his easy chair, a book in his lap, headphones on. Will was standing in his playpen, crying. "Nephi, the alarm!"

"What? Huh?" Apparently he'd dozed off, too.

"We're evacuating! Go find Marva, and get the kids out of here!"

"No, *you* go with Marva! There's stuff I need to take care of."

From outside, the sound of sirens added to the alarm. Siri turned on the TV; they had a link to the same security camera feeds that MacGuiness and Larsen had. The view down the street showed armored personnel carriers rolling down the street. On the roof view, several choppers were approaching from downtown. Will stopped crying and stared at the monitor, apparently thinking it was a TV program.

"Not good!" Nephi grabbed Siri and kissed her quickly. "Grab your suitcase. I need to grab the backups. We don't have time to take the systems; I'll need to do a self-destruct."

"Harris can do that. Nephi, we need you!" Siri was feeling light headed.

"I'll be along with JL and Mac. You know the way, get going!"

Below the apartment complex were utility tunnels that had been closed years before. Mac's people had cleared them out and extended them a few feet to the charter school next door. That place had gone bankrupt and was now occupied by a handful of homeless squatters. The squalor provided a perfect cover for the Brigade's emergency exit.

"Siri! I was trying to call you." Marva wore a large backpack. The two older kids each had one as well. Siri wished she had one of those, instead of the rolling suitcase she'd packed.

"Mom, I scared!" Will said.

"Don't be scared; it's an adventure!" Marva said. "It'll be fun!"

"Don't believe her. It's just a creepy tunnel," said Duane, Marva's middle child. She shushed him.

The HQ was a frenzy of activity, people running through the halls with weapons and fire-fighting equipment. Siri was sick with worry about Nephi, but she kept those thoughts to herself as they hurried down the stairs. At the end of a hallway was the entry to the tunnel.

"Damn this old door!" Marva fiddled impatiently with the padlock.

"Let me try, Mom!" Keenan, her oldest boy, grabbed the lock; it opened with a cracking sound. He lit the flashlight and led the way into the tunnel. Marva and Siri carried the babies.

A boom echoed through the tunnel. All the kids shrieked. Siri gripped the baby tighter. "Are you sure this is safe?"

"We don't expect explosives, just incendiaries," Marva said quietly. "That's Uncle's favorite strategy; smoke the rebels out like rats."

It was the longest half hour in Siri's life, as she shuffled bent over through the dark tunnel. Twice she banged her head on low hanging conduits. Eventually they emerged into a dark dusty stairwell. Marva pulled a pistol out of her purse, keeping it ready as they climbed the stairs. Siri shuddered; despite Nephi's efforts to teach her marksmanship, guns still made her uncomfortable. At the top of the stairs was a workshop or garage, empty except for an old station wagon. Siri opened the vehicle's door, and recoiled at the smell.

Marva made a face. "Somebody's been sleeping in here."

Siri felt her skin crawl; they'd all need de-lousing before bedtime.

Marva pulled up the garage door and jumped in the driver's seat; they pulled into the street, ignoring the ongoing SWAT raid like typical city dwellers. Helicopters circled overhead. Smoke poured into the air from the Brigade HQ next door. *Please,* Siri prayed to the Buddha, *let him be OK.* To her horror, a police car zoomed up behind them, lights flashing.

Just then an explosion rocked the street; the cop car behind them swerved to avoid a rain of bricks and hit a light pole. Another explosion assaulted their ears, then another!

"Yes!" Marva punched the air with one hand. "Everything's going according to plan. We set the fire ourselves to destroy the evidence, then escape out the tunnels on either side!"

Siri nodded. There was nothing she could do but hope and pray.

★ ✪ ★ ★

"Serena, behave yourself!" Joel's sweet dream evaporated when he opened his eyes to the morning sun and an otherwise empty bed. He groped along the edge of the mattress, and found his glasses. Brown eyes stared at him from a black and white face, above a lolling pink tongue.

"*Oy*, Groucho, you need some doggie breath mints!"

The animal stopped wagging its tail and lay down on the tiny rug in front of the bunk. Ignoring his furry friend, Joel sat up and looked out the window. There were RV's parked on both sides. This was a good place to hide, but bad if you had to get out quickly.

Around two AM, Joel and Groucho had rolled into the encampment in their circa-1990's pickup camper. As usual they'd gone to the back of the enclosure, which had been a greyhound racetrack before the hard times hit. People called these places 'Wiltonvilles', in homage to the Hoovervilles of the previous century.

Evicted from their houses by the thousands, the dispossessed made their homes in their vehicles. At first they invaded the public lands, filling all available camping spaces and staying for weeks on end. Soon afterward, the Agriculture and Interior Departments closed down the campgrounds and booted everyone out, lest the masses of uprooted city people disturb the spotted owls or other endangered critters.

Joel yawned, stretched, and threw on yesterday's sweatshirt and jeans. He stepped out of the camper's back door and walked around to cab's driver side door. Groucho bounded enthusiastically behind, crawling over Joel's lap to take his spot in the passenger seat.

"Sorry, Pal, we're not ready to go yet."

Scheisse, the fuel gauge said 'E.' Joel didn't panic, because he knew there was probably a fuel source nearby.

Due to the conflicts in oil producing countries, as well as rampant inflation, the price of gas hovered at 20 dollars a gallon. People economized any way they could. Joel's method was to use a Vespa scooter for everyday transportation. He hooked up a bike trailer behind, and loaded it with empty five gallon paint cans. With the narrow lane between vehicles and all the pedestrian traffic, it was slow going. Groucho kept up easily, trotting on long lab-spaniel legs, ignoring the ferocious barking of his fellow dogs in the surrounding campsites.

At the far end of the grounds was a silvery van labeled "SNACK BAR". The proprietor, a portly Hispanic man, was cranking open the awning to open for the morning business.

Joel shut off the Vespa's engine. "Good morning, sir. Do you have any used cooking oil?"

"That depends. I get a lot of people asking for that these days."

"How about a trade?" Joel held out a handful of cigars. "Genuine Cuban tobacco. Even if you don't smoke, I'm sure you can move 'em."

The man frowned "That could get me arrested. I don' t have no tobacco sales license."

Joel laughed. "I'd wager you don't have a food vendor's license either, or you wouldn't be working in a Wiltonville."

They struck a quick bargain, and Joel left with three cans of oil for conversion to bio-diesel. As he and Groucho made their way back, he marveled that such a place could exist, considering that the inhabitants were breaking a hundreds of laws and regulations just by being here. It might have been his imagination, but he thought he saw more sunburned white faces among the darker-skinned people who'd originally dominated these encampments.

Joel stopped to wait for a young man and woman, tattooed and pierced biker-types, as they crossed in front of him. Despite their menacing

330

appearance, they smiled and waved; Groucho answered them with a friendly bark. The pair wore bright red "Vote American" t-shirts. *Ah, more anti-Lopez partisans.* That California had elected a governor who'd once been an illegal immigrant, pardoned by the most recent amnesty, had enraged a lot of people.

Yet, for a politician, Manuel Lopez hadn't been that bad. One of his first acts in office was to forbid the police from hassling the homeless. In principle, Joel disagreed, since he and his fellow squatters were occupying other people's property without permission. Though considering the circumstances, where could they go? Do-gooders who tried to erect temporary housing ran afoul of building codes and zoning laws. 'Not in my back yard,' indeed!

As Joel pondered these weighty matters, he almost ran into another group of people crossing the path. He screeched the Vespa's brakes and sat there, heart pounding, as four swarthy men glared at him. One gave him the finger. Groucho growled menacingly, which was quite out of character for him. Joel grabbed the animal's collar. These men did not look liked dog lovers.

The biggest of the four, at least in terms of muscles and mustache, approached Joel and spoke in a thick accent. "Watch where you going, asshole!"

"My apologies," Joel said. *Don't antagonize them, but don't show fear, either.*

The man sneered and walked away. Joel sighed in relief. He had a brief flashback to two weeks before, when another group of foreign-looking men had flagged him down to ask for help with their apparently disabled vehicle. When he stopped, one of them reached an arm in his window, grabbed his neck and shouted to the others in an unknown language. Only by putting the car in reverse and punching the gas had Joel managed to escape. After all that time, his neck still bothered him.

Could they have been bounty hunters? He'd been worried about that ever since his near-miss earlier that year. The avaricious store owner hadn't succeeded in getting a photograph of Joel with his new 'Kojack' look, but he could have easily called the Feds with a description.

After his breakup with Serena, Joel abandoned the idea of staying in one place. He no longer felt safe, despite his expensive fake credentials and another change in appearance. His remaining barter credits went toward a diesel pickup with camper shell. The dog Joel had found was eating garbage behind a Korean restaurant. *Living dangerously,* Joel chuckled to himself.

As he traveled, Joel was appalled to see what had happened to the once-prosperous West Coast. He took pictures and made notes but kept them to himself. Occasionally he posted to the 'Stooge' blog, but he was careful not to mention anything that might infer his location. Even so, he got hundreds of emails per day over the satellite link. Not like the old days, when they were mostly kudos from like-minded folks and flames from supporters of the government.

Nowadays people sent Joel stories of their daily struggles, plus rumors and conspiracy theories, some crazy, some believable. Lately they centered on the China Lake incident. According to the media, militia types had stolen advanced weaponry from the naval testing grounds. *Yeah, right.* Most people believed it was one of those ethnic gangs the government hired as 'security contractors' going rogue. That seemed more plausible than the official story.

Back at his campsite, Joel poured the used oil in his handy-dandy diesel cooker, then added the alcohol and catalyst. He hoped he'd have some time here before the next crisis. The truck's tank was almost empty, and he hated to keep the cooker inside the camper. It was five feet tall and *heavy.* One spill would release enough toxic fumes to render his home uninhabitable.

While he waited for oil to be converted, Joel stuck the satellite dish on the mounting, fired up the computer, and checked his 'Seventh Stooge' email. Groucho lay at his feet, a living throw rug. Not a replacement for Serena, but still a good companion.

Another two hundred messages. Joel didn't have time to read them all, so he'd set the email program to extract those with certain keywords. He scanned the resulting lists, all with anonymous handles, many of them familiar. One was 'Yusef Islam.' Joel was so surprised, the cigar dropped out of his mouth and burned a spot on the plastic surfaced camper table.

"Hello my Judaic friend," the message began. "I apologize for not communicating sooner. I promised myself I would do whatever I could to make up for the inexcusable actions of myself and my family. Once again, I have information for you."

It had to be Emal Ahmedaj again. Joel was glad the guy was still alive. Having fled his extended family and the crime syndicate they served, and later defied the leadership of the militant Islamic Aid Society, the Albanian had made a lot of enemies. As before, Emal had some critical information, something the world had to know.

Using the highest encryption, Joel posted an urgent message for Nephi's anonymous ID. His friend had joined Mac MacGuiness' Butler Brigade, though lately the Feds had them on the run. Joel had worried for several days before receiving Nephi's latest email. What a *mensch*, to keep him informed, despite the considerable trouble and risk involved.

Joel lit another cigar and puffed nervously as he stared at the screen. Suddenly a message popped up, 'Voice-only secure call.' The voice was familiar. "Hello, Joel! Is everything alright?"

"Siri! Your voice is music to my ears." He wondered if she'd had the new baby yet, but this was no time for small talk. *Are those two crazy, or having trouble finding condoms?* "How's your other half, and the little guy?"

"Our son is well. As for my husband" a fleeting worry crossed her face, "let's just say he's out in the field."

"I'll take your word for it." Joel knew better than to ask where. Rumor had it the Brigade was raiding the posts of the so-called North American Command all over the Southwest, stealing weapons and performing acts of sabotage. The exception was Texas, where they had the tacit approval of Governor Davis, who seemed to already have one foot out of the Union. Joel said a silent prayer for Nephi and hoped the Lord was listening.

"Anyway, Siri, remember my Albanian friend from the pod-cast?"

"Yes, the man who liked to play with snakes. He's not up to his old tricks again, is he?"

"No, he said he turned over a new leaf, and it's still turned." *Assuming he's not back with his rotten extended family.* "He has some pretty explosive news for us."

"Are you sure you can trust him? That 9/11 attack plot he was pushing never happened."

"That's true, but my other sources say it was because their plot was exposed. Plus, he came forward at great risk to himself. So I think he's trustworthy."

"I can't promise I'll believe it, but you've really piqued my curiosity. What did he say?"

"You know how the Feds have been hiring gangsters to do their dirty work. My friend has an inside source, one of his in-laws, who says the Albanian Mob gave them an ultimatum. If they weren't paid in something other than dollars, they'd walk. Looks like it worked because suddenly the black market is awash in *real* money, especially pre-1965 silver coins."

"I've noticed that, but why would the government need these gangsters so badly? They have thousands of soldiers in the Liberty Legion."

"Yes, but it's been a fiasco. Those foreign mercenaries haven't even been able to defend the FEMA camps and the Fusion Centers from attacks by the rebel groups. Our source says the Feds have a new strategy, targeted assassinations."

"You're kidding. Who are they planning to kill? It's not like we're hiding Osama bin Laden or Anwar al-Awlaki."

"This is the scary part. Rebel leaders like MacGuiness and Tole. Governors of rebellious states like Texas and California. Maybe even the technical gurus like JL, Nephi and you."

"What?" Siri gasped. "That just can't be true."

"I wish it wasn't. I hear the Brigade has a pretty good intelligence arm. I'd be surprised if Mac doesn't already know this."

"If he did, Nephi and I would know about it."

"Don't be so sure. You know how military units operate, and the Brigade is no different. Information is on a 'need to know' basis."

There was a long pause on the other end. "If it's true, we may owe you our lives. In any case, we need to be a lot more careful. Did your friend say anything about when?"

"It's gotta be soon, and– oh crap, there's the sirens!"

There was alarm in Siri's voice. "What's happening, Joel?"

"The cops are clearing us out, probably. Damn, they're not supposed to do that! We've got to get going!"

"Who's 'we'?"

"Me and my dog. Purebred AKC mongrel. Goodbye, Siri. Give my best to your husband and the little guy. I'll keep you posted." He signed off and shut the computer down. With a grunt he lifted the still-processing diesel cooker into the back of the camper and secured it with straps.

"Groucho, get in the truck. Now, where are my cutters?" The security in places like these was a joke; in this case, a chain-link fence. Nothing a pair of sturdy wire cutters couldn't handle. The cops would be doing their sweep, checking ID's, looking for fugitives, But Joel, Groucho, and the lucky campers around them would be heading out the back way.

Chapter 15 – The Sacramento Massacre

Interstate 5 was almost empty that morning. A few years ago, that would have been unthinkable. These days most people couldn't afford to drive, unless, like Joel, they could make their own fuel.

Groucho sat in the passenger's seat, tongue hanging out, happily gazing out the window. Joel patted the animal's head. "You've got the life, Buddy." He envied the dog, living in the moment, not worrying about what the next day would bring.

There was plenty to worry about. The e-Barter system was still off-line. Joel was lucky he had contacts left from before the Internet crackdown. Old fashioned barter was a hassle, but it was a living. "I like to *kvetch*, Groucho, but we're both lucky. We're both still eating, and not being eaten." Lately it seemed there were fewer dogs in the 'Wiltonville' camps where Joel stayed, with suspicious-looking meat on some of the barbecues.

"Tonight, my furry friend , we're staying with friends in Coalinga. Ha, gotta love that name!" His hosts were an older Jewish couple he'd met through his computer repair business. Despite the risks in befriending a stranger, the two had been like a surrogate family to him.

They arrived in Coalinga early that evening. As usual, Herb and Diana invited Joel to dine with them. Joel accepted, despite his guilt about the cost of his hosts' hospitality. They didn't even know his real name, as he was still using his 'Ed Zigurdregy' alias.

"Ed, have some more roast beef." Diana could be pretty insistent.

"No, I couldn't. It must have cost a fortune."

"What fortune? We get it by barter from a rancher in Napa."

Afterwards, Joel retired to the living room to have a drink with his hosts. A comedy was on TV. Nobody was watching, but the laugh track provided background for their conversation.

"It's ridiculous," Herb said. "How can they increase military spending when the schools don't have enough money?"

Joel was about to respond when the television caught his attention with a special news report. The announcer said. "CNN's Don Guerrera is live at the state capitol, with more details."

"In an apparent terrorist incident, Governor Manuel Lopez was shot by unidentified assailants on motorcycles while leaving the Capitol in his limousine this evening. The Governor was flown to the University Medical Center and pronounced dead on arrival. The shooting suspects are still at large and an Islamic extremist organization has taken responsibility."

"Oh dear!" Diana exclaimed. "Could things possibly get worse?"

"I guess Puloski is governor now," her husband said. "I have mixed feelings about that. He's not as radical as Lopez, but I hear he's in the pocket of big business interests."

"In any case," Joel said, "I expect us to lose more of our freedom. The politicians never fail to take advantage of a crisis."

The newscaster confirmed Joel's fears. "Acting Governor Puloski has declared a state of emergency, including a dusk to dawn curfew."

"On that encouraging note," Joel said, "I'm going to hit the hay. I need to leave tomorrow at sunrise."

Joel had not been surprised at the news. This was what Ahmedaj had warned him about. The 'Seventh Stooge' had published the story, but with the Internet clampdown, who knew how many people actually read it?

Groucho barked happily when Joel entered the camper, especially when he saw his master had brought a treat. As the dog devoured the fat trimmings from dinner, Joel cracked open a window, lit a cigar, and thought about tomorrow's journey.

He dreaded returning to Sacramento, because it was where, a few months back, he'd nearly been kidnapped by unknown foreigners. Tonight's news made him even more reluctant, since the 'emergency' was likely to be more stringently enforced in the capital city. But financially, he couldn't afford not to go. These days, he had to accept barter as payment, and hold on to what clients he still had. When a client had commodities that could easily be traded (in this case nutritional supplements) he was loath to pass up the opportunity.

Joel and Groucho rolled into Sacramento around noon. The city seemed eerily quiet. The relative absence of traffic was a big change from when he'd first come here, but there was something else, a kind of tension in the air.

They got off the freeway and headed east on J Street. As they waited at a red light, Joel was startled by a thrumming sound. An olive drab helicopter thundered by overhead. A bit further on, he had another surprise, something he hadn't encountered in ages – a traffic jam.

"Damn!" Was it an accident, or some stupid roadblock? As always, there was the danger of hidden DHS agents who'd pounce on anyone making a suspicious turn-around. The late Governor Lopez had stood up to the Feds on numerous issues, but that was a battle he'd lost.

Joel lit a cigar, took a drag, and waited. The next traffic light was green, but nothing moved. Surprisingly, people started getting out of their cars. He leaned out the window as two young Latinos passed by. "What's going on?" he yelled.

"Don't you have a *phone*, man? We just got the tweet, big protest at the Capitol."

He grabbed his phone from the console. There were two new messages from #calpatriots:

Manuel Lopez death was no terrorist attack! The Feds did it to put their puppet in power. 7th Stooge was right.

Join us at Capitol to demand Puloski resignation and Web-election of new governor. Support democracy, end Federal tyranny!

"Hey, Groucho, I still have readers." For a moment he pondered the message's authenticity. In his younger days he'd dreamed that one day, the people finally get fed up and revolt. Now he was more cynical. Was it a plot by some asshole group like the Raptors to incite rebellion? Or was it the Feds, luring their opponents into a trap?

Anyone who followed these young fools to the Capitol needed to have his head examined. Yet it was likely to be history in the making, and the way the dog was acting, if they didn't get out soon, there'd be stains on the upholstery.

Joel slipped the leash on his companion. "OK, fella, you be my guard dog." With his perpetually wagging tail, Groucho wasn't intimidating, but at least he had a good growl.

They left the camper in the street and followed the river of people. These days the Capitol Park was surrounded by a tall fence and protected by concrete traffic barriers. Today the gates were closed, probably due to the so-called emergency. The crowd pounded at the gates, until some smart Aleck with a bolt cutter snapped the padlock. The people poured through.

Against his better judgment, Joel let himself be swept along. With so many bodies around them, the air was stifling. Poor Groucho panted furiously. Joel looked around for a way out, then spied a metal light post on a wide concrete pillar which probably doubled as a secondary vehicle barrier. With a grunt, he lifted the dog onto the pedestal and pulled himself up after. The two of them sat and waited for the fireworks.

To the south of the Capitol was the chopper he'd seen; a huge two-rotor troop transport, its blades still moving slowly. A line of uniformed men emerged, carrying clubs and riot shields. To the east along the building's facade stood several Humvees and military trucks, some with pivot-mounted machine guns in the back. In the midst of it all was a tank, one of the newer Abrams 'M1A3' models. The uniformed men took their places next to the vehicles, forming a ring around the statehouse.

The men were not soldiers. Their uniforms were darker than any US military branch, and the vehicles bore the Earth-and-Eagle logo of KBR-Schwartzwasser. Judging by their looks they'd come from numerous countries in Africa, Asia, and Latin America. People said KBR-S hired foreigners because they accepted sub-standard wages, but Joel suspected another reason. Being outsiders, the contractors would not hesitate to use deadly force.

As Joel gripped the dog's collar, he felt a deep growl from the animal's throat. "Groucho, *no!*" Not that he could blame the poor animal. Joel wished he had a camera, then remembered he did. With his free hand, Joel got his smart phone from his pocket and started recording. If and when video streaming came back to the Undernet, he'd post it to his blog.

There were hundreds, maybe thousands of civilians massed in the park. The majority of the crowd appeared to be Latino, here to support their late lamented governor, but all ethnic groups were represented. An excitable crowd plus nervous mercenaries; not a good combination.

Joel panned the phone's camera over the park, then zoomed in on the tank. An officer emerged from the hatch. He was a tall man with very dark skin, and a geometric pattern of scars on each cheek. He scanned the crowd, then raised a megaphone to his lips.

"This is a restricted area!" His English was barely intelligible. "All civilians disperse in an orderly fashion. I repeat: For your safety, you are ordered to leave the area at once!"

The crowd didn't budge, perhaps out of anger, perhaps because they were hemmed in by the security fences surrounding the park. At the front lines a shirtless white guy with dreadlocks began to shout, "Hell no! We won't go!"

The crowd took up the chant, which gradually changed to "Puloski must go!" The shouts became louder, until it became a thunderous roar.

The African scowled and spoke into a walkie-talkie. The armor-clad mercenaries pushed the masks they'd been wearing around their necks onto their faces. White clouds of tear gas billowed into the crowd. The contractors raised their plastic shields and advanced into the mob, swinging riot batons at anyone unlucky enough to be in their way. People coughed and wheezed as they fled from the gas; stumbling toward the fringes of the park.

As the smell wafted in their direction, Joel raised his shirt collar over his face. Groucho sneezed. Joel glanced over his shoulder, looking for a possible way out. He wasn't so worried about himself. Would the dog, with his keen sense of smell, be affected more severely?

There were sirens in the distance. Joel craned his neck to see. Down the street came a procession of armored police vehicles, at least seven of them. It was difficult to read the inscriptions, but they appeared to be from various jurisdictions. "Uh-oh, Groucho, the jig is up." Hundreds of people would be arrested and hauled away to God-knows-where. Joel wondered if they should leave now, or wait until Hell broke loose, and take advantage of the chaos.

"There's something funny going on..." Joel said to the dog. This operation seemed to be cobbled together from random agencies, yet any given city would have more firepower than this. Was it because they expected trouble in their own areas as well?

Less than a hundred yards from where Joel stood, an armored personnel carrier rolled up slowly, parting the crowds as it approached the Capitol. The sign on the door said 'Oakland Police.' When it reached the edge of the cleared area in the center of the plaza, it stopped.

From the vehicle came the shriek of feedback as a public address system turned on. The contractors stopped their advance, as if awaiting the announcement. "This is a message to Acting Governor Puloski. On behalf of the people of California, and our patriotic comrades in law enforcement, the Pledge Keepers, we demand your immediate resignation." The voice was deep, confident, and strangely familiar.

Joel pointed his camera phone at the APC and zoomed it in. Though no one was visible, he recognized the voice. He'd seen this man in the mainstream media, as well as on the Undernet. It was DeLane MacGuiness, the Butler Brigade's second in command.

MacGuiness continued, "We also demand an investigation into the death of Manuel Lopez, and the appointment of an interim governor by the Legislature. Come out with your hands up, and we promise you a fair trial. Please call off your legions of foreign mercenaries; we sincerely wish to avoid bloodshed. You have thirty minutes, starting now."

That explained the hodge-podge of police vehicles. Some of the cops had joined the rebels. Joel was surprised to see so many. But something about this situation stank, and it wasn't just the tear gas. Were the protesters just pawns to be sacrificed to the cause?

For the time being, the tear gas was stopped, and contractors stood their ground as the people retreated. Joel was horrified to see children among them, but at least they were getting out of harm's way. Though a large number of others, mostly young men, remained in the park, tying scarves around their faces as they waited for the battle to resume.

Despite his own fear and Groucho's squirming, Joel stayed as well. This was the journalistic opportunity of the decade. As his Pop used to say, "No guts, no glory."

It was like a bone dry forest, just waiting for a spark. Up in front of the crowd, the dread-locked white guy was at it again. The man was either high, crazed with adrenalin, or both. He let out a battle cry and charged toward the soldiers through the empty area. From the back of one of the trucks, the gunner fired a burst, knocking the assailant to the ground in a bloody heap.

The remaining crowd screamed, charged and trampled, as the mercenaries fired at them indiscriminately. Joel tried to take cover, such as there was, behind the lamp post. He watched in horror as a man clutched a motionless young woman, covered in blood. Through it all, the phone was in Joel's hand, still recording.

"Cease fire! Cease fire!" DeLane's anguished voice boomed over the chaos. "Stop!"

They did stop, and the contractors began falling one by one, writhing in pain. The two gunners fell off their trucks to the ground. As the maddened crowd rushed forward to attack them, they too, fell down heaving as if hit by an instantaneous flu.

Over the shouting, Joel heard a hum from MacGuiness' APC. For the first time he noticed a large dish antenna mounted on the top. Now it made sense; this was one of those 'non-lethal' microwave weapons. The men inside the tank, however, were immune from the ray's effects. Its gun swiveled and took aim at the rebel vehicles. Before the tank could fire, a projectile was lobbed from one of the armored police cars; it landed near the tank's open hatch. Two men erupted from the tank, hacking their lungs out.

Now the other SWAT vehicles, which had been hanging back, crept forward. The mercenaries were struggling to get up. Though the pain ray had stopped, it was too late for the contractors. As their trucks neared the enemy line, the rebels poured out, clad in body armor, and proceeded to disarm and zip-tie the mercenaries. From the distance there were more sirens; this time, firetrucks and ambulances.

Joel grinned. "Where's the fat lady? She's missing her cue." With his hired guns subdued, Puloski had no choice but to surrender. Though, being a politician, he wouldn't necessarily take the sensible way out. Groucho panted heavily; the suspense was killing them both. Joel reached into his pocket and pulled out a cigar. He lit up, ignoring dirty looks from the folks below. If they were crazy enough to risk being shot, surely they could endure a little second hand smoke.

Joel sat on the concrete base and stroked Groucho's neck as they waited. Though reluctant to surrender his viewing post, he feared that the 'official' police or perhaps the Guard (if any had returned from Nigeria) would arrive to renew the conflict. There was an eerie calm as the rebels loaded the captured mercenaries into a prison bus. The park was strewn with casualties, both dead and injured, but the paramedics seemed to have the situation in hand.

It was difficult to tell if anything else was happening. If there were any deliberations they were no doubt taking place by phone. Nearly an hour had gone by when the PA system switched on, and DeLane's voice boomed over the crowd. "Acting Governor Puloski has agreed to resign."

A loud cheer went up from the crowd. Ironically, some of them chanted, "USA, USA!"

The APC started up and drove to the foot of the capitol steps. DeLane MacGuiness emerged from the vehicle; he wore simple olive drab fatigues and body armor. As he walked up the steps, there was a loud crack. DeLane was knocked off his feet, and slammed to the concrete walk. Immediately the rebels returned fire, directing the fusillade on an open window on the top floor of the west wing. Whoever shot DeLane, Joel thought, was probably history.

As medics rushed the Lieutenant away, the APC started up again. The remaining onlookers shrieked as the heavy vehicle bounced over the few steps and slammed into the front door. Dust and mortar flew everywhere. The APC backed up and the rebels poured in through the enlarged doorway. The crowd of civilians milled around excitedly; a few brave souls tried to get in closer but a line of Pledge Keepers stood in front to keep them back.

As the breeze brought a new whiff of the remaining tear gas, Groucho began to cough and hack. Worried for the animal's life, Joel decided to leave, scoop or no scoop, but now the people were now streaming around them back toward the capitol. "Just hang in there, Buddy," Joel said. "When the lemmings finish their trip to the sea, we'll go."

A few tense moments later, an escort of four Butler Brigade soldiers appeared at the hole in the statehouse with a small gray-haired man between them. Joel zoomed his camera phone to get the action. The former Governor was handcuffed and disheveled, a morose expression on his face. Once again the crowd cheered. For a moment, Joel feared another riot, but the people were subdued. It appeared that the day's tragedies had ruined their mood for celebration.

"OK, Groucho," Joel said. "Time to get you to a vet." He knew a place on the south side of the city that accepted barter. The dog limped along for a few blocks, then Joel bent down and picked him up. Oy, he was heavy! It was a long walk to the truck.

Groucho seemed a bit better as Joel drove out through the snail-paced traffic. There were frenetic news reports on KFQQ about the Sacramento Massacre. There was endless speculation about what would happen next, but little more information than Joel already knew. He was about to change the station when they interrupted with breaking news:

"Surviving members of the legislature have nominated House Speaker Julius Chang as the interim governor, then unanimously passed a resolution removing California from the United States. Governor Chang has already signed the bill. The California Republic has been reborn!"

The border guard stared at the computer screen. "Nobody told us to expect any missile components."

"I assure you, Sir," Nephi said, "This is a communications satellite, and it's totally legitimate. This thumb drive has the manifest, as well as Governor, I mean President Davis' electronic signature." He handed the man a small plastic object imprinted with a hologram of the Great Seal of the Texas Republic.

The guard plugged the drive into a slot on the front of his computer. "Sorry, I've only been here a few weeks." He made a few mouse clicks and stared at the screen some more. "It appears to be authentic, but I still need to call my supervisor."

Nephi looked back at the highway behind them. From his vantage point, the line of vehicles stretched back all the way through Ciudad Acuna. "If you'll pardon my asking, how did things get so messed up? You look like you're fully staffed."

"A lot of the customs people were anti-independence and quit when the Legislature voted to secede. Some of 'em got arrested when they tried to stay on but wouldn't take orders from Austin." He picked up the phone and dialed. Horns honked in the distance.

Emal peered down at them from the cab of the semi-truck. "What is the problem? Is a gratuity in order? I have some silver coinage."

Nephi shook his head vigorously, then put a finger to his lips. The Albanian meant well, but he needed to shake the habits of the Old Country. Though America was becoming more like Albania – or at least, its negative stereotype – with each passing day. He turned back to the guard. "We hoped the security would have relaxed a bit, because of the blockade and all."

"All the more reason to be careful; Washington could be sending spies and saboteurs. And with things so crazy in Mexico... Yesterday we had a guy come in with a truckload of marijuana. He thought just because they legalized it down there, that we had, too."

"You'll find no drugs in our trucks," Nephi said.

"Uh-huh. Yes, Sir." The guard hung up and let out a deep breath. "You're free to enter. But next time I hear there's rockets coming over the river, I'm calling in sick."

Nephi climbed back into the cab's passenger seat. "It's a go!"

"Praise to..." the Albanian paused, "Jesus." He started the truck; they were on there way.

"Indeed." Nephi was aware of Emal's true identity; the man was a Muslim masquerading as a Latino named Julio. "I thank the Lord that we've made it this far. Just pray the Feds don't bomb us to smithereens. Siri would never forgive me if I got myself killed."

Emal laughed. "My wife, either." His expression became serious. "Do you think the Texas Air Guard will try to protect us?"

Nephi shrugged. "I don't know if they can stop an air attack, but I'm sure they'll try. Because Richard Branford sank an awful lot of money into the place. He might finally get his the space tourism business off the ground, so to speak."

"I wish he was going to be here. I have always wanted to meet the man."

Nephi braced himself with a hand on the dash. "Julio, are you sure you know how to drive this thing? You almost ran that Subaru off the road!"

"I am a licensed commercial driver. He needs to stop texting and watch the road."

"Just slow down and take it easy." Nephi felt bad for his outburst. No doubt Emal was as nervous as he was; luckily they didn't have far to go. Their destination, formerly Laughlin Air Force Base, was just a few miles east of Del Rio.

Laughlin was one of the many bases whose personnel had sided with Texas after the secession vote. Nephi found it amazing they'd done so well in this regard, when California was under siege from within its own territory. Probably it helped that Texas had enough in its treasury to keep a lot of soldiers on the payroll. Still, the new republic was forced to downsize several facilities, including Laughlin, half of which was sold to Branford's company.

The truck complained as Emal hit the air brakes. "Here we are, Nephi!"

The 'Maiden Galactic' sign at the gate was so new the paint looked wet. Workers were tearing down the old chain link fence, replacing it with prefabricated sections. This was one of Branford's innovations; the wall had intrusion sensors were embedded in the material.

The guard was a short Asian man in a blue uniform that looked like something out of Star Trek. As Larsen rolled the truck up to the kiosk, the man hit a switch and the gate swung open. "Welcome, Gentlemen. We've been expecting you."

Emal put it in gear and they rumbled through.

"I'm surprised the Feds haven't bombed this place already," Nephi said. "Surely their 'no fly zone' includes rocket launches. We should have done it in Mexico like we first planned."

"I agree with your concern. However, I'm also more familiar with corruption in my, um, home country. We have already paid far too much to the drug lords just to get our shipment through. Either path would have been dangerous."

"True, but this is a lot more important than our personal safety. If we succeed in getting FreeStar up there, it's good-bye to government censorship and surveillance. If we fail, we've wasted a whole bunch of time and money, and may not get another chance."

"Unless the Feds shoot it down." Emal turned at a big sign marked 'LAUNCH SITE 1.'

"Let's pray they don't. It helps that we're using their own technology against them." Nephi looked up as they approached a large building. "Is that the control bunker? Looks like it could survive a nuclear war."

"If the President makes good on her threats, we may need to."

Nephi frowned. "I know the woman is desperate, but she'd never resort to nukes. That's just the rumor mill going overboard. Even Wilton isn't that insane."

The Albanian didn't answer; he just turned down what appeared to be a runway, toward a skeletal metal structure which towered over the arid scrub land. As they neared the launch pad, they saw a huge cylindrical object lying on its side on the tarmac. The end facing them narrowed to a circle about ten feet in diameter. This was where the nose cone would go.

Emal stopped the truck near the site. A stocky, red-bearded man in a yellow hard hat approached them. He mounted the step to the semi's cab and peered through the open window. "It's about time you guys got here. Our baby sitters were ready to scrub the launch."

"There was some confusion at the border," Emal said.

"I'm not surprised to see you here, JL," Nephi said. "You must be like a kid in a candy store, getting to work on an actual satellite launch."

"I wish. That jerk from Branford's corporate office won't let me touch anything, because I'm not a licensed electrician. The Raptors sent over some guys from Louisiana, supposedly they're qualified, but you've never seen such a bunch of rubes."

"Let's not worry about our egos," Nephi jumped out of the cab and walked around. "As long as we get this baby into space. Emal, could you back the trailer up to the booster?"

"Hold on, just one minute!" A slight short man, also wearing a hard hat, came running up from behind the booster. Despite the heat and humidity, he was wearing black pants and a black shirt and tie. "Who are you, and what authorization do you have to be on this project?"

"Nephi Snow, chief communications officer, Butler Brigade." He extended a hand to shake, but the black-clad man made no move to accept it. "Call Commander MacGuiness; he'll vouch for me. I also have a crypto-signed authorization from President Davis for the satellite."

"Alright, then. As long as you understand who's in charge." He turned and chased after Emal. "You there, in the truck! Not so fast, this is a sensitive installation!"

Larsen grinned. "His name's Meader. He's not quite as big of an asshole as he seems. A real germophobe, he won't shake *anybody's* hand."

"I'll call MacGuiness." Nephi pulled out his cell phone. "He'll straighten this guy out. We can't afford to keep anybody on the sidelines right now."

"Don't bother, Mac's not accepting any cell calls. We're pretty sure our secure cell protocols have been compromised."

Nephi exhaled in a huff; he was running out of patience today. "I've been working on some better algorithms, but until then, we can't just stop communicating entirely."

"It's not that. It's the hit squads they're worried about. After what happened to Lopez, not to mention the attempt on Davis' life." The latter incident was not public knowledge, but widely known in rebel circles.

"I understand," Nephi said, "But we're all taking risks here."

"Right. So, let's get 'er done!" Larsen picked up a walkie-talkie from a clip on his belt. "Hey Deveraux, can you get over here with the crane? We've got the nose cone ready to go."

Larsen strode off to where Emal and the others were unloading the contents of the semi-trailer. From the other side of the gantry a diesel powered crane rolled up. As Nephi watched them, he felt an uncharacteristic tightness in his gut. It didn't seem plausible that the Feds were going to let them get away with this.

Meader returned. His earlier anger seemed to have subsided, but his forehead was creased with lines of anxiety.

"Your friend Larsen insists on wiring the nose cone, against my explicit instructions. He's not qualified to do that. If our provider finds out, they'll cancel all coverage for this launch."

"He knows the satellite as well as anybody. The company in Singapore manufactured it according to his specifications."

"Nevertheless, I'm personally responsible if anything happens..."

"Listen, I know you're just doing your job. Who's in charge here? I'll go talk to them."

"Ms. Sims, at the Command Center, but she's no more likely to approve this travesty."

"Tell you what. I'll have a word with Ms. Sims. You keep an eye on Jon Larsen while he works. You *are* qualified to do that, aren't you?"

"Of course, but..."

"What's the quickest– oh, never mind." Nephi spied an open electric cart parked just past the rocket's side booster. He turned and ran quickly in that direction.

"Wait, you can't..." Over his shoulder Nephi saw Meader throw up his hands and head for the nose of the rocket.

Nephi hadn't thought to ask for the key, but luckily it was still in the switch. He got in the cart's driver's seat, switched on the motor, and drove toward the big concrete building.

At the door there were three guards, two black and one Hispanic, dressed in fatigues and carrying rifles. A pale wiry man with graying blond hair stood between them, smoking, "Nephi, so glad you could make it." He took a last drag, threw the cigarette to the ground, and crushed it under foot. "The Boss Lady is expecting you."

"Please to see you, too, Sergei." Nephi was not fond of Sergei Gorkachev; he had to remind himself they were on the same side. The Russian had two decades experience in the Russian aerospace industry. After his emigration to America, he went to work for the Free Speech Foundation. Many people credited him with holding the organization together in the grim years since 9/11. The trouble was, he'd never let anyone forget that fact.

Sergei sent one of the guards back to the launch site with the cart. Then he and Nephi entered the building and walked down a long hallway to the control room. Though the room had no windows, there was a giant video screen on one wall with a view of the outside. Right now it showed a close-up of the empty metal gantry.

Standing over a row of consoles, which were staffed by four men and a woman, stood a smartly dressed dark-haired lady. She turned as the newcomers approached.

Sergei stepped up, having apparently promoted himself to a leadership role. "This is Nephi Snow. He is the Butler Brigade's liaison for the Free Star project. Nephi, this is Victoria Sims, COO of Maiden Galactic."

Nephi extended a hand. "It's a pleasure to meet you."

"Mister Snow," she replied. Her hand was cool and warm. "We almost had to cancel the launch due to your tardiness." Her accent reminded Nephi of Siri, whose speech had a British inflection.

Sergei furrowed his brow. "Apparently Robert Branford didn't trust us to do what we said we would, since he felt compelled to send his babysitters."

Victoria smiled, showing surprisingly perfect teeth. "Yes. *Sir* Robert supports your cause, but he has ample reason to be concerned. If your cobbled-together launch vehicle were to explode or fall on a populated area, the corporation could be held liable."

"Ms. Sims," Nephi interjected. "We're all very grateful to Sir Robert for letting us use these facilities, and practically for free. Your boss is a great friend of liberty."

"True. Though to be honest, it's partly because he's brassed off about all the trouble the US government gave us at his first launch facility in New Mexico. But that's neither here nor there. You men know computers, we can use all the help we can get."

Nephi and Sergei took their places behind two empty consoles. "I wish I could help you," she continued. "But my computer expertise is confined to financial modeling programs."

"That's OK. I don't envy your job. You're between the proverbial rock and hard place."

She laughed dryly. This time her smile seemed genuine. "Tell me, Mr. Snow, are we wasting our time here? Is this new stealth technology all it's cracked up to be?"

"You mean, can we prevent the US government from shooting it down?" He shrugged. "I'm no expert, but the DOD itself developed the technology. It's not so much a satellite as a swarm of micro-satellites that communicate by radio. In theory it's impossible to take them all out, because it has redundant components spread out over an area of several cubic miles."

On the big monitor they watched the assembled rocket rise slowly to its upright position. An enormous sky-crane did the lifting. It was large as the machines used to build high rise hotels back in Vegas. Nephi shook his head. *I'm as bad as JL, better get to work.*

There was plenty to be done. Nephi and the others monitored the systems while Victoria paced the control room, giving orders and arguing with Sergei. When the gantry connections were complete and the main engine was fueled up (the side boosters, as on the Space Shuttle, used solid fuel), it was almost time to launch. Larsen returned in the shuttle with Meader, Emal and the first two of the launch site workers. As he entered the building he shouted, "Yes! We did it!" He made the rounds, and high-fived or fist-bumped everyone, even Victoria. As she returned the gesture, a smile flicked across her face.

She picked a microphone off the console and spoke into it. "Good work everyone, but let's not celebrate too soon. We have a tight launch window. Where's the fire suppression crew?"

A man in blue coveralls spoke up. "Next door at the Air Guard base. They had some equipment trouble, but they'll be here in a quarter hour."

"Thank you, Mr. Devereaux," Victoria said. "Alright then. Countdown to launch is 60 minutes." The numbers went up on the big screen, superimposed over the view port.

Nephi had caught Larsen's enthusiasm. It felt like the time he'd drank a whole liter of Pepsi while driving cross-country. He checked his console again. At that moment, the virtual gauges which showed the fuel and liquid oxygen pressure dropped to zero and flat-lined.

"Excuse me, Ms. Sims? I'm seeing a problem with the fuel system, or maybe it's just the sensors. I'm getting a reading of zero."

She leaned down to look at the screen. "Hmm..." Her perfume was subtle but familiar; it made Nephi miss Siri even more than he already did. "Not good."

Victoria spoke into the mike again. "Pause the countdown. We have a problem, the launch is on hold."

"What is it?" Larsen peered at Nephi's screen. "I know where that is; it shouldn't take more than an hour to fix" He looked at Victoria. "Permission to return to the launch pad?"

"Granted, provided you take Mr. Devereaux along in case you run into trouble."

In a minute the two were in the electric shuttle, speeding toward the launch site. The monitor showed the dust trail as they crossed the dry land between the runways A nervous tension filled the room as they watched the two men enter the tower.

"Ms. Sims, we have another problem." A young Hispanic woman was sitting at the radar screen, which tracked incoming weather as well as any aircraft hearing the launch site. "I've got two bogies coming in from Mexico, 300 kph."

"Let me see." Victoria's face went white. Seconds later, she was knocked off her feet by a blast that echoed through the concrete bunker, and the place shook. One of the Brigade's guards was there instantly to help her up. The picture on the big screen went white, then was replaced by the image of a dust cloud and in the distance, flames.

"What the hell?" Sergei shouted, "The God damn Mexicans just let them through!"

"The cartels run the border states; if it doesn't hurt their business, they couldn't care less." Nephi said. "But the Texas Air Guard is right next door, can't they do something?"

Victoria was already on the phone. "Colonel? Yes, we've been hit! They missed the rocket but there's a fire at the bottom of the gantry."

Nephi jumped out of his seat. "No! JL's up there! Where are the fire fighters?"

"There's a tanker truck out back," Emal said. "Quickly, where are the keys?"

"No!" Victoria was livid. "I can't let you do that! The Texas Guard will be here any moment. Leave this building and I'll have you both arrested. "

The guards at the door didn't move to stop them. As he and Emal got into the firetruck, Nephi looked up and saw the drones returning from the north. At that same moment two surface-to-air missiles streaked in from the east. As Emal started the truck, a fireball appeared over their heads. "Praise the Prophet! They stopped at least one of them!"

Nephi braced himself as they bounced over the half mile to the launch pad. Their path was strewn with rocks and chunks of asphalt thrown up by the earlier strike near the bunker.

Emal handed him a fireman's helmet with a face shield. "You get the hose. I'll turn on the pump, then I'll be right with you!"

It took Nephi precious seconds to unhook the hose. They were dangerously close the burning gantry. They had to stop the fire before it reached the rocket's solid fuel booster.

"Hold on tight; it will kick when the pump turns on!" Emal's voice came over the truck's loudspeaker. Though Nephi tightened his grip, the hose almost leaped out of his hand. Emal appeared from around the back, "We need to get closer; I'll reel it out."

Nephi struggled forward with the hose. The heat was overwhelming. Despite the mask, he could hardly see, and the sparks whipped up by the Texas wind singed his clothes. There was a cloud of steam as the foamy liquid hit the blaze. Larsen and Devereaux might not burn to death, but the heat would soon cause the structure to collapse.

"We're making progress!" Emal shouted. "Good thing we didn't wait!"

The roaring sound returned followed by another explosion; Nephi was knocked to the ground. He lifted his head to see the tower. The areas they'd just extinguished were burning again. He tried to get up, but something had him pinned. Then he saw the truck was gone and there was what looked like an engine block on his leg. The pain was excruciating.

He lay there, half conscious, as the sirens approached. A second firetruck pulled up beside him; two paramedics rushed over. "Stay still, we'll get this thing off your leg."

"Where's Emal, I mean Julio? He was right here! And we have two men on the gantry!"

"Don't worry, we've got a ladder crew." In the background there was shouting and another explosion.

"JL! The rocket!"

"Keep still!" Two men lifted him onto the stretcher. "That was the second drone going down. If they hit the rocket, we'd all be dead."

Nephi twisted his neck to see. Smoke rolled off the gantry, but there were no visible flames. From nearby somebody yelled, "There were only two, right? Come on, let's get everybody out of here!"

As the men strapped Nephi down, he fought to stay conscious. "What happened to Julio? He was by the firetruck when it got hit."

"That must have been the guy who got thrown. Lots of broken bones, probably a major concussion, but it looks like he'll recover. We got the two men off the gantry in time, but we lost two of our own, and two more being air-evac'ed to the hospital."

The ride away from the launch pad was even rougher than the ride there. Nephi let out a moan of despair and prayed. *Oh Lord, we needed this satellite so badly...*

"Mendoza!" Came the driver's voice from up front. "You're not going to believe this! They're launching the rocket!"

"What? That's insane! It's not safe! The control structure suffered serious damage."

"Really?" Nephi's voice was hoarse. "It's going up?"

The paramedic picked up his phone. "Base, what's the status on the launch?" He listened for a second, then said, "It's almost out of the atmosphere. They got lucky, but there's going to be hell to pay, for whoever authorized this."

"Sergei, I'd guess." Nephi hissed through clenched teeth. "Darn it, my leg really hurts."

"I'm giving you a morphine shot, try to relax."

Nephi gritted his teeth at the poke of the needle. "Whew, that's better already. Between the pain and the stress it felt like my heart was gonna explode. It's just so... important and yet... was it worth people dying for?" He sniffled. "Sorry, I feel stupid, my wife and kids are in hiding and I can't reach them and I'm so worried." He began to weep softly.

"Take it easy, Sir, you're in shock. Don't worry, I'm sure your family will be OK."

"It's not just that. I feel so flipping overwhelmed. I can't believe we did it. We've got our own satellite! The Feds can't shut us down now."

The paramedic gave him the kind look usually reserved for lunatics. "Good for you, Kid."

"Do you have a tissue? Thanks." He blew his nose. "All I know is, it makes me really proud to be an American."

The medic laughed. "I'm just a Texan now, and even I'm a bit choked up."

Siri awoke with a start, drenched in sweat. Where was she? Where was the baby?

She leaped out of bed, pulled on a robe and threw open the door. Now she remembered where she was, but where was little Padmi? This house was so tiny, she couldn't be far.

Her search was very brief. Lottie Two-Arrows sat in a kitchen chair, cradling the tiny baby in her arms, singing softly. "Good morning," she half-whispered. "I hope you don't mind. I heard her fussing, and I figured you could use the sleep."

"Looks like she's in good hands," Siri exhaled in relief as she sat down across the table. Then she felt another wave of panic. "Where's Will?"

"Outside playing with Jimmy. Don't worry, I'm keeping an eye on them."

Siri hoped she was just being paranoid. It was hard not to be, with Nephi out on his 'top secret' mission. And those horrible rumors about Wilton authorizing death squads. At first she doubted Joel's revelation, but then Lopez was assassinated. The Sacramento police had suspects in custody, and they were not *jihadis* but mobsters – just as the Albanian had predicted.

"Help yourself to cereal and toast," Lottie said. "I made coffee."

"Thanks." Siri poured a third of a cup of coffee and topped it off with milk. Sipping it, she grimaced, then looked at Lottie. "Any news from your parents?"

"Mom sent a message this morning. She never says much, just asks if we're OK. She said the weather's hot, so they must be somewhere south. Sure hope they're not in California."

Considering recent events, Siri understood her concern. "Knowing your parents, they're probably someplace else. They seem to have a knack for avoiding the trouble spots." Lottie's parents frequently traveled for business; they dealt in untaxed cigarettes and other contraband. Here in Pine Ridge, South Dakota, there wasn't much in the way of economic opportunity.

Though Siri appreciated the Two Arrows' offer of asylum, she also felt like a babysitter. They'd left 16-year-old Lottie in charge and were no doubt glad to have an adult around.

Siri peeked out the kitchen window. Will was laughing and shouting as Lottie's little brother chased him around the shaggy grass of the yard. Despite Siri's worries about the constant danger and frequent moving, Will seemed pretty well adjusted.

Her biggest worry was, were they safe here? So far she and Nephi had managed to stay a step ahead of the Feds. After the death squad rumors, Nephi insisted she find a safe place to hide. In her younger days that would have infuriated her, but these days, their first priority was the children. She worried about Nephi as well. The last time he'd checked in was a week earlier. "Sorry, Love," he'd told her. "We're working on a critical operation, so I won't be able to use my phone, even the secure one." All she could do was pray for his safety.

"Lottie," she said, as the girl set Padmi in her playpen. "May I use your Internet?"

"Be my guest. It's satellite, sometimes we have problems connecting. You might have to try a few times before you get on."

Siri logged on, and entered her password for the Undernet. Access was still anonymous, and fairly secure from government surveillance, but running as it was on the computers of volunteers, the bandwidth was insufficient for video or even audio. It was text-only, like the dark ages before the Web.

As in the 1970's, people used virtual bulletin boards, where a person could post encrypted messages, and the recipient with the proper key could download and read them. The list looked like gibberish, some aliases but mostly numeric identifiers. Siri sighed, nothing from Nephi.

She scanned the list again, in case she'd missed it. These were long strings of numbers, and unlike her phone, this computer didn't have an app that would automatically match Nephi's ID. As she read the message headers, a non-numeric handle caught her eye: 'Seventh Stooge.' Somehow, amidst all the craziness, Joel was still writing. She clicked and opened it.

You all heard the big news from California, and I'm the schmuck for missing this one. California, declaring independence? Texas I expected, maybe even Vermont. But seriously, folks, the Grizzly Bear Republic was never for real, not even in 1846. Yet they did it, and all it took was for Wilton's poodle Puloski to badly botch the crowd control. Of course, it didn't hurt that they caught the gangsters who waxed Lopez, the ones what were supposedly crazed towel heads.

That's what it took for California to get off its collective sun-tanned ass. Not that they had contingency plans like the Texans, oh no. Governor Angelita batted her eyelashes and got the military commanders on their side. "We got oil money to keep the bases open, y'all." No, California Just Did It, and ended up with the US Army occupying everything from Bakersfield to the Mexican border. The Feds would've taken it all, but for

a rash of mysterious equipment failures and lots of their guys going AWOL. By the way, anybody see our friend MacGuiness lately?

Joel's news didn't make Siri feel any better. If Mac's people stirring up trouble in California, he might be there with them. She understood the need for security, but being kept in the dark about his whereabouts made her furious. One more time she checked the list for new messages, and there at the bottom was Nephi's ID. With trembling hands she entered her private key; the message appeared, dated two days ago. *A curse on this crippled Undernet!*

Sweetheart, I want you to know I'm safe, and nowhere near California; can't say much more. Give Padma and Will a kiss, tell them Daddy loves them. Also, be very careful, the plot 7S warned about didn't stop with Lopez. There was an attempt on the Commander's life, Albanians again, so they're not just targeting rebel governors. I don't want to worry you, but be ready to relocate within the week. I'll send you details as soon as this operation is done. Love always, Nephi.

Lottie entered the room, cell phone in hand. "This probably nothing, but..."

Siri stopped breathing for a moment. "What? What's going on?"

"Just got a text from my cousin Jim; you know, the one in the NAM. They got volunteer security patrols along the highways now. Jim saw those guys from the picture you gave me."

"Who? You mean the Albanian Mafia?"

"Yeah. There were two vehicles with Florida plates, a big white crew cab and a black Hummer, traveling together. Stopped for gas just across the Nebraska border."

"Oh my God... Lottie, I have to take the kids and get out of here. I'm putting you all in danger." Except for its remoteness, Pine Ridge was not a good hiding place. Everything for miles around was empty grassy hills.

"Are you sure, Siri? There's lots of foreigners running around in fancy cars these days. Like my dad always says, 'It doesn't help to panic.' "

"Considering what I've heard about these guys, I'm not taking any chances."

Lottie nodded. "You're right, we better all get out of the house, just in case. I'll round up the kids." She headed for the door, then turned back. "Shouldn't we just call 9-1-1?"

"No! These men may be Federal contractors; the local police might just turn me over to them. They could arrest you, too, for harboring me. Then what'll happen to the kids?"

"Those are my people, they wouldn't..." Lottie stopped in mid-sentence. "Though if they have badges... oh well, let's be on the safe side."

Quickly Siri threw her things together. She and Lori strapped the kids in the back seat of the Two Arrows' old Suburban.

"Everybody ready?" Lottie emerged from the house with a rifle and a shotgun. The sight startled Siri; her mind had refused to believe she and her children were in mortal danger.

Siri barely had her door closed when Lottie peeled out of the gravel driveway.

The seat belt warning dinged loudly as Lottie struggled to put hers on. "They were going west on 18. We'll head for the Badlands; maybe we can lose 'em there. Siri, maybe we *should* call 9-1-1, these are Rez cops, they all know me and my parents. If those gangsters are as bad as you say they are, will we be able to get away from them?"

"I see your point, but let's give it a try, OK?"

One thing about the prairie, it was a tough place to sneak up on someone. "Somebody's following us," Lottie said, glancing in the rear view mirror. "Looks like the truck they mentioned. But how would they be able to find us like that? Could they be tracing your phone?"

362

"No, we only use stealth phones. Somehow they must know I'm with you, and of course they can get the plate number from the DMV." Siri stared at the white truck. It was gaining on them, even though Lottie was going at least 75. As they rounded a curve, she could see the black Hummer close behind it.

"OK, I'll call." Siri dialed, waited a moment. "Damn! It went through to voice mail. What's with this place?" She waited impatiently for the beep. "Hello, we're on highway 165 being followed by two suspicious vehicles. I think they're trying to kidnap us." She described their pursuers and hung up.

"They're getting closer," Lottie said. "We've got to go faster. If the highway patrol stops us, good; we'll have witnesses."

The engine complained as Lottie stepped on the gas and put it in high gear. Siri glanced at the speedometer. They were going nearly ninety on this pot-holed two lane highway. The white truck and black Hummer were still gaining on them.

From the back, Will yelled. "Mommy, I have to go potty!"

"Hold on, OK?" Lottie shouted. "We'll stop soon!" Lowering her voice, she said to Siri, "You have your husband's pistol? Make sure it's loaded; we may need it!"

"OK, but I'm a terrible shot!" Nephi had taken her to the firing range several times, but firing his .45 made her flinch so badly she could hardly hit the target at all. This .22 was the largest caliber she could handle, and he'd practically forced her to carry it, despite her reluctance.

"Then let me do the shooting."

For a while they sat in silence, while Lori kept the kids busy singing 'Old MacDonald.'

Siri kept glancing back nervously. "Do you think we can make it to the Badlands before they catch up? We might find a hiding place there."

Lottie's usual confidence had evaporated. "Probably not. Hey, I have an idea! See that hill?" To the west a single butte rose above the prairie. "I know it pretty well. My dad used to take me deer hunting there. Anyway, if there's one thing Betsy here can do, it's climb."

"But won't we be sitting ducks?"

"It'll slow them down. It's been raining; maybe they'll get stuck. And I know the way to get down the other side."

Lottie slowed the Suburban to a crawl, and turned onto a trail that was barely more than two wheel tracks. It was a brutally rough. They hit a bump so hard, Padmi started crying.

As they drove further up the hill, the trail narrowed. The earth rose abruptly on their right, forming sort of a wall. On their left they were only a few feet away from a steep drop off.

"Lottie, it looks really muddy. Be careful so you don't get stuck."

Lottie grinned. "Don't worry, this beast can go anywhere." She stopped and shifted the old-school manual transmission into super low. The engine roared as they resumed their laborious climb. As they entered the muddy area, the teenager gunned the engine. The truck slid to the left, toward the drop off. They came to a halt as it stalled with the check engine light on.

"Don't die on me now! No, no!" Lottie turned the ignition key again and again. Each time the starter turned the engine but it it was no go. "Shit, I mean shoot, I flooded it!"

"Don't panic," Siri said, her fears overwhelmed by necessity. "We'll continue on foot. You get the kids together. I'll go off on my own and lead them away. It's me they want."

"No, I can't let you face them alone." Lottie turned to her sister, still in the back. "Lori, take the kids. A few yards up the hill there's kind of a small cave you can hide in."

"But," Lori wailed, "I can't take all of them, what about the baby?"

Struggling to keep herself calm, Siri jumped out of the truck. Her sneakers sank in the thick sucking mud. She opened the rear door and grabbed the duffel she'd thrown a few things into. "Here, I've got a baby backpack so you can carry Padma. Quick!"

"I hafta potty!" Will screeched.

Beside him, Jimmy began to cry. "I'm scared! I want my mommy!"

"You can pee by that bush," Lottie said. "Then Lori will take you all on a hike, OK?"

Lori wiped her tears and smiled. "Come on, you guys, we're going on a hike. It'll be fun!"

Once Lori had the baby on her back, Lottie handed her the shotgun. "Don't point it at anybody you don't want to shoot." She grabbed the rifle. Siri reluctantly took Nephi's pistol.

They hurried a hundred feet or so up the trail, then Lottie directed Lori to take what looked like a cow path up the side of the hill. As she watched the kids over her shoulder, Siri once again felt terror in her gut. She prayed they could somehow stay hidden from the bad guys.

Lottie forged on ahead. Siri double-checked the gun's safety, then hurried to catch up. The weapon was like an anchor in her pocket. Despite Nephi's shooting lessons, she felt completely out of her depth.

"Here, those rocks at the top!" Lottie called. "We'll take cover there."

They reached the summit none too soon; they could see the white pickup inching around the stalled Suburban as the Hummer waited behind.

"I think I can slow them down a bit. Cover your ears." Lottie crouched behind one of the lower rocks, resting the rifle on the flat surface. She squinted through the telescopic sight, pulled the trigger and crack! A hole appeared in the truck's front grill. Another shot, and they could see the steam rising from the vehicle's hood.

"Lottie, you're an amazing shot!"

The girl grinned. "Got my deer three years in a row, before Mom and Dad left town."

The women watched intently as the doors opened on both vehicles. Lottie squeezed off another shot and laughed as the men scrambled for cover. "Just scaring 'em. I don't want to hurt anybody if I can avoid it. In case we're wrong about who these guys are." Again she fired a shot above their heads. The men crowded into the Hummer; it began to back down the trail.

For an instant Siri thought they were saved, but she knew the hoodlums wouldn't give up easily. "Now what are they doing?"

"Probably trying to find another way up, where they've got better cover. Lucky for us, we can see the entire hilltop. Bad thing is the whole western slope's out of our view."

Siri craned her neck; there was nothing moving in her field of vision. Again she wished Nephi were here. He was an excellent marksman, which would have evened their odds.

"Let's switch weapons." Lottie handed Siri the rifle, and took the pistol. "Just do what you saw me do. Come on, try it." She put a hand on Siri's shoulder. "Keep your head down! Now look through the scope. This rifle has laser sights, just put the red dot on your target."

Her heart beat like crazy. Siri swung the rifle around and sighted in on a round protrusion atop an oblong rock. It seemed easy, but when the time came to pull the trigger, could she do it?

They waited, almost not daring to breathe. Then a bullet whizzed over their heads. Lottie popped up and fired three rounds. There was a ringing in Siri's ears.

"There's two of em, just behind those rocks. I almost got one!"

"Lottie, what are we going to do?" As if in answer, Siri's phone rang. The display flashed 'Unknown Number.' Her mouth was so dry she could hardly answer. "Hello?"

A man's voice replied, with an East European accent. "Mrs. Snow, I presume?"

"Don't get any closer, we're armed!" She put the phone in speaker mode.

"Obviously, but you're outnumbered," said the voice. "There are six of us and only two of you. Nobody needs to get hurt, especially not the *children*."

"He's bluffing!" Lottie whispered.

"I don't know," Siri whispered back. The accent reminded her of the Albanian guy who'd been on Joel's show. *Oh my heavens, it's the Albanian Mob, just like they warned us.* Finally she responded, "There are no children with us."

"Go back where you came from." Lottie shouted at the phone. "This is a sovereign nation, and you don't belong here!" Lottie shot a glance at Siri, and mouthed "what now?"

"I see you're not taking us seriously. Hold your fire, ladies. Ahmed, show them what we found." Siri watched in horror as Lori and the boys appeared over the ridge, flanked by two of the gangster. Behind them came a well-dressed man wearing a headset.

As the man spoke, the voice on the phone continued. "We relieved the middle schooler of the shotgun she was carrying." He clucked his tongue disapprovingly. "Giving firearms to a child, that's a Federal offense. Now, enough fucking around. Mrs. Snow, you have thirty seconds to surrender or the children might be *accidentally* hit by the crossfire. Hands up, both of you!"

Lottie put down the pistol and started to raise her hands, but Siri shook her head. "No deal. First give the kids to my friend here, then I'll come with you peacefully." To Lottie, she whispered. "I'll leave you the cell phone so you can call for help."

They saw the man gesture, apparently talking to someone who wasn't visible. He turned back to face Siri and Lottie, and roughly grabbed Lori by the hair. "You think I'm joking? I'll shoot the girl and the baby, two for one!"

The two little boys started screaming. The Albanian waved his gun at them. "Shut up, you two, I swear I'll..." Before he could finish his sentence, his head jerked back and he fell to the ground. Siri's head snapped to Lottie, who had Nephi's gun in her hand. *Total insanity; she could have easily hit her own sister.*

Lottie stood up and shouted. "Kids, over here!" They dashed across the hilltop, with Padma still in Lori's arms. Everything seemed to go in slow motion as one of the henchmen raised his gun and took aim at the fleeing children. Another trained his gun on Lottie; there was no way she could defend herself; the children were between her and the bad guy.

There was one thunderous crack, and then another, as the first henchman fell on top of his comrade. The second shot was not so lucky; the man cried out and spun around, a spatter of red erupting from his left shoulder. He swung around to aim at Siri; she squeezed the trigger a third time only to produce a barely-audible click. *This is it,* "Buddha help us," Siri prayed.

The bullet didn't come. The remaining two mobsters dropped their weapons and raised their hands. Three men came into view, wearing police uniforms. Pine Ridge cops.

Siri looked down at the rifle in her hands. *I've killed a man.* She fought the nausea and staggered to her feet, then ran across the hilltop toward her children. Padma was wailing, still on Lori's back. Just a few yards from her goal, her foot hit a gopher hole and she went sprawling. A tan, acne-scarred face peered down at her, and a big hand helped her up. She threw her arms around him and sobbed uncontrollably.

"It's OK." The officer's voice was calm and deep. "It's over now."

"Captain?" said the officer who'd been checking the Albanian's corpse. "You won't believe this, but this man has a deputy Federal Marshal's badge."

Chapter 16 – The Beginning of the End

As Joel got out of the Jeep, he encountered the smell of pine and a slight breeze on his face. He had just arrived at an undisclosed location in the mountains of West Virginia. Commander MacGuiness invited him here for an exclusive interview, in his role as the 'Seventh Stooge.' Joel's escort, a stout, mannish woman, had blindfolded him at the Ohio River crossing.

"Can I take this *verkakte* thing off?"

"Certainly," said a familiar voice. "Kowalski's caution was commendable, but we're only here for a short time."

When he removed the blindfold, Joel was taken back. The voice belonged to a man in a motorized wheelchair. No doubt a quadriplegic, his arms rested motionless on the chair's armrests. He looked around 30, black skinned with close cropped hair and an athletic frame. He wore military fatigues, and a monocle-like device hung from a headband in front of one eye.

"Welcome to the Butler Brigade," he said. "Shall I call you Mr. Stooge?"

"Moe is fine." Joel had gone through so many aliases lately, he'd soon need a score card.

"Forgive me; I can't shake your hand. I'm Lieutenant DeLane MacGuiness, operations coordinator, Region 3."

"I'm honored to meet you." Joel paused a moment, overwhelmed by the Lieutenant's tragic condition. "I was there at the state capitol in Sacramento when Puloski resigned, and I was lucky enough to get video of those events. I must say I consider you to be a true hero. I only wish I'd been able to do more for the cause of liberty."

"Thank you. I have regrets of my own, though they don't change anything. The risk comes with the territory, and I'm a lot luckier than the seventeen who lost their lives that day."

"Certainly." Joel nodded, though he doubted he could maintain such a positive attitude, had their positions been reversed. "I was fortunate enough to escape without injury, though my dog nearly died from all that tear gas."

DeLane grimaced. "Are you crazy, bringing a dog to an insurrection?" He smiled. "Just goofing on you. There were plenty folks who brought their kids along, now *that's* crazy." The young MacGuiness blinked at the monocle device, and the wheelchair motor whined to life. He turned and headed toward a wooden building that looked like a western style bunkhouse.

"I really appreciate this interview," Joel said as he walked beside DeLane. "Between the depression and martial law, people don't have much hope. They look to the Commander for inspiration."

"Yep," the younger MacGuiness grunted, "Our thoughts exactly. Unfortunately it's not going to happen. Circumstances have forced us to pull up stakes immediately."

"What? Is it because of the President's ultimatum? Do you think she's serious?"

"I'm not at liberty to say. The important thing is to get out before all hell breaks loose."

"You won't get any argument from me," Joel said. He looked back, realizing the Jeep that had brought him had disappeared. "Though I'd rather not hang out here and wait for the bombs to drop. Could your group use an embedded reporter? I promise I won't get in the way."

DeLane gave a short harsh laugh. "There'll be nothing for you to report. Chatting with the Commander is one thing, but we can't have you transmitting our actions to Uncle."

"Of course not." Joel said. "I wouldn't expect to have a live feed, and even afterwards I'd leave out any sensitive details. But people need to know what's happening. Most Americans are on your side."

"Are you sure about that? The latest polls show a lot of people supporting the President."

Before Joel could answer, he heard footsteps in the gravel, and turned to see another man approaching. He stood an inch or two shorter than Joel's six feet, and was quite slender in build. His thick dark hair matched well with his olive complexion. Unlike DeLane, he wore civilian garb, a matching tan shirt and pants. He also had a wireless headset, the bleeding-edge kind with tiny monitors on the sides that could be flipped in front of his eyes.

The newcomer glanced at Joel, then spoke to DeLane. "Lieutenant, the MCU is loaded and ready."

"Very good. Mahmoud, this is Moe. He came here to interview the Commander, but the situation changed. We need to get him out of here, so he'll be riding with you."

For a moment, Mahmoud stared open-mouthed at the Lieutenant. "I've been meaning to talk to you about that. There's no way I can do this alone. I was counting on Tranh and DeSanctis; now I've got to do everything myself and babysit this reporter on top of it all."

"I'm sorry, it can't be helped. And I'm sure Mr. Moe can take care of himself; he seems like a pretty bright guy."

"I guess I've got you fooled," Joel said. "But seriously, I'll do whatever I can to help."

"Good," DeLane continued, "First, some ground rules. You're free to ask questions about anything you want, but no calls or data transmissions until we've dropped you off."

"Agreed." Joel felt his stomach doing flips. "I've got the major incentive of personal safety. I'm not about to call the drones down on myself."

Joel followed DeLane and Mahmoud around the building and past a couple of non-descript construction trucks. "Like I just said, is there anything I can do to help?"

"As a journalist, you're not supposed to take sides, are you?" DeLane chuckled. "But we won't hold it against you. Do you know how to read a map?"

"Of course. Though it would help to know where we're going."

"Sorry, we can't tell you any more than absolutely necessary. You are to obey Mahmoud's orders, or he's authorized to drop you off anywhere, even in a battle zone, understood?"

"Yes. Where's our ride?"

"Right in front of you." There stood a fifth-wheel-type pickup, attached to a trailer which was decorated in rocket ships, medieval knights, and popular anime characters. "You'll be hiding in plain sight." DeLane looked up at Mahmoud. "Be safe." He turned and rolled away.

"Don't let the outside fool you, Mr. Moe" Mahmoud said as they entered the trailer through the side door. "This is our Mobile Communications Unit, MCU. It's a converted video game party trailer. There's no armor, but as long as we're not noticed, we'll be OK."

The trailer had no windows, but there were four huge video monitors on the walls. Facing the monitors was a row of long, padded, couch-like seats. Joel set his computer bag on the floor near the front. "So, Mahmoud, what are your duties on this mission?"

The young man smiled wanly. "It's called C-cubed: Command, Control, and Communications. Can't do the first two without the third." He sat at an office chair facing the central monitor. The chair's wheels had been removed; it was bolted to the trailer's floor. A TV-tray table was attached with a swivel bracket; it held a keyboard, trackball, and joystick. Jose fastened a lap belt and swung the tray inward. "Sorry, this is the only one with a restraint."

"No problem. Mind if I step out for a quick smoke?"

Mahmoud was already engrossed in the monitor. "You have five minutes."

Joel stepped out, lit up and puffed furiously.

From behind, he heard a voice. "Are you authorized to be here?"

He turned to see a stocky man with a gray beard framing a ruddy face. Like most of the others, he wore civilian clothes. "Certainly. Lieutenant MacGuiness himself assigned me to ride with Mister..." he realized he didn't know the man's last name, "Mahmoud."

The man nodded. "Can't be too careful. I'm Corporal Roberts, your driver."

"Good to meet you. If you're here to complain about the smoke, I'll be done in a minute."

Roberts smiled. "Nah, I love the smell of a good cigar."

"No kidding? Most places the villagers come after me with torches and pitch forks." He held out a cigar for Roberts, who accepted it gratefully. "This place reminds me of a summer camp I went to when I was a kid. Good place for a secret base."

Roberts lit up and took a puff. "Not really. There's not much that escapes Uncle Sam's attention. That's why we have to move quickly, and why we dress like civvies and drive civilian trucks. Looks are deceiving, though. Mine's got armor plate and a bulletproof windshield."

"Let's hope you don't need it." Joel stubbed his cigar on the ground and re-entered the trailer.

Mahmoud was typing rapidly, simultaneously speaking in low tones with someone, possibly the senior MacGuiness, over the headset. Joel sat and unzipped his equipment bag. There was a rumble as the pickup's diesel engine started; they began moving with a lurch.

"So," Joel said when Mahmoud was between conversations. "I've been hearing a lot about FreeStar. I'm surprised the Feds haven't shot it down. Is that how you're communicating?"

The young man frowned. "I'm not allowed to say. Though I do know a bit about the satellite. It uses the DOD's own technology against them. It's not one bird, it's a flock, small mini-satellites networked together. Developed after the Chinese launched their own satellite killer."

Joel grinned. "I don't suppose Wilton's very happy about that."

"No, she's not," he laughed dryly. "You asked for a job, right? See the screen to my left? It's got a composite radar map of the area. We need to keep track of the dots, especially the moving ones. Green are our guys, red are probable enemies, black are neutral, yellow are unknown. Watch where they're going and watch for any unusual activity."

"OK." Joel's stomach tightened; he should have brought antacids. "And what do I do if I see a red one headed this way?"

"Tell me immediately, and I'll inform the rest of the team."

The trailer swayed as they headed down the mountain. Although there were no windows, the big monitor at the front showed a camera view of the road. Mahmoud ignored it; he was focused on his own monitor, which showed several colorfully animated charts and bar graphs.

Joel looked over at Mahmoud. "We seem to be headed east. Is this a retreat or an attack?"

He answered without looking up. "Like I said before, I can't tell you, but you're a smart fellow. I'm sure you'll figure it out."

"True. I'm also very humble." Joel studied the map. It showed the local topography, though none of the features were labeled. Across it ran the dotted lines of state boundaries and the spidery tracks of highways. The biggest red dot was on a river that ran east toward a jagged bay. *Washington!* He hated to bother Mahmoud again but his nerves were so jangled, he had to get his mind off the danger. "Do you mind if I ask about your background? You don't sound like you were born in the US."

He shrugged. "That I can answer. I was born in Iran, in Qom, the holy city. I came to the States with my family when I was 16."

"Lucky you left before the Israelis bombed it." *He's Iranian.* Joel winced involuntarily, though he'd strongly opposed that war. "How did you end up in the Brigade?"

"When the troubles started, and the government stepped up its persecution of Muslims, I joined the underground. But I was expelled from my group due to," he paused, "lifestyle issues."

Joel nodded. Some kind of sex thing, he figured, or maybe they caught the kid eating a bacon sandwich. "Hmm, the IAS?" He looked at Mahmoud for a reaction, but the young man averted his eyes. "That's an interesting group. One of the few non-sectarian Islamic organizations I've encountered. Still, they're not exactly a Reform-type congregation, are they?"

Mahmoud's face darkened. "Not to be rude, but I need to concentrate on what I'm doing."

"*No problemo*, my Persian amigo." *Besides, schmuck,* he told himself, *you should be focusing on your own screen, or you'll get us all killed.* In a moment, his worries were confirmed. "I see red dots, at least eight of them, converging on the green square to the west. That's where we came from, right?"

"Thanks." Mahmoud's face was expressionless; he spoke into his headset in hushed tones. "Region Four command, do you copy?"

Joel shuddered. There must have been dozens if not hundreds of rebels there; he hoped they got away. He watched the red dots cluster around the green, no doubt obliterating it. Meanwhile green dots began appearing on the highways, coming from all directions, all heading toward the capital city. *If this isn't an invasion, I don't know what is.*

Meanwhile he kept glancing to the big screen on the front. The view was jarring, since the truck was not visible; obviously the camera was mounted way up front. *So far, so good, no tanks or snipers in sight.* At the same time, Joel tried to eavesdrop on Mahmoud but all he could pick up was vague military jargon like "Bravo Company, report status."

As they continued east, the Washington-bound traffic increased, mostly trucks, vans, and other commercial vehicles. The lanes in the other direction were virtually empty.

"Is everybody who's with us in the Brigade?" Joel asked.

Mahmoud sighed. "You are persistent, aren't you? I'm sure you've figured it out by now. If, theoretically, we were making a move on Washington, we'd want to marshal all our allies, not just the Raptor Group militias but the Pledge Keepers and IAS as well."

"I heard the Ohio and Pennsylvania National Guard switched sides. They're under Mac's command now, aren't they?" No response. "Sorry, I shouldn't ask so many questions."

"It's OK, I just won't answer them. Especially right now; I need to be on the mike."

Joel wished he could risk taking notes. Then he remembered his phone. *I'm such a putz,* he told himself. He reached into his pocket and turned on the 'record' function. If something interesting happened, he'd at least get an audio recording.

At that moment, they came to a sudden halt. In front of them the traffic was stopped in all lanes. "What's happening?" Joel asked. The nervous churning in his gut had returned.

"I have a report that the Shenandoah River bridge was taken out. "Good thing we have some temporary pontoon units. Just one of the many good uses our reservist friends are putting our Federal anti-terrorism dollars to."

"How long will that take?" Joel asked. "This situation scares me. There were a lot of green dots on this road. If *we* can tell who's who, so can the Feds, probably. What if they decide to bomb us all to smithereens?"

Mahmoud put a finger to his lips, then radioed ahead to Roberts, the driver, putting the channel on the trailer's loudspeakers. "What's the ETA on the temporary bridge?"

"About two hours, Neo." Apparently that was his code name. "You may want to take cover, in case the Feds have a welcome planned for us."

"Good idea." Joel headed out the door; he needed fresh air and a smoke. In the east, he saw what looked like a small flock of strange geese high in the sky. His mental question was answered when he saw an explosion in the roadway ahead, followed by two more.

"Drones!" Mahmoud yelled. "Moe, it's not safe out there!" The trailer rocked as the bombs exploded nearby.

Joel ducked back inside. Mahmoud had donned a combat helmet but remained in his seat. His fingers flew over the keyboard; he seemed to be conversing with a dozen people at once.

"Sorry, Friend, but I don't think I'm needed on the radar, the bad guys are already here!" Joel grabbed his backpack plus a spare flak vest and helmet, and was out once again. *Better to die outdoors than in that stuffy rolling coffin.*

Roberts had gotten out of the pickup cab; he was crouching beside it, rifle pointed at the sky. As Joel approached, he gestured toward the ground. "Get down, you fool!"

Joel ignored the advice. Instead he ran along the freeway fence, looking for an opening. He hated to look like a coward, but what else could he do? Without a weapon, the most useful thing he could do was to find a good vantage point to record the action.

Another drone swooped down on them; Joel hit the ground. There were explosions ahead and behind. As he got back to his feet, he saw that there were indeed other rebels in this traffic jam, and they were fighting back.

A few yards away was a Chevy pickup with its fiberglass bed cover propped open. From inside the bed a cannon fired at the sky. The shot clipped the wing of one of the robot aircraft as it flew overhead. The drone dove toward the ground, but one of its cousins came close behind. Its bombs set the Chevy ablaze.

Joel got it all on video. He'd linked his smart phone, which had a high-res camera, to the computer inside his backpack. An antenna mounted on his backpack telescoped above his head and swiveled its tiny dish to point at FreeStar. Even if he died today, the world would witness this historic battle.

With all the noise of drones, bombs, and rebels returning fire, Joel could hardly hear his own voice. He shouted at the top of his lungs, and hoped his mic would pick it up. "This is Surly Moe, live from Virginia, where rebel forces are moving on Federal positions, and encountering a fierce aerial bombardment..." Try as he might, Joel couldn't think of a way to make that funny.

His phone buzzed insistently. It was a text message from Mahmoud: **Moe, where are you? More drones coming from east. Deploying stingers.**

Joel turned the camera to the east, and sure enough, three white gull-like craft flew over the horizon. They passed over his head toward Mahmoud's location. From the west came a finned projectile trailing smoke, followed by two more in quick succession.

Nobody needed to tell Joel to hit the dirt. He threw himself on the ground, praying the bombs would miss them all. Then there was a much louder explosion very close by.

Moments later, Joel looked up. On the other side of the freeway fence, smoke rose from some commercial buildings. He ran as fast as he could back toward the trailer.

"Mahmoud! Roberts! You OK? Answer me!" Joel was greeted by a grisly sight. The Corporal, or rather half of him, lay ten feet away from the pickup. He felt bile rising in his throat. A few feet away, Roberts' sidearm lay in the dirt, still in its holster. Joel grabbed the gun and clipped the holster on his belt. He felt ghoulish, but its owner had no use for it.

Mahmoud appeared beside him. He stared at Roberts for a second but said nothing. "C'mon, let's get out of here!" The trailer was on fire. There was a hole in the midsection.

"But what about Roberts, the trailer?"

"Nothing we can do. Help me unhitch it from the truck. Is that a satellite antenna on your pack? We need to..." A noise made him look up. "More drones! Get down!" From his vantage point on the ground, flat on his back, Joel saw one of the craft do a nose dive, another make a barrel roll, and the third spin out of control. Judging by the explosions, all hit the ground nearby.

"What happened?" he asked Mahmoud as he struggled to his feet.

"They got through! We've got teams out west doing sabotage at the command centers in Vegas and Sierra Vista. They force the drones to autopilot, then we use jammers to confuse their navigation. Hurry! We don't know how long it'll take the Feds to bring the systems back up!"

"But we can't leave Roberts' body lying there like road kill!"

"Oh for the love of the Prophet." Mahmoud blanched. "Should we wrap him up or...?"

"Surely the Brigade has medics. You're the communications guy, call someone!"

"Uh, right." He pulled out his phone. "Hawk-eye, this is Neo requesting assistance..."

Joel felt a rising panic. He rummaged behind the pickup seat and found an emergency blanket. He used it to cover Roberts and, with some trepidation, closed the man's open eyes. "God, filled with mercy, dwelling in the heavens' heights, bring proper rest..." He rushed through the English version of the prayer; the Hebrew seemed inappropriate, given the small golden cross around the dead man's neck. "Now let's make tracks!"

Joel got into the truck. Mahmoud was behind the wheel with the engine running. "Your computer still working? We need to contact Butler command. There's a secure Wi-Fi bridge behind the seat. The password is Z-X-W-one-five-nine..."

"I'll try." Joel was able to connect to the satellite, but for some reason the Butler command network appeared to be off-line. *Have faith, they'll get it back up,* he told himself.

Mahmoud eased the truck forward on the shoulder. They crept past the halted traffic toward the river, where a dozen or so men struggled to erect a temporary pontoon bridge. Mahmoud got out and spoke to the crew's foreman, who seemed skeptical of the young man's authority. While the two of them argued, Joel retrieved the communications equipment and their battery packs from the truck. After a quick call from the Commander, the foreman found a man with a boat to take Joel and Mahmoud across. On on the other side, they found an idle Humvee and were once again on their way toward Washington.

As Joel sat in the passenger's seat, he logged back on to his tablet computer. This time the Griffin connection to the Butler HQ succeeded. A female voice answered with a random-sounding code phrase. Mahmoud leaned over toward Joel's i-Pad and half-shouted, "HQ this is Neo, requesting instructions."

"Your orders are to proceed to Washington," the woman replied.

On the empty highway, and without the trailer, Joel and Mahmoud could travel much more quickly. "Is the loss of the MCU going to put the mission in jeopardy?" Joel asked.

"Not good, but at least we have the spare equipment. Say, we're almost to the Perimeter."

The Perimeter– Joel had yet to see that outrage in person, but photographs of it were featured on hundreds of websites as a symbol of Federal arrogance. It was a twelve-foot security fence surrounding the capital, running just outside the Beltway, with guard towers every mile or so. They'd started building it after the suicide bombing at the Washington Monument some years ago; as far as Joel knew, it was still not finished. Each entrance to the Imperial City would be a security checkpoint, manned by KBR-Schwartzwasser or some other species of goon.

By now Mahmoud and Joel had been joined by other vehicles, obviously all fellow rebels. They had abandoned their attempt to simulate normal civilian traffic. They approached the capital at 70-80 MPH, unimpeded due to the recent downing of the drone fleet.

The rebel advance halted just west of the Outer Beltway, the new freeway that routed Baltimore-bound traffic around the Perimeter wall. Here it was more like gridlock than an invasion. There were hundreds of vehicles, especially military surplus and modified trucks.

"This is not good," Mahmoud said. "The Feds have bombed so many roads they've got us all bunched up here. We're got to break through or spread out, or we'll be massacred."

From here they could just barely see the wall. Joel grabbed his phone to get a photo; he was leaning out the truck window when unseen government forces fired from somewhere, destroying two of the trucks at the leading edge of the rebel forces.

"What are our orders?" Mahmoud demanded into the headset. "Advance or retreat?"

"Everyone hold your positions. We'll be breaching their defenses momentarily."

The voice was DeLane MacGuiness! To Joel, it was strange to think of a disabled man leading an invasion.

"Acknowledged."

From the east came an ominous sound: helicopters, at least six of them, flying directly at them. There was the sound of gunfire hitting the metal plate on the vehicle's roof, and peppering the reinforced windshield with star shaped cracks. Joel threw on the helmet and hunched down in his seat."Why do I imagine I'm hearing 'Flight of the Valkyrie'?"

Nephi gazed at the lights of Billings as they got nearer. Despite his exhaustion his heart beat faster. "Thank you, Lord," he whispered.

Next to him sat a wealthy rancher he knew only as Jim. Jim had been stranded out east after the President's ban on "non-essential" travel. This aircraft, Liberty Charters Flight 101, was openly defying the prohibition. The cost of Nephi's ticket (very expensive, due to pent-up demand) had come out of the Brigade's treasury. "Least I can do," Mac told him, after Nephi's team had put up the FreeStar satellite that made anonymous communications possible again.

A hand clapped Nephi on the shoulder, startling him. "Cheer up, Buddy," Jim said. "We're almost there."

Nephi smiled wearily. "Yep." The plane descended toward an illuminated strip of darkness on the prairie. A gentle bump told them they had finally landed.

Jim grinned broadly. "We made it, son! Didn't I tell you those Feds were blowing smoke? They wouldn't dare attack a civilian flight."

"For once, I'm happy to be wrong." Nephi hadn't expected them to shoot down the plane, either. But he'd been certain the government would do *something* about this widespread defiance.

The DC-9 was packed. "We were lucky to get on," Jim said. "Most pilots are afraid to fly. But with the Feds busy in California, Texas, and Vermont, who's gonna enforce the ban?"

Nephi shrugged. "Considering how desperate they've gotten, I figured they might hire the Russian Mafia or one of the Cartels to take out the fight crew." He laughed. "But I couldn't wait any longer. I haven't seen my wife and kids for weeks."

"I hear ya, man. These days, you've got to go when you get the chance."

Over the loudspeaker, the flight attendant was reciting the standard admonition to stay seated. Jim chuckled. "They don't want us fighting our way to the luggage bins." The rancher unbuckled his belt and leaned forward in his seat, like a runner at the starting line.

A roaring sound from above made them both jump, dumping Jim's cowboy hat on Nephi's lap. "What the hell was that?"

A deep voice came over the intercom. "This is Captain Young. Please remain seated. There is no cause for alarm. This appears to be some sort of military exercise. We'll continue to the gate as soon as we determine everything is safe."

There was immediate pandemonium in the plane; everyone was talking at once. "Did you see that?" "Are they attacking us?" People craned their necks, and got out of their seats for a better view. Young children cried and screamed.

The stewardess grabbed the mic. "Everyone, please stay seated. We've been told to proceed to the jet way. Please keep your seat belts fastened until we come to a complete stop."

Jim got up anyway, popped open the overhead luggage compartment, and grabbed Nephi's crutches. "Here you go. Which was your bag, the green one?"

"Gosh, you don't have to..." he began, but Jim had already grabbed Nephi's backpack and set it by his feet. "Thanks, Jim!"

"No, thank *you.*" Nephi was puzzled until he remembered he was wearing a Guardsman's jacket. Had the man assumed he was a veteran?

"Actually, Jim, I'm not..." But the man was already fighting his way down the aisle. The plane rolled to a stop. The passengers stood up en masse; they could hardly hear the stewardess giving them permission.

Nephi got up, carefully swinging out his stiff, painful leg. A gray-haired couple smiled and waited for him the move his suitcase and extend the handle. "Thanks." He turned to hobble down the aisle. Somehow he managed to get up the ramp with the suitcase in tow.

When he came through the door into the terminal, his mouth fell open in shock. The place was packed. *When did they start letting non-passengers on the concourse?* Then he remembered; Montana had begun nullifying Federal laws and regulations. There were rumors it might even follow California, Texas, and Vermont in declaring independence.

"Daddy!" He was almost bowled over by a brown-skinned boy. Nephi propped himself against a wall and lifted his son off the floor. "I think you grew an inch while I was gone!"

"Mommy needs a hug, too." Siri, looking haggard, but radiant in a yellow t-shirt and jeans, squeezed through the crowd to give her husband an embarrassingly passionate kiss. When they came up for air, she said, "I was so worried. They were talking about closing the airport."

"Daddy, did you see the jet planes? Were you afraid?"

"Yes, it was pretty scary. I'm just glad nobody got hurt."

"People say it was Wilton, giving us a warning. With the civil unrest everywhere, I'm amazed that she could find the time." It took a moment for Nephi to realize the speaker was Siri's father. "But we're thankful you made it. How's your leg, is it healing well?"

The question failed to register in Nephi's tired brain. "Pradeep! And Chandrika! So good to see you! I forgot you were out here now."

Siri glanced back at her parents. "We got them out of Madison just before the travel ban."

"While you were on your top secret mission," Pradeep said with a grin.

"We're standing in everybody's way." Chandrika motioned for them to move down the concourse. She was holding little Padma, who had somehow slept through all the commotion.

"Come on." Siri grabbed Will's hand. "It's a long drive home, and it's way past the kids' bedtimes."

Nephi grabbed his crutches and hobbled along with them. "How long can the drive possibly be in a small town like this?"

"Daddy!" Will cried out. Everybody stopped and listened, their eyes lifted to the sky, as if they could see through the terminal roof. The roaring sound had returned.

Through the big terminal windows, the jets were no more than streaks of light as they streaked by. Bright yellow flashes erupted one after another as the bombs struck the runway. The floor beneath them vibrated with the shock waves of the blasts. The last one was even louder, as the control tower exploded in a fountain of flame.

The crowd's silence ended, replaced by screaming. People stampeded toward the door, and streamed around Nephi and his family, threatening to trample them underfoot in their rush.

"Stay together!" Nephi shouted. He dropped his crutches and put his arms around Will and Siri. The pain radiated up his leg from where the titanium reinforcements bound his bones.

A female voice came over the loudspeaker. "Everyone remain calm! Do not leave the building! There is room for everyone down in the underground shelter." The lady on the speaker sounded like she was on the verge of panic herself. Meanwhile, Nephi struggled to stay standing. Luckily, in this small terminal, there couldn't be more than a few hundred people.

Finally the pain got the best of Nephi; he collapsed to the floor. After a few harrowing moments, the area where they were standing cleared out, though there was still a crowd jostling around the hallway on the other side of the security check. Other people were exiting backwards through the metal detector, the airport security staff wisely standing out of their way.

"Your crutches!" Pradeep pointed toward the exit; they lay crisscrossed on the floor where the mob had dropped them. "I'll retrieve them!"

"Thanks," Nephi's wife and father-in-law helped him to his feet. Seeing everybody was OK, he laughed. "You couldn't have asked for a more dramatic homecoming." He immediately felt remorse, thinking of the controllers who'd surely perished in the tower explosion.

"It doesn't look like the bombers are coming back," Siri's mother observed. The baby in her arms had ceased her crying and already returned to sleep.

"Then let's be off, soon as the rush is over." Once again, Nephi hugged Siri and Will. "So Pradeep, where are you and Chandrika staying? Are you close by?"

"You might say that," Siri interrupted. "Right down the hallway." To his look of surprise she said, "Sorry, there's a severe housing shortage here."

"It's all good," Nephi said. *I should be thanking God for my blessings, not sweating the small stuff.* "Let's go home."

Behind it all, he couldn't help feeling another twinge of guilt. JL, Mac, and even the now-paralyzed DeLane were out risking their lives while he was here safe with his family. It seemed that the rebellion was just beginning in earnest.

"I suppose we can't wait any longer. Get out your brushes and let's get started."

Serena's art class was unusually small today. That meant the payments would barely cover the cost of gas. In the old days, teachers' pay had never been spectacular, but at least it had been steady. These teaching gigs were far more informal. Teachers could be paid miserably or quite well, depending on whether they kept the students interested enough to show up.

"Today we'll be using color as an expression of emotion. Let's begin with sadness."

"Shouldn't be hard, with the way things have been going," quipped a scrawny guy with a goatee, one of the few males in the class.

Serena tried to cover her irritation with a smile. "Very good, Curt. Draw on those emotions and express them on the *canvas*."

There was a rapping on the classroom door. A balding, gray bearded man Serena had never seen poked his head inside. "May I interrupt?"

Serena smiled again. "Sir, we only have 90 minutes, and we already got a late start."

Mildred, the mousy little woman in the front, looked up from her easel, startled. "That's my husband! George, what's going on?"

Taking that as an invitation, George stepped inside. "I don't want to start a panic, but they sent us home early from the office. There are rumors of an attack..."

The alarmed murmurings made it sound as if there were a lot more than seven students. Curt gave a snort of derision. "By the Feds? Good luck to them. They got their asses kicked in Reno and Medford ." He didn't mention the Feds still controlled the southern third of the state. Unlike Texas, California had not managed to control the military bases within its borders. LA had been under siege for weeks. Despite strict rationing, the city was running out of water.

"Not that. It's Wilton's ultimatum. Against all three states that seceded, Vermont, Texas, and us. I just read on the Undernet, it could happen any minute now."

Serena realized she'd lost the battle. "What do you mean? How could things be more serious than they are now?"

"Haven't you heard?" George said. "Dire consequences! Everybody's sure she means nukes, what else could she do?"

Curt laughed. "Dude, don't believe that bullshit. Not that I don't hate that bitch Wilton, too. But they'd have to launch from one of our subs; no way the crews would attack America."

"I wouldn't be so sure," George said. "They say the President's at Livermore working on a last-minute defense with some anti-missile experts from the Brigade."

Serena was puzzled. "Wilton's in California?"

"No, President Chang," Mildred interjected. "Though it's weird to think of him that way."

Serena sighed. "We'll put it to a vote. How many want to cancel class? Sorry, George, you're not a paying student."

Four hands went up. Serena abstained. *Much as I love art, if this is the end, there are other things I'd rather be doing.* That reminded her of Joel, and she was filled with sadness. "OK, class is canceled. We'll reschedule for next week, assuming we're all still here."

As if on cue, the power went out; not like the brownouts they'd been experiencing for the last few weeks, but completely dark. One of the younger girls shrieked.

"Everybody chill! Even if they do attack, it probably won't be here."

"Your teacher's right," George held up his hands. "Everyone stay calm! I know where the nearest shelter is! Everyone, follow me."

Outside there was shouting and honking horns, but no air-raid sirens. People were abandoning their cars in the street, though where they were escaping to was not apparent.

"Are you sure this isn't some kind of a trap?" Serena asked. "Like Katrina. We get to the shelter and they'll try to keep us from leaving?"

"Beats being caught in the fallout," George looked up. "Holy Christ!"

It was almost evening, but for some reason, there was a glow on the eastern horizon.

"My God!" Mildred grabbed George, almost knocking him down. "Don't look, it'll make you blind!" Two of the younger students, both teenage girls, clutched each other and wailed.

Curt snorted in exasperation. "It could be Sacramento, but how could we see the flash that far away? And it doesn't make sense! Wouldn't the missile have had to fly over us?"

"Depends on where they launched it from," said another class member, a goth-looking college girl, who seemed to Serena to be morbidly fascinated.

"Enough arguing, we need to find a shelter." Serena felt strangely calm. Under her breath, she said, "Adiós, Sacramento." She hadn't heard from Joel since shortly after he'd left, when he'd told her he'd settled there. If Joel had been there, she prayed his death was painless. Perhaps his ashes were in the mushroom cloud now rising in the southeast.

Chapter 17 – The Battle of Free Columbia

Joel's gut churned with fear. "How are we going to get out of here, with those burning trucks ahead? We don't have any way to move them!"

"Like the old TV show said, we have the technology." Mahmoud spoke into his radio. "Tranh! Holloway! What're you guys doing? Take down those copters!"

"Yes, sir!" responded a voice. There was a mechanical whine from the right and behind them. Long cylindrical objects rose slowly from the beds of both pickup trucks.

"Let's see how well Larsen's rocket trucks work."

"Larsen? Would that be anybody I know?"

"Unlikely." As the choppers returned, they met a nasty surprise. The launch tubes were loaded with some serious-looking m, probably pilfered from a Guard armory. As the rockets streaked into the sky, the gunships fled. One took a hit in the rotor and spun out of control. There was a crash and more flames as it landed in the middle of the highway.

"Woo-hoo!" Joel shouted. "Glad they got the bastard, but now the road's worse."

"Med teams!" Mahmoud shouted into his headset. "The pilot might still be alive. Is anybody there?" Joel, my headset's gone dead, see if you can raise HQ for instructions."

"No connection. Nothing but static on that channel. Feds must be jamming us!"

"Curse it all!" Mahmoud pounded the steering wheel. "We need a way out of here!"

"We can take out the wall," came the response over the radio.

"Do it!" Someone jumped out of the lead escort truck and loaded another rocket.

"That one looks different," Joel said.

"Refurbished dud from the Iraq war," Mahmoud explained. "We need more firepower for this task." The barrier walls were not rocket-proof; in a minute the two of them were driving through the breach and onto the frontage road. From behind they heard the sound of sirens.

Mahmoud clenched his fists. "What's wrong with my radio? Companies Alpha and Bravo, report! Joel, try yours again."

The tiny external speakers on Joel's tablet crackled with static, then cleared up. "Holloway here! Company Alpha, northwest perimeter gate. We're under enemy fire!"

"Plan B, deploy the UAV's!" To Joel, he added, "Use their own technology against them."

"What, you have Predators? Why haven't I heard about this?"

Mahmoud grinned. "Not exactly Predators. UAV's are a pretty big category. Let's just say we're lucky we have allies among the local police."

"True," Joel hadn't forgotten how the Pledge Keepers had intervened on the rebel side in California. "But how can we fight artillery with a bunch of flying cameras?"

"When are you going to learn that I won't answer your questions? At least not before the battle's over. Just be patient and watch the fun."

Joel was about to deliver a smart Aleck comeback, when more jets screamed above them,. A bomb struck the truck ahead of them; it burst into flame. Mahmoud slammed on the brakes.

" Tranh's hit! We need medics, now!"

Without thinking, Joel jumped out of the car. *I can't let the man die.* Out of nowhere came another jet. Another bomb hit Tranh's truck, making the rescue effort moot.

"Joel, get back in here! Nothing we can do for him."

They got back on the freeway, the Inner Beltway this time, and negotiated around the craters, the remaining trucks accompanying them. The threat of death had a profound effect on Joel's bladder. He concentrated on filming with his cell phone, to keep his mind off the urge. Mahmoud's headset resumed functioning; whoever was jamming that frequency had stopped.

Mahmoud split from the group and left the Beltway at an exit marked Virginia Highway 267. This was definitely a war zone, with blasted buildings everywhere. They sat at a non-functional traffic light, watching a long line of vehicles, presumably rebels, where streaming back onto the highway that would take them to the capital.

"Well, Mr. Journalist, I feel bad that I've had to ignore your questions. But now I need to check on my techno-toys, and you may find it interesting." Slowly Mahmoud inched into the traffic, then floored it and darted across the highway in front of a big truck.

"We survived the bombs, now you want to kill us on the highway?"

Mahmoud ignored Joel's complaint. He followed a nearly empty road northward across the Potomac river. A few minutes later, he pulled over by a pile of rubble, dominated by chunks of concrete with mangled protruding re-bar. Joel realized it had recently been part of the Wall.

"I'm sure you guessed it," the young man said. "This was one of the security checkpoints that were giving us so much trouble." Everywhere there was broken glass, twisted metal, and pieces of brick, as well as parts of vehicles.

"My God, is that a severed hand?"

Mahmoud glanced at it and shrugged. "We hit several of the guard stations at once, so they couldn't warn each other. Looks like our plan worked better than we expected."

"There!" Mahmoud pointed to a cracked rotary blade that looked like it came off a toy helicopter. "I can tell you now, since it's already happened. UAV's, the same ones the police and the military have been using to spy on us all. We removed the cameras, filled them with C4 explosive, and did the kamikaze thing. Hey, look, one of them survived!"

"Wait, is it safe to pick that one up?"

Too late; Mahmoud had already grabbed it. "Don't worry, this one is unmodified. We had to keep a few cameras so we could see where we were going." He turned the device over in his hands. "This looks fixable; I'll keep it. As for the rest of them, who knows if there are any duds left. When this is over, we'll send in a de-mining team."

"So what happened to all the contractors? It sounded like there were hundreds."

"The survivors must have run like the spineless cowards they are." He pulled a phone out of his pocket. "We need to get going, but first, something I've got to check." He pushed a button and said, "Charlie Company, report. DeSanctis, is that you?" Mahmoud nodded; then smiled and repeated the news to Joel, "Raptors got through from the east, we're hitting 'em from both ends!"

"Fantastic! But how do we know it's not some kind of trap?"

"Only one way to find out." They got back in the Hummer and drove slowly over the broken ground to where the road resumed on the other side of the wall. Mahmoud looked at the display in the dash. "The nav system says we're on the right track."

The streets were deserted. "Where are the others? This hardly looks like an invasion."

"We're sticking to the same strategy; stay spread out, so they can't attack us all together. Modern communications technology has definitely changed guerrilla warfare."

As they headed down the boulevard, each stoplight they encountered had mysteriously been set to blinking yellow. Probably the rebels were also hacking the traffic control system.

"I don't trust it," Joel said. "I wish I knew where all the contractors went."

"Don't worry. I'm sure they're trying to ditch their uniforms and sell their equipment." The street was deserted. "Supposedly, at one time Schwartzwasser had some good soldiers. When the inflation got really bad, they all demanded 100 percent pay raises, and the company went for cheaper help. The guys they have now will steal anything that isn't nailed down."

Joel continued recording with his cell phone through the window as they drove; the video would be shaky but better than nothing. He was amazed the buildings were still standing and the streets passable. Though a lot of store windows were broken, and a few buildings were on fire.

Minutes later they passed a sign that said, 'Welcome to Free Columbia – The Fifty-First State. Warning: All Public Areas Monitored for Your Safety.'

They were now in Washington proper. Joel put his phone to his eye and zoomed the camera in on the Capitol dome to the east. Neither the civilian population nor the mercenaries were anywhere to be seen. "Wish we could have been in the thick of the invasion. I'd like to see a little more action."

"This way was a lot safer." Mahmoud grinned and added, "Besides, from what I've been hearing, the battle's almost over."

The two men fell silent. Joel pondered the magnitude of the day's events. The scenery wasn't changing much, so he stopped recording. He was irritated that his recordings had been so mundane. This was history in the making, and he'd missed most of it.

"I hate to break my promises," Joel said, "but will it hurt anything if I make a live broadcast? I think you're right; it looks like the war just might be over."

Mahmoud glanced at Joel, eyebrows raised, He said nothing for a minute or two. "Oh, go ahead, why not? What are they going to do, shoot us?" He grinned. "After all, that's the kind of security-fascism we're fighting against, isn't it?"

"You can say I held you at gunpoint while I shamelessly defied Mac's orders." Joel laughed. "But I don't think it'll be an issue. We've definitely let the Feds know we're here."

Joel disconnected his computer from the Brigade's transmitter and hooked it back up to his mini satellite dish. No doubt they were routed through the same place, the FreeStar satellite, but he didn't want to risk connecting through the Brigades' own network. The connection was elusive at first, but after some frantic button pushing he established an up-link.

"Hello, world, this is Surly Moe, AKA the Seventh Stooge, reporting from the Imperial City of Washington. Get ready to pinch yourselves. I'm black and blue from doing just that. Possibly I'm hallucinating from all those magic mushrooms I ingested in my college days, but so far no sign of Mescalito. But back to the present: I'm traveling with rebel forces as they enter the city, ostensibly to remove the female Mussolini from her throne in the White House.

"As you can see, the streets appear to be quite deserted; it's downright spooky. As for our comrades in arms, they're at other undisclosed locations in the city." As they drove, he focused the cell phone a few blocks ahead for a more stable view. "Sadly, the fighting, combined with the inevitable looting, has caused significant damage to this historic city. It's enough to bring tears to the eyes of any American, even a hardened old cynic like myself."

As they turned a corner, the connection indicator on his computer screen fell down to zero bars. "*Oy*, I'm off line!" Joel wiggled the connection to the satellite antenna. He tried extending the mast, but it was out as far as it would go. "What a piece of *dreck*!"

"That's not all. The navigation system just crapped out." He held up a cell phone and pressed a button. "No connection to HQ, either."

"So what do we do?"

"We *could* simply meet at the final rendezvous point. I'm sure we can find Pennsylvania Avenue without much trouble. The question is, is it safe? Just because we're in the city doesn't mean the fighting's over. Like in the Israeli war, when the Iranian patriots..." Mahmoud slammed on the brakes. "Trouble! Stay still, don't say anything!"

A large truck stood in the middle of the street, blocking their path. Three dark, very tall men, perhaps Somalis or Sudanese, approached them. They wore Schwartzwasser khaki uniforms and carried automatic rifles, two of which were currently pointing in their direction.

Now this, Joel thought, *would be exciting journalism, if I dared record it.* Quickly he closed the computer and stashed it under the seat. He expected that taping the mercenaries would make them pretty cranky. As he stashed the phone in his pocket, he felt the holster he'd forgotten he was wearing. He still had Roberts' gun! It was comforting to know he had it, though he doubted he could pull it out without getting shot.

The tallest of the three men stepped up to the driver's side window, which Mahmoud had rolled down just a crack. "By authority of US gov'ment we commandeer vehicle."

"Whose authority? Can't you see we're part of a military convoy?"

The African grinned. "Rebel convoy. You lucky if we let you live." The two underlings pointed their guns right at them. Suddenly Mahmoud punched the accelerator and the truck peeled out in reverse.

"Joel, get down!" The Africans fired. The bullets were small caliber, and rather than shattering, the windshield was riddled with tiny holes. Mahmoud was crouched down, driving blind; he slammed the Hummer rear-first through a store window. Thankfully it was unoccupied at the moment. The shock of the crash finished off the damaged windshield; it crumbled into bits of safety glass all over Joel and Mahmoud's laps.

"Good, now I can see." Mahmoud shifted back into drive and gunned the engine. The wheels just spun; somehow he'd gotten the bumper caught on some kind of rack. Then something snapped, and they lurched forward.

"Are you insane?" Joel yelled. He tried to take shelter behind the dash, but the space was too small for him to squeeze into. His heart beat so hard he thought it would burst. In a moment of panic, he pulled out Roberts' gun, a .44 magnum, and realized he didn't know if it was loaded. *Do you punks feel lucky?*

They must have felt lucky indeed, because the three of them stood their ground, spraying bullets into the cab and radiator, but the big vehicle kept on going.

Without stopping to think, Joel sat up and aimed at the Africans, pulling the trigger six times in rapid succession. It was loaded after all, and the noise was deafening. With the gun empty, Joel ducked his head down again. By some miracle he had managed not to get hit.

As a bullet zinged through the cab, Mahmoud slammed on the brakes. The Hummer fish-tailed and careened into a light post. Somehow this impact caused both airbags to deploy. At that moment, Joel was half-crouched, and the bag bounced off his head as it exploded outward.

Joel sat slumped forward, dazed, for several minutes. His head pounded like he'd been hit with a brick. Then he cautiously peered over the dash. One of the Africans lay sprawled out on the pavement, a huge red stain on his chest; the others were gone.

"Holy shit," Joel muttered, "Did I take that man's life?"

To his left, Mahmoud sat silently, apparently unconscious. "Hey Kid, are you OK?" There was no response. "Mahmoud, answer me!"

He grabbed the man's shoulders to shake him awake, when he noticed the blood splattered on the head rest, and the red mess in the Iranian's dark hair. In revulsion, Joel pushed him away. There was a tiny bullet entry wound in the center of Mahmoud's forehead.

"Oh merciful God!" Joel cried out like a man who'd lost his mind. "How could you allow this young man's life to end so brutally? This good man, with his whole life ahead of him?" Head in his hands, Joel curled into a ball and wept. His shoulders convulsed with sobbing.

Though he was dimly aware that he was in danger, that the surviving mercenaries might return at any time, Joel didn't care. He sat and wept, not just for this young man who'd recently befriended him, but for every casualty of this time of trouble. He wept for the American soldiers killed and injured in Nigeria, the lives lost in riots like the one in Sacramento, the untimely death of Manuel Lopez, and for DeLane MacGuiness' ruined body. He cried for families split and relationships ended, and for the friends, lovers, and relatives he missed so badly.

"Neo, is that you?" It took Joel a second to realize the voice was coming over the radio. "Come in, Neo!"

The interruption brought Joel back to reality. He sniffled and picked up the radio. "Um, bad news, Neo's been shot. I'm..." he paused. Was it safe to reveal his identity? "This is Moe. What's happening? What are our orders?"

"Is this the famous Stooge? Moe, this is Commander MacGuiness. We had a temporary network outage. How is our communications officer, is he seriously hurt?"

"He's... he's dead, Sir. We had a run-in with some foreign mercenaries."

There was a pause. "I'm very sorry. And you, are you hurt? Do we need to send help?"

"I'm fine." Joel reached past Mahmoud's lifeless body and turned the key. The Hummer's engine rumbled to life. "My vehicle is still operational."

"Good. We're at 18th Street and F, which is a few blocks west of the White House. We're facing the remaining Federal forces there, so proceed with caution. Do you know the way?"

"I think so." Joel swallowed hard. At the moment, this mundane discussion seemed ghoulish. "Sir, did I hear you correctly? The White House, does that mean it's all over?"

"Not quite, but there's a light at the end of the tunnel. If you make it in time, you'll get the scoop of a lifetime. Then later I'll give you that interview I promised."

"Thank you, Sir. I'm on my way."

Of course, he couldn't drive anywhere without first moving the body. Joel swallowed hard and fought back the nausea as he unbuckled Mahmoud's lifeless body and pulled him over the center console into the passenger's seat. Mercifully, the man's eyes were already closed.

For the second time that day, Joel said the prayer for the dead, this time in Hebrew. After that, he thought to check Mahmoud's pockets for weapons, since Roberts' gun was now out of bullets. There was nothing but a cell phone; as his own was no longer working, Joel pocketed it.

He got out to check the damage to the vehicle. Although the front driver's side quarter panel was pretty badly crumpled; the tire was still inflated. With a bit of effort he pulled off the smashed fender to free the wheel. Surprisingly, the radiator was intact. He opened up the back and dug through the supplies, finding a plastic tarp, which used to cover the bloodied driver seat.

Although the navigation system was inoperable, Joel had a vague recollection of the city's layout from a previous visit, so he started the Hummer and drove in a southeasterly direction. He flipped the radio on; it still worked. He tried several presets; most produced static instead of a signal. When he found a station that was working, the news gave him yet another shock.

A deep male voice was speaking. "...reports are still coming in about the apparent nuclear detonation in Lodi, California. The state's disaster agencies report that most of the city has been flattened. The death toll has been estimated in the tens of thousands and still rising."

A female voice broke in. "So what do we know about the perpetrator of this horrible crime? Has anyone claimed responsibility?"

"As I said, Susan, the rumors are going wild. Some say it was Iranian terrorists exacting revenge for Israel's attack on their country a few years ago. Others blame domestic rebel groups such as the banned Raptor Militia. Still others say this was done on the orders of the President herself, to destroy Sacramento as punishment for California's secession."

"But how could it have been delivered? There were no sightings of any missile."

"That's true. This just in, we have reports that the President is currently negotiating with a rebel army that has breached the Perimeter Wall and entered the city of Washington."

Joel said nothing; he was in shock. Was Serena safe? *If she stayed in San Francisco, she should hopefully be OK, unless people panic and all hell breaks loose.* He said a silent prayer, *God if you're out there, please let Serena be OK!*

"Stop right here," MacGuiness said. "Man, I can't believe we've got this far. Just a few blocks from the White House." They'd reached Eighteenth Street, the easternmost extent of the rebel advance from the west. The defenders, the few remaining government and contract troops, were dug in one block east, on Seventeenth Street.

Larsen parked the Explorer behind a Land Cruiser equipped with do-it-yourself armor plates. "Cool, I haven't been there since third grade."

Mac gave one of his famous guffaws. "I bet you'll get to see a little bit more of it this time." The two men put on combat helmets and got out of the vehicle. The street was filled with cars and trucks of all sorts. Some were occupied; others had doors open, with men and women standing outside, smoking or talking in small groups. The sounds of rap, heavy metal, or country western music mixed with the occasional bursts of gunfire in the distance. Despite the cacophony, there was an eerie quality to the scene, like an massive bomb ready to detonate.

Mac and Larsen rounded the corner of the museum, they duck-walked to the concrete barricades a few yards down F Street. Enemy soldiers knelt behind their own barricades a block away. On the rebel side, a 100 mm cannon stood in the middle of the street. Mac and Larsen joined two nervous-looking guys wearing hunting cammo and police vests crouched beside it.

Larsen was wide-eyed. "Holy shit! Is that a World War II Howitzer? You guys gonna shell the White House?"

The older looking of the two men, grinned and replied, "If the bitch doesn't surrender, we will. We've already fired a couple shells into the grounds, want to see?"

Mac shook his head. "No, the cease-fire still holds, for the moment. The President has about 30 more minutes before the deadline. Then we move."

Larsen shook his head. "To be honest, I don't understand how we did it. I know the country's broke, and most of our own troops are overseas, but they've still got a lot of foreign mercenaries, and those guys hate our guts."

"Maybe so," Mac said, "But they're not fighting for the home team. It's like Vietnam, Iraq or Nigeria, except now the roles are reversed."

"Doesn't make me feel better," the younger gunner said. "They've still got superior firepower."

"True," Mac replied, "But Lodi changed everything, tragic as that was. We just got word that the Chairman of the Joint Chiefs resigned, and what little regular army that was out in the streets got pulled back to their barracks. It's just us and the contractors now."

The older guy looked at Mac. "So Commander, why don't we move in then?"

"Good question. I'm actually waiting for a phone call." At that moment, a few riffs of Bob Marley issued from Mac's pocket.

Mac raised the phone to his ear. "Yes, Lieutenant?" The response brought a smile to the Commander's face. "It's official then, await instructions." To Larsen and the others, he said, "It's official, the Pentagon has ordered its troops to stand down." He made another call. "Holloway, send a message to all units, move in immediately. We rendezvous at the White House."

The older gunner looked concerned. "Sir, I thought we were going to give the President 30 more minutes."

"Screw her," Mac said. "Time to go, before the bitch can talk the brass out of it. What do you say we give them a little warning shot?"

"Can I try it?" Larsen interjected.

Mac shook his head. "Some other time, JL. Fire, Soldier." The older guy nodded to his younger teammate, who slid the shell into the breech, pushed the lever, and jumped out of the way. The was a loud boom and a hiss as the shell left the tube, then a shower of earth as a crater appeared in the formerly well-manicured White House lawn.

"Awesome!" Larsen exclaimed. He and MacGuiness got up, ran back to their SUV and jumped in. Everywhere men scrambled and engines started. Armored vehicles of all sorts poured into the streets and smashed the government barricades. There were Vietnam-era amphibious 'tanks,' SWAT team armored cars, and construction and farm trucks customized with metal plate. The sound of gun fire was punctuated by an occasional rocket blast. The noise was amplified as it echoed off the historic buildings.

"Keep going!" Mac had switched his phone to walkie-talkie mode. "We've got them on the run!"

As they advanced down the block, they saw mercenary position being hit hard. Men dropped their weapons and ran. Others raised their hands.

Again Mac spoke. "All units, the mercs are surrendering, hold your fire! Any law enforcement personnel or anyone with handcuffs or restraint, take them into custody!"

In a few minutes it was over, with the contractors now giving up en masse. Mac shouted into his walkie, "Armored dump truck, blue Land Cruiser, move aside immediately for black Explorer. Sheridan tank crew, we need an opening."

To their right, a tank turret swiveled and fired a shell at the White House fence, now protected by permanent concrete barricades. The explosion threw twelve-inch chunks everywhere; when the smoke cleared, there was an opening.

"Take her in, Mr. Viking." Larsen put the Explorer in gear and drove down the street toward the now-open grounds of the White House.

It was bad enough to get lost in a normal situation. But to get lost in a city in the midst of a civil war, with a dead body in the passenger's seat– that was another kind of hell. Finally Joel stopped at a souvenir shop, where a very frightened lady handed him a map, "free of charge." Joel thanked her, plunked a twenty dollar bill on the counter, and walked out. It wasn't worth much more than the paper it was printed on, but at least it was a gesture of appreciation.

Finally he found his way to the 18th and F Street. Three Butler Brigade soldiers– he could tell them by their non-uniform uniforms, and the prevalence of blacks and Hispanics– stood at the street corner guarding a government building with a huge hole blown in the side.

"It's all over but the shouting, Man," a young black man told him.

His teammate, a middle-aged Latino, ambled over to the Hummer. "Holy shit! Is that Neo? God damn it, he was a good kid!"

"Mercenaries tried to take our vehicle," Joel said. "I wish he hadn't tried to be the hero."

"They would've killed you guys anyway." The black man turned to one of the others. "Neo was Muslim, right? The body needs to be buried quickly, it's their way." They called a medical team and took Mahmoud's body out of the passenger's seat. This side was now stained with blood, too, as Joel had only thought to cover the driver's seat.

"Now, you know how to get to the White House, right?"

Joel nodded, and got back in. This time he did not get lost. Rounding the corner, he saw it. Its wall had been knocked down; pieces of the older fence were piled on the grass. A dozen rebel vehicles, including a WWII era tank, were brazenly parked on the lawn. Joel was forced to leave the Hummer on the street, as the drive was blocked with vehicles.

Though the shock of the rebel attack had driven the thought from his mind, Joel suddenly remembered he needed to use the bathroom, badly. At the White House entrance there were two guards and a long line of rebels waiting to get in. He'd never get through in time, and he hated to show up in the Oval Office reeking like a vagrant. "Oh screw it!" Joel ducked between two trucks and did something he'd never imagined: urinate on the White House lawn.

Feeling guilty but greatly relieved, Joel zipped up and proceeded to the White House. The line had disappeared; the entrance was now was guarded by a single green-clad rebel fighter.

"Hello, Soldier," he said. "An amazing day, isn't it?"

As he tried to enter, the guard said, "Sir, I have orders not to let anyone else pass!"

Joel gritted his teeth. "Is the Commander here? I'm supposed to meet him for an interview. I'm Surly Moe, I do the 'Seventh Stooge' blog on the Undernet."

"Really? I read your stuff all the time. You don't look at all like I'd imagined." The guard radioed ahead, then looked up with a smile. "You may proceed."

Halfway down the corridor, Joel met a man in an electric wheel chair going the opposite direction. "Hello, Mr. Stooge," he said. "I understand you proved yourself under enemy fire."

Joel shrugged, embarrassed. "I did what I had to do. I feel terrible about Mahmoud, though. He didn't deserve to die like that, when everything was almost over."

DeLane nodded. "Nobody does, especially not a city full of civilians." He sighed, then turned the chair around. "Follow me; we're holding a press conference in the Oval Office."

Before Joel could ask for clarification, DeLane continued, "The Joint Chiefs opposed the strike, and they countermanded the launch orders that the sub commanders had already refused. But Wilton had another trick up her sleeve. She sent a couple of hired gangsters to Sacramento, with a portable nuke in the trunk of their car. When the State Police stopped them, it somehow it got set off accidentally."

"Unbelievable!" Joel shook his head sadly.

The guard at the door saluted DeLane, then looked at the .44 in Joel's holster and said, "He'll have to check his weapon."

"You take it. It's not mine anyway," Joel said.

Joel pushed his way into the Oval office, the place was jam-packed, mostly with rebel fighters, with a scattering of journalists. MacGuiness stood at the podium with a stocky red-bearded man beside him.

"Ladies and gentlemen, let me introduce a man without whom we wouldn't be here today– Jon Larsen, chief technology officer for the Butler Brigade, computer hacker extraordinaire, and all-around engineering genius. Without his work on the Griffin System, we wouldn't have had the Undernet, and we could not have ended the tyranny of Wilton's regime."

The crowd applauded enthusiastically, though it wasn't the fracas Joel would have expected from such a motley assortment of people. It was like the ghost of recent tragedy hung over them, damping the celebration. Joel looked around, trying to burn this moment indelibly in his memory. Among the varied military-type fatigues there were some suits. Joel recognized a number of perfectly coiffed talking heads from the network news. He expected that this gang of toadies and butt-kissers would soon claim they'd supported the rebellion all along.

As he scanned the crowd further, he saw another familiar face. The man turned and approached him. "Joel Walter!" He exclaimed. "What are you doing here?"

"I was about to ask the same of you, Mr Ahmedaj. I should have known you'd end up among the good guys."

"I felt I had no choice." He cast his eyes down. "I owe you an apology and a great debt."

"Water under the bridge, my friend."

The applause drowned out their conversation as Larsen stepped up to the podium. He grinned broadly and began. "Thank you, Commander MacGuiness, Captain Roe, Ms. Standing Bear, Mr. Ahmed X, General Tole." He paused as each leader stood up in turn. The last man grimaced as Larsen called his name. There was obviously some bad blood between them. "And to everyone else who helped make this popular rebellion a success, thank you!

"Which brings me to another couple of heroes of the Revolution, who could not be here today. The White House staff was kind enough to bring in this big screen TV so we can hear from these luminaries via satellite – the FreeStar satellite, of course." There was renewed applause. "May I present, live from Billings in the Republic of Montana, the two people who *really* made this all possible, Nephi and Siri Snow!"

This brought actual cheers. The fair-skinned blond Nephi was a stark contrast to the deep brown skin and lush black tresses of his wife. As camera zoomed in, Nephi's face reddened a bit.

"This is a truly humbling experience. I'm not accustomed to public speaking, but I want to thank all the men and women whose sacrifices were so much greater than our own. Most of all I want to thank my dear wife, Siri Jayasuriya Snow, the real brains behind this operation. Siri?"

The camera moved to Siri, who feigned a moment of exasperation with her husband. "Thanks, Honey. Our gratitude goes out to all who have fought so hard to bring freedom back to our beloved country. On this historic occasion, we must remember the words of Thomas Jefferson. 'The tree of liberty must be refreshed from time to time, with the blood of patriots and tyrants.' Of course, any shedding of innocent blood is the greatest tragedy..."

Next to the podium, Larsen scanned the crowd. When he saw Joel, he motioned for him to join them. It took a couple of minutes for Joel to fight his way through the crowd. When he reached MacGuiness, the Commander clapped him on the shoulder, and said in a hushed voice (as Siri was still speaking), "Good job, Mr. Stooge!" I'll see you get the Medal of Freedom. He extended his hand and they shook. "Don't I know you from someplace?"

"As a matter of fact, Commander, we met in Phoenix at the Senator Bishop protest. My real name is Joel Walter; at the time I didn't have the beard and the schnoz was a bit bigger. I've been doing the Abbie Hoffman shtick for a while, you know."

Mac guffawed. "So you're that troublemaker? Love your work! Glad you could be here for the celebration. We'll also toast to the memory of those who perished. You drink scotch? This is 70-year-old Glenlivet, the President's personal stash. It's amazing!" He accepted a glass from Larsen, who already had one in his other hand, and passed the whiskey to Joel.

Joel took a too-large sip and coughed. "Smooth!"

In the far corner of the room were seven men, none of had joined in any of the applause. Six wore heavily decorated uniforms; the seventh was the Vice President, who had recently resigned his position in protest. "We're about to complete our preliminary negotiations," Mac said, "after Mrs. Snow finishes her speech. You may record the proceedings if you wish."

"Thanks, Commander." At that moment, Siri finished speaking. The room burst into applause once again as Nephi and Siri signed off. Joel followed Mac to the corner of the room. When they reached the generals he pulled out Mahmoud's phone and resumed taping.

"As I was saying, Sirs," Mac began, "We'd like to keep this totally legitimate. Has Ms. Wilton signed the resignation papers?"

"No sir," answered a man whom Joel recognized as General Wilcox, chairman of the Joint Chiefs. "There were other priorities, given the circumstances."

"We need to do that; have the Chief Justice swear in Vice President Frommage. Then there's the matter of the Constitutional Convention. By all the polls, the people demand it."

"Our attorneys are reviewing the press release as we speak," Frommage said. His eyes met Mac's for a second before looking away.

Moments later, two military police escorted in the former President and her husband Robert Wilton, who was also Secretary of Homeland Security. Both were in handcuffs.

"Madame President." MacGuiness handed her the documents and a pen.

She stared at him icily. "I'll need to have my hands free." The MP unlocked the cuffs. The former President signed several forms without reading any of them. She then held out her hands and the MP cuffed her wrists again.

"Madame President," Joel interjected. "If I may ask, what would you say to those who claim you committed a war crime in the destruction of an unsuspecting American city?"

There had been subdued conversation before; the room was now silent. Even the network newscasters stopped their hushed commentary. Everyone stared at Joel, then at Wilton.

Her face flushed red. She spoke, in a barely controlled fury. "I have no regrets. I am the lawfully elected President!" Unlike Frommage, she had no problem looking MacGuiness in the eye. "All you people had to do was submit to our legitimate authority!"

As they led the former President and her husband away, MacGuiness turned to address the cameras. He was the logical choice to be spokesman for the Rebellion, even if certain others were transparently envious. "I'd like to offer a prayer for all those on both sides who have lost their lives in this conflict, especially the innocents in the unfortunate city of Lodi. Nonetheless, this is a happy occasion. We will have our convention, and we will regain our liberty. This is our Yorktown! We have won the Second American Revolution!"

The audience erupted into cheers, many of the voices hoarse with emotion. From the corner, Jon Larsen, apparently feeling no pain, yelled, "Speech, speech!"

The Commander laughed. "Screw the speeches! Let's party!" The somber mood disappeared; the room was filled with laughter and loud conversation. Over the objections of the Acting President (reputedly a sober alcoholic) two burly men in Raptor uniforms entered the room, pushing a cart loaded with booze. Jon Tole began handing out ten-thousand-dollar bottles of cognac. Roe and Standing Bear lit cigars. Joel wanted one himself, but kept recording.

A sweeter smell impinged on his senses. MacGuiness had lit a joint. He took a drag and passed it one of his lieutenants. When it came round to Joel, he took a long hit, burning it a quarter of the way down. He handed it to Emal, who grimaced and handed it to his neighbor.

Was the war really over? There was still Congress to contend with, most of whose members were heavily invested in the old system. Would they accept the changing of the guard? Despite the challenges, Joel hated to be the pooper of the party. He remembered a Ben Franklin quote, a response to a question about the new nation's form of governance: "a Republic, if you can keep it." They'd almost lost that Republic forever. It was up to Joel's generation, as well as those to come, to ensure that it never happened again.

Chapter 18 – E Unibus Plurum

"Rough night, Sweetie?" Rosa smiled at Siri as she emerged from the bathroom looking pale and disheveled.

Siri smiled back, weakly. "Night was OK, it's the morning sickness. As much as I love Will and Padma, I swear to you, this is the last one."

"You're so lucky to have a man like Nephi. He's one in a million. Though to be honest, I thought you two were crazy to start a family in the middle of a rebellion."

"Well," Siri poured herself a cup of weak green tea, "we talked a long time about that. Both of us expected the troubles would last for years, so why wait?"

"Life goes on," agreed Rosa. Siri had never asked why she and Jack never had children. Now Jack was gone, killed in a shootout with DHS agents. Scant comfort the agency was gone; the killers would never pay for their crimes. Siri felt like weeping. She brightened as a boy entered the kitchen, followed by his sister, toddling unsteadily behind him.

"Good morning, my little pumpkins!" She grabbed Padma and hoisted her into the air, then bent down to give her son a kiss. "Aw, Mom!" complained Will. He turned to go, but couldn't escape an additional kiss from Aunt Rosa.

After the kids had eaten, Rosa said, "Don't worry, Siri, I'll clean up. You can get to your work. It's such a beautiful day; I'll take the kids to the park."

"That would be great, Rosa." It was not easy to concentrate when the kids played inside.

The house now quiet, Siri shuffled to her office. Her computer was the newest super-parallel server from Larsen Electronics. It was powerful enough to render 3D video in real time, far more muscle than she needed,

Returning to her notes, she considered the latest security issues with e-Barter. Scammers had figured out how to con the system into giving credit multiple times for a single trade. At least the problem wasn't widespread, yet. Maintaining public confidence in the system was as important as protecting its confidentiality.

After working for over an hour, she realized the solution she'd devised was unworkable. She closed her eyes and took cleansing breaths, trying to keep her stress level down. Not to worry, though, she'd been quite stressed with the first two pregnancies, and they'd gone just fine.

Her video chat program beeped, a welcome interruption. A window opened with Nephi's face in it. "Hi, Hon! Sorry to interrupt your work!"

"Don't be. I could use a break right now. How did your testimony go?"

"Could've been better. I only got to speak for two minutes; they wouldn't even watch my Power-Point. I think the Legislature already has their minds made up."

"So we'll be forced to spy on our customers." She shrugged. "I expected that. Utah, I mean Deseret, doesn't like people working under the table any more than the Feds did."

Nephi frowned. "Yeah, they were a hostile audience, especially when I questioned the *need* for income taxes. We don't fight foreign wars anymore, and welfare's a thing of the past. They get enough property taxes to pay for streets, police and emergency services. If they charged tuition, with private charity for the poor kids, the schools could be self-supporting."

She nodded. "Though we'd still have the baby boomer problem. Since the US broke up, no more money for Social Security and Medicare."

"Sell off the assets. Now that we're independent, Deseret controls millions of acres of formerly Federal land. Keep the system afloat long enough to phase it out."

She laughed. "We both know that's not going to happen. They should listen to you. You're smarter than the lot of them."

"Good grief, woman, you'll give me a swelled head! Doesn't solve our problem, though. Now that we're a legal, money-making business, if the government orders us to put a back door in e-Barter, what can we do?"

Siri shrugged. "We could move to Dakota Republic. They've got no plans to bring back the income tax. But I'm not worried. Between the Undernet and competition between the former states, not even California or New England can get away with high taxes."

"What amazing times we live in," Nephi said. "Five years ago, who would have thought the US government would fall? And the Constitutional Convention end up in a shouting match?"

Siri nodded. "It's human nature. There's a kind of centrifugal force that acts on any entity that gets too big. Remove the chains, it flies apart, like the USSR or Yugoslavia."

"True." He sighed. "Maybe I'm too stubborn for my own good, but I refuse to act as a government spy. I want to be free to develop my– *our* product," Siri smiled at his rephrasing, "the way we want it, not the way the politicians in Salt Lake City want it."

"You worry too much, Sweetie. Even if Salt Lake forces Snow Technologies to cooperate, *we* don't have to. Your family would be happy to buy our share. They won't mind playing ball with the government. We can go make trouble somewhere else."

Siri heard a noise behind her. "Mommee!" A brown-skinned little boy leaped through the air and landed in her lap, almost knocking her off her chair.

"Hello there, Big Guy!" she turned the chair to face the screen. "Say hi to Daddy."

"Hi, Daddy!" Will frowned for a moment as if pondering what to say next. "How's your work, Daddy? You having fun today?"

"It's OK," Nephi grinned. "But it'll be much better when I'm back home with you guys!"

"Yay! Daddy, when you get home will you teach me how to use the 'puter?"

"*I* already taught you how," Siri said, a little irked.

"That's just *games*," he said disdainfully. "I want to invent stuff, like you and Daddy."

"Of course!" She blew a kiss to her husband, who did the same. His image disappeared.

★ ◎★ ★

Larsen stood at the podium, smiling broadly. "*Bon jour monsieurs et madames.* I apologize for my appalling French. I haven't tried using it since high school. So please, don't throw any rotten fruit." The audience laughed politely.

Actually, Larsen had been working with some intensive language-learning software. This was his first trip to Montreal, a good time to put it to the test. Years ago, when he'd gone to Paris, his French had been so poor, people actually suggested he speak English.

"I don't often give talks outside of the former USA. My subject makes governments nervous. South of the Forty-Ninth Parallel, the days of high-taxing, big-spending government are over. But here in the Great White North, my talks in Vancouver and Toronto were mysteriously canceled. Perhaps your government is letting me speak just to spite the Canadians. Big mistake. The Quebecois need tax relief, too." That prompted some nervous chuckles.

"But my main focus is technical. How can we build an information system from open source components, and yet make it secure enough to resist the world's most dedicated cryptanalysts?" Larsen clicked the remote; a photo of NSA headquarters appeared behind him.

"This isn't the same NSA we had before the USA broke up. It's now a private company, working all sides in a world rife with industrial espionage. Yet another thing for security professionals to worry about."

"What makes a system secure? As security guru Bryce Schneider put it, security requires more than just hardware and software..." Larsen had delivered this speech so many times, he'd go to auto-pilot. It was refreshing to attempt it in another language.

For Larsen, things hadn't gone the way he expected since the Revolution. First of all, Andrea was married, not that he'd have been interested. His FBI file showed she'd been most cooperative with their agents. Embittered, he'd plunged himself into his work, turning his hobby into a successful computer firm in a few short months. But that didn't satisfy him, either.

So he sold the business and wrote *The Anarchist Farmer*, a memoir of his recent times in and out of trouble. His agent had advised a speaking tour, which turned out to be much more fun than he'd expected. He enjoyed shooting his mouth off, and there was a side benefit: women, of all types and descriptions.

Today the audience held one particularly interesting specimen. It was difficult to tear his gaze away. She was tall and slender, with creamy white skin and short dark hair. He couldn't help thinking he'd seen her somewhere before. He'd try to speak to her, and he really hoped she was single. Celebrity of any sort, even his own geeky version, had advantages.

His mind wandering to erotic fantasies, Larsen stumbled over his speech. Luckily he had notes on his JL-Pad, a high tech cheat. When he finally finished, he was a nervous mess, but there was still the Q and A to contend with.

The questions were pretty basic. "What was the most secure encryption algorithm? How do you protect against a brute force attack? How do the two sides of a transaction synchronize keys?" Forgetting some of the French nomenclature, he ended up resorting to English phrases.

"Any more questions?" He was about to call on a young fellow in the front row, when he saw another hand go up. It was the dark-haired woman who'd caught his fancy.

"Mr. Larsen," she began in perfect, Parisian dialect French. At that moment, Larsen realized who she was. How could he be so forgetful? He was so busy berating himself, it was hard to concentrate on her words as she continued.

"Your talk has been fascinating. But you haven't told us about your career. How did you go from being a 'glorified hobbyist,' as you describe yourself, to a leading technologist? What motivated you? Did the government wrong you, or was it simply a love of problem solving?"

A grin appeared on Larsen's face. "Well, Ms. Sims, all my life, I've been skeptical of authority. But I honestly never expected to bring down the government! All I wanted to do was read subversive websites without ending up on FBI surveillance, and swap a few MP3's now and then." He omitted the joke about porn he often used when speaking to these mostly-male groups.

"Also, I can't take credit for the technology that spawned the Revolution. Most of the kudos go to my friends, people like Nephi Snow, his wife Siri Jayasuriya Snow, and of course, the notorious Joel Walter, AKA the 'Seventh Stooge'..."

Victoria Sims smiled, glanced at her watch, and retrieved her purse from beneath her seat. There were a few more hands up in the audience. Larsen began to panic.

"Sorry, no more questions, I have a previous engagement." The surprised moderator thanked him, the audience applauded once more, and Larsen quickly gathered his things.

Larsen pushed his way through the crowd and into the corridor. The conference center was huge, and its neighboring hotel could have housed the entire population of Larsen's home town. He saw his target heading toward the elevators and quickened his pace.

"That was a great question," he said breathlessly as he caught up with her.

She stopped in the middle of the busy hallway. "Really?" Victoria said in her charming British accent. "I was afraid I'd offended you. Some people find me a bit overbearing."

Larsen laughed. "Not necessarily. After all, you could have pressed charges, and you never did. I'm surprised you still don't want to slug me."

"Let's reserve judgment on that one, shall we?" Victoria smiled sweetly. "Actually, since the launch went off well and the satellite didn't fall on Houston, no harm done."

"Except for those poor firemen. But that was the Feds' fault for bombing the launch pad." He paused, and the two of them stared at each other in the middle of the crowded lobby. Suddenly Larsen felt extremely awkward, "I'm free at the moment. Can I buy you a drink?"

"Certainly," she said with a little laugh. "If you'll let me use the ladies' room first."

"OK. Meet me in the lounge, I'll be at the bar." As Larsen waited, he pondered his own surprising reaction. Certainly Victoria was attractive. There'd been a bit of chemistry between them at the Command Center in Del Rios, which was strange since they were such opposites. He hadn't thought about her at all since then, because he'd immediately dismissed his chances as nil. How could Victoria, who hobnobbed with billionaires and commanded thousands of employees, possibly be interested in a rough-edged farm boy like him?

Then again, they'd both gone through the same difficult, life threatening situation. Maybe the inherent camaraderie would work to his benefit. Plus, her finger was unencumbered by a wedding ring. At this point in his life, Larsen had no desire to settle down, but if anyone could change his mind, it would be a brainy, beautiful, take-charge woman with a cute accent.

To his surprise, she sat down at the next stool, a wry smile on her face. "Sorry I kept you waiting."

"No problem," Larsen said. "No problem at all."

Emal's prayers finished, he immediately checked his cell phone. There was a message waiting but from a blocked number. "I have a message for Zacarias," said a deep male voice with an Arab accent. "Call the following number within the hour."

Emal called the number and gave the pass-phrase: "The imam sends greetings."

The same voice answered. "We've determined the subject's location." He paused, giving Emal time to press the phone's 'record' button. "520 West Sierra Street, Laramie, Yellowstone Federation." He followed with a phone number and email address. "Target is living under the name Livia Meisner. According to county records, she has recently married."

"Thank you." Emal hung up.

After all this time, he'd located her. Amazing luck that it was now, when he just happened to be in the same country. Again it looked like divine providence, though Emal would have preferred the call to be a little earlier in the day. He was tired, not in the mood for confrontations.

No, he had to act now. Tomorrow would take him to the Dakota Republic. Border crossings weren't bad for an individual, but for an 18-wheeler carrying goods that might be regulated or taxed, they could be a hassle. Also, he'd paid the investigator in gold. If she moved before he returned to the Yellowstone Confederation, it would be a huge waste of money.

Emal climbed in the cab and headed down the Interstate. He repeated the address to the truck's nav system, and it displayed a map to her house. "Show nearest truck stop." He didn't want to come rumbling down the street in his Freightliner. That would attract unwelcome attention, and in some towns, a stiff fine. Luckily, he still had his 350 Yamaha. The visored helmet would provide extra anonymity for his side trip.

It didn't take long to reach Arjana's neighborhood. It was upscale but not gated. Her house was a white two story on a cul-de-sac, with a late-model SUV in the driveway. *The whole bourgeois thing.* He parked next to the SUV, and hung the helmet on the handlebars. At the door, he hesitated a moment.

Finally he rang the bell; no answer. While he waited, he silently recited the thirty-sixth Sura of the Koran. He wondered if anyone had heard him, then rang the bell again. Halfway through the Sura a second time, he pushed the bell again.

As he was turning to go, the door opened, and Emal found himself staring down the barrel of a 12 gauge shotgun. "What do you want, Emal?" Arjana demanded.

Emal was not as scared as he would have expected; a Believer needn't fear death. He furrowed his brow. "That's not a very sisterly greeting."

"I'm sorry," She lowered the gun to her hip. "I have good reason to be cautious. Tell me, Brother, did the Corporation send you?"

He shook his head. "I haven't associated with them for years. They tried to kill me, and almost succeeded. I don't even know who's alive and whether they're still in business."

She smiled weakly. "I'm sure they are. Come in, Emal, the neighbors will get suspicious." "Thanks," he said, without sarcasm. He followed her through the vaulted living room into the kitchen, which was almost as big as the apartment Emal shared with Esma and the children. "You heard about Egon."

She nodded. "Yes. A tragic waste, though I must say I wasn't surprised. But Enver is out of prison now. You should look him up. With your influence maybe he'll make better choices."

"I appreciate your confidence in me. And I will contact him. Do you have his number?" "Certainly." She picked up a phone. "I'll text you his information right now."

As he waited for his sister's text, Emal looked around. "You have a beautiful home." He glanced at a photo of a woman in a white dress, Arjana. "You've gotten married. How wonderful! I wish Esma and I could have been there."

"Look closer at the picture."

"Oh," The groom in the picture wore a yarmulke. Though Emal felt no strong emotion, an image came to his mind unbidden. He saw himself with a hand around the groom's neck and a knife in the other. He forced the grisly scene from his mind. Violence had never been his way. *They are also People of the Book,* he reminded himself. "Have you converted to his religion?"

Arjana's silence was good as an answer. "So *now* do you want to kill me?"

His anger returned. "You insult me! You think I'd do such a thing to my own sister?"

"You disapprove rather strongly, though don't you? I saw the expression on your face!"

"Of course I don't approve! But it's your life. And if you love him, I'm happy for you."

"Emal, please understand, no matter how strongly you feel about religion, I've never been a Muslim, so I'm not an apostate. Same with Mother and Egon.

Father, on the other hand, was in the Sunnah before he became a Communist. Do you suppose he's in Hell now?"

Emal shrugged. "Only Allah knows that."

She got up from the table and walked to the sink, where she loaded some plates into the dishwasher. "I've made coffee, would you like some?"

"Yes, please."

She handed him a mug and sat beside him. "You know, Brother, I never imagined it would be like this. I thought here in America, we'd be Americans, and we'd leave behind the old world feuds and the tribal bullshit. Mom and Dad would retire to Sun City or Miami, and we'd bring our grandchildren to visit. But that drunk driver..." Arjana sniffled, blinking back tears.

"I understand, Sister. I believe that if Mother had been alive our family would have never gotten involved with criminal elements."

"I assume that means you've been keeping to the straight and narrow."

Emal nodded. "Of course. I used to rationalize our actions; we were only corrupting the infidels..." He laughed. "Not that it's a big deal these days. *Everybody's* doing it now, buying and selling drugs and such. People thought the underground economy would go away when the United States fell apart. Ha! It's bigger than ever."

"Yes. The politicians in Helena make lots of noise, but nothing gets done. Still, it's much, much better than before. The camps are closed, no more disappearances."

"I was frightened, too," Emal stirred another spoon of sugar into his coffee. "That's why I ran, to keep Esma and the children safe. When I heard the government had hired the Corporation as enforcers, I was terrified. My two biggest enemies working together! I had to do something. Because I went public with that information, they sent men to kill me.

"That was you? I heard the rumors on the Undernet. No offense, Emal, but somehow I'm not surprised." She put a hand on his shoulder. "It makes me very proud to be your sister."

"Why not? It's my country, too. Or it was. Now it's just the Republic of Michigan."

"I guess our dream was pretty foolish," she said with a bitter smile. "We can never become Americans now, because America is gone."

"That depends on what you think America is. It didn't cease to exist just because old government went away. It's the people, all of us who live here, or an idea, an ideal."

Arjana glanced at the clock. "Levi will be home soon, if you'd like to meet him."

"I'm sorry, Sis, I need to be in Rapid City tonight. But let's keep in touch. Do you have the Griffin program? I know the bad times are supposed to be over, but it doesn't hurt to be careful. Here." He scribbled a private email address on his business card and handed it to her.

There were tears glistening in Arjana's eyes. They hugged. Emal got on his motorcycle and headed back to the truck stop where his rig was waiting for him. He felt a serenity he hadn't experienced in many months. He'd give Esma a full report this evening.

Maybe all that prayer was finally paying off.

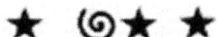

Joel looked up and smiled. The kids from his third period class, sophomore American history, shuffled in. "Good morning, people!" he boomed. "We have new textbooks, hot off the press. Everybody grab one."

"Hey, look!" said Robbie Garcia. In a dramatic TV announcer voice, he read, *Techno-Rebels: The Second American Revolution.* Hey Teach, how'd your face get on the back?"

"I wrote it," Joel tried his best to sound indifferent. "A lot has happened since your old books were published."

"Of course!" exclaimed Heather Jones. "My parents say you had a big part in the Revolution. So of course you're the man to write it."

"I hate to bring this up," said Billie Cooper. "But isn't this what you'd call a conflict of interest? Telling the school to buy your own book?"

"You've been listening, ten points for you." Billie seemed disappointed, the girl loved to argue. "It *would* be a conflict, but I don't have any input into what books the district assigns."

"I thought the *government* picked the books," said another boy.

"The district *is* part of the government," explained Billie in an exasperated voice.

This was how most of Joel's History and Government classes went, the discussion jumping from one topic to another. It wasn't easy keeping thirty teenagers on task, and Joel was out of practice. He hadn't taught since his early thirties.

Finally he got them settled down. "The first two chapters of the book should be familiar to you. We've been going over that material for the last couple weeks. Now," Joel gave them his best exasperated smile, "what factors laid the groundwork for the collapse of the US government?"

"The Oil Wars," said Keisha Warren from the back of the room. "After Afghanistan and Iraq, the Armed Forces were seriously over-extended. Nigeria pretty much did them in."

"Very good," said Joel. "Anybody else?"

"How about hyper-inflation?" said another student.

"Neglecting the veterans," added Robbie Garcia, who was, for a change, not joking or making fart noises. "The private contractors were paid way better than our soldiers."

"Patriot Acts I, II and III," said Billie. "Suspending habeas corpus. Interference in local government. It got so bad even the local police stopped cooperating."

Joel nodded. "Excellent answers. If you didn't get good notes, or if, like me, you can't read your own handwriting, you'll want to scan the first two chapters to refresh your memory. Next assignment, read Chapter 3, which covers the Techno portion of the rebellion."

"They're all friends of yours, aren't they?" asked Billie. "That's what my dad says. Like Nephi and Siri Snow, and Jon Olson from Minnesota."

"Jon Larsen, from Dakota," Joel corrected, just as the bell rang. "Chapter 3!" he repeated over the din, as the kids threw books in their bags and stampeded out the door.

Joel sighed with relief. *Thank God for lunch, stogie time.* Since the Revolution, there'd been backlash against all the 'health and safety' laws of the early twenty-first century. There were actually places where you could smoke indoors.

As Joel closed his briefcase, his phone rang. He picked it up, "Hello, Joel speaking." It felt wonderful to be able to use his real name again.

"Hi, Dad! Are we still on for lunch?"

"Certainly, Sweetheart. If you don't mind my usual haunt."

He could imagine his daughter's nose wrinkling; she sighed audibly. "It's OK. Normally it bothers me, eating where they let people smoke, but I have to admit their ventilation systems are extremely effective. Oh, and Dad, you don't mind if I bring a friend, do you?"

"Of course not, if it's one of your cute single girlfriends."

"Dad!" she cried in mock outrage. "You dirty old man! I think Mom is right about you!"

"Did I ever deny it?"

Like him, those teachers who shared his vice hung out in the tavern across the street, where they'd eat their lunch and gossip. The cigarette smokers wrinkled their noses at Joel's pungent habit. But years of persecution had created a kind of solidarity.

Joel remembered he hadn't logged off his computer. As he did that, he heard a quiet knock at his door and looked up.

"Dad?" said a female voice. "Can we come in?"

He sprang to his feet. "Esther, how'd you get here so quickly? Were you calling me from outside the door?"

As his daughter entered with her 'friend,' Joel's mouth fell open in shock. "Serena! My God, what are you doing here?" They hugged in the doorway. He looked at his daughter. "You brat, you tricked the old man once again."

"I didn't say *whose* friend I was bringing along," Esther grinned.

"My mother passed away last week." Serena said. Her mother had been in her nineties, so the news was not a surprise. "I flew to Phoenix to sort out her affairs. I should have called you, but I've been an emotional wreck."

"I'm sorry to hear about Kathleen."

Serena looked down. "I know we left things on a bad note; I always meant to get back in touch. After the Lodi thing, I thought you might be dead! I had to get away from the fallout, so I went back to Florida. By the way, have you heard from Soozie? She was in the camps for over a year. She's in Taos now. I'll probably stop on the way back."

The two women followed Joel out the door, and waited while he locked up.

"Speaking of moving, the immigration laws here in Aztlan are still relatively lax, for people with a family connection here." He looked her in the eyes. "Serena, I still feel terrible about how I bailed on you, but things were insane then. When it was all over, I thought you wouldn't want to hear from me. But I would've come back here come hell or high water. It's great to be close to so Esther," he flashed a smile at his daughter, "and the grandkids."

Serena nodded. "No use agonizing about the past. I'm so happy your family is together again!"

"Yes!" Esther said. "I was telling Serena how hard it was for me not to be in touch with you. I was so worried that I'd unintentionally lead me into a government trap."

"Somebody did a good job raising her," Serena took Joel's arm as the three of them headed for the campus gate. "I'm getting sick of Florida; all the crime, the high cost of living. I might move to Cuba; it's so old-fashioned and quaint. They're talking about federating with Florida, so I'd be an automatic citizen. On the other hand, I've always liked the desert. Know any good property for sale?"

"I know an old guy who could rent you a room," he said with a grin.

"I don't know. Some of those old guys are real bastards to live with." She winked at Esther to let her know she was joking.

"Not if you know how to do him a *favor* once in a while!"

"You are such a pig!" She gave him a playful sock in the arm.

"Dad," Esther groaned, "Too much information!"

"Sorry, Honey. Serena's right, I'm a pig, but at least I'm the kosher variety. Let me make it up and buy lunch for both of you."

"What do you mean make it up? We expected you to pay anyway."

As they stood at the corner waiting for the light, there was an awkward silence. Joel looked over at his daughter. She had moved a discreet distance away from him and Serena, and was pretending to be engrossed in the school's front sign, with its 'Student of the Month' and 'Go Jaguars!' announcements.

"So," Joel adopted a serious expression. "I understand if you're angry with me, but– are you seeing anybody right now?"

Serena just smiled and kissed him, a long, sensuous lip-lock. When they came up for air, several of Joel's students were standing across the street, cheering and clapping.

"Did I get you in trouble?" Serena laughed nervously.

"Yes, with my daughter."

Esther was standing there giving them an evil look. "If you guys are finished *reminiscing*, we'd better get going."

When Joel Serena, and Esther arrived at the New Sonora Lounge, there was a commotion outside. Five state police vehicles– *national* police, Joel reminded himself– were parked in front, blocking the street, backing up traffic.

Six or seven locals were standing on the sidewalk gawking. One was a man Joel knew from the local PTSA, Jesus Ramirez .

"What's going on?" Joel asked him.

"It's a raid, undocumented workers."

"That's a shame. I hope they don't shut the place down. I love the Sonora."

Jesus shook his head. "I don't know, man. It's their second offense."

The suspects being led out in handcuffs were fair skinned young people, bleached blond girls and guys with surfer haircuts.

"Damned Californians," There was a smirk on Jesus' face. "They think they can come to our country and work any time they want."

"And why shouldn't they?" Joel's remark elicited a look of puzzlement from Ramirez. "Isn't that one of the reasons we got rid of the Feds?"

"People say the Rebellion changed everything," Esther said. "But I tell them, 'It may be a smaller government, but it's still a government.' Those politicians need somebody to keep them on their toes. That's why the Seventh Stooge should come out of retirement."

"She's right, Joel," Serena laughed. "Isn't there an old saying, that if you want freedom, you need eternal vigilance?"

"You do," Joel said. "Plus a whole lot of *chutzpah*."

About the Author

Vaughn Treude grew up on a family farm in North Dakota. The remoteness of his home, with few children his age nearby, made science fiction and fantasy a welcome escape. His favorite writers were Isaac Asimov, Robert Heinlein, and JRR Tolkien. He always planned to become a sci-fi writer, but the demands of life kept his various projects from completion. After several years as a software consultant, he realized that the same kind of discipline required for writing code could be applied to creating fictional worlds.

Politics have exerted a strong influence on science fiction ever since HG Wells speculated on the future of human civilization, to *1984, 2001* and beyond. Treude's writings are no exception. He has always had a strong belief in freedom and the value of the individual. *Centrifugal Force* is the result of speculation on how a measure of freedom might be achieved in today's unfree world.

Treude lives in the Phoenix, Arizona, area where he has one teenage son and two domesticated hell-hounds.

Coming soon from Vaughn Treude

Fidelio's Automata

It is the dawn of the Twentieth Century. America has defeated Spain and acquired a global empire. An anarchist assassin targets President William McKinley– and would have succeeded if not for the revolutionary new Roentgen device. Technology is transforming the nation in unexpected ways.

In the year 1901, a radical young Cuban engineer arrives in New Jersey to work for Thomas Edison, and becomes embroiled in America's most famous scientific rivalry. A Rough Rider turned Quaker seeks to atone for his participation in the War by trying to stop American atrocities in the Philippines. Meanwhile, a new conflict is brewing south of the Rio Grande. A chance meeting of these two individuals produces an alliance that will change America's destiny and rewrite the history of the steam era.

www.ingramcontent.com/pod-product-compliance
Lightning Source LLC
Chambersburg PA
CBHW062001170626
46813CB00001B/2